THE WAR OF THE FATTIES
AND OTHER STORIES
FROM AZTEC HISTORY

The Texas Pan American Series

SALVADOR NOVO IN HIS LEANER YEARS.

Photograph by Manuel Alvarez Bravo

The War of the Fatties
and Other Stories
from Aztec History

as told by Salvador Novo
Translated by Michael Alderson

University of Texas Press
Austin

FIRST EDITION, 1994

Frontispiece: Copyright © Manuel Alvarez Bravo,
Mexico City, Mexico.

LIBRARY OF CONGRESS
CATALOGING-IN-PUBLICATION DATA

Novo, Salvador, 1904–1974.
   The war of the fatties and other stories from Aztec history / as
told by Salvador Novo ; translated by Michael Alderson.—1st ed.
      p.   cm.—(The Texas Pan American series)
   Includes bibliographical references.
   ISBN 0-292-79059-7 (alk. paper).—ISBN 0-292-75554-6 (pbk. : alk. paper)
      1. Aztecs—Literary collections. 2. Novo, Salvador, 1904–1974—
Criticism and interpretation. I. Title. II. Series.
   PQ7292.N7W37   1994
   862—dc20   93-7030

Grateful acknowledgment is made to the following for permission to reprint
previously published material:
   Fernando Rivera Novo and Guillermina López Espino: For English translations and poetry excerpts from Part V of *Never Ever*; "Historia," *Espejo: Poemas antiguos*; "La parábola del hermano," *Poemas de adolescencia*; "La novela de
la Revolución," *Poemas proletarios*; "Resúmenes," *XX poemas*; the epigraph
from *Nuevo amor*; "La poesía," *Espejo*; and "Adán desnudo," *Poesía*.
   Manuel Alvarez Bravo: For the use of his photograph of Salvador Novo.
   Grove Press: For excerpts from *The Labyrinth of Solitude* by Octavio Paz.
Copyright © 1985 by Grove Press, New York, New York. Reprinted by permission of the publisher.

TO PEDRO ALMODÓVAR AND PAULINE KAEL.
TO TERESA G. NAVARRO.

Contents

Introduction:
About the Author

ah but sometimes we wake up with the soul of an operetta
and we wish we had a carriage with white horses
white as the clouds we watch go by stretched out on green grass
while the sky like a perfect Moroccan binding
while nothing but one says while as one reaches for something
    else
and we feel great urges to cry rabidly
and say bad words or be infinitely sweet . . .

(from Part V of *Never Ever*)

I

If he had been born just a little darker, and if his Mexican mother had not married a man from Galicia, Salvador Novo might never have become aware of nationalism's most superficial aspects. But as things turned out, Salvador looked the way he looked, and his mother married whom she married, and young Salvador wrote a poem called "History" about some time during his childhood:

> ¡Mueran los gachupines!
> My father is a gachupín,
> full of hate the teacher looks at me
> and tells us of the War of Independence
> and how the Spaniards were evil and cruel
> with the Indians—he is Indian—
> and all the children shout death to the gachupines.
>
> But I object
> and think that they are very stupid:
> That's what history says
> but how are we to know it?[1]

And if Salvador's family had not left the capital and moved to Torreón to escape the Revolution; and if they had not had a house near the entrance to the city; and if Salvador's uncle had not looked like someone else; and if Salvador had not seen him shot by the troops of Pancho Villa; and if Pancho Villa had not then spared Salvador's father's life—even though he was a Spaniard—on the condition that he leave the country; and if Villa had not later accepted a hacienda as a bribe from the government to give up fighting; and if that bribe had not been so ironic, since after all, it had been somewhat of an agrarian revolution Villa had been fighting in, Salvador might never have realized that popular heroes are not always what they are cracked up to be, and the obituary he wrote in 1923 upon Villa's assassination might have turned out a little differently.[2]

And if more of the thinking and less of the fighting had taken place in "the barbarous North" where Novo grew up; and if the schools had not been forced to close because of the various military occupations—by the Villistas, by the Huertistas, by the Carrancistas—and Salvador had not been forced to stay inside, where he spent the time reading through his uncle's library, he might never have come across Enrique González Martínez, whose influence turned up later in Salvador's early poetry, and he might never have come across that poet's famous line (from "Tuércele el cuello al cisne," *Los senderos ocultos* in *Poesías Completas,* p. 135) which sounded the death knell for modernist aesthetics in Latin America, "Twist the neck of the swan with the deceitful plumage," and he might never have realized that literary traditions are not sacred, not inviolable, and he might never have broken a few on his own, and he might never have been called brother to Eliot and heir to Jules Laforgue, the Mexican Cocteau, the modern Molière, the only poet in Mexico besides Paz who ever understood André Breton, and many of the other things Novo was called during his lifetime, not all of them good.[3]

And if in 1910, after Francisco Madero had led the *anti-reeleccionistas* and Pancho Villa and Pascual Orozco had revolted in Chihuahua against the dictator Porfirio Díaz, forming a pact with Madero and storming Ciudad Juárez; and if after Porfirio Díaz had been forced into exile and Madero had been installed as president, Bernardo Reyes had not then revolted against Madero in the Northeast, and Zapata had not revolted in the South, articulating his Plan de Ayala; and if in February of the next year Madero's military commander in Chihuahua, Pascual Orozco, had not then rebelled for a second time—this time against Madero—and Madero had not sent Victoriano Huerta (later president) to put him down; and if Félix Díaz, Porfirio Díaz's nephew, had not revolted in Veracruz, and Huerta, supposedly defending the Madero government, had not conspired with Reyes and Díaz's nephew to kill Madero's brother Gustavo, at a meeting held inside the U.S. Embassy; and if Huerta had not then persuaded President Madero and Vice-President Pino Suárez to resign; and if four days later, after

Huerta became president, Huerta's forces had not killed both Madero and Pino Suárez; and if back in Chihuahua, Villa, along with others in Sonora and Carranza in the Northeast, had not then revolted against Victoriano Huerta, and Carranza had not announced his Plan de Guadalupe; and if in the North, Villa and Carranza had not formed a pact, and Zapata had not continued fighting in the South; and if in 1913 in Sonora, Alvaro Obregón, Plutarco E. Calles, and Adolfo de la Huerta had not teamed up to join the battle against Victoriano Huerta, and the United States had not invaded Veracruz, angering forces on all sides; and if in 1914, World War I had not broken out, and in May of the same year, Carranza had not been afraid of Villa getting to Mexico City before he did and had not cut him off from shipments of coal and other supplies coming by train and by sea; and if Carranza and Obregón had not made it to Mexico City and turned down Zapata's Plan de Ayala and then installed Carranza as president; and if factions in Sonora had not continued fighting, and Obregón had not gone north to solicit Villa's support in Sonora and then ended up betraying Carranza by forming an alliance with Villa; and if Zapata, still not satisfied with Carranza's lukewarm agrarianism, had not kept fighting— now not against Madero or against Huerta but against Carranza—and if, in response to a national convention convoked by Carranza, Villa had not called his own convention in 1914 in Aguascalientes and received the support of many national leaders; and if the convention had not been attended by a representative of the Zapatistas as well, and Villa had not convinced the convention to set up a government headed by General Eulalio Gutiérrez and had not named himself military commander; and if it had not soon become apparent that Villa would not even recognize the government he himself had set up; and if in 1915, Villa and Zapata had not entered Mexico City, and Carranza and Obregón had not retreated to Veracruz; and if Obregón had not eventually been able to regain military control of the capital; and if in 1916, a new convention had not been held and it had not produced the quasi-liberal, quasi-radical Constitution of 1917 and marked what many consider the end of the Mexican Revolution; and if that had been all, and Carranza had not run unopposed in 1917; and if after all that, Carranza had not then been accused of doing nothing to advance reforms and of maintaining the status quo, and Zapata had not been considered a threat to Carranza and been assassinated in 1919, and the president had not then managed to get the support of Zapata's followers by rewarding them with positions of power in the Morelos state government,

Salvador might once in a while have referred to the Revolution as something more than "the shootout that was the Revolution." But as things turned out, he never did.

And if Salvador had been born just ten years later, in 1914 like Octavio Paz was, and had been only three when the end of the Revolution was declared, Salvador might have taken a little more interest in its history, or written an "Ode to a Barefoot Soldier" or "to the División del Norte," and he might never have learned the first axiom of cynicism, "Idealism increases in direct proportion to one's distance from the problem," expressed so succinctly by John Galsworthy. But even Octavio Paz was forced to admit, in an interview with Claude Fell, that much of the fighting that took place seemed to have had no reason.[4]

But that is as far as the ifs go. There comes a time, no matter how much we are products of our environments or victims of circumstance, when the human will takes over, and we become responsible for our own lives, or so goes the story. For Novo, it can be said that this moment arrived late in 1917, when in order to attend high school at the Preparatoria Nacional, he moved to Mexico City where he lived with an uncle who worked for the railroads. Novo was thirteen years old when he came of age.

. . . The storm that howls

will throw up a stone to me . . . And when the Sun awakens
my brother and he continues along his path, death

will have perhaps covered me with its dust. And my brother
will pass over me . . . and seeking me in vain
he will go to die alone in a distant country . . .

("La parábola del hermano," *Poemas de adolescencia*)

II

High school is a fun time for Salvador Novo. His first year he tests out
of English and Spanish literature and spends much of his time playing
hooky, going to the movies, exploring the city, and visiting book-
stores.[5] In high school Novo meets Xavier Villaurrutia, and in 1919 they
publish their precocious poems for the first time in *El Universal Ilustrado* and more, soon afterward, in *El Heraldo de México*. Xavier becomes what is euphemistically called Novo's *amigo íntimo* and is later
the subject of several poems. He is also part of the group that comes
to be known as the Contemporáneos.

The Contemporáneos are a group of poets and playwrights, a group
of friends, who come together for the first time in the late teens and
early 1920s: Bernardo Ortiz de Montellano, Enrique González Rojo,
José Gorostiza, Jaime Torres Bodet, Jorge Cuesta, and Gilberto Owen.
Others sometimes associated with the group but who did not participate in any of the group's major endeavors are Carlos Pellicer, Octavio G. Barreda, Elías Nandino, and Rubén Salazar Mallén.

As a group, the Contemporáneos are the most exciting development
in Mexican literature since modernism. Their work prompts José Joaquín Blanco, in his excellent *Crónica de la poesía mexicana,* to assert that
though "Mexican poetry has not had its Siglo de Oro, it has had its
decade: the thirties of this century. Pellicer, Villaurrutia, Gorostiza,
Novo, Owen, Ortiz de Montellano . . ." Blanco notes their influence
in many of the poets who come after: "The real influence of the Contemporáneos occurred in other poets who, although they didn't submit
themselves docilely as disciples, did revise and reevaluate earlier poetry
and assimilated from it whatever freely mattered to them: Octavio Paz,

Ali Chumacero, Rubén Bonifaz Nuño, and later, Gerardo Deniz, Tomás Segovia, Eduardo Lizalde, Gabriel Zaid, José Emilio Pacheco, and José Carlos Becerra. It can be said that the influence of the Contemporáneos is still of the first order in Mexican poetry, and even in essay and theater."[6]

Salvador Novo's contribution to the legacy of the Contemporáneos is substantial. Between 1915 and 1945, he writes three experimental plays, *Divorcio: Drama Ibseniano en cinco actos* (1924), *La señorita Remington: Diálogo fingido de cosas ciertas en que se demuestre que el tiempo no es dinero* (1924), and *Le troisième Faust: Tragédie brève* (1937); and translates three, *Ligados* (1928) and *Diferente* (1934), both by Eugene O'Neill, and *El dólar plata* (1935), by William P. Shea.

In poetry, his impact is felt even more: *Poemas de infancia* and *Poemas de adolescencia* (unpublished until 1955), *Adytias, poemas* (1924), *XX poemas* (1925), *Espejo: Poemas antiguos* (1933), *Nuevo amor* (1933), *Seamen Rhymes* (with drawings by Federico García Lorca, 1934), *Romance de Angelillo y Adela* (dedicated to García Lorca, 1934), *Décimas en el mar* (with illustrations by Julio Prieto, 1934), *Poemas proletarios* (1934), *Frida Kahlo* (1934), *Never Ever* (1934), *Canto a Teresa* (1934), *Dueño mío* (1944), *Decimos: "Nuestra tierra"* (1944), *Florido laude* (1945), and many satiric poems that are circulated in carbon-copy manuscript form but are not published until 1955 in *Sátira*, or are later included in the posthumous *Sátira, el libro ca. . .*

Novo's output is great and varied, so varied, in fact, that critic Eduardo Colín says, "He is like a box of surprises,"[7] and Emmanuel Carballo says:

> As a poet, Novo is a conqueror who for strange reasons doesn't colonize the territories he discovers: graciously—satanically—he leaves the poets of his age and younger to industrialize his discoveries. In his poems from his adolescence, he imitates Darío and González Martínez, and his "pastiches" possess such merit that an unsuspecting reader could easily confuse them with the poems on which they were originally based. His López-Velardian poems prove his enormous capacity for mimicry. Later, to make fun of the *estridentistas* (particularly Maples Arce), he writes the most lasting poems that that avant-garde trend ever produced, *Entre azul y buenas noches*. Immediately after, he shows up in surrealism, and it isn't an exaggeration to say that he and Octavio Paz are the only Mexican poets who have understood Breton and his disciples. Novo's surrealist texts stand out for the way their images are created: a writer of powerful

imaginative capacity and of numerous, efficient mental mechanisms, he seasons his metaphors with irony and tenderness, with the "poetic" and the "prosaic," the classic and the modern, the purism in art and the populist elements, his own finds and the discoveries of others. His images and metaphors are like going from hot to cold water in the bathroom sink with no transition: using the element of surprise, they catch the unsuspecting reader off guard and move him, they produce in him the bittersweet sensation that Novo has proposed to communicate. . . . Together with Gorostiza, Pellicer, and Paz, Salvador Novo is one of the four most important poets of the Mexican twentieth century.[8]

In essay, Novo is known for his wittiness and his elegance: *Ensayos* (1925), *La educación literaria de los adolescentes* (1928), *Return Ticket: Viaje a Hawai* (1928), *Jalisco-Michoacán: 12 días* (1933), *Continente vacío: Viaje a Sudamérica* (1935), and *En defensa de lo usado y otros ensayos* (1938). Blanco calls him one of the best prosists in Mexico and describes *Ensayos* saying "[Novo's] innocence has been lost completely; in prose he is an erudite dandy, boasting of modernity and encyclopedism, full of humor and of twentieth-century wisdom to oppose to the wisdom of museums and archaeologists."[9] Antonio Castro Leal says, "His prose—so clear, so efficient, with a syntaxis of multiple, well-oiled hinges—almost makes one want to call it functional because it is made exactly for its purpose and because it has the sober and daring elegance of all the adornments it has spurned because they don't serve its end. One finds in it, naturally, a long education in the classics . . ."[10]

Novo also produces several anthologies which help establish him as an expert on world literature, particularly modern English-language literature, which had not been studied much in Mexico since Poe: *Antología de cuentos mexicanos e hispanoamericanos* (1923), *La poesía norteamericana moderna* (with poems translated by Novo, 1924), *La poesía francesa moderna* (1924), and *Lecturas hispanoamericanas* (1925), as well as several other anthologies for children. As early as 1922, when he is just 18, he translates *"Almaida de Entremont" y "Manzana de anís" y otros cuentos* by Francis Jammes (with a prologue by Xavier Villaurrutia), and in the late twenties is the first in Mexico to comment on lesser-known poets like Langston Hughes and Countee Cullen and Christopher Morley's "Translations from the Chinese," as well as on most other modern poets from the United States.

In 1928, bored and unimpressed by what the theaters of Mexico City have to offer, Novo and Villaurrutia take what little theatrical experience they have (some acting history and two musical revues they had written for the Teatro Lírico), a handful of friends (including Gilberto Owen and Celestino Gorostiza), and set up their own theater, Teatro Ulises, in the house of their friend Antonieta Rivas. Though the theater lasts only a few months, and though they had not intended it, Novo and his friends in Teatro Ulises set off a literary explosion whose shock waves are felt until well into the 1940s. Antonio Magaña Esquivel, in his *Medio siglo de teatro mexicano,* calls it "the arrival of the poets to theater," a line that would also later be used in the 1950s to describe Octavio Paz's Poesía en Voz Alta movement.[11]

The state of Mexican theater in the 1920s was deplorable. It had been dominated by cabarets and musical revues, comedy acts, zarzuelas, and other short pieces. According to Magaña Esquivel and others who have studied the subject, Mexican theater was overrun with Spanish influence. It was dominated by Spanish impresarios. Its repertoire was mostly Spanish, and the few Mexican playwrights who attempt anything serious at all imitate the Spaniards, Benavente, Linares Rivas, and Dicenta. Both actors and acting techniques are imported from Spain. So pervasive was the Spanish influence that even Mexican actors felt compelled to speak with a Castilian accent![12]

Teatro Ulises has two modest seasons, from January to August 1928 and then the first months of 1929. It stages six plays in translation: *La puerta reluciente* by Lord Dunsany, *Simili* by Claude Roger-Marx, *El peregrino* by Charles Vidrac, *Orfeo* by Jean Cocteau, *Ligados* by Eugene O'Neill, and *El tiempo es sueño* by Henri Lenormand. Nevertheless, Teatro Ulises is the only theater at the time to stage foreign or experimental works. Teatro Ulises also introduces new acting techniques and staging theory. When the theater closes in 1929, others quickly pick up where Teatro Ulises leaves off: Teatro de Orientación (led by Celestino Gorostiza and in which Villaurrutia participates), Proa Grupo, Teatro de Ahora, Escolares del Teatro, et al. continue to experiment on their own and to stage the experiments of young European playwrights.

In 1920, after the fall of Carranza, General Alvaro Obregón is elected president. Though he is remembered for many of his actions, especially for finally setting in motion the early stages of agrarian reform and stimulating the labor movement, Obregón's legacy to his country, at least with respect to cultural history, rests on his nomination of José Vasconcelos as the Minister of Public Education. José Joaquín Blanco here gives some idea of Vasconcelos' importance: "The struggle between the factions decided in favor of the Sonorans [Obregón and later Calles were both from Sonora], what they called the 'constructive revolution' began. With Vasconcelos in the University and later in the Ministry of Public Education, the dawn of our culture seemed to have begun and the enormous amount of energy in the arts and technology was explained by the Vasconcelan motto of substituting the troops of destruction with new contingents of construction, whose vanguard would be youth and the progressive intellectuals."[13] Vasconcelos, called the Maestro de la Juventud (Teacher of Youth) in Mexico, continued the tradition of Simón Bolívar by opposing a sort of Pan Americanism to the Monroe Doctrine. He was a member of the influential group Ateneo de México, which included other writers, like Alfonso Reyes. He built a reputation as a philosopher and intellectual with the publication of his books *Indología* and *La raza cósmica* and authored the phrase, ubiquitous in Mexico, "Por mi raza hablará el espíritu [The spirit will speak for my race]." He is also responsible for giving Diego Rivera, José Clemente Orozco, and David Alfaro Siqueiros the public walls they needed to launch their careers as muralists.

José Vasconcelos is the person most responsible for bringing the young Contemporáneos together as a group, by appointing them to fill the vacancies in the Ministry of Public Education left by the dismissal of Porfirio Díaz's *científicos*. Because he provides intellectual leadership as well as bureaucratic patronage, both Vasconcelos' presence and his absence have a profound impact on the group.

Under Vasconcelos the Contemporáneos participate in the first of the series of magazines that turns the assortment of young writers into a cohesive group and later gives the group its name: *México moderno* (1920–1923), *Vida mexicana* (1922), *La Falange* (1922–1923; the Fascists had not yet appropriated the word for themselves), *Ulises* (1927–1928; edited by Novo and Villaurrutia), *Contemporáneos: Revista mexicana de cultura* (1928–1931; the magazine that gives the group its name), and *Examen* (August to November 1932), to name the most important.[14] Novo does not play a major role in any of the magazines except *Ulises*, but through them his fate is nevertheless linked to the fate of the group. He also, with others from *Ulises*, is one of the editors of *El Espectador* in the early 1930s, in the areas of theater, art, and literature.

Shortly before the elections of 1924, when General Plutarco E. Calles is selected to be Obregón's successor, Vasconcelos resigns his position as Minister of Public Education. The loss of Vasconcelos' patronage, his subsequent exile, and political events in general in Mexico under

Calles have a disastrous effect on both the morale and the unity of the Contemporáneos.

For Novo, this is the second time in a year that he has suffered a loss. Though he was always associated with the group of Contemporáneos and with Vasconcelos, he has also been closely allied to a certain linguist and historian from the Dominican Republic working in the Escuela de Verano at the National University, Pedro Henríquez Ureña. It was Henríquez Ureña who gave Novo his first job in the government bureaucracy, teaching at the university, and it was Henríquez Ureña who served as Novo's mentor, guided his readings, encouraged him to compile his first anthologies, helped Novo to publish, and incorporated him into his small group of friends that published *Vida mexicana:* Antonio Caso, Vicente Lombardo Toldeano, Eduardo Villaseñor, the Nicaraguan Salomón de la Selva, and Daniel Cosío Villegas. However, in 1923, shortly before Henríquez Ureña's marriage to Lombardo Toldeano's sister, Henríquez Ureña and Novo have a falling out over Novo's gay activities. (Novo had gotten in the habit of picking up taxi drivers, and he even began making contributions to the taxi-driver-guild's newsletter in order to meet more.) Henríquez Ureña fires Novo from his position in the university and then, because Henríquez Ureña plans to leave the country, he leaves instructions that Novo should not be rehired. In his memoirs, Novo tells the story of how his own attendance at Henríquez Ureña's wedding ceremony later gave rise to a rumor (initiated by fellow writer Julio Torri) that Novo knelt down on the floor during the ceremony, opened his arms, and prayed aloud, "Lord, keep him for me. Lord, protect him. Lord, what's he going to do with a woman?"[15] This is probably the same Pedro who appears in Novo's poem *Never Ever*.

With Vasconcelos' resignation and Henríquez Ureña's departure, *La Falange, México moderno,* and *Vida mexicana* all suspend publication in 1923. Most of the Contemporáneos are forced to seek new positions in the Ministry of Health under Dr. Bernardo J. Gastelum, and must wait until they have established themselves there before they can resume publication of another magazine.[16] Novo, fortunately, is given a job as editorial director of the Ministry of Public Education by Vasconcelos' replacement, José M. Puig Casauranc.

Politics in the 1920s was beginning to take on the qualities that have characterized it ever since. Plutarco Calles, originally thought to be a radical, is elected in 1924. His most important appointment is Luis Morones, whom he puts in charge of the Ministry of Industry. Morones has risen to power as a labor boss, and under Calles, he, in the words of Robert Jones Schafer in *A History of Latin America,* "continued to accumulate an unsavory reputation for corruption, for subservience to employers rather than care for workers, and for the strong-arm methods of his Grupo Acción. Calles' reliance on labor became offensive to *agraristas,* and reinforced their support of Obregón."[17]

In 1926, nine years after the end of the Revolution, war breaks out again when Christian fundamentalists, the Cristeros, backed by conservative Catholics in Mexico and the United States, revolt in reaction to Calles' restrictions on the church. That same year, Calles names Obregón to be his successor as president. Because Obregón has already served as president, Calles moves to amend the constitution to allow a second term. (The Constitution of 1917 had been careful to include limits on the term of office for president, since the memory of Porfirio Díaz's multiple reelections was all too recent.)

Two generals are shot by Calles' forces for opposing Calles' nomination of Obregón. However, in 1928 Obregón himself is shot, and it is rumored that Calles' own forces are responsible, through Grupo Acción, the hit squad run by Morones. Some attribute the assassination to Calles' need to limit the power of Obregón and of the agrarian reformers.

Gastelum resigns from the Ministry of Health, again forcing many of the Contemporáneos to scramble for positions elsewhere, scattering them everywhere. Jaime Torres Bodet, José Gorostiza, and Gilberto Owen find positions with Genaro Estrada, head of Foreign Relations and an author (*Pero Galín*) as well, and leave the country. Ortiz de Montellano also obtains a post in Foreign Relations, but stays around to continue publication of the magazine *Contemporáneos.* Xavier Villaurrutia, Jorge Cuesta, and later Celestino Gorostiza end up with Novo back in the Ministry of Public Education.

With Obregón dead, and over the objections of the other generals from the Revolution, Calles imposes Emilio Portes Gil, who serves as interim president until another election can be held in 1929. At this moment, realizing that he needs institutional support and some political mechanism to unify the disparate elements that fought in the Revolution, Calles organizes the Partido Nacional Revolucionario (PNR), the party which eventually becomes the Partido Revolucionario Institucional (PRI), ruling today.

At the end of the interim term, when Calles attempts to impose another president, Pascual Ortiz Rubio, through the party mechanism of the PNR, the army revolts but is quickly put down. José Vasconcelos appears on the scene again and announces he will oppose Calles and Ortiz Rubio on the tried and true platform of *anti-reeleccionismo* (Madero's platform in 1910 against Porfirio Díaz). In its intellectual nature, Vasconcelos' campaign bears a certain resemblance to Adlai Stevenson's. He seeks an end to corruption, to military domination of the government, and to Mexican subservience to the United States. Vasconcelos "loses" what was likely a fixed election and in 1929 goes into exile, where he bitterly condemns the Calles/Ortiz Rubio government. Just two years later, in 1931, Ortiz Rubio is forced to resign because of his failure in dealing with the oncoming depression. Calles, now known as the Jefe Máximo de la Revolución (Maximum Boss of the Revolution), chooses another Sonoran, General Abelardo Rodríguez, to complete the term.

Novo makes it through this "consolidation of the Revolution"—messy as these leadership changes always were in the 1920s—fairly safely in the Ministry of Public Education, but after Vasconcelos' exile, he must leave to work in the Ministry of Industry, Commerce, and Employment, a job he never mentions in any of his writings. Novo has been left absolutely cynical by the recent turn of events, and allusions to Calles later appear in several of his writings, including *The War of the Fatties*. José Joaquín Blanco describes the effect of Vasconcelos' fall on the Contemporáneos:

> Vasconcelos is the knot that holds the generation of the Contemporáneos together; the first job this group had was *Lecturas clásicas para niños,* directed by Vasconcelos himself. And here the slight difference of ages among the Contemporáneos becomes a brutal division, as indicated by the drama of Vasconcelos. The oldest, Pellicer, Gorostiza, and Torres Bodet, were each in his own way left marked by the messianic, positive, and spiritual impulse during Vasconcelos' stay in power; the younger ones: Novo, Villaurrutia, Cuesta, and Owen, were left marked by the disaster and skepticism. . .[18]

To complicate matters, the Contemporáneos had not weathered the ten years of Callismo without picking up a few enemies along the way. Their interest in foreign literature made the Contemporáneos an easy target. Although, for example, *Ulises,* directed by Novo and Villaurrutia, included mostly contributions from the group, with some by Julio Torri and Mariano Azuela, it also included a good number of contributions from foreigners like Carl Sandburg, James Joyce, Max Jacob,

Benjamín Jarnés, Massimo Bontempelli, and Marcel Jouhandeau, and it was the inclusion of these foreigners that caused nationalists to object. *Contemporáneos* was similar. Villaurrutia cooperated with his expertise in French literature, and Novo with his in English-language literature. Almost from the start, the Contemporáneos ran into strong opposition from the most nationalistic elements of society, which accused them of being "antinationalist."[19] Emmanuel Carballo recalls some of the most typical criticism:

> Like any group with its own physiognomy, the Contemporáneos were open to the wrath and insults of other bands. Manuel Maples Arce believes they are united by a certain indeterminate "complicity." Ermilo Abreu Gómez says, referring to it, this group "has tried, without capacity of sufficient *culture*—and I don't say information—without being men enough, without an effective relationship with the land it lives in, to govern the effectiveness of the literature that ripens outside the small parcel it has rented for its debates." Time—to which the nationalistic voice of the author of *Canek* has appealed—has in part proven the Contemporáneos right. Although well sifted, their work still lives, while that of their antagonists has suffered alarming discredit. They, those who sought stimulus from abroad, grasped some of the notes that distinguish between being Mexican and the way of being Mexican in poems, essays, and works of fiction. Their "enemies" often wrote works that were more Mexicanist than Mexican.[20]

Novo was not oblivious to the literary situation of the country and answers nationalists' criticism himself, as one of the editors for *Ulises:* "We have not set out to procure whatever is national about our work, and with our words we do not wish to compromise our country."[21] Issue number six of *Ulises,* the last issue, carried yet another disclaimer: "[I]t is honorable to declare that *Ulises* does not represent 'national opinion' in any way . . . *Ulises* implies no more than two criteria, more or less in agreement the one with the other. Villaurrutia and me."[22] What Novo does not point out is that admiration of foreign literature does not imply foreign loyalties or in any way separate one from one's "people," the basic premise of the whole discussion. Worth mentioning, however, is the fact that in a country with only 20 percent literacy, like Mexico at the time the Contemporáneos began their careers, the very act of writing at all separates one to a certain extent from one's "people."

After the inauguration of Teatro Ulises, criticism of the Contemporáneos was stepped up, because it did not go unnoticed that all the works presented were by foreign authors.²³ It did not seem to matter to critics that all the actor-directors in the group were Mexican, or that much of what was commercially produced was also foreign, that is, from Spain.

Partly in reaction to the charges of "un-Mexicanism," in 1928 the Contemporáneos, although not Novo, produced an anthology of modern Mexican poetry, which, though possibly well-intentioned, ended up causing a storm of criticism by the unfortunate, though intentional, omission of various poets, particularly the modernist poet Manuel Gutiérrez Nájera. Reviews of the anthology brought on some rather colorful and nasty anti-intellectual responses, e.g., "We do not know why, nor do we care to find out, but the compilation of this anthology, circumscribed around the finicky ephebic phalanx [a reference to *La Falange*] of this suspiciously fraternal Parnassus, smells to us like the work of the university."²⁴ (Vasconcelos, in exile at the time, had been very closely identified with the university.) As Novo later recalled, "Those who were upset brandished all sorts of vile insults: they called them homosexuals, isolationists, *précieux,* criminals, bad Mexicans."²⁵ Although most of the group had participated in producing the anthology, the cover carried the name of Jorge Cuesta, and he bore the brunt of the criticism.

In 1932, Jorge Cuesta is again the center of a scandal that draws attention to the Contemporáneos when *Examen,* the short-lived magazine Cuesta edits, publishes excerpts from *Cariátide,* by Rubén Salazar Mallén. The crude language in the piece scandalizes writers at *Excelsior* and others, and José Gorostiza, head of Fine Arts, Xavier Villaurrutia in the editorial department, Jorge Cuesta, Carlos Pellicer, and the department supervisor are all forced to resign from their positions in the Ministry of Public Education. What Novo calls a "picturesque 'trial'" begins centering around the scandal at *Examen.*²⁶

Everybody seems to have gotten in on the act at one time or another. And as lasting proof of what can best be described as a campaign to discredit the Contemporáneos is the section of the murals Diego Rivera painted in the Ministry of Public Education after Vasconcelos' resignation, in which Rivera depicts the Contemporáneos as decadent lushes.

Carlos Monsiváis provides a description of the campaign against the Contemporáneos in his excellent biographical article "Salvador Novo: Los que tenemos unas manos que no nos pertenecen":

The persecution defines them pitilessly. Orozco draws cartoons of them and baptizes them "los anales" [the anal ones]. Antonio Ruiz el Corzo paints Novo and Villaurrutia as feminoids leading the protest against the "pueblo." Rivera belittles them on the walls of the Ministry of Public Education. The persecution grows: in 1932 the Porfirian Committee of Public Health is reestablished in the Chamber of Deputies to purge the government of counterrevolutionaries. October 31, 1934, a group of intellectuals (José Rubén Romero, Mauricio Magdaleno, Rafael Muñoz, Mariano Silva y Aceves, Renato Leduc, Juan O'Gorman, Xavier Icaza, Francisco L. Urquizo, Ermilo Abreu Gómez, Humberto Tejera, Jesús Silva Herzog, Héctor Pérez Martínez, and Julio Jiménez Rueda) asks the Committee, since it is attempting to purify the public administration, to "extend their policies to the individuals of doubtful morality who hold official posts and who, through their effeminate acts, in addition to constituting a punishable example, create an atmosphere of corruption, to the extreme that it impedes the instilling of the virile virtues in youth . . . If it is a question of fighting the presence of fanatics, of reactionaries in public offices, the presence of hermaphrodites incapable of identifying themselves with the workers of social reform must also be fought." In the campaign against the Contemporáneos, the most mentioned name is that of Novo (who is ridiculed as "Nalgador Sobo"). [The spoonerized version of his name means, roughly, "bun fondler."—Tr.] Gossip, accusations of transvestism, rumors about his predilection for taxi drivers—Novo's atrocious reputation grows day by day, and, not so paradoxically, such demonization is the solid and serious source of his recognition.[27]

In 1934, General Lázaro Cárdenas is elected president. Cárdenas' first task is to consolidate his own power, but to do so he must get out from under the shadow of Calles, who has come to be known as the Maximum Boss of the Revolution, who has dominated politics for ten years, who has chosen three puppet presidents to represent him, and who, furthermore, has the support of his Partido Nacional Revolucionario. Cárdenas is smart enough not to break from Calles immediately. He begins by appointing a few of Calles' men to his cabinet, Tomás Garrido Canabal as minister of agriculture and Emilio Portes Gil as head of the PNR. However, he soon moves against them, replacing Garrido Canabal with General Saturnino Cedillo, a caudillo from San Luis Potosí, and firing Portes Gil. Cárdenas also seeks to consolidate his power by shutting down Calles-run gambling and prostitution, and gains populist sympathies by refusing to live in Chapultepec Castle. He also strengthens policies favoring labor and peasants. Eventually he is able to portray Calles as a Fascist, and succeeds in exiling both him and Morones in 1936. Cárdenas further asserts his authority by reorganizing Calles' PNR, renaming it the Partido de la Revolución Mexicana. (Miguel Alemán Valdés makes it the Partido Revolucionario Institucional, the PRI, in 1952.) Much of what Cárdenas did as president is known in the United States: his nationalization of the oil industry, his granting of asylum to Leon Trotsky and refugees from the Spanish Civil War, and the lip service (for, despite everything, it was only that) he gave to socialist elements in Mexican politics.

Although Calles was hard on the Contemporáneos, their lot does not improve under Cárdenas. On the contrary, it gets worse. According to Octavio Paz, "Cárdenas' policies in cultural matters suffered from serious limitations. He was not at all attracted to the University or the higher aspects of culture, I mean to science and disinterested learning and to free art and free literature. His artistic tastes—or those of his close collaborators—tended toward pseudorevolutionary didacticism and nationalism."[28]

Under Cárdenas, literature becomes more politicized than ever, and the nationalism which previously was used to condemn the Contemporáneos now takes on an added dimension of pseudoproletarianism. Thus the experimentalism of the Contemporáneos falls into direct conflict with the populist social realism of the muralist movement, just as in Europe the avant-garde movement could not be incorporated into the tenets of social realists. In this context, what Paz refers to as the "handful of the older [writers]" or the "new literature" can be applied to the generation of the Contemporáneos:

> When a society decays, it is language that is first to become gangrenous. As a result, social criticism begins with grammar and the reestablishing of meanings. This is what has happened in Mexico. Criticism of the present state of affairs was begun, not by the moralists, not by the radical revolutionaries, but by the writers (a handful of the older but a majority of the younger). Their criticism has not been directly political—though they have not shied away from treating political themes in their works—but instead verbal: the exercise of criticism as an exploration of language and the exercise of language as an exploration of reality.
>
> The new literature, poetry as well as the novel, began by being at once a reflection on language and an attempt at creating a new language: a system of transparencies, to provoke reality into making an

appearance. But to realize this proposal it was indispensable to cleanse the language, to flush away the official rhetoric. Hence these writers had to deal with two tendencies inherited from the Revolution and now thoroughly corrupt: nationalism and an "art of the people." Both tendencies had been protected by the revolutionary regimes and their successors. The resemblances between the official aesthetics of Stalinism and the officious aesthetics of Mexican politicians and hierarchs are instructive. Mexican mural painting—originally a vigorous movement—was a prime example of this mutual accommodation between the regime and the "progressive" artists. The criticism directed at a showy nationalism and an art of patriotic or revolutionary slogans was more moral than aesthetic: it criticized imposture and servility. . . . Setting art free was the beginning of a wider freedom.[29]

Even today, it is tempting but misleading to compare the work of the Contemporáneos in literature with that of the popular muralists in art. As José Joaquín Blanco points out, what the muralists of the 1930s were trying to achieve with respect to the visual arts had already occurred in poetry during the Romantic movement of the nineteenth century, and had given as its product, for example, the national anthem, and later manifested itself as the *novela de la Revolución*. The latter, despite its proliferation, produced only one novel still remembered today, Mariano Azuela's *Los de abajo*, written more than fifteen years before Cárdenas, in 1916.[30] With respect to the *novela de la Revolución*, Novo, in a 1965 interview, says,

> [It] is very boring, and what's worse, it was born dead. As a body of literature, it isn't worth the trouble reading; individually, some works are excellent. For my taste, the focus this last generation [including *Pedro Páramo* by Juan Rulfo in 1955?—Tr.] has given the theme is more interesting. Most of the novelists of the Revolution did not have the integrity to say what really happened in the battlefields and in the private cabinets of the great bosses and ideologues. The most authentic novel is *Tropa vieja*. Its author, Francisco Urquizo, has always written—and his bibliography is extensive—the same novel. He and his congenitors have wished to make a specimen into a genus, which is a zoological aberration. These brutes—the revolutionaries like Zapata and Villa—the writers made into men: they conceded to them the faculty of reasoning, class consciousness, the possibility of indignation and of love faced with given social circumstances. In other words, they invented them.[31]

Elsewhere in the interview, Novo says, "We liked [Mariano] Azuela; today it was many years ago that he was 'discovered.' If I were to reread him, I don't know if I would still like him. *La luciérnaga* interested me more than *Los de abajo*." In *Poemas proletarios*, Novo dedicates one section of the opening poem to the *novela de la Revolución* and the so-called revolutionary literature:

> The literature of the revolution,
> revolutionary poetry
> about three or four anecdotes about Villa
> and the flourishing of *maussers*,
> the rubrics of the lasso, the woman soldier . . .[32]

Cardenismo had its representatives in literature, though they certainly did not include the Contemporáneos. No review of Mexican poetry would be complete without at least passing mention of what was the Contemporáneos' only real competition in the literary sphere, the fiasco of the *estridentistas*, an affected, self-conscious bohemianesque movement, today virtually forgotten. The *estridentista* movement is best described by José Joaquín Blanco:

> *Estridentismo* means "noise," the only thing they didn't make because, as [writer Carlos] Monsiváis explains, "a bourgeoisie that still hadn't taken shape didn't have the slightest interest in letting itself be ridiculed." The silences of the Contemporáneos, on the other hand, caused so much noise that they were persecuted as homosexuals and thrown out of their jobs, a trial was held over one of their magazines, and they were insulted with phrases like "the literary *asalta braguetas* [fly swatters? zipper burglars?] will never be able to understand the sweaty new beauty of our century." But that populist sweat, which invoked Marx and futurism, was nothing more than "infantile bravado," impotent in the face of the Edisonian reality of mechanized, industrialized urban life. Many other "poets," even more radicalized and populist, fought the Contemporáneos, though they left no seed, seeds they never had, nor noise, which they used up on themselves.[33]

To be fair, the harshness of Blanco's assessment of *estridentismo* is, though not quite unbiased, at least justifiable. As in the cultural polemics of Hitler's Germany, McCarthy's United States, Stalin's Russia, what was ostensibly a spirited, often vicious debate over aesthetics was more often than not confused and exacerbated by personality clashes, political expediency, and sexist prejudices. Carlos Monsiváis gives some indication of the (low) level of the debate between the Contemporáneos and the *estridentistas* who, along with the Mexican muralists of the Treinta-treintista group, opposed them.

The literary historians usually give a concrete limit to the *generational* work of the Contemporáneos: 1920–1932. Their collective influence and the hatred they incite are prolonged until the decade of the forties. In his *Poesía mexicana moderna* (1940), the anthologist [and *estridentista* poet] Manuel Maples Arces does not shy away from partisanship in his presentations: "Of the poets who in a symbolically Mexican revue locked themselves into the circle of the 'Contemporáneos,' drawn together by similar complexes and tendencies, Salvador Novo is one of those who has most tempted the demon of frivolity. 'Style has a sex,' Marivaux used to say, 'and one can recognize a woman through one sentence.' Here the identity is evident in an intention of triviality; no longer are desires hidden under any sexual euphemism, as in the other comrades of his tribe, but textually and without beating around the bush they proclaim the relationship that exists between individual privacy and imagery." With the subtlety that was given to him, Maples Arce continues: "Fruit of that impure vice spoken of by Valery Larbaud, Villaurrutia's poetry is offered marked by the fatalities of the sex . . . Making use of inversion [i.e., homosexuality] as a poetic device . . . Thus, in its frozen surfaces, this poetry depicts nothing more than scenes naturally inverted in the dead waters of reflection."

In the twenties, the aggression is daily and multiple. The polemic in which Julio Jiménez Rueda denies and Francisco Monterde affirms (giving Mariano Azuela as an example) the existence of a "virile Mexican literature" has an explicit context: the Contemporáneos. In 1929 or 1930, the group of realist painters, Treinta-Treinta, demands the resignation of various officials, including a few homosexuals: "And we are against homosexualism, imitation of the current French bourgeoisie; and between them, now favored, and us, tireless fighters, there is the abyss of our honor, which cannot be bought for a post. The government should not maintain those of doubtful psychological condition in its ministries."

Novo, model of the bad example. He is harassed, stigmatized. Without making him retreat: he is homosexual, he never denies or conceals it, he makes of it a symbolic badge for the daily annoyance of good manners. In the twenties, in full effervescence of machismo as the theory and praxis of the Latin American reality, Novo's attitude is a scandal. His heterodox choice is expressed as a challenge, defiant exhibition of fragility, dandyism, femininity of plucked eye-

brows. He responds to the attacks—as he is preserved in the portraits of him from the twenties and thirties—by heightening the
provocation. There, congregating ridicule and ill will, he is a Wild-
ean aesthete, a very refined snob in a golden vest, with an expression
of sweet ennui on his face and the back of his hand on his hip. He is
not the only one singled out, but he is the most ostentatious, who
accepts any insult and returns it with interest. In newspapers, magazines, and conversations, he is viciously ridiculed: he is by far the
most attacked of the Contemporáneos.

A typical attack: The Bolivian emigré Tristán Marof publishes
México de frente y de perfil (Editorial Claridad, 1934) and, in his way,
summarizes part of the climate of ferociousness against the Contemporáneos in his chapter "Effeminate Literati":

> Though against our better judgment, it is not possible
> in this chapter to leave out a strange group whose mor-
> bid tendencies from the first day I arrived in Mexico
> caused me certain pity . . . These lads write to please
> themselves. Their prose is acrobatic, movable, and insig-
> nificant. Each phrase of theirs seeks a certain "objective
> in rectitude" and they do not use Vaseline! They believe
> themselves to be disciples of Freud, of Cocteau, of Gide.
> They do pirouettes on country trapezes and, believing
> that they are cultivating a certain "Saxon humor," they
> are ridiculous. The traveler or the observer is surprised
> right from the start by the literary abuse of the word
> "joto" [faggot]. One might even guess it referred to
> some sacred name. The charm fades quickly, since the
> "joto" literary masters are sad and languid bureaucrats
> who fill inferior posts in the Mexican administration.
> They don't even constitute a picturesque band of *pillos*
> or *boleros* [blackguards or bootblacks]. Be it a Salvador
> Novo or a Villaurrutia, or a Genaro Estrada, or some
> other, the disappointment is the same . . . They have no
> imagination. Salvador Novo is the author of a dull,
> boastful book for certain lesbian women . . .
>
> Abroad those of the "jotista" literary group are in-
> transcendent; nobody pays any attention to them or is
> interested in their literature, but in Mexico they write in
> the reactionary newspapers—the only ones that circu-
> late; they are entrenched in the bureaucracy, they give
> classes in the school to boys, from whom they should be
> distanced for the sake of appearances, and, finally, they

stroll through the streets and beaches making a gala ball
out of an insolent reactionaryism and inciting people
with their stares, which are not exactly literary . . .

The embargo, the psychological pressure, the social and moral
lynchings are very intense. To them Novo opposes his literary and
journalistic prolificacy, and the ironic civic values which later, in order to assimilate them, will be marked almost unanimously by cynicism. In everything he is too much: precociousness, talent, work capacity, genius, calumny, culture, affectation. . . . The effect of the
persecution of the twenties and thirties will last in Novo the rest of
his life and, once the long years of resistance are past, it will little by
little be transformed into a desire to please and be praised, in the
truce implicated by the gradual abandonment of harassment, in the
languid photo in the kitchen or the daring toupée that stimulates,
once again, provocation. But before the suspension of hostilities, the
overwhelming disdain and sarcasm will magnify Novo's satiric dis-
position, they will justify or explain his verbal excesses, and will get
for him an abundant audience at the slightest staging of his defiance.
Novo's moral sideshow, to put it that way, will never go unnoticed;
from there he will obtain the tone and initial impact of his legend
and from there will come (from the desire to finally be accepted) his
most serious and harmful concessions.[34]

Although the Contemporáneos are faced with overwhelming unpopu-
larity in the 1930s, Novo has an initial stroke of good luck in 1933, just
before he is purged from the bureaucracy and from his position as a
teacher of history of the theater at the Conservatorio Nacional by
President Cárdenas, ironically the year before Cárdenas promulgates a
law protecting the jobs of civil servants. Back in the Ministry of Public
Education in 1933, Novo is sent to represent Mexico at an international
conference in South America, where he meets Federico García Lorca.
The experience inspires Novo to write *Continente vacío,* about the voyage, the conference, and the writers he meets in South America; *Canto
a Teresa* and *Décimas en el mar,* reviews of sea-related poetry; *Seamen
Rhymes* (the second half of which is in English and is considered an
outright act of provocation by nationalists), about the sea; and "Romance de Adela y Angelillo," a love ballad about a Mexican woman
and an Andalusian man, a bullfighter, who meet in Buenos Aires and
fall in love (as García Lorca, an Andalusian, and Novo, a Mexican, have
met in Buenos Aires). Novo also writes a play, *El tercer Fausto,* a gay

love story, tragic, despite Novo's usual funny irrelevance, which, given the mood of the country, he doesn't dare publish in Mexico until twenty-two years later. (He does, nevertheless, translate it into French and publish it in Paris in 1937 in a very limited fifty-copy edition.) In 1933 Novo also publishes *Espejo: Poemas antiguos,* memories of his childhood, and *Nuevo amor,* his best-known book of poetry, which is highly acclaimed and immediately translated into both French and English. In 1934 he publishes *Poemas proletarios,* a sort of short *Spoon River Anthology* that attacks the prevailing pseudorevolutionary populism of the times by mocking the stock phrases of official history and the Cárdenas administration's hypocritical self-portrayal as a pro-proletarian government and by portraying the pathetic lucklessness of four soldiers; *Never Ever,* one of the first attempts in Mexico at a sort of free-association or stream-of-consciousness poetry; and *Frida Kahlo,* written in the same style, a portrait, not entirely flattering, of the surrealist painter. (Earlier, Novo had written *La Diegada (1926)* in response to Frida's husband's mural in the Ministry of Public Education; however, the virulent verses are only circulated in carbon-copy manuscript form until 1955, when they appear as part of *Sátira.*)

After this short burst of energy, Novo apparently becomes disgusted with the cultural scene in Mexico under Cárdenas and goes into a sort of poetic hibernation. He researches and writes "Las aves en la poesía castellana" in 1935, as an escape from the world, but doesn't make it public until 1952. He works in advertising, develops "spots" for the television and radio, and serves as a consultant in the movie industry, where he writes dialogue and script for a variety of movies, including *Perjura, Gil de Alcalá, Los dos mosqueteros, La venganza del zorro,* and *El signo de la muerte,* starring Cantinflas.

Merlin H. Forster, who has studied the Contemporáneos extensively, puts the end of the group as a group as early as 1932, after the *Examen* scandal. Some had left the country in 1928 after the assassination of Obregón, taking up the foreign service jobs Latin America often affords its dissidents, and especially its writers, as an alternative to exile. Those who had stayed around had later been purged from the bureaucracy during the *Examen* affair or shortly afterward by Cárdenas.

Novo contributes columns to several newspapers, *Excelsior, Novedades,* and *Ultimas Noticias,* often writing anonymously, and publishes occasionally (*En defensa de lo usado,* 1938, a collection of previously published columns; *Dueño mío,* 1944, in limited edition, a collection of four of the funniest and most exquisite gay love sonnets ever written [included, with others, only in the two *Sátiras*]; *Decimos: "Nuestra tierra,"* 1949, which reflects a nostalgia for less complex times; and *Florido laude* in 1945, a rather uninteresting series of verses about flowers written for the Fiesta de la Flor). Nevertheless, Novo is beaten, and he does not really come back to the literary scene until after the last Cárdenas appointee leaves office, twenty years after the *Examen* scandal.

José Joaquín Blanco describes the options for writers of Novo's and our times:

> In general [the Mexican writer] finds himself situated between very narrow options. There are obsessive taboos: not to be outdated (how is the Mexican going to go on writing sonnets when the North Americans have already gotten to the moon?); not to be European-ized (betrayal of one's country!); not to be personal (the privileged condition of forming part of the "very few" implies an awareness of that injustice and tries to resolve it speaking as representative of those who don't have a voice); not to be too cultured or present one-self as such (the successful writer is he who appears anti-intellectual, the intellectualized writer gives the impression of a gentleman who attends a gathering of beggars in coat and tails), etc.
>
> Poetry in this way appears as either a messianic apostolate or as a *déraciné* luxury. Apostolate if it seeks to morally and emotively con-solidate the basic aspects of the national personality (which is equal to a moral defense of the Fatherland), to give a voice to those who lack one, to register the poor reality that surrounds it. Luxury, ivory tower, and *malinchismo* if it dares break the taboos mentioned.[35]

Novo by 1934 had broken all the taboos mentioned. With his expertise in foreign literature, he appears intellectual, "too cultured," and Euro-peanized. He is personal, even intimate, in many of his poems (Rivera, in fact, in his mural depicted Novo as a gentleman in tails); he refuses to be the Voice of the Oppressed Masses, at least in the way that is expected of him; and he is in a way outdated. Though he introduces many new innovations in poetry, in his longing for less industrialized, less standardized times (in cummings-esque poems like "El mar" and "Diluvio" in *XX poemas*), he at times appears outdated, if for no other reason than his insistence on the value of writing for writing's sake in an age of utilitarianism, when poetry too must be made "useful" to the new nation. In the 1930s under Cárdenas, Novo loses his resolve and at some point writes this burlesque sonnet (published in *Sátira* but probably written earlier) about the futility of writing, which for the sake of form, and to avoid the funding censors of the Jesse Helms committee, is perhaps best left in the original:

Escribir porque sí, por ver si acaso
se hace un soneto más que nada valga;
para matar el tiempo, y porque salga
una obligada consonante al paso.

Porque yo fui escritor, y éste es el caso
que era tan flaco como perra galga;
crecióme la papada como nalga,
vasto de carne y de talento escaso.

¡Qué le vamos a hacer! Ganar dinero
y que la gente nunca se entrometa
en ver si se lo cedes a tu cuero.

Un escritor genial, un gran poeta . . .
Desde los tiempos del señor Madero,
es tanto como hacerse la puñeta.[36]

In 1936, García Lorca is killed by the Fascists in Spain. Jorge Cuesta commits suicide in 1942.

When we resurrect
—I'm planning to do so—
between us and this century
there will be an association of ideas
in spite of our format.

("Resúmenes," *XX poemas*)

III

In 1949, under the presidency of Miguel Alemán, toward the end of
Salvador Novo's self-imposed silence, poetic hiatus, government black-
listing, exile in his own country, or whatever one chooses to call it, an
archaeologist named Eulalia Guzmán announced that she had discovered the long-hidden remains of Cuauhtémoc, last Aztec emperor,
symbol of the heroic resistance to the Spanish Conquest, and subject
of two of the plays contained here.

According to accounts by Cortés in his fifth *Letter of Relation* to the
king of Spain, after the Conquest, in 1525, Cuauhtémoc was hung for
allegedly plotting a rebellion against Cortés' troops during a Spanish
expedition to the Gulf of Honduras. In the four centuries that followed, poets from both Mexico and abroad variously used the figure
of Cuauhtémoc as a symbol of bravery and passion; as the romantic
reminder of the nobility of a bygone era (with emphasis on *bygone,* as
illustrated by the words of Cuauhtémoc in these verses by the Romantic poet Ignacio Rodríguez Galván, 1816–1842, "My century has
passed: my people all / will never lift their dark face, / now sunken in
loathsome mud"); and as justification for a new empire, independent
from Europe (under Iturbide), or for a new republic, led by a Native
American (under Juárez).[37] Nothing, however, was known about the
whereabouts of Cuauhtémoc's body during those four hundred years
other than that it had been left hanging on a ceiba tree somewhere
near a town once called Acallan.

Then, in 1949, *Excelsior,* one of Mexico's most respected newspapers,
ran a report of a Native American man in a small town in Guerrero
who claimed to have documents proving the whereabouts and burial

place of Cuauhtémoc's body. The documents had allegedly been signed by Toribio de Motolinía, a sixteenth-century Franciscan monk known as Protector of Indians, and told the story of how Aztec subjects still loyal to Cuauhtémoc had secretly recovered his body and transported it to a town, Ichcateopan, for burial. As the tradition of the town goes, Motolinía swore the locals to secrecy out of well-based fears that Spaniards would exhume the body.

The furor and excitement triggered by the claim was similar to what would happen if Amelia Earhart's body were suddenly discovered, or Adolf Hitler's, for lack of a better comparison, or Leif Eriksson's, or the holy grail.

The government immediately directed the National Institute of Anthropology and History to investigate, and it in turn commissioned Eulalia Guzmán, a respected archaeologist with a Ph.D. in anthropology. Guzmán had studied in both Mexico and Germany, was up-to-date on recent technological methods, and had assisted Alfonso Caso in his momentous discovery and excavation of tomb number seven at the Zapotec-Mixtec ruins in Monte Albán. Though some of her colleagues openly scoffed at her from the start, saying the idea of finding Cuauhtémoc's body was preposterous or impossible, Guzmán duly began her investigation.

The details of the case are rather complicated (they are more thoroughly described in Dolores Roldán's *Códice de Cuauhtémoc* [Mexico City: Orion, 1984]), but briefly, Guzmán, using the information found in the documents supposedly signed by Motolinía, and inspired by the oral tradition of the townspeople and by accounts from various Aztec codices that indicated that Ichcateopan had been Cuauhtémoc's birthplace and kingdom, eventually discovered what she believed to be the bones of Cuauhtémoc, under the main altar of a sixteenth-century church in Ichcateopan. They were covered by a few semiprecious beads, a spearhead, and a copper plaque with the words "1525 1529 Lord and King Coatemo" crudely etched in it. (The year 1525 was the date of Cuauhtémoc's hanging; 1529, the date of his burial by Motolinía, according to the documents of Ichcateopan. According to local sources, bodies that are hung dry out like a piece of fruit, rather than decaying, which explains how the four-year span between death and burial was possible.) A deformed foot bone, the third metatarsal, seemed to attest to the identity of the skeleton, since shortly after the fall of Tenochtitlan, the capital of the Aztec Empire, the Spaniards, convinced that Cuauhtémoc knew the hiding place of Moctezuma's treasure, had tortured him by burning his hands and feet.

The governor of Guerrero quickly rushed to the scene, followed by Alfonso Caso, director of the Instituto Nacional Indigenista, and other dignitaries. Reports describe the emotion of the townspeople at the tomb—some crying, some shouting "My King! My King!"—and the vigil set up by the community to guard the remains, which had been sealed in a box and wrapped in the Mexican flag.

Newspapers speculated about what should be done with the bones, whether they should be interred with other national leaders, whether a new monument should be built, whether they should remain in Ichcateopan. Guzmán was popularly acclaimed for her success in unraveling the clues of the documents to discover the bones of a national hero, lying in oblivion for four centuries.

Almost immediately, however, for whatever reason, be it professional rivalry, sexism, fear of the political consequences for the still largely non-Indian government (what if Cuauhtémoc's royal heirs could be traced, some speculated), or just healthy scientific skepticism, the charges of fraud began. There were claims that the documents by Motolinía were forgeries, that Ichcateopan had not been the town's name in the sixteenth century, that the bones had been taken from a nearby cemetery, that the plaque and other artifacts had been chemically aged. Although all these suspicions were eventually discredited, fellow archaeologists began to ridicule Guzmán as the victim of a hoax, or even its originator.

The Mexican government promptly appointed a commission of "experts"—"wise men," as the headlines sarcastically called them—to review Guzmán's evidence. Swamped in publicity, the commission began an investigation which some charged was more political than scientific. (The credentials and objectivity of some of the commissioners were doubtful.) Passions ran high. Popular sentiment against the commission increased with its every pronouncement about the inconclusiveness of the evidence.

In an effort to vindicate Guzmán's claims, the popular muralist Diego Rivera was summoned to attempt a portrait of the Aztec prince. His rendition, based on a reassembly of the bones, was then compared with descriptions of Cuauhtémoc in accounts by the conquistadors. José Vasconcelos, now back in the country, was called upon to attest to Guzmán's character, which he willingly did, declaring, "Eulalia Guzmán is no charlatan." Everybody who was anybody was forced to take one side or the other.

By all accounts, the investigation became somewhat of a monkey trial. Dolores Roldán, passionate in her attempt to vindicate Guzmán, to the extent that she bordered on the melodramatic, compared the commission to the church tribunal that considered Galileo's theories on the universe, and to the "scientists" of Columbus' day considering his claim that the earth might not be flat. The commission, to the surprise of nobody, ended up declaring that all of the evidence had been fabricated.

Nevertheless, thousands of school children marched down Paseo de la Reforma in Mexico City to cover Cuauhtémoc's statue with flowers. High school students marched at night by torchlight in a homage to the fallen prince. Even the armed forces organized an act to honor Cuauhtémoc as Mexico's greatest military strategist, and the Senate proclaimed the need to raise a monument and inscribe Cuauhtémoc's name on the walls of the Senate building.

Under pressure, in 1950, the case was reopened and another commission was formed, pompously called La Gran Comisión Investigadora sobre la Autenticidad de los Restos de Cuauhtémoc (The Grand Investigative Commission on the Authenticity of the Remains of Cuauhtémoc). Though less contrary than the first commission, in the sense that it admitted that forgery of many of the artifacts was not likely based on chemical analyses and other tests, the commission still refused to authenticate Guzmán's discovery.

What Guzmán did then is unclear, although it is known that she was left to live in near poverty. Marginalized and ridiculed by the scientific community in Mexico, did she persevere, ceaselessly petitioning the government in attempts to have the remains authenticated and to clear her name, thus becoming a modern version of the pathetic Carlota la Loca, wife of Emperor Maximilian, who for years after her expulsion from Mexico attempted, rather ridiculously, to have Napoleon restore her to the throne? Or did Guzmán retreat in disgrace? Details are not available—not for Guzmán in any case. Carlota, subject of one of the plays here, eventually went insane and lived the last sixty years of her life in a demented state. She died in 1926, when Novo was twenty-two. (Refer to the glossary for more details.)

Regardless of what Guzmán herself did, however, the issue of the authenticity of the Ichcateopan discovery is still a hot one twenty-five years later. In 1973, under pressure, President Luis Echeverría declares the town a national monument, and in 1976, under President José López-Portillo, yet another commission is formed to review the methodology and conclusions of previous commissions.

The commission of 1976 is more objective but still falls short of authenticating the claims. What is worse, when the bones are transported to Ichcateopan for display in a glass tomb at the site of their discovery, it is discovered that someone has removed the first cervical vertebra and the misshapen third metatarsal, which had proven a key factor in establishing the identity of the bones.

What Novo's opinion was on the authenticity of the Ichcateopan discovery is hard to judge. Nevertheless, it is likely that Guzmán gained his sympathy, never awarded lightly, at least with respect to the unfair treatment she received before the Gran Comisión. It is certain to have reminded Novo of the treatment Novo's friends, the editors of *Examen,* had received during an earlier monkey trial, one that was the culmination of a long smear campaign against the Contemporáneos, including Novo. In any case, Guzmán's story was enough to motivate Novo to include her as a character in *Cuauhtémoc and Eulalia,* in his set of *Diálogos,* published in 1956, five years after the results of the second commission were disclosed. And it is likely that the affair was also influential in his decision to write *Cuauhtémoc,* published in 1962.

Ironically, while Eulalia Guzmán's career is coming to a crashing halt, Novo's seems to have taken off again. The election of Miguel Alemán in 1946 marks the end of the long series of military presidents in Mexico. Alemán is the first leader since the 1910 Revolution who has not been chosen from among the many generals of the war, or from among the participants in any of the factional battles. Though many deplore this as the end to what they call the revolutionary period, for Novo the civilian government means an end to persecution, more tolerance for cultural innovation, and a chance to win back the public exposure and admiration so long denied him. In 1946, Novo wins the Premio Ciudad de México and $2,000 pesos with his monograph *Nueva grandeza mexicana,* based on Bernardo Balbuena's eighteenth-century *Grandeza mexicana* and Francisco Salazar's earlier works, *Crónica de la Nueva España* and *Diálogos latinos.* It also incorporates certain elements of Novo's 1923 serial novel *El joven* or *¡Qué México! Novela en que no pasa nada.*[38] Novo splits the prize money, donating half to the National University and half to the national literacy campaign.

What Novo's unfettered opinion of Alemán might have been is difficult to say. He satirizes the president's wealth and corruption in *The War of the Fatties* and in *In Ticitézcatl,* but owes to him the fact that he is once again allowed to work in the government bureaucracy. With

Alemán's approval, Carlos Chávez, composer of *Sinfonía india* and director of the newly reorganized National Institute of Fine Arts, names Novo head of the institute's theater department, a position Novo holds until the next change of presidents.

(It is no wonder that Novo later organized his chronicles of cultural life in Mexico around the different presidential periods; and if we are to believe what he says in a 1965 interview with Emmanuel Carballo, Novo would probably have considered arranging a literary anthology the same way. Carballo: "Based on what you've just told me, do you believe that in Mexico, more than literary *movements,* we have political *moments,* translated into the printed word?" Novo: "Yes. In Mexico everything happens according to the spasmodic ejaculations of its politics." [39] Indeed, Novo's own works can be grouped very comfortably into presidential periods.)

As theater director for the National Institute of Fine Arts from 1946 to 1952 (Alemán's term as president), Novo's impact on the Mexican stage is substantial. He organizes the Escuela Nacional de Teatro to train young actors, scenery artists, production workers, and directors. The new pool of trained professionals is largely responsible for the boom in the number of theaters inaugurated during the 1940s and 1950s. Antonio Magaña Esquivel, in his *Medio siglo de teatro mexicano,* lists twenty-five new theaters that open in Mexico City alone during that period. [40]

Xavier Villaurrutia and Celestino Gorostiza are also involved in the efforts to rejuvenate theater in Mexico, and in a real way, it is as though the group from Teatro Ulises had returned to dominate the stage, this time with near unanimous approval. (Novo may indeed have been gloating over this fact when he thought up the title for his play, *Ha vuelto Ulises* [*Ulysses Has Returned*], published some time later.)

During his first season at the National Institute of Fine Arts, Novo produces three plays written by Mexicans: *La huella,* by Agustín Lazo; *El pobre Barba Azul,* by Xavier Villaurrutia; and *El gesticulador,* by Rodolfo Usigli. However, no one objects when in 1948 Novo produces four foreign plays and one of his own, an adaptation for children. The year 1949 even sees August Strindberg's *Danza macabra* (*Dance of Death*), and the season of 1950 must have made nationalists turn over in their graves. Five works by Mexican authors were staged: *Rosalba y los llaveros,* by Emilio Carballido; *Antonio,* by Rafael Bernal; *Los de abajo,* by Mariano Azuela; *Xicaltépec,* by Roberto Blanco Moheno; and *Cuauhtémoc,* by Efrén Orozco; and *fourteen* foreign plays: Jean-Paul

Sartre's *Muertos sin sepulcro* (*Huis clos*), Eugene O'Neill's *El emperador Jones* (*The Emperor Jones*), Luigi Pirandello's *El hombre, la bestia y la virtud* (*L'uomo, la bestia e la virtu*), Ramón María Valle Inclán's *La marquesa Rosalinda,* Euripides' *Medea,* Lillian Hellman's *The Little Foxes* (performed in the original English!), Prosper Mérimée's *La carroza de la Perricholi* (*La carrosse du saint-sacement*), Alejandro Casona's *Fablilla del secreto bien guardado,* Edmond Rostand's *Cyrano de Bergerac,* Evelyn Williams' *Trespass* (performed in English), T. S. Eliot's *The Cocktail Party* (performed in English), Emmanuel Roblès' *Monserrat* (*Montserrat*), Conrado Nalé Roxlo's *Una viuda difícil,* and Noel Coward's *Un espíritu travieso* (*Blythe Spirit*). Needless to say, the scales tipped back the next year when only works by Mexican authors were staged, including the premier of *Corona de sombras,* by Rodolfo Usigli; *Los signos del zodiaco,* by Sergio Magaña; and *La culta dama,* which is Novo's first full-length success, a satire of the bourgeois lady in Mexico. The play causes a small scandal in the newspapers, proving that the organizer of Teatro Ulises has not lost his bite.

Novo's old enemies, on the other hand, seem to be losing theirs. In 1959, Novo lends his support to the Poesía en Voz Alta movement (a theater group started in 1956 whose proponents included Emmanuel Carballo, Juan José Arreola, Héctor Mendoza, Nancy Cárdenas, and later Octavio Paz) by allowing the group to use one of the theaters under his jurisdiction to produce Jean Genet's *The Maids* (*Les bonnes*). The few who object with cries of "Homosexuals!" and "Enemies of Mexico!"—the same charges once leveled at Teatro Ulises—are outnumbered.

In the late forties, Novo dedicates much of his time to the foundation of children's theater for the nation. In conjunction with the 400-year anniversary of Cervantes, Novo writes a stage adaption of *Don Quixote* for children. The farce and two *entremeses,* humorous one-act plays, (with music by Carlos Chávez, among others) are a major success and reach nearly 55,000 children. The next year he writes and directs *El coronel Astucia,* based on *Astucia,* by Luis G. Inclán.

Although Novo leaves the National Institute of Fine Arts when Adolfo Ruiz Cortines is elected president in 1952, he is named to the Academia Mexicana de la Lengua, and with the backing of investors, led by none other than President Ruiz Cortines, is able to inaugurate his own small theater, Teatro de la Capilla in Coyoacán, with only ninety-eight seats. There Novo produces several experimental plays, most of which he translates himself, and is the first in Mexico to stage

Samuel Beckett's *Waiting for Godot.* He also writes and stages all six of his "dialogues": *Joven II* (between his old self and his young self), *Adán y Eva* (between Adam and Eve), *Cuauhtémoc y Eulalia* (included here), *Diego y Betty* (between Diego Rivera and a reporter from the United States), *La Güera y la Estrella* (between actress María Félix and La Güera Rodríguez, a character created by Artemio de Valle Arizpe), *Malinche y Carlota* (included here), and *Tercer Fausto* (published in French in 1937, but appearing in Spanish for the first time, a dialogue between a young gay man and Mephistopheles, and later between the man as a woman and his lover). In the style of the Drama Quartet (Charles Laughton, Charles Boyer, Agnes Moorhead, and Cedric Hardwicke), the productions are limited to readings by Novo himself and actress Marilú Elízaga. (Dramatic readings were also one of the techniques explored by the Poesía en Voz Alta movement.)

Toward the end of President Ruiz Cortines' term, Novo is named director of the Escuela de Arte Dramática, which he had helped create. He also writes and produces another successful three-act play, about the political corruption of the news media, *A ocho columnas,* and his name is promptly banned from the newspaper alluded to. The editor threatens not even to publish Novo's obituary. (The "eight columns" of the title refer to the eight columns of text on the standard newspaper page.)

The presidential period of Adolfo López Mateos, beginning in 1958, is Novo's most important with respect to theater. In 1963, he wins the Premio Juan Ruiz de Alarcón, amidst some controversy, for *The War of the Fatties* (*En pipiltzintzin* [*Los niñitos*] *o La guerra de las gordas: Comedia en dos actos*). He translates and directs several works (Rattingham's *Mesas separadas* [*Separate Tables*], Robert E. Sherwood's *Camino a Roma* [*The Road to Rome*], Alan Jay Lerner's *Brigadoon,* William Shakespeare's *Otelo* [*Othello*], George Bernard Shaw's *Santa Juana* [*Saint Joan*], and *Un hombre contra el tiempo* [*A Man for All Seasons*] by Robert Bolt).

In addition to *The War of the Fatties,* Novo writes three other successful plays under President López Mateos: *Yocasta, o casi* (1961), *Ha vuelto Ulises* (1962), and *Cuauhtémoc* (1962). The first two pieces are based on classical legends. *Yocasta, o casi* is the story of Oedipus' mother projected into modern times. The title is a play on "I, chaste, or almost" and "Almost Jocasta." *Ha vuelto Ulises* centers around Penelope's mixed emotions upon Ulysses' return from Troy. Its prologue, with several long, optional passages about the structure of classical

Greek theater, is typical of Novo's interest in literature that talks about itself. The same year *Ha vuelto Ulises* is published, Novo publishes *Letras vencidas,* a series of essays on literary history and criticism, several specifically about history of the theater. Novo's interest in theater history and classical theater is significant, because its influence is seen and (typically) commented upon, both in *The War of the Fatties* and later in *In Ticitézcatl.*

Much more important than any classical influence that can be found in the plays contained here, and an important cultural event for Mexican society in general, is the publication, in the late 1950s and early 1960s, of a series of books that makes previously inaccessible Aztec culture available to the general public. In the context of Mexican literature, the importance of these works cannot be understated, for they make Novo part of the first generation of Mexican writers to be legitimately considered heirs to pre-Hispanic literature. (Novo, incidentally, is one of the first Mexican writers to have seriously studied Nahuatl, which served him not only in his capacity as a writer but also as Official Historian of the City of Mexico from 1965 to 1974.)

Despite claims to the contrary, earlier writers cannot, except in limited cases, claim any literary connection to their Aztec predecessors. José Joaquín Blanco explains why:

> To consider the poetry of pre-Hispanic Mexico and New Spain as the origins [of modern Mexican literature] implies giving them an intentionality they didn't have. In the importance that the liberals gave to pre-Hispanic texts, Menéndez y Pelayo saw a cultural falsification, given that, on the one hand, only enigmatic fragments existed in the 19th century, from which only very fantastically could any interpretation at all be derived, and on the other, as a cultural fact, the cultured Mexicans, like the Europeans, knew more about Mesopotamian cultures than they did about Teotihuacan or Chichén. . . . Recall too that it was only until well into the 20th century that pre-Hispanic poetry was translated, studied and conveniently distributed.[41]

With that in mind, the novelty and importance of the plays included in this book cannot be thoroughly understood without considering the publication of Alfonso Caso's famous book *Los Aztecas: El pueblo del Sol* (in the second half of the 1950s), which Novo ridicules in the "Presentation" of *The War of the Fatties;* Miguel León Portilla's *Veinte himnos sacros nahuas* (in 1958), parts of which are paraphrased in the deliv-

ery room scene in *The War of the Fatties;* a second book by León
Portilla, *La visión de los vencidos: Relaciones indígenas de la conquista* (in
1961), which influences the perspective of *Cuauhtémoc;* Novo's own
Breve historia de Coyoacán (in 1962), which serves as the basis for a
longer, never-published book, *Historia de Coyoacán,* from which "Ahuítzotl and the Magic Water" is excerpted; and, in 1964, Angel María
Garibay Kintana's *La literatura de los aztecas,* following up his earlier
Epica náhuatl. The latter two pieces serve as the basis for *In Ticitézcatl*
and other adaptations Novo prepares to be performed on-site in Teotihuacan as part of a spectacular light show, *Luz y sonido,* for the cele-
bration of the 1968 Olympics. All published in the late 1950s and 1960s,
these above-mentioned books, which Novo uses as sources for his stories from Aztec history, have, to use the reviewer's phrase, been both
long awaited and much anticipated. Their publication is one of the
most exciting events in the history of Mexican literature, and certainly
one of Novo's intentions is to communicate the find.

But Novo is not Pablo Neruda encountering the heights of Machu
Picchu. Though the two were born the same year, while Neruda was
reading Walt Whitman, Novo was reading Dorothy Parker.[42] Needless
to say, Novo's attitude, even when he considers the sacred history of
the Aztecs, is not reverential. Since 1927 he has been the "curioso im-
pertinente," a name he borrowed from Cervantes for his column in
Ulises. Cynicism is his calling, his responsibility even, if we let Carlos
Monsiváis tell it:

> In the 20th century in Mexico it falls to Salvador Novo to initiate a
> singular task of demolition: to chip away at the Sacred Institutions,
> to prove that myths are vulnerable, to find the flaws in our Great
> Names. *To demythify, to desacralize,* are verbs that, in Mexico, Novo
> has cultivated more than anybody: in a country where the people are
> regimented by respect, paralyzed by it, satire is a sin. If we don't
> know how to praise, we are told, much less can we exercise our fac-
> ulties of discrimination, the critical powers that reveal the faults, the
> Achilles' heels of a country and its way of noticing or not noticing
> reality. Therein lies the reason the labors of Novo—who has in-
> vented new forms of attack, who has made aggression into an art
> and has given combative possibilities to a respectful literature—have
> become so indispensable.[43]

Novo's curious impertinence or satiric irrelevance is still evident in each
of the plays contained here. In each, he unmasks or, to use the word
he coined, "demythifies" a national myth. They abound in Mexico, at

least according to Octavio Paz: "Mexico's public art is state art, swollen like a circus athlete. Its only major rival is Soviet art. Our specialty is the glorification of official figures painted or sculpted with the well-known method of amplification. The mass production of cement giants. Our parks and squares smother under a vegetation of heavy civic monuments."[44]

In *The War of the Fatties,* Novo unmasks the myth of the sad-faced Indian, the myth of the Pueblo del Sol, the myth of the ethics of the Aztec rulers and of the PRI (ruling party in Mexico today), and, particularly, of Calles, Cárdenas, and Alemán. As Emilio Carballido says, *"The War of the Fatties* is medicine for our ancient pre-Hispanic world, so sick from solemnity and rhetoric, it injects it with a shot of life-giving humor, confers on it the vitality of laughter."[45] In *Malinche and Carlota,* Novo unmasks the myth of the complete indefensibility of those two women's positions, and the myth of complete independence under Juárez. In "A Few Aspects of Sex among the Nahuas," it is the myth of women's lack of sexual desire, and the myth of the modern origin of creative sexual practices (further developed in his "Las locas y la Inquisición," in *Las locas, el sexo, los burdeles*). In "Ahuítzotl and the Magic Water," if it can be considered in this context, it is the myth that the old empire had no problems whatsoever, and the myth that early historians understood the use of the period. In *In Ticitézcatl,* it is the myth that the legend of Quetzalcóatl's return is all there is to know about him, and the myth that classical Nahuatl culture is incompatible with classical Western form. In *Cuauhtémoc,* it is the romantic myth that contemporary Native Americans do not share the same virtues as their ancestors (achieved by casting Cuauhtémoc as "A Young Native American Man," i.e., any young Native American man), and the myth that everyone was satisfied with the imperial structure (an important reminder in a country that has occasionally looked toward monarchy as a form of government and has concentrated the powers of a monarch in the office of the president). And, finally, in *Cuauhtémoc and Eulalia,* it is the myth that we are ready to face the facts and give up our myths, replacing them with a handful of beads and a rusty spearhead, and the myth that we ought to.

The role of a cynic is rarely appreciated by one's contemporaries, but by the mid-1960s Novo has been able to cut a place for himself in the history of Mexican literature, and he enjoys a popularity he has never had but long deserved. He has been awarded the Premio Ciudad de

México for *Nueva grandeza mexicana* in 1946, been appointed to the Academia Mexicana de la Lengua in 1952, won the Premio Ruiz de Alarcón for *The War of the Fatties* in 1963. In 1964, Novo's 813-page collection of his best prose, *Toda la prosa,* which he publishes on the insistence of Nobel laureate Gabriela Mistral, is heralded by the press.

Novo's triumph over past adversities is worth gloating over, and in 1965, it is motive enough for his friend and colleague Emmanuel Carballo to write, somewhat vindictively:

> Novo is a cynic, a human being who calls things—as prohibited as they might be—by their first name. Since his youth he had known how to be what some of his contemporaries refused to accept: a distinct human being. Without euphemisms, in prose and in verse, he faced up to his destiny and lived all his hours as they came. Today after many long years of slights and hypocrisy, readers and critics recognize in him a writer, a great writer, an agonist who has sneered at his tragedy, a human being who has lived according to his desires, his insecurities, and also to the roles he played, both great and small.[46]

In 1966, in a volume that also includes *In Ticitézcatl* and *Cuauhtémoc,* Novo publishes two more short plays, *El sofá* and *El diálogo de ilustres en la Rotonda. El sofá* is a debate on the relative worth of tradition and money, as seen by three generations of tailors (the oldest is blind; the youngest wants to be an electrician) and a woman from the United States who wants to buy their sofa. *El diálogo de ilustres en la Rotonda* is a one-act comedy that includes just about anybody who is anybody in Mexican letters. Gathered in the rotunda mentioned in *Cuauhtémoc and Eulalia* are the ghosts of Alfonso Reyes, Enrique González Martínez, Amado Nervo, Juan José Tablada, Mariano Azuela, Luis G. Urbina, Virginia Fábregas, and Angela Peralta. Novo parodies them as they discuss their reception speeches for Ramón López Velarde, who is scheduled to be interred but who is preempted by a Dr. Mora who "brings with him credentials of Intellectual Father of the Reforma." As they wait, they discuss Novo's contemporaries Jaime Torres Bodet and Bernardo Ortiz de Montellano.

In 1968, a street is named after Novo in Coyoacan; he is one of the very few writers to have received this tribute during their lifetimes.

Thy bosom is endeared with all hearts
Which I by lacking have supposed dead . . .

(epigraph, *Nuevo amor*)

IV

Forty years of marginalization and personal attacks do not go by without taking a toll on even the most noble of leaders, and despite his ultimate success, their effect on Novo is obvious. When in 1968 the government of Gustavo Díaz Ordaz fiercely puts down the student movement by attacking a peaceful demonstration in Tlatelolco, the government calls upon Novo as Official Historian of the city to defend the action. His complaisance seems particularly cowardly in comparison with Octavio Paz's resignation of his ambassadorship to India in protest. However, unlike Paz, Novo had a show to put on, in Mexico, not New Delhi (his show *Luz y sonido* was scheduled to be performed in Teotihuacan during the Olympics), and, unlike Paz, Novo had already experienced enough government retaliation for noncooperation in his lifetime, on his own, without asking for it. Perhaps he reasoned that little would have been gained by his resignation. But his support!

As late as 1959, old-line critics had still not forgiven Novo, or the Contemporáneos as a whole, for their so-called lack of patriotism, for their definition of themselves as twentieth-century individuals rather than nineteenth-century nationalists, for their distaste for the ostentatious proletarianism of Rivera and Cárdenas, for the ubiquitous sloganism, for the concept of literature as an arm of propaganda. Nor had the Contemporáneos been forgiven for their interest in foreign as well as national literature.[47] More contemporary critics, however, who have dismissed these issues as absurd and have condemned the witch hunt of Contemporáneos under Cárdenas—which must seem to them as ridiculous as the HUAC, the Cold War, and the McCarthy era seem to critics in this country—still struggle to appreciate Novo because of his apparently ambiguous sympathies.

Carlos Monsiváis (born in 1938) explains Novo's seeming slide to the right thus:

> "Nothing," declared Jean Cocteau, "is as difficult to maintain as a bad reputation." That of Novo's cracks during the presidency of Miguel Alemán. At the luncheon in his honor, flanked by Vasconcelos and Torres Bodet, there is a homage by the democratic left for his work *La culta dama,* interpreted as a criticism of the bourgeoisie. Almost the ultimate: in 1947 Novo becomes a founding member (secretary of propaganda) of the then-leftist Partido Popular . . . [Later], at the beginning of the government of Adolfo Ruiz Cortines, Novo (48 years old) gives up counting on his provocations. . . . From defiance to complacency: very honored among the continual visits from the First Lady, doña María Izaguirre de Ruiz Cortines; very happy about the profusion of bankers, renowned professionals, politicians, intellectuals that fills the theater to capacity and admires the menu . . . To give in a little is to give up too much. Novo, clutching the pardon, makes fun of the subversives, finds in his friendship with the oligarchy his greatest vainglory, he even renounces defense of "the tribe." When a controversy arises in 1955 because of the prohibition of a play about lesbians, Novo intervenes to speak of "libertinism," of protecting the public from "sordid instincts," of the right of the authorities to protect morality and good manners. Such degradation reaches perfection: "If the Government did not have guardianship over such concepts [morality, good manners], its right to persecute thieves, to jail murderers, punish delinquents, would be invalidated—in a word, to repress antisocial manifestations, whatever kind they are, and thus they recur to the sanctuary of art to there take refuge like a thief that takes refuge in a church . . . May the day come when our robust health is freely repulsed by such exotic dishes."[48]

Like Novo's earlier defenders, José Joaquín Blanco (born 1951), perhaps the youngest and most objective critic, attempts to explain Novo's incongruous political shifts by blaming the torturous political climate:

> *The great disadvantage* of the Contemporáneos, as with the generation of the Ateneo de la Juventud, was their enemies. These stupid, opportunistic enemies little by little forced them into positions that were ever more asphyxiating, until they ended up in aberration. They didn't leave them alone until they had justified their literary activity in the same terms as the prevailing Powers. . . . In Novo it is clear: he became abject by entering into the game of the interlocutor. . . . Inevitably, literature is in contact with its enemies: what we

wish we didn't know about the Contemporáneos . . . reveals the prevailing moral space, which they succumbed to perhaps out of fatigue . . . or from disenchantment, and from personal weakness. . . . The Contemporáneos, exiles in their own land, are also exiled in their poetry. . . . The poet, as expatriot, as a treasonous exception, as a bloody denunciation of the cultural failure of the country.[49]

Blanco is more successful with a second approach, explaining Novo's actions, his life in fact, as a sort of expedient but undenied hypocrisy, in which Novo makes it painfully clear to all that, under duress, he has compromised himself:

The figure and poetry of Novo are invaluable despite his political corruption and mercenarism, for the sincerity with which he faces up to his disaster and takes it, in his satirical poems, to its cruelest consequences, a bitterness without tears, without complaint:

> I can write perfect verses,
> measure them and avoid assonances,
> poems that will move whoever reads them
> and that will make them exclaim:
> "What an intelligent boy!"
> . . . .
> I shall seek the best of histrionics
> to make them believe that what
> moves them also moves me.
>
> But in my bed, alone, sweetly,
> memoryless and voiceless
> I sense that the poem has not come from me.

Novo doesn't try to fool himself nor does he try to fool us: within the *very narrow* mark of opinions in his time, he chose the one that was most to his advantage. For a frivolous, intelligent, educated homosexual, in the twenties and thirties the "caminos del bien" were not open to him. The governments of Calles and Cárdenas had treated him like a dog: he accepted the sweetest servitude in private initiative, and when the government opened the doors under Avila Camacho and Alemán, he entered, happy to charge a good price for his efficient services. To have chosen another path in his conditions would have demanded greater moral force than that which he was disposed to employ. As in the biblical scene, he traded his literary inheritance for a bowl of lentils, he knew exactly what he was losing, and that awareness destroyed him in the most consciously and voluntarily bitter life in the history of our literature. And even inside that literary inferno that reflected his own internal disaster, there remained many, very many good qualities, perhaps more and better than those of the professional "caminantes del bien."

Certainly Novo pretended before the public his whole life: he wrote things on the Patria, good manners, family morality [Pancho Villa, we should add], etc., and charged well for his services, not only in money: his bosses as well as society had to accept him with his "maldita" appearance as an evident homosexual, plucked eye-lashes, in make-up, with rings and wigs, saying things in his news-paper chronicles that others lacking his vocation of bitterness and emotional suicide would never have dared. When, on television, dur-ing the regime of Díaz Ordaz, Novo expounded on patriotic virtue, a clear clash of lies *insinuating a farce* was set up between him and the public: the sexagenarian, in make-up, dandified, and with his mannerisms and jewels, made a show of educating an easily scandal-ized society (the *Maestro de la Juventud* as a transvestite!), which in turn pretended—comedy of histrionics—to let itself be educated by him. But in his invaluable texts he doesn't pretend.[50]

With that in mind, that Novo never pretends in what he writes, and the suggestion that he meant his television appearance supporting Díaz Ordaz in Tlatelolco to be taken tongue in cheek, it is best to turn to Novo's poem "Adán desnudo," in which he apparently throws his sup-port to the student movement. Abridged and in translation it follows:

> Yes, we are still standing, but like the dust
> that stands on statues: preserved
> by the salt that covers us, petrifies us
> . . . .
> captive in the walls
> that one by one were raised
> to build a hereditary world
> by the men who abdicated their potential:
> who fearfully fled
> the forest and the sea to close themselves off in cloisters:
> to divorce their languages into countries,
> to congregate their fear in the cities,
> isolate themselves in houses and close doors on one another;
> to protect their vanity of gods in the temples,
> humble themselves in palaces;
> to stockpile bravado and cowardice in closets
> to love one another sadly in bedrooms,

to live on in bookshelves, in file cabinets,
in coffins, tombs, monuments.

. . . .

And suddenly,
the light of dawn offends and blinds our eyes.
New Adams with firm teeth bite into apples without sin,
plunge their strong arms into the crystal of the rivers,
tear down walls, doors, niches,
borders;
they appear on all the horizons
in search of themselves,
unsurprised, made in their own image;
they see themselves, they dance

. . . .

The world is theirs alone.
The one they take back:
the one we didn't know was ours
and which we traded for this one which they now tear down.

A world without borders, or races, or cities:
without flags, or temples, or palaces, or statues.
A world without prisons or chains,
a world without past or future.
The world unforeseen
by the men captive in the crypts of our world:
dreamed perhaps, scarcely imagined
by the naked Adam in Paradise.[51]

"Adán desnudo" was published in 1969, shortly after Novo had suffered a serious pulmonary infarction which forced him to greatly reduce his activities. It has, in this context, the strength of words spoken in articulo mortis, especially in light of the fact that that same year Novo also published "Mea culpa," in which he expresses his—by his own admission—maudlin regrets about not having had children. Although "Mea culpa" has nothing to do with the student movement, it attracts the attention of Elena Poniatowska, author of the definitive *La noche de Tlatelolco*. Significantly, she gives Novo a sympathetic interview.[52] (It is worth mentioning, too, that the gay movement, of which Salvador Novo was a very early predecessor, and whose underground newspaper was the only Mexican publisher to print Novo's scandalous memoirs, first went public on the ten-year memorial march of Tlatelolco.)

The year after "Adán desnudo" and "Mea culpa" are published, Novo is awarded the Trofeo Calendario Azteca by the Mexican Association of Radio and Television Journalists in 1970. In 1972, he publishes his last collection of essays, *Las locas, el sexo, los burdeles,* from which "A Few Aspects of Sex among the Nahuas" has been taken, and which includes a second dialogue with Sor Juana, *Sor Juana recibe,* between the poet-nun and Don Carlos de Sigüenza y Góngora. The book also includes several essays on theater. Novo died in 1974, twenty-four years after Xavier Villaurrutia and one year after Pablo Neruda.

In assessing his work, and considering his life, particularly his political actions, it is most beneficial not to confuse the two. As Blanco notes, "Novo pretended before the public his whole life," but "in his invaluable texts he doesn't pretend." Sociological critics of Latin American literature have long noted that in Latin America (as elsewhere) literature has often been born from the need to express somewhere and somehow what cannot be expressed publicly, from the need to outwit the compilers of the *Index Librorum Prohibitorum,* to avoid the wrath of a humorless dictator or the retaliation of an insecure government. Carlos Fuentes, in his introduction to *Todos los gatos son pardos* (published eight years after Novo's *Cuauhtémoc,* but on the same theme), says:

> . . . in our country, to talk to oneself is to talk to the others: poetry has always been the central artery of Mexican literature: we only tell the truth in secret. And even when we talk out loud, we continue to speak in a low voice; remnant of the sweet Indian accent, some call it; voice of the slave, I say, voice of the subjugated man, who had to learn the language of his masters and who directs himself to them with elaborate respect, prayer and confession, circumlocutions, abundant diminutives and—when the señor turns his back—with the knife of the double entendre and the war cry of a nonchalant remark. . . . Because in Mexico public speech, from Cortés' *Letters of Relation* to the king all the way up to the last presidential address, has been held prisoner by the powers that be . . .[49]

Certainly, unlike Paz, Novo did not show himself to be a hero at Tlatelolco. But writers are not chosen by the valor they display in war. Generals and politicians only exceptionally make anything more than heroic couplets or crafty blank verse, just as writers only exceptionally make hyperbolic budget requests. Nevertheless, despite Tlatelolco, or including it, Novo has all his life fought to regain what Fuentes calls "captive public speech," and he has used the best weapons he, as a writer, as a seemingly frivolous, intelligent, educated homosexual, has had available to him, "the knife of the double entendre and the battle cry of the nonchalant remark." It is to those weapons, appearing here as razor-sharp *macanas* and ironic parallels, that we owe some of the best literature of our time.

Notes to Introduction

Translations are mine unless otherwise noted.

1. Salvador Novo, "La historia," *Espejo: Poemas antiguos,* in *Poesía, 1915–1955.*
2. Salvador Novo, "Ya viene Pancho Pistolas," in *Toda la prosa,* pp. 73–76. Actually, except for the ironic epigraph—Novo's uncle was a cotton seed dealer—it is a fairly complimentary obituary.
3. Frank Dauster (*Cuadernos Americanos,* May–June 1961) calls Novo "brother to Eliot and heir to Jules Laforgue." Jean Clarence-Lambert (*Les poesies méxicaines*) calls Novo the Mexican Cocteau. Antonio Magaña Esquivel (*Salvador Novo,* p. 74) compares Novo to Molière. Emmanuel Carballo (*Diecinueve protagonistas de la literatura mexicana del siglo XX,* p. 260) comments on Novo's understanding of André Breton. Some of the "other things Novo was called" are cited elsewhere in the introduction.
4. "Claude Fell: '. . . You greatly insist that the Mexican Revolution had no ideological bases.'
   Octavio Paz: 'This is how it differs so much from the last century's liberalism. To call *revolution* the changes and upheavals that started toward 1910 is to yield, perhaps, to a linguistic expediency.'"
   Octavio Paz, "Return to the Labyrinth of Solitude," trans. Yara Milos, in *The Labyrinth of Solitude,* p. 339.
5. Much of this is described poetically and humoristically in *Poemas de adolescencia, XX poemas,* and *Espejo,* in Novo, *Poesía.*
6. José Joaquín Blanco, *Crónica de la poesía mexicana,* pp. 256, 263–264.
7. Eduardo Colín, "Salvador Novo," *Rasgos,* pp. 111–118.
8. Carballo, *Diecinueve protagonistas,* p. 259.

9. Blanco, *Crónica*, p. 209.

10. Antonio Castro Leal, *Salvador Novo: Antología 1925–1965*, p. xi.

11. Antonio Magaña Esquivel, *Medio siglo de teatro mexicano (1900–1960)*, p. 55.

12. Antonio Magaña Esquivel and Ruth S. Lamb, *Breve historia del teatro mexicano*, p. 122; Magaña Esquivel, *Novo*, p. 97; Michelle Muncy, *Salvador Novo y su teatro (estudio crítico)*, pp. 35–54.

13. Blanco, *Crónica*, p. 181.

14. Most of these magazines have been reprinted as recently as the 1980s by the Fondo de Cultura Económica in Mexico City.

15. Salvador Novo, *Nuestro cuerpo*, nos. 2–3 (July 1980): 10. These memoirs have been translated into English in *Now the Volcano*, ed. Winston Leyland.

16. Novo has written a little parable with respect to the changes in the bureaucracy: "Job," in "Confesiones de pequeños filósofos," in *Ensayos*, in *Toda la prosa*, pp. 53–54. Novo also discusses Vasconcelos in Carballo, *Diecinueve protagonistas*, p. 235.

17. Robert Jones Schafer, *A History of Latin America*, p. 563.

18. Blanco, *Crónica*, p. 183.

19. Merlin H. Forster, *Los Contemporáneos (1920–1932)*, pp. 15, 23n.

20. Carballo, *Diecinueve protagonistas*, p. 232; Forster (*Los Contemporáneos,* pp. 15, 23n) lists criticism specifically of the magazine *Ulises* in *El Universal*, January 11 and 12, 1928.

21. Magaña Esquivel, *Novo*, p. 33.

22. *Ulises*, no. 6, cited in Forster, *Los Contemporáneos*, p. 14.

23. Forster (*Los Contemporáneos*, pp. 15, 23n) cites, for example, criticism appearing in *El Universal* and *Excelsior* in May and June.

24. *Excelsior*, May 28, 1928, quoted in Forster, *Los Contemporáneos*, pp. 17, 23n.

25. Carballo, *Diecinueve protagonistas*, p. 236.

26. From a letter by Novo, in Forster, *Los Contemporáneos*, p. 121. According to Novo, in 1957, Salazar Mallén published a pamphlet on the hearings called "Adela y yo." Though it is impossible to verify (the pamphlet is not easily obtained), the title seems to be a reference to Novo's poem "Romance de Adela y Angelillo" or to the popular song "Adela," which seems to indicate something of the focus of the trial.

27. Carlos Monsiváis, "Salvador Novo: Los que tenemos unas manos que no nos pertenecen," in *Amor perdido*, p. 277.

28. Paz, "Return to the Labyrinth of Solitude," trans. Yara Milos, in *Labyrinth,* p. 343.

29. Paz, "Development and Other Mirages," in *The Other Mexico,* trans. Lysander Kemp, in *Labyrinth,* pp. 263–264.

30. With respect to the Romantic movement and the visual arts, see Blanco, *Crónica,* p. 37.

31. Carballo, *Diecinueve protagonistas,* pp. 242, 243.

32. Novo, *Poesía,* p. iii.

33. Blanco, *Crónica,* p. 257.

34. Monsiváis, "Salvador Novo: Los que tenemos unas manos," in *Amor perdido,* pp. 273–275.

35. Blanco, *Crónica,* pp. 17–18.

36. Salvador Novo, *Sátira, el libro ca. . . ,* p. 9.

37. Blanco provides an uncommon review of the portrayal of Native Americans in "La invención de los orígenes," from his excellent, down-to-earth *Crónica,* cited above.

38. Refer to the Bibliography for the publishing history of this novel, and of Novo's other, never completed novel, *Lota de locos.*

39. Carballo, *Diecinueve protagonistas,* p. 241.

40. Magaña Esquivel, *Novo,* pp. 95–96.

41. Blanco, *Crónica,* pp. 19–20.

42. Carballo: "What literatures have influenced principally in your work?"

    Novo: "U.S. and English literature. I can cite, among their authors, the classics and many moderns who have lost their relevance, like Erskine. . . . I carefully read Shaw, Thackeray. The U.S. poets—Whitman, the imagists—are felt behind my *XX poemas.* In my cynical poetry, Dorothy Parker had a very powerful influence." Carballo, *Diecinueve protagonistas,* pp. 255–256.

43. Carlos Monsiváis, "Su sátira apta para el ataque y la contienda," in Magaña Esquivel, *Novo,* pp. 296–297.

44. Paz, "Return to the Labyrinth of Solitude," trans. Yara Milos, in *Labyrinth,* p. 343.

45. Emilio Carballido, "'Don Quixote' 'La culta dama' 'A ocho columnas,'" in Magaña Esquivel, *Novo,* p. 292.

46. Carballo, *Diecinueve protagonistas,* p. 262.

47. Raúl Leiva, *Imagen de la poesía mexicana contemporánea,* cited in Forster, *Los Contemporáneos,* p. 222.

48. Monsiváis, "Salvador Novo: Los que tenemos unas manos," pp. 289–290.

49. Blanco, *Crónica*, pp. 253–256.

50. Blanco, *Crónica*, pp. 213–215. Poem quoted is "La poesía," from *Espejo*, in Novo, *Poesía*.

51. Novo, *Poesía*, 1st reprinting, 1977.

52. Elena Poniatowska, "Lamenta Salvador Novo el no haber tenido un hijo," dated December 16, 1969, in Magaña Esquivel, *Novo*, pp. 271–272.

53. Carlos Fuentes, *Todos los gatos son pardos*, pp. 5–6.

Translator's Note

This translation first started as an effort to understand the many Nahuatl terms and historical references in *The War of the Fatties*. Consequently, producing the glossary has been of primary importance, and I hope it will be as valuable to both English- and Spanish-speaking readers as it was for me while preparing it, while at the same time saving readers the chore of combing through cumbersome dictionaries in 6-point type, with no guide words, and entries run into each other on the same line.

I worry that more than a few readers will be scared off by the long Nahuatl names and their many variations. It is worth mentioning, however, that even the longest, Tlahuizcalpantecuhtli, is no longer than Franklin Delano Roosevelt—one syllable shorter, in fact, depending on how you pronounce the president's surname—and that by removing the *-tecuhtli* suffix, which means "prince" and is a title given to exceptional warriors, the word is almost as manageable as the phrase "Jack be nimble." Additionally, a pronunciation guide has been provided in the glossary along with a note for Spanish-speakers. Also included are the meanings of many proper names, since, as is often the case with agglutinative languages like Nahuatl, their length is due to the fact that they are actually compound words.

The many variations of characters' names, as annoying here as they are in Russian novels, are often due to the simple addition of a suffix, usually *-tzin,* which means "noble" or "cherished"; *-tecuhtli* or *-tli,* mentioned above; or to spelling inconsistencies due to problems the mostly uneducated Spanish conquerors had in transcribing Nahuatl words whose pronunciation was certainly foreign to them and likely varied from town to town.

One issue worth mentioning with respect to the translation is the writing style of the many historians Novo quotes. Some, like Fernando

Alvarado Tezozómoc, were not native Spanish speakers, and the resulting accounts often have a sort of naïve quality about them which I have tried to preserve. Others, like Sahagún, translated from Nahuatl texts without the help of dictionaries or grammars. Not one, of course, was familiar with contemporary rules of punctuation and style, and several were quite long-winded, as the quotations included in "Ahuítzotl and the Magic Water" demonstrate. Many of the abnormalities in the text are due to these factors, and though I have intentionally tried to preserve them in English as part of the "flavor" of the text, I hope I have not made them any worse than they already are.

In Ticitézcatl, like many an opera libretto and many an epic poem, has been translated into prose because of the near impossibility of rendering the sometimes very short rhymed verses into like form in English without drastically altering the content. It is, I fear, in places rather "unbeautiful," to recall a word Gore Vidal once used in describing his own translation. Nevertheless, opera, as I'm sure Novo would have snootily agreed, should always be performed in the original.

The texts brought together here, which take readers chronologically from the fall of Tlatelolco in 1473 to shortly after the Spanish victory in Tenochtitlan in 1521, with a detour through the Reform and the timeless world of the gods, include all of Novo's Aztec-related prose, with the exception of passages in a few other essays, his speech "Huehuetlatoalli," written in homage to Cuauhtémoc, and the texts for his later *Luz y sonido* productions which are not available.

"Mexicans Like 'em Fat" (Appendix A) is an attempt to avoid criticism by fat libbers (who have recently and inexplicably joined the growing tide of book censors by demanding that Judy Blume's *Blubber* be removed from the shelves of school libraries in my hometown). It also shows Novo's understanding of one aspect of sexism and his perspective on fatness.

Finally, I cannot overemphasize how much richer the texts become in light of the information provided by the glossary, which includes entries for all proper names, all non-English words, and many English words marked in the body of the text with an asterisk. Entries of particular interest to those unfamiliar with Aztec culture might include *causeway, Triple Alliance,* and *century.* A genealogical chart (Appendix B) is included to help sort out the relationships between the kings and queens who figure as characters in these works. The map of Anáhuac (Appendix C) will help to visualize the layout of Tenochtitlan on Lake Texcoco and to locate the territories of the kingdoms that made up the powerful Triple Alliance, mentioned so often here.

THE WAR OF THE FATTIES
AND OTHER STORIES
FROM AZTEC HISTORY

A Few Aspects of
Sex among the Nahuas

Translation of "Algunos aspectos del sexo entre los nahuas."
In *Las locas, el sexo, los burdeles*. Edo. de México: Novaro, 1972.

Even when our illustrious forbearers the Nahuas practiced polygamy, the enviable privilege of changing *petate* partners at will was reserved for the ruling classes. It was the *pipiltin*, or "nobles," who, with the example of the Tlatoani, maintained a convenient assortment of female cornfields in which to deposit the fine seed of their descendance. The harvests from select warriors, priests, and legitimate candidates to the throne always turned out to be as abundant as they were assured, despite the fact that one or another lady—like Acamapichtli's first, called Ilancuéitl, or "old skirt"—might be sterile.

Not everyone, however, could afford such luxury. But for the less fortunate, and for the young bachelors going off to battle, occasional refreshments, who would substitute for the sole wife or the one yet to be contracted, were wisely provided. Destined to the noble service of the boys and the men with only one wife were girls whose name is derived from their function: *Ahuianime*—the cheerer-uppers—from the verb *ahuia*, "to cheer-up," plus the suffix *ni*, "one who does something," and the plural *me*.

The praiseworthy Sahagún has preserved his well-informed indigenous sources' detailed description of these girls, whose name in the Castilian, to which the Padre rendered it, sounds to our chaste modern ears more violent than that of "cheerer-uppers." In Book X of his *General History of the Things of New Spain*, he devotes chapter 15 to speaking "of the many manners of evil women." In fact, he doesn't include many, only four: "about the public women," "about the adulteress woman," "about the hermaphrodite," and "procuress."[1]

---

[1] In contrast, in chapter 11, Sahagún lists eleven kinds of evil men: "the deranged man, the madman; the lewd youth; the old whoremonger; the pro-

It is in the first of these four divisions where the venerable Padre transcribes the sonorous Castilian word of four letters [i.e., *puta,* "whore"—Trans.] for the sweet Nahuatl denomination, *Ahuianime:*

1. The whore is a public woman and has the following: that she goes about selling her body, she begins when she is young and doesn't cease even when she is old, and she walks about as if she were lost and drunk, and she is a gallant, polished woman, and with this she is very immodest; and any man she runs into, she sells her body to, because she is very lustful, dirty, and shameless, talkative and very full of vice in the carnal act; she adorns herself quite heavily and is so curious in her accoutrements that she looks like a rose after she is very made up; and to dress herself up, first she looks in the mirror, bathes, washes herself very well, and refreshes herself in order to give more pleasure; in order to have a good face and shine, she also is used to anointing herself with a yellow lotion from the earth that is called *axin,* and at times she puts colors and rouge on her face, being a lost and worldly woman.

2. She also has the habit of dying her teeth with cochineal, and of letting her hair loose for more beauty, and at times of having half of it loose and the other half over the ear or over the shoulder, and of braiding her hair, and even putting it over the crown of the head, like little horns, and then walking around, strutting, like an evil woman, shameless, dissolute, and despicable.

3. She also has the habit of perfuming herself with fragrant perfumes, and of going around chewing *tzicli* to clean her teeth, which she has for show, and when she chews, her chomping sounds like castanets. She is a walker, or a tramp, in the streets and the marketplace, she walks around strolling, seeking vices, she goes around laughing, she never stops and is disturbed to the core.

4. And through the delights she continually seeks she follows the way of beasts, she joins with some and with others; she also has the habit of calling out to the men, making signs with her face, making eyes at them, choosing the one who pleases her most, and wanting them to covet her, tricking the boys, or young men, and wanting them to pay her well, and going around procuring other women for the men, and going around selling other women.

If we were to attempt a comparable sketch of the contemporary descendants of those ladies today, we would find that—though they

---

curer; the pervert; the murderer, the murderer of people; the traitor and the storyteller; the buffoon; the thief; the dancer with a dead woman's forearm, the dancer with the forearm; and the highwayman."—Trans.

share them with many "decent" women—they preserve their ancestors' habits of meticulous grooming and provocative make-up; that their hairstyles are equally complex and ostentatious, just like their strut; that their fragrant perfuming is today achieved with an atomizer; and that the *tzicli* those women chewed and popped is no longer a characteristic strictly limited to their profession. Ever since our good neighbors of the north industrialized chewing gum (which, like so many other indigenous contributions to Western culture, comes from Mexico), the *chicle,* which, though deformed, preserves its Nahuatl name, is available sweetened and in different flavors for the ruminating preferences of all kinds of women. And even though among the Nahuas it was looked on as bad and censured for men to chew it, the commercial advertising of the industrialized product has resulted in extending its occasional or daily use to the men as well, who may chew without fear of punishment, who today are not labelled as effeminate for using it, like the "sométicos" were, who were also described by Sahagún in section V of chapter II of Book X, which we have been making a running commentary of: "The passive sodomite is abominable, heinous, and detestable, worthy of being ridiculed and laughed at by the people, and the stench and ugliness of his sin cannot be suffered because of the disgust it gives men; in everything he shows himself to be womanly or effeminate, in walking or in talking, for all of which he deserves to be burned."

The sodomite has his feminine equivalent in the *hermaphrodite, whom Sahagún describes thus: "The woman who has two sexes, the one who has the nature of man and the nature of woman, who is called hermaphrodite, is a monstrous woman, and has *supinos,* and has many girlfriends and maids, and has a gentle body like a man; she uses either of her natures; she is usually an enemy of the men because she uses her masculine sex."

Throughout the world of sex schemed the woman who, among the Nahuas, practiced the trade that, with slight variations, has become more respected in our time, even earning the classification of "public relations manager," and that Fernando de Rojas immortalized with his character Celestina; she was the procuress, described thus:

"The procuress, when she employs bawdry, is like the devil and brings the devil's ways, and is like the eye and ear of the devil, in short, she is like the devil's messenger. Such a woman is used to perverting the hearts of other women and draws them to her will, to what she wants; very rhetorical in her speech, using savory words to coax, she goes about using them like roses to allure the women, and so also with her sweet words does she charm and stupefy the men."

Although we are not able to induce that this might be the general rule among our ancestors, there are various illustrious examples that indicate their inclination for fat women.[2] The great Huémac made his orders for concubines very precise; he would order his public relations officials to go out and look for those with hips not less than four out-stretched hands in latitude. And King Moquíhuix, last autonomous king of Tlatelolco, scorned his noble wife, sister of Axayácatl, for her thinness, and he would instead comfort himself with his collection of robust concubines, whom, during the war with the Mexicas, he let loose naked to face the Aztec army, whose faces those Amazons on foot bathed with squirts from their teats.

But, if the Mexican men have preferred them fat ever since then, the Nahua women, for their part, yielded to the call of the masculine at-tractions upon discovering their magnitude through the eventual ab-sence of the *maxtli* or loincloth, as illustrated by the story of Tohuenyo. One day, the mischievous god Titlacahuan decided to tempt the daughter of King Huémac, who "estaba muy buena," to quote verba-tim from the poem which I will try to condense in prose, and which uses the expression that, with respect to the classification of women, we continue to use today in Mexico.

Many princes had asked for the princess's hand; "but Huémac made concessions to nobody, to nobody did he give his daughter." The mis-chievous god "transformed himself, he took the face and figure of To-huenyo, walking about naked no less, the thing hanging there, he set himself to selling chile and went to set up in the market, across from the Palace."

Huémac's daughter looked toward the market and began to watch Tohuenyo: "There he is with the thing hanging. As soon as she saw him, she immediately closed herself up in the Palace. Because of this,

---

[2] . . . and their prejudice against thin women, as illustrated in this description of the mature woman in chapter 14 of Sahagún's *General History:* "The mature woman is candid. The good mature woman is resolute, firm of heart; con-stant—not to be dismayed; brave. . . . The bad mature woman is thin, totter-ing, weak—an inconstant companion, unfriendly. She annoys others, chagrins them, embarrasses, shames, oppresses one. Extremely feeble, impatient, loses hope, becomes embarrassed—chagrined. She goes about in shame; she persists in evil. Evil is her life. She lives in vice." (Translated directly from the Nahuatl by Dibble and Anderson; *see* Bibliography.) Novo further explores this theme in his essay, "Mexicans Like 'em Fat," included in Appendix A—Trans.

Huémac's daughter fell ill, became tense, got a fever, as if she were feeling bad because of Tohuenyo's birdie."

Upon discovering the cause of his daughter's illness, the good father ordered that Tohuenyo be found, as though recurring to some heroic medicine. As soon as the princess had achieved her caprice, she got better. She married Tohuenyo. The nobles looked upon such an unequal marriage as a bad thing, and the king, to rid himself of the chile vendor, sent him into a war from which he was sure not to return. Nevertheless, as he was really a god, he returned victorious, was acclaimed by the nobility as a hero blessed with virtues beyond the specifically curative one he had exercised with the princess, and they all lived happily from then on. The moral of this episode continues to be applicable and useful in our time. We could summarize it in this aphorism: He who doesn't advertise, doesn't sell.

In the *Florentine Codex,* folio 99, recto and verso, there is a short poem that illustrates the staying power of the Nahua women's libidos into old age, and with poetic elegance [in Nahuatl, that is—Trans.], lays out the reasons for this endurance:

> In the days of the lord Nezahualcóyotl
> two old ladies were taken prisoner
> with frosted hair
> white as the snow,
> stiff as dried maguey fiber.
>
> They were locked up
> because they were apprehended
> when they were about to commit adultery:
> as their respective husbands
> were also very old,
> they were going to have carnal relations
> with some little students, with some little youths.
>
> Lord Nezahualcóyotl
> asked them, said to them:
> "Our ladies,
> what is this we hear?
> What would you have me believe?
> Surely you don't still
> desire the things of the flesh?
> Aren't you already satisfied,
> being now as you are?
> How did you live

when you were still young?
Tell me, state it for me,
it is for this that you are here."

They answered him:
"Lord, king, our lord,
receive, listen:
You men who are already old,
you have no appetite for the flesh
because potency has abandoned you,
you spent it quickly and now you've none left.
But we women don't tire of this
because there is in us
like a cave, a valley.
It only waits for what you will throw into it
because its place is to receive."

And who would dare deny that these women, our sweet and ardent grandmothers, were right?

In Pipiltzintzin
(The Children)
or

The War of the Fatties

COMEDY IN TWO ACTS

Translation of *La guerra de las gordas*. [Full title: *In Pipiltzintzin (Los niñitos) o La guerra de las gordas: Comedia en dos actos*.] Mexico City: Fondo de Cultura Económica, 1963.

NOTICE

The events dramatized in this comedy are real historic events, according to the authorities Durán, Tezozómoc, Alva Ixtlilxóchitl, and Sahagún, with no more license than a chronological adjustment between the War of Tlatelolco and the chicanery of one queen, the sterile Ilancuéitl, wife, not of Axayácatl, but of Acamapichtli; and a similar displacement in time of the successive kings of Tezcoco: Nezahualcóyotl and Nezahualpilli.

PRESENTATION

We tend to approach our ancient history with solemn faces, reiterating only those episodes, characters, and settings that give strength to the legend of the "Sad Indian"; to the anguish of the "Pueblo del Sol" (perpetually engaged in arduous battle against the chance destiny of floods, fiery eyes, earthquakes, and the periodic risk of yet another *extinction); and to the tiresome necessity of paying the taxes of survival in blood. From Quetzalcóatl to Cuauhtémoc, we review a long—and in a way, monotonous—list of austere monarchs whose affable, beneficial deeds for their people are matched, upon closer examination, by the number of their conquests and the cruelty of their victory celebrations.

In this survey, two or three figures usually manage to win our admiration: the legendary Quetzalcóatl, a model of virtue and wisdom, and the enlightened Nezahualcóyotl, father of Mexican poetry, whose influence in poetry has surely filtered down to us and prevailed through the mixed blood of the mestizo. From time to time, Quetzalcóatl and Nezahualcóyotl have provoked the imagination of Mexican novelists, poets, and playwrights, and of more than one foreigner. To an even greater extent than these two, Cuauhtémoc has seen the interest in his heroic resistance and *combustion rekindled, and the "coward" Moctezuma has been known to reappear, reinterpreted, in our literature.

Legend and history—beautifully Siamese in our Indian past—are so rich and so intricate that they could well have inundated our many Sophocles and Euripides with valuable subject matter. If that had been the case, we would already have our tragedy: the human reflection of the war between the gods, between Tezcatlipoca and Quetzalcóatl. But our Sophocles and Euripides have instead preferred to climb other Olympuses. The closest they usually get to that ancient world is to describe the moment of its destruction by the conquistadors, when it is already history—Malinche and Cortés—that inspires their palinodes.

Nevertheless, the history and legend of our ancestors also has plenty of less tragic material. It awaits its Aristophanes—disappointed perhaps by having waited in vain for a Euripides. Again, if Quetzalcóatl and Cuauhtémoc are the alpha and omega of the indigenous world, between the two of them, and throughout the times of the many characters who lived in the interval between them, many episodes and situations occurred that had an aspect of humor and bite, which we haven't noticed, or haven't taken advantage of, or haven't used in our efforts to give our theatrical ventures our own unique anecdotal content, also worthy of universal and even contemporary appreciation if we compare it to other important literatures. Our Indians knew how to laugh; they practiced sex; passions burned in them. To ignore these facts, not to take notice of anything in their lives except their austerity, is to perpetuate among us the European thesis that classified them as different from the "men of reason."

In order to write *In Pipiltzintzin* or *The War of the Fatties,* all I had to do was rely on the documents that gave me the story. The story of the War of Tlatelolco and Tenochtitlan, which in 1473 put an end to the independence of the small kingdom founded on the lake seven years after Tenochtitlan (in 1337),[1] can be found in more or less the

---

[1] This is not the place to take into account the version of the Mexicas who, beaten in Chapultepec in the year IX *ácatl* 1243, took refuge—some of them—in Xaltelolco, which would mean that Tlatelolco, as it would later be called, had been founded earlier than 1325.—[S.N.]

same form in the *Anales de Cuauhtitlán (Códice Chimalpopoca)* as in Fernando Alvarado Tezozómoc's *Crónica Mexicáyotl;* with variations, and with more detail, in Fray Diego Durán and in Torquemada.

Here is how it is told in the *Códice Chimalpopoca:*

> (197) 7-Calli. In this year the Tenochcans and the Tlatilolcans contended among themselves, in the time of King Axayacatzin. Also in those days Moquihuixtli reigned in Tlatelolco. Here is the story they tell. Before there was war, Moquihuixtli did many bad things with the women. One daughter of Axayacatzin, king of Tenochtitlan, was the woman of Moquihuixtli; and this woman passed everything on to Tenochtitlan; she let Axayacatzin know how many secret war talks Moquíhuix had had. About this time Moquihuixtli scandalized the city with many things. He flattered all the women so they would swell up a lot. He stuck his forearm from the elbow to the wrist in between the legs of the lady who was daughter of Axayacatzin, and with his hand he felt something of her parts. And they say that the nature of the lady spoke and said, "Why are you ailing, Moquíhuix? Why have you abandoned the city? It will never be; it will never dawn." Later it happened that he spilled his fluids in the inside of the palace. For sport he would bathe his fluids with cactus spittle. He would strip his women, who came there daily to anoint him; and he was seeing each one, et cetera.

And it adds in (239): "In Tlatilolco Moquihuixtli reigned when the city was conquered."

Let us see now how it is told in the *Crónica Mexicáyotl:*

> (213) Princess Chalchiuhnenetzin's teeth reeked terribly, for which she never lay down with King Moquihuixtli. (214) In the year 7-House "1473 years" was when Tlaltilolco was conquered, when this town lost itself through concubinage; it has already been said that it was due to Chalchiuhnenetzin, the older sister [not the daughter, as the *Códice Chimalpopoca* says—S.N.] of the lord Axayacatzin, who felt greatly overcome with spite, according to what the elders say, because her husband, Moquihuixtli, no longer cared for her at all, because she was feeble, had an ugly face, was skinny with no meat on her, and he deprived her of all the cotton blankets that Axayacatzin, her younger brother, sent her, by giving all of them to his concubines. (215) The Princess Chalchiuhnenetzin suffered a lot; she was forced to sleep in a corner, next to the wall, where the grinding stone was, and only had a rough, raggedy blanket for herself; and it has already been said that this was because her husband, Moquihuixtli, king of Tlatelolco, did not care for her at all, although he housed her

in a different house from his concubines; and surely sometimes Moquihuixtli saw her lying on the "machochtli" [(?)—S. N.], and it has
already been said that in no place was she considered to be worth
anything; and inevitably King Moquíhuix never did want to lie with
Princess Chalchiuhnenetzin, and he slept only with his concubines,
very handsome women ["very good women"—S. N.]. It has already
been said that this Princess Chalchiuhnenetzin was not strong, but
skinny, nor did she have much meat on her, but had a very bony
chest, and for that reason Moquihuixtli didn't want her, and he
treated her very badly. Because of that, she came to Tenochtitlan to
tell her younger brother, Axayacatzin, what Moquihuixtli did to her,
as well as how he talked of going to war against the Tenóchcatl; she
came to tell him everything. Axayacatzin, on hearing it, had become
very angry and worried, and he decided to declare war, for which it
was said that Tlatilolco was lost because of concubinage.

Let us see how Fray Diego Durán tells it in chapter 33 of his *Historia:*

> The lord of Tlatelulco was married to a daughter or sister of the king
> of Mexico, Axayácatl, and while asleep, says the story, she dreamed
> a dream and it was that she dreamed that her shameless parts were
> talking and that with a doleful voice they were saying, "Oh, my lady,
> and what will become of us tomorrow at this time!" Waking up from
> the dream very afraid, she told her husband what she had dreamed
> and begged him to tell her what it had meant; he told her what he
> had decided to do, and that it could be that it meant what would
> happen the next day . . . The lord of Tlatelulco came outside here to
> see if in his house there were any people around and found that in
> the kitchen of his house there was an old man of many days, whom
> he believed he had never seen, and who was talking to a little dog
> who answered everything he asked, and that on the fire there was a
> boiling pot, next to the old man, and inside it some birds dancing,
> which the king took as a very bad omen, and that a mask that was
> hanging on the wall began to complain very dolefully, at which point
> the king took it down and shattered it . . .

A little farther on, in chapter 34, Durán is the only one to describe
the war with the battle that I have incorporated into this comedy:

> Moquíhuix and Tecónal, seeing that they were lost and that the
> people were fleeing more than they were fighting, used a trick, and
> it was that, getting together a great number of women and stripping
> all of them naked and making a squadron with them, they sent them
> towards the Mexicans who were fighting furiously, and these

women, thus nude with their shameful parts and chests uncovered, came slapping themselves on their bellies, and others came showing their teats and squeezing milk from them and showering the Mexicans . . . Seeing such an awkward thing, King Axayácatl ordered the Mexicans to do no harm to any woman, but they were nevertheless taken prisoner . . . and so following the victory and the women's release, the king climbed to the top of the temple with others of his soldiers . . . but when he got there, he found that Moquíhuix and Tecónal had taken refuge in the altar where Vitzilopuchtli was. The king, bravely going in to where the very idol and altar were, killed them and dragged them out and threw them down the stairs of the temple.

Torquemada is much more tenuous, even though he is more prolix in the description of Moquíhuix's wedding. In chapter 50 of the second book of his *Monarquía indiana,* he talks "Of how Moquíhuix, king and lord of Tlatelulco, married the daughter of Tezozomoctli of Mexico, sister of Tízoc, Axayácatl, and Ahuízotl, who were Mexican kings . . ." and says that "Moctecuhzoma Ilhuicamina, king of Mexico, knowing the bravery of Moquíhuix, lord of Tlatelulco, ordered that he marry the daughter of Tezozomoctli, sister of Axayácatl, who reigned after him, whose wedding was ordered by this said king, and by Nezahual-cóyotl, who was king of Tezcuco, which wedding was celebrated with great majesty and pomp; it took place at his house with the solemnity that such lords required, and many lands were given to him from this part of Mexico, in an area that is called Aztacalco, as you come out of Chapultepec forest . . ."

Farther on, in chapter 55 in the fifth year of the reign of Axayácatl, he tells us that

> about this same time, Moquíhuix, lord of Tlatelulco, brother-in-law of King Axayácatl, married to his sister, ordered another temple to be made, that was called Cohuaxólotl, just to trick the Tenochcans; and from here there began to be dissent between these two parties, bringing back to life ancient passions (as if they were not all one and the same, and of the same blood and family) which caused Axayácatl to become somewhat disgusted with Moquíhuix, his brother-in-law, and Moquíhuix showed himself to be displeased with Axayácatl. To this was added the fact that the one from Tlatelulco, not much loving his wife, the sister of Axayácatl, didn't treat her with the love or respect that was owed to a sister of such a great king as the king of Mexico.

All of chapter 58 is dedicated to telling at length of "the war that [Axayácatl] had with the Tlatelulcans, where King Moquíhuix was killed and his kingdom became subject to the Mexicans." It repeats here that

> this king had a sister of his married to the lord of that part, who, as he was arrogant and a little loose in his life and dishonest, the woman felt very bad about, and she was motivated by her jealousy to go to her brother with her complaints. King Axayácatl spoke to him a few times begging him to treat his sister—whom Moquíhuix abhorred, either because the message angered him (as happens with many married couples) or because he couldn't put up with her ordinary jealousy—well. They say that this evil king was so vicious that on that day (and the days before then) he would go into the women's quarters and, from among those that worked sewing the ornaments and robes of the goddess Chanticon, would rape those that seemed best to him, and with this he caused a great scandal in the republic. Not content with committing this scandalous sin, this bestial man also betrayed many of his stewards and captains, all of whom were very upset, and were even more motivated to kill him than to fight the enemy.

Once the war is under way, Torquemada doesn't say anything, or doesn't know anything, about the deed of the naked fatties. In contrast, he preserves for us the fact that "many of the very Tlatilolcans who saw themselves dying and ending helplessly, and who heard the shouts of Moquíhuix urging them on, told him: 'Bugger, pansy, come down here and take up arms, the place for men in war is not to stand watching those who fight, and if you won't, we will climb up there and throw you off the temple for having gotten us into a war that we never wanted.'"

Torquemada denies Axayácatl all part in the death of Moquíhuix (which he attributes to Quetzalhua, who according to him is the one who throws him off the temple) except for opening his chest and taking out his heart "in the district of Copolco, that is next to Tlatelolco; although when Moquíhuix was delivered to Axayácatl's hands, he was already dead from the great blow he got when he fell from the temple." And, in passing, heartily contradicts Padre Acosta: "This war happened this way and for the causes given, and not because the Tlatelulcans had rebelled against the Mexican king, like Acosta says; because, as we have proven in this long story, some had a king just like others had theirs, and each one was a republic in itself, nor did the Mexican king capture the Tlatelulcan king, he only took out his heart once he was already dead, as we have already said." (The chapter in which Padre Acosta affirms what Torquemada contradicts is chapter 18 of the seventh book of his *Historia natural y moral de las Indias:* "On the Death of Tlacaélel and the Deeds of Axayácatl, Seventh King of Mexico"; in which he errs, as he was the sixth.)

With these historical testimonials, I believe I have sufficient basis to assert the authenticity of the episode which I've dared dramatize. And I dare assume that such notorious variations among such respectable, serious, and accredited historians authorize me to fuse them into a new version (because I don't pretend to resolve history, just to create theater from it), and to put to use those parts of each one that are most suited to and best fit my modest proposal. To conclude the quotations, I will only add the condensed version that Sahagún (Eighth Book, chapter II, paragraph 4) gives of the War of Tlatelolco and the end of Moquíhuix, to whom he concedes a voluntary suicide: "The fourth lord of Tlatelolco was called Moquihuixtli, who governed nine years and in whose time the lordship of those from Tlatelolco was lost, due to the hatred and animosity between him and his brother-in-law the lord of Tenochtitlan called Axayácatl, and desperate in the end, the said Moquihuixtli climbed the stairs of the *cu* of the idols, which was very high, and from the top of the said *cu* he flung himself off, and thus ended his life."

I admit that I have taken greater license, in that it affects the chronology, by exaggerating and repositioning both in time and space the episode that I make coincide with the war of Tlatelolco: that is, the inconvenient sterility of a queen, Ilancuéitl, who indeed was not the wife of Axayácatl, but of Acamapichtli.

According to Durán (chapter 6),

> this king [Acamapichtli] was married with a great lady, native of Culhuacan, named Ilancuéitl, who was barren and sterile, for which the king and all the greats were very grieved; and fearing that his kingdom would be left without an heir, the lords gathered in council and decided that each one of them would give him one of their daughters, so that, taking them as his women, from them would be born heirs and successors to the kingdom. . . . But so we don't forget to mention the first lady of the king, at first, although she was not scorned, she was so sad that her eyes were fountains day and night. Seeing her sadness, the king, who held her very dear and loved her affectionately, tried to console her as much as he could, and she,

seeing how much the king loved her, asked a favor of him, and it was that since the Lord of Children had denied her the fruit of benediction, that in order to get the people of the town to give up the bad opinion they had of her for being barren, that he should give her the children that were born of the other women, so that as they were born she could put them to her breast, lie down and feign she had given birth, so that those who came in to visit her would wish her well for the birth and the new baby. The king gave in to her pleas, ordered that it should be done, and thus at a birth by any one of those women she would lie down in the bed and take the child in her arms and feign she had given birth, receiving the gifts and graces of those who visited her; and although in reality she was not truly the one who had given birth, as far as she was concerned, she was . . .

Another chronological liberty that will be noticed by the ever fewer connoisseurs of our history is the one I take in making Nezahualcóyotl coincide not only with Axayácatl, but also with his son and heir Nezahualpilli. The fodder for the rumors of the Tenochcan court ladies that I present here is the episode of Chalchiuhnenetzin (who has the same name as the wife of Moquíhuix), whose weak will and harsh punishment by Nezahualpilli are narrated in detail by her descendant Don Fernando de Alva Ixtlilxóchitl in chapter 64 of his *Historia chichimeca*. We might mention in passing that this author gives a very brief account of the Tlatelolcan war in chapter 51 of the same *Historia*.

Equally real, with respect to our history, is the influential and long-lived figure who, incarnated in various *Calles- or *Cárdenas-like patriarchs, kept ruling for several, let's call them, presidential periods that go from Izcóatl to Axayácatl. If in this comedy he already appears a little "gaga," I don't believe I am excessively adulterating the probability of his mental state at the time of the episode in which he participates from the sidelines. I am referring to Tlacaélel.

The scene about Ilancuéitl's birth: with respect to both the therapy that is alluded to and the ceremonial oratory of invocations by the elders or the midwife, my version, although abbreviated, is again faithful to the pertinent texts collected by Sahagún from his indigenous informers. In this scene, the greatest liberty I have taken has been architectural, but it was indispensable for me: giving "closeable" doors to a room that, like all the rooms of that time, would have had only feather curtains or *pétatls*.

The probability of women's participation in palace life, besides being necessary for me theatrically, is supported by the historical fact that, as noted by Orozco y Berra, Axayácatl showed himself to be less misogynistic on the issue than his ancestors: "Recovering from the wound, although left scarred and with a limp, Axayácatl had a great feast, to which he invited the kings of Acolhuacan and Tlacopan, with the lords of the subjected provinces; the emperor's women attended as well, an uncommon thing in the customs of those days." (Orozco y Berra, Book III, chapter 5.)

I have taken other necessary and excusable minor liberties by assuming, or rather, by attributing, writing and fractionary currency to the Nahuas; and by calling the students of the Calmécac of Tlatelolco "cadets from the military school." With respect to the names of the secondary characters in this comedy, I've only forged two: that of Tomahuazintli and that of Cuitlacuani, with Nahua words that seemed fitting: with her, the impressive amplitude of her behind; with him, his symbolic coprophagy.

Dramatis Personae

(in order of appearance)

Moquíhuix, (last) king of Tlatelolco
Tecónal, his prime minister
Tomahuazintli, maiden of Chalchiuhnenetzin
Chalchiuhnenetzin, wife of Moquíhuix
Soothsayer
Chicomexóchitl, lady of honor to Queen Ilancuéitl
Xochichihua, lady of the court, (Lady I)
Xochihuetzi, lady of the court, (Lady II)
Tlacaélel, the Cihuacóatl (90 years old)
Axayácatl, king of Tenochtitlan
Tepecócatl, Tenochcan general
Calcimehuateuctli, Tenochcan general
Cocipantli, Tenochcan general
A captain
Epcóatl, Axayácatl's court minion
Nezahualpilli, prince of Texcoco
Cuitlacuani
Two (or more) slaves

Act I, Scene 1: Daytime. Royal hall of Moquíhuix in Tlatelolco. Scene 2: Queen Ilancuéitl's antechamber, in Tenochtitlan. The next day, in the morning.

Act II, Scene 1: General quarters of Axayácatl at four A.M. Near La Lagunilla. Scene 2: Hall in Axayácatl's palace, in Tenochtitlan.

The War of the Fatties

In Pipiltzintzin or The War of the Fatties was premiered at Teatro Fábregas on April 19, 1963, under the direction of the author and with the following

CAST

Tecónal	Guillermo Zetina
Moquíhuix	Enrique Aguilar
Tomahuazintli	Mónica Miguel
Chalchiuhnenetzin	Alicia Montoya
The Soothsayer	Guillermo Zarur
Chicomexóchitl	Rosamaría Moreno
Xochichihua	Marinela Peña
Xochihuetzi	Alicia Gutiérrez
Tlacaélel	Carlos López Moctezuma
Axayácatl	Raúl Ramírez
Tepecócatl	Mario García González
Calcimehuateuctli	Helio Castillos
Cocipantli	César Castro
Epcóatl	Rogelio Quiroga
Aztec captain	Bruno Márquez
Nezahualpilli	Darío Vivien
Cuitlacuani	Guillermo Zarur

Scenery and production by Antonio López Mancera.

ACT ONE

Scene 1

Tecónal appears before the curtain and speaks to the audience.

TECÓNAL: Ladies and gentlemen, good evening: I've come to fulfill
the ritual function that in their plays the Greeks used to assign
to gods and goddesses: that is, to speak the Prologue.

As you know, a goddess appears, says her little speech (in
which she gives the audience the background for what they are
about to see), disappears (or does a "mutis" as we say in theater), and the action begins.

Now I'm not exactly a goddess—or a god for that matter;
nor are you about to see a Greek tragedy. This is a Mexica
tragedy—that seems Greek. Our Hellene, the Hellene of this
Tlatelolcan Troy, is the Queen Chalchiuhnenetzin, sister of
Axayácatl, the sixth king of the Tenochcans. Because of her this
war breaks out, which will wipe Tlatelolco, its autonomy and
self-government, off the map of Anáhuac.

TlatElolco, not TlaLtelolco. It's worth your while to learn
to correctly pronounce the name of this now ancient neighborhood of Mexico City, whose restoration is revealing its beauties,
and that was, at the time of our story, a separate kingdom.

The chroniclers and historians tell us that Tlatelolco was an
island. Yes, an island, like Cuba; founded on the lake years before Tenochtitlan. But Tenochtitlan did not like having an independent kingdom so close, on the same waters, as you shall see.

We open, then, in Tlatelolco. But I was going to tell you
who I am. I am Tecónal. That's TeCOnal, not TeconAL, which
sounds like the name of a medicine. Remember, in Nahuatl,
there are no words with accents on the last syllable, they all are
accented on the next to the last syllable. It is a mistake, which
we owe to the Spaniards' incapacity to pronounce any language
right, including their own, that people say TenochtiTLAN,
TehuaCAN, CuauhtiTLAN. It should be TenochTItlan, Te-
HUAcan, CuauhTItlan.

In any case, I am Tecónal, prime minister and court advisor to the young and impetuous king—fourth and last king of
Tlatelolco—called Moquíhuix. Chroniclers and historians have

lent their ears to some of the most scandalous rumors about his behavior. They say horrible things about him. But, I am his advisor. I'm not going to judge him. Besides, people always exaggerate, and they make up thousands of things about the powerful.

You will now get to meet Moquíhuix for yourselves. I have just given him a diplomatic note (well, not very diplomatic) from his brother-in-law, Axayácatl, and it has Moquíhuix boiling like water for a pot of hot *chocolate.

Let us go, then, to the throne room of King Moquíhuix.

(*The curtain opens. Tecónal goes to his place at left.*)

Tlatelolco. Throne room. Moquíhuix and Tecónal.

MOQUÍHUIX: (*Crumpling a document, holding back his anger.*) But have you read this?

TECÓNAL: I've *deciphered it, yes. Several times.

MOQUÍHUIX: (*He blows up.*) This is war! Who does Axayácatl think he is? Does he think that I'm going to put up with this kind of attitude in his messages? That, come the time, I'll be alone and at his mercy and that of the old fart Tlacaélel? Are they wrong! Both of them! He tells me off, as if it were nothing! He talks about public decency! Did you read that?

TECÓNAL: (*Serenely.*) Yes. I read it.

MOQUÍHUIX: (*Letting down a little.*) Intruders! Nomads! My grandfather should never have allowed them to set up camp on the lake, so close to here!

TECÓNAL: (*Condescending.*) Unfortunately, this time they're right. I've investigated. The boys—there are twenty of them—have confessed without any pressure.

MOQUÍHUIX: What happened?

TECÓNAL: (*Informative.*) It was . . . a month ago. A group of noble women from Tenochtitlan came to the *tianquiztli* market. There was a sale on duck. It was the day of 2 for 1. They'd come with their daughters and slaves. In choosing this and that, bargaining, and because there wasn't any *change, they weren't able to start back to Mexico until late; on the way, they ran into a group of cadets from the military school.

MOQUÍHUIX: (*Reproachful.*) What were they doing in the streets at that hour?

TECÓNAL: (*Explaining.*) They were out on maneuvers. You will recall that you yourself ordered that all the boys of Tlatelolco, twenty years old and up, would compete in target practice—with arrows, of course—and in tearing down stone statues with slingshots and *macanas*. For the Moquíhuix cup . . .

MOQUÍHUIX: Naturally! We have to be prepared for war. *Si vis pacem, para bellum.* And then?

TECÓNAL: (*Excusing himself.*) They say that the women provoked them, with smiles. They followed them, joking, playing; it was already dark: and in the cornfield . . .

MOQUÍHUIX: (*Sententiously.*) Uncomfortable, but very natural. What's wrong with that?

TECÓNAL: In my opinion, nothing; but the ladies went to complain to Axayácatl.

MOQUÍHUIX: (*Intrigued.*) To complain? All of them?

TECÓNAL: The mothers. The oldest ones.

MOQUÍHUIX: (*Final.*) Oh, I see! They probably didn't touch them at all. And they said they were worried about their money . . .

TECÓNAL: Well in any case, Axayácatl is using the incident to justify his demand for higher tributes. He calls them, let me see [the document] . . . reparations.

MOQUÍHUIX: (*Irritated.*) So that's what it is! A pretext! Because there's no logic at all in demanding that, besides giving the best of Tlatelolco away to the tourists, I would have to pay such a fine! No, Tecónal! This is war! I won't take any more!

TECÓNAL: Your anger is justified, Moquíhuix, but it is not the best counselor. Calm down.

MOQUÍHUIX: (*He calms down.*) I am calm! You can't accuse me of unjustified violence. What haven't I done to get along peacefully with the Tenochcans? Isn't it enough of a sacrifice to have accepted Axayácatl's sister for my wife? That ugly, skinny, black, bony woman with the flat chest?

TECÓNAL: (*Compassionate.*) Our poor queen. She has a good appetite, but nevertheless . . . She eats better and more capriciously than any of your other ladies. Something must be wrong with her thyroids.

MOQUÍHUIX: If that were the only thing wrong with her!

TECÓNAL: (*He knows.*) Yes, I understand. She hasn't given you any children. It's sad.

MOQUÍHUIX: (*Clarifying.*) I haven't asked for any! Just the thought of spending a night with her!

TECÓNAL: (*Insinuating.*) Yes, of course. But an heir, born of Chalchiuhnenetzin, would win you the good favor of her *uncle, Axayácatl. After all, that's how all those kingdoms were made: by marriages of political convenience. Your grandfather Tezozómoc . . .

MOQUÍHUIX: (*Making excuses.*) Yes, I know. He used the system, but the Tenochcans have perfected it, forging an empire through blood ties: They need cotton from Cuauhnáhuac? Well, ask for their princess's hand, and inflate her belly. They want to ingratiate themselves with the Texcocans? Well, just add one more to Nezahualcóyotl's harem. That's what I call blackmail!

TECÓNAL: (*Resigned.*) And what a system! Every day the Tenochcans are more powerful.

MOQUÍHUIX: (*Examines the list.*) Nouveau riches! *Bug-eaters! We admit the boys did wrong. We can punish them by marrying them to the women they broke in. But higher tributes: he's doubling it, nothing less! And how? Where am I supposed to get everything Axayácatl demands? He wants everything: blankets, lip-rings, necklaces, bracelets, parrots . . . And if we give him all the ducks he wants, we'll depopulate our lake! His demands aren't even original. They are exactly the same as the tributes Tezozómoc imposed on them when these, these . . .

TECÓNAL: (*Obliging.*) *Refugees.

MOQUÍHUIX: ("That's it.") When these refugees first got here!

TECÓNAL: (*Consoling.*) They aren't that harsh. Tezozómoc sure put them in a tight spot, though, when he ordered them to bring him one of those floating *chinampas* they used when they first established themselves: with a mother heron whose *eggs had to hatch chicks in his august presence. And they managed it.

MOQUÍHUIX: (*Disgusted.*) That was just a magic trick. I'm not a magician. And we're talking about ducks, not eggs. And not ten, but a thousand! And on top of that . . .

TECÓNAL: (*Practical.*) We can bargain with them, get a reduction, come to an agreement.

MOQUÍHUIX: (*Imperative.*) Find a way! That's your job!

TECÓNAL: (*Wise.*) But that would not definitively remedy a situation of tyranny, which is what we ought to try and solve. He would only postpone the demands, and raise them later. All that about the rape of the merchant women has no real importance. It's just a good pretext. It wouldn't be the last.

MOQUÍHUIX: (*Eloquently.*) But don't they already have enough with what they get in tribute from the others that they call their good neighbors? The Xochimilcans, who provide them with the flowers to satisfy their neurotic olfactory inclinations? The Coyohuacans, who sculpt favorable portraits of their families for them? The Huitzilopochcans, who color them up with feathers? *Triple Alliance! I'll eat poison if there's anything triple about it! Those spineless wimps from Tlacopan and Texcoco . . . those pedantic shrimps, most of all, with their poet-kings and their language academies . . . Bah!

TECÓNAL: The ones from Tlacopan are ours. I've talked at length to them about it. If it were necessary, they'd pull through.

MOQUÍHUIX: But they're part of the alliance!

TECÓNAL: But they've proceeded skillfully, face it. Spineless wimps and all, they get along all right with Axayácatl. He doesn't come down as hard on them.

MOQUÍHUIX: (*Flustered.*) So why does he treat me so badly?

TECÓNAL: (*He explains.*) Because the Tenochcans don't feel safe, or at ease, as long as there's no blood bond between us. (*Persuasive.*) Pardon me for insisting: I'm sure that if you would go along—sacrificing yourself, I understand—with making Chalchiuhnenetzin pregnant . . . just one night . . .

MOQUÍHUIX: (*Horrified.*) Not for an hour! Not for a minute! Oh, Tecónal! I can see plainly . . . you don't know what you're asking of me.

TECÓNAL: (*Begging.*) Half a night! Just enough to leave your royal seed in her. Then you can satisfy yourself, stretch out, get the

bad taste out of your mouth with one of the others. (*Tempting.*)
I was just going to tell you, an order of twenty splendid Totonacan women just came in, just the way you like them: fat, hot-
blooded, with behinds worth their weight in gold. I have them
ready for you tonight.

MOQUÍHUIX: (*Delighting.*) Twenty! Not bad . . . I'll see them tonight. But just them. Don't insist on forcing me to lie with
that . . .

TECÓNAL: (*Terse.*) I'll respect your allergy; but I would like to know
your motives. Are they that strong that nothing will manage to
persuade you to commit such a minimal sacrifice, of such important political consequences?

MOQUÍHUIX: (*Definitive.*) That strong. (*Solemn.*) Since you must
know—and nothing can be hidden from you—her teeth smell
atrocious!

TOMAHUAZINTLI: Lord, my lady the queen is here to see you.

MOQUÍHUIX: (*Surprised.*) The queen, here? In the Hall of Counsel?

TOMAHUAZINTLI: Seeing that you wouldn't answer her call, she decided to . . .

MOQUÍHUIX: (*Furious.*) Well tell her . . .

TECÓNAL: Receive her, my lord. Calm down, I beg you. I will be
here, nearby. If you need me . . .

MOQUÍHUIX: (*Frightened.*) You don't mean here . . . now?

TECÓNAL: Of course not. That will be, if you agree, whenever you
wish it to be: tonight or tomorrow . . . The sooner the better, of
course.

MOQUÍHUIX: (*To the slave, eyeing her.*) What's your name?

TOMAHUAZINTLI: Tomahuazintli, my lord.

MOQUÍHUIX: (*Sizing her up.*) Descriptive. Are you from Tlatelolco?
I've never seen you.

TOMAHUAZINTLI: I serve my lady Chalchiuhnenetzin. I came in her
entourage. I'm Tenochcan.

MOQUÍHUIX: Virgin?

TOMAHUAZINTLI: Of course, my lord.

MOQUÍHUIX: Which shift do you cover for the queen?

TECÓNAL: (*Admonishing him.*) Your Highness!

TOMAHUAZINTLI: What should I tell my lady?

TECÓNAL: (*Curtly.*) That the king, her husband, will be very pleased to receive her at once.

MOQUÍHUIX: But . . .

TECÓNAL: Go tell her.

TOMAHUAZINTLI: (*Flirting.*) Please accept these flowers, my lord. They have just come from Tenochtitlan.

MOQUÍHUIX: Nothing would be more useful. Give them to me. (*He holds them to his nose.*) Let the queen come in, then.

(*Exit Tomahuazintli.*)

TECÓNAL: While you talk to her, I will go over these papers, here, nearby. And I will start composing the answer the ambassadors should take.

MOQUÍHUIX: (*Losing heart.*) Don't go very far. If you hear me cough, come quickly.

TECÓNAL: Don't worry. I'll be on the alert.

MOQUÍHUIX: (*Pompously.*) As for the response, you already know. Energetic. No concessions. Let them see with whom they're dealing.

TECÓNAL: (*Taking notes.*) With whom they're dealing. (*He sticks his head out.*) Here comes the queen. By your leave. (*Exits to hide himself at the door on the left.*)

(*Moquíhuix adopts a royal posture in his* icpalli, *with the flowers still to his nose.*)

CHALCHIUHNENETZIN: (*Entering. Cold. Incisive.*) Excuse me for daring to come seek you here; but what I have to tell you is urgent. And since you hadn't answered my call . . .

MOQUÍHUIX: (*Nonchalant.*) I was going to go see you as soon as I had finished my agreement with the prime minister.

CHALCHIUHNENETZIN: (*Dryly.*) That's what you said yesterday.

MOQUÍHUIX: (*Tolerant.*) Yesterday I had to receive the ambassadors from your brother. And take them to inspect the new works: the *tianquiztli* market, the *causeway of Tepeyácac . . . Every day

there are pilgrimages. Between that and sacrificing twenty Tlaxcaltecans in his honor, the whole day slipped by.

CHALCHIUHNENETZIN: And the night?

MOQUÍHUIX: (*Final.*) I ended up exhausted. I went to bed very early.

CHALCHIUHNENETZIN: (*Antagonistically.*) It's not that I'd imagined
you would visit me in my bedroom . . . In your house, I've already resigned myself to staying in the place for the grinding
stone that shows me your disdain.

MOQUÍHUIX: (*Trying hard to control himself.*) Not that again. Have
you come to interrupt an important agreement with your ridiculous complaints and conjugal woes?

CHALCHIUHNENETZIN: (*Swelling.*) But you could have understood
that if, in spite of everything, I insisted on talking with you a
moment, it would be because I had good reasons to place
the . . . affection I profess to what I must consider my new
country, and its threatened well-being, before my tattered
dignity.

MOQUÍHUIX: (*Exploding.*) I will worry about the well-being of your
new country, which is more mine than yours. My kind has ruled
Tlatelolco well for more time and better than those from your
oversized island. Your * artificial oversized island.

CHALCHIUHNENETZIN: (*Conceding him a point.*) I'll concede you
that. And it's precisely because I want you to continue on the
throne you exclude me from that I must tell you what I have
persistently been dreaming, and it can't be anything but
significant.

MOQUÍHUIX: I well know what you dream, dear. Wake up.

CHALCHIUHNENETZIN: (*Solemn.*) Save your irony. It's evidently prophetic, this dream that repeats itself, disturbing me every night;
I can scarcely sleep. Nevertheless, I haven't told it to anyone.
But yesterday it was so clear, so impressive, that it woke me up,
and I told it to the palace soothsayer, who came to my call. I
asked him for a simple interpretation; but he immediately saw in
my dream a clear omen.

MOQUÍHUIX: (*Disdainfully.*) I don't know how to interpret dreams.
It's not the duty of a king. You're in good hands with the soothsayer. What is it you were dreaming?

CHALCHIUHNENETZIN: (*Solemn.*) That my private parts were talking . . .

MOQUÍHUIX: (*Quickly.*) Did you dream it, or is it true?

CHALCHIUHNENETZIN: . . . and they said to me with all clarity: Oh, my lady! What will become of us tomorrow at this time!"

MOQUÍHUIX: (*Quickly.*) What time was it?

CHALCHIUHNENETZIN: (*Normal.*) Eleven, or twelve, I suppose, because the soothsayer was still awake studying the stars, and he came in the middle of it to see me.

MOQUÍHUIX: (*Explicit.*) Well, it wasn't too hard to predict the status of your inquisitive private parts. The next day, at the same time, the only thing that could have changed . . . But you say they were talking?

CHALCHIUHNENETZIN: (*Firmly.*) Out loud.

MOQUÍHUIX: (*Reproachfully.*) And you had the gall to confide it to the soothsayer?

CHALCHIUHNENETZIN: (*Excusing herself.*) If you had been at my side . . .

MOQUÍHUIX: (*Offended.*) They would have taken care not to talk to me.

CHALCHIUHNENETZIN: (*Coldly.*) That's why I called the soothsayer.

MOQUÍHUIX: (*Scoldingly.*) And I'm sure he prescribed that you should not have such a heavy dinner. At this altitude, and at your age, one shouldn't have dinner. It causes nightmares. Even if you were to benefit from what you stuff down your throat . . .

CHALCHIUHNENETZIN: (*Practical.*) I've brought him with me. I already knew that even in the remote possibility that you would see me, you wouldn't pay any attention to me.

MOQUÍHUIX: (*Disconcerted.*) What? You've brought him? The soothsayer? And what for?

CHALCHIUHNENETZIN: (*Firmly.*) So that you could hear what happened afterwards from his own lips.

MOQUÍHUIX: (*Coughs loudly.*) After what?

CHALCHIUHNENETZIN: After finding out about my dream and going out to consult the oracles.

(*Enter Tecónal, called by the password of the cough.*)

TECÓNAL: Oh, excuse me, my lady.

MOQUÍHUIX: (*Saved.*) Stay, Tecónal. (*Royally.*) For you there are no secrets.

TECÓNAL: May I, my lady?

CHALCHIUHNENETZIN: (*Coldly.*) If the king commands it . . . (*She goes to the door, signals. The soothsayer appears.*)

MOQUÍHUIX: Hello, old man.

SOOTHSAYER: My lord! (*Kneels.*)

CHALCHIUHNENETZIN: (*Imperative.*) Tell the king what happened the night before last.

SOOTHSAYER: (*Slowly.*) I came back from looking for maguey spines, I pierced my *tongue, I threaded up to seven maguey threads through it . . .

TECÓNAL: To the point, Huehue.

SOOTHSAYER: (*Slowly.*) I took my icy midnight bath, and was contemplating the stars . . .

CHALCHIUHNENETZIN: (*Nervously.*) . . . When I called you and told you my dream. Tell what happened next.

SOOTHSAYER: (*Terrified.*) Oh, my lordship! The queen's dream was already significant enough by itself. The *tonalpohualli* wasn't favorable: a day of the *Fox, in the year of the Rabbit. And there, in the very antechamber of the queen . . . I shudder to even think of it!

MOQUÍHUIX: What happened? What did you see?

SOOTHSAYER: (*Solemn.*) An old man, squatting, carrying on a conversation with . . . four dogs!

MOQUÍHUIX: (*Skeptical.*) Talking dogs! Impossible. Our *dogs don't even bark. They're mute! Tasty, but mute.

SOOTHSAYER: (*Confidently.*) These talked. Like you and I. And with more polish; like Toltecs, or like Texcocans.

TECÓNAL: The influence of the Triple Alliance is spreading.

SOOTHSAYER: (*Convinced.*) That was a warning, without a doubt. But it wasn't the only one. Another hair-raising sight caught my attention: in a pot over the fire, a lot of birds, all colors of the rainbow, were boiling, but they were unhurt and happy as larks.

MOQUÍHUIX: (*Sardonically.*) Did they speak too?

SOOTHSAYER: (*Clarifying.*) No, my lord. They cheeped and sang like they usually do; but their situation didn't seem to bother them one bit. And the fire didn't bother them at all. Then I heard a voice . . .

MOQUÍHUIX: (*To Chalchiuhnenetzin.*) Did your . . . start talking again?

SOOTHSAYER: (*Solemn.*) It was a jade mask that was hanging on the wall. Suddenly, its eyes came to life, they looked at me, and its stone lips, curled back sarcastically, pronounced words.

TECÓNAL: What did they say?

SOOTHSAYER: (*Fatal.*) They were saying, "Moquíhuix's days are numbered."

MOQUÍHUIX: How dare you!

SOOTHSAYER: (*In a trance.*) "Because he unwisely persists in scorning his legitimate queen and our lady; and seeks his pleasure among his numerous concubines whom he, like King Huémac who came to no good end, requires meet uncommon and hard-to-find specifications; and he hoards them and collects them like an army; and lies with them and wastes his royal seed; he shall perish in a war that he hasn't had the good sense to avoid through the dignified behavior of the king that he doesn't deserve to be."

MOQUÍHUIX: (*Furious.*) Have him flogged! Skin him! Rip out his guts!

TECÓNAL: He's in a trance, can't you see? And his person is sacred. Let him speak. Let him say what he knows.

SOOTHSAYER: (*Comes out of the trance.*) Overcome by my natural indignation, I ripped the mask off the wall and threw it on the ground. It broke into pieces, but, ah! the pieces kept talking, each one on its own, mixed up phrases that all together formed one terrible, sarcastic, cackling laugh.

> (*The warnings have noticeably worried Moquíhuix,
> who moves away, deep in thought.*)

TECÓNAL: And what else?

CHALCHIUHNENETZIN: (*Impatient.*) Isn't that enough? (*Moquíhuix returns, authoritatively.*) The voice of the oracle didn't wait for the Soothsayer to invoke it in the temple. It expressed itself through the mask. (*Glancing at Moquíhuix.*) It was the mask of your grandfather Tezozómoc.

MOQUÍHUIX: (*Disbelieving.*) What! How could it be, since he was cremated with it on in Azcapotzalco!

CHALCHIUHNENETZIN: (*Explicit.*) My brother gave it to me as a present when he sent me here. The decorator found it very decorative and decided to hang it in my antechamber. He said it gave a symbolic touch to the union of our two houses.

MOQUÍHUIX: (*Making fun.*) Union!

CHALCHIUHNENETZIN: That's what he said. How was he to know?

TECÓNAL: (*Worried.*) What's important is that the voice of Tezozómoc has come back to speak.

MOQUÍHUIX: But if it spoke like that against me, it couldn't be his. I was his favorite. And come to think of it, he doesn't have any room to criticize. In any case, I've inherited his . . . inclinations.

CHALCHIUHNENETZIN: (*Whining.*) The Mictlan is like a repair shop for souls. Those who come back from there try, in their prophetic way, to amend their own fatal errors in their descendants.

MOQUÍHUIX: It's a family obsession—repairs and reparations.

SOOTHSAYER: (*Obvious.*) That's the way it is. What other meaning or purpose would there be in dying if it isn't to prevent our children from suffering or going astray?

TECÓNAL: That's a question of metaphysics. What did you do afterward?

SOOTHSAYER: From there I went to the temple, where I bled myself again. At daybreak, I helped with the sacrifices of the day, participated in the goddess Huitzilopochtli's breakfast with a few sips of *chalchíhuatl,* and quickly convoked a meeting of priests and seers.

MOQUÍHUIX: Well done. And what did they say?

SOOTHSAYER: I'm sorry, King. They all concurred by affirming that, according to the signs that appeared in my lady Chalchiuhnenetzin's dream and in the other omens already described, the war you are secretly hurrying towards will mean your end.

TECÓNAL: The priests seem to know more than I do. If there were some war on the horizon here, I would be the first to know.

SOOTHSAYER: Do you doubt their wisdom?

TECÓNAL: Not in their territory; in mine, yes. Otherwise, I'd be a priest or a soothsayer, and they prime ministers.

CHALCHIUHNENETZIN: The Cihuacóatl . . .

MOQUÍHUIX: There is no Cihuacóatl here, dear. That's in Tenochtitlan, where, it seems, your brother is not happy ruling just one city, and he consults with old Tlacaélel about everything.

TECÓNAL: Tlacaélel is the power behind the throne in Tenochtitlan. His place is at the side of the king and as a counterweight to the monarch; endowed with both priestly and military power, he embodies a dangerous marriage of Church and State and foreshadows an eventual division of powers that is most dangerous. But here in Tlatelolco there is only one will: the will of King Moquíhuix.

MOQUÍHUIX: Well said.

TECÓNAL: Thank you. Consequently, and with all the respect your age accords you, you did wrong to consult with the other seers about the queen's dream and the supposed omens of the loquacious dogs and the rainbowlike birds. And even about the mask of our beloved Tezozómoc.

SOOTHSAYER: Who else was I going to consult with about it?

TECÓNAL: Why, with the king, of course.

CHALCHIUHNENETZIN: That's what we've come to do, in the end. (*To Moquíhuix.*) Now you know everything. Decide.

MOQUÍHUIX: Decide? What?

CHALCHIUHNENETZIN: If in spite of all these clear warnings from beyond, you will throw your people into a war against my brother.

TECÓNAL: (*Conciliatory.*) Nobody's thinking of war, my lady, believe me. A few ambassadors have come, it's true; they seek punishment for an infraction, which we are willing to accept; and they propose an *alliance for the simultaneous progress of Tenochtitlan and Tlatelolco; a joint plan of action, that would have ramifications for our underdeveloped neighbors, to stimulate them to higher production; a plan, I must say, whose complexity forces us to analyze it, carefully measuring the feasibility of the . . . contribution we would have to make. But that is all! Nobody is thinking of war . . .

CHALCHIUHNENETZIN: (*To Moquíhuix.*) Can I guarantee my brother that?

MOQUÍHUIX: You? And why you?

TECÓNAL: (*Superior.*) The negotiations have already started, my lady, through the proper channels.

CHALCHIUHNENETZIN: Because I have to go to Mexico some time soon.

MOQUÍHUIX: (*Surprised.*) To Mexico, you? With whose permission?

CHALCHIUHNENETZIN: (*Ironically.*) I'm not surprised you forgot. But you yourself agreed that I would attend, alone, representing us both, the baptism of my nephew, who will be born in two days.

MOQUÍHUIX: Oh, yes, yes, of course. With so much going on . . .

CHALCHIUHNENETZIN: (*Dryly.*) May I go then?

MOQUÍHUIX: When?

CHALCHIUHNENETZIN: (*Conclusively.*) Tomorrow.

MOQUÍHUIX: (*Glancing at Tecónal.*) Well . . .

TECÓNAL: (*Obsequiously.*) The king has already set aside the gifts that he is sending to your dear brother Axayácatl, with his best wishes. A convenient entourage will escort Your Majesty. At daybreak?

CHALCHIUHNENETZIN: Yes.

TECÓNAL: Everything will be ready, my lady. (*He bows.*)

CHALCHIUHNENETZIN: (*Under her breath.*) You're going to pay for it dearly, Moquíhuix.

(*Chalchiuhnenetzin exits, followed by the Soothsayer.*)

MOQUÍHUIX: Whew! What gibberish! (*Throws down the flowers which he has been holding under his nose.*) I hope they assault her on the way, or that she stays in Tenochtitlan!

TECÓNAL: (*Skeptical.*) The road is very safe. After the incident with the cadets, we've doubled the guards. We watch it cooperatively.

MOQUÍHUIX: Is that true about the gifts? I'd completely forgotten about that little nephew.

TECÓNAL: (*Superior.*) I'll worry about the gifts. The Tenochcans love our tanned hides.

MOQUÍHUIX: They smell awful.

TECÓNAL: They perfume them afterwards.

MOQUÍHUIX: If we were already ready for war, what I would send Axayácatl is embalming fluid for the dead and the funeral flags!

TECÓNAL: But everything in its time. Now it's to our advantage to ingratiate ourselves with them and avoid a war, if possible. We still don't even have an army.

MOQUÍHUIX: Do you believe in omens? In what the soothsayer said?

TECÓNAL: If your grandfather Tezozómoc's mask talked . . .

MOQUÍHUIX: That's what disturbs me.

TECÓNAL: He was always wise. A hundred and eighty years old. Now he must be even more so. (*Quickly.*) One thing occurs to me.

MOQUÍHUIX: Yes?

TECÓNAL: (*Illuminating.*) Let the queen be the one to take Axayácatl your response to his memo. Name her ambassador extraordinaire for the royal holiday of the baptism of Axayácatl's heir. That way you make what would otherwise be just a visit to the in-laws into a State affair.

MOQUÍHUIX: But how! A woman ambassador?

TECÓNAL: (*Explicit.*) Not just any woman: your wife. That way you will set a revolutionary precedent of maximum political importance. Chalchiuhnenetzin will be the First Lady of Tlatelolco: who, because she has no children of her own, watches over those of others and aids her royal husband in such an intelligent manner that he doesn't hesitate to confide in her tactfulness to express his official reasons for protesting the size of the tribute the king of Mexico asks for. She herself asked if she could guarantee her brother that you didn't want war, remember?

MOQUÍHUIX: Yes; she dared ask me that.

TECÓNAL: (*Insinuating.*) What's it cost you to placate her? And if she herself is the one to take your message, Axayácatl will believe your words all the more, guaranteed by the voice of his own sister.

MOQUÍHUIX: (*Exploding.*) But I do want war! And I can't stand Axayácatl, or his disgusting sister, or that old hag of his wife! What's more, I don't even believe she's going to give birth. Not at that age!

TECÓNAL: Stranger things have happened . . . But they've already made the official announcement . . .

MOQUÍHUIX: (*Calming down.*) A man, that's different. At any age he can . . . more or less . . . But, Ilancuéitl! How long have they been married?

TECÓNAL: (*Reflecting.*) Well, if it's the same one . . . since the reign of Acamapichtli! It can't be. She has the same name, but it must be someone else. Older than the king, that's for sure.

MOQUÍHUIX: There you have it. And Axayácatl doesn't get hot even when it's boiling. It seems to me there's something fishy going on here.

TECÓNAL: We'll know soon enough. But that's not what's important now. I beg your leave to retire to finish up the response and plan the gifts and the queen's trip and her entourage and her nomination as ambassador. I'll bring you the papers to sign tonight.

MOQUÍHUIX: Tonight? What about the Totonacan women?

TECÓNAL: Well, a little earlier then: while you're bathing and getting ready. They'll be ready for you.

MOQUÍHUIX: Did you get a look at . . . what's her name? Tomahua-zintli? What a beaut!

TECÓNAL: You'd fall for anything! You're already going to see these Totonacans.

MOQUÍHUIX: I believe you; but some other day . . .

TECÓNAL: I'll make sure she doesn't go with the queen. Really, you liked her a lot?

MOQUÍHUIX: Well, for a little while she wouldn't be bad.

TECÓNAL: Tonight then.

MOQUÍHUIX: That's it. What did you do with Axayácatl's ambassadors?

TECÓNAL: I put them up in my guest house, after the protocol banquet.

MOQUÍHUIX: In good company?

TECÓNAL: For them. They're old, all five. I sent them ten girls.

MOQUÍHUIX: Ten! Isn't that a lot for them?

TECÓNAL: I don't think so. They're second hand.

MOQUÍHUIX: Weren't there any new ones?

TECÓNAL: They'll never find out.

MOQUÍHUIX: You're a genius! What would I do without you? If we beat the Tenochcans . . . When we govern over Mexico, I'll make you my . . . What position does Tlacaélel have?

TECÓNAL: Cihuacóatl, the female snake.

MOQUÍHUIX: I'll make you my Cihuacóatl.

CURTAIN

Scene 2

Queen Ilancuéitl's antechamber. A door in the center, through which an old lady (Chicomexóchitl) leaves at the same time as two others (Xochichihua and Xochihuetzi) enter from the right in a hurry, with big jugs of hot water. She stops them in front of the door with her first line:

CHICOMEXÓCHITL: No, don't go in. Give me the water. (*They give her a jug, she tests the water, leaves it in the doorway; touches the other with her hand.*) This one's cold. It needs to be very hot. (*The lady that was holding it makes a false exit.*) But we don't need it that much. This one's enough. Wait here. (*Takes the first jug in and closes the door.*)

XOCHICHIHUA: (*Confiding.*) Do you think now it'll finally be?

XOCHIHUETZI: That's how it looks. (*She moves closer to the door, listens. Returns.*) Poor queen. At her age . . .

XOCHICHIHUA: Who would have thought! Did you notice her pregnancy? I didn't, not at all.

XOCHIHUETZI: The truth is I didn't notice. She always wears such big *quexquémetls* that there's no way one could tell. But it was about time, that's for sure. Ten years of marriage and nothing, until now.

XOCHICHIHUA: Well, we'll see if now she'll get it over with. Will you wait here for me? (*Picks up her jug.*) I'm going to heat up this water.

XOCHIHUETZI: (*She touches it, burns herself.*) But it's boiling!

XOCHICHIHUA: Well, you heard her. She wants it hotter. They must be going to cook the little coconete.

XOCHIHUETZI: They're born cooked, silly. Leave it here. (*Xochichihua leaves it at the door.*) Don't leave me alone. These things make me really nervous. I remember the first time . . .

XOCHICHIHUA: Oh, it's not so hard! And mine came out upside-down. But the midwife straightened things out, she invoked Quilaztli and Yoaltícitl, put me in a hot *temazcalli* . . .

XOCHIHUETZI: They gave me ground *cihuapactli*. It helps with the pushing.

XOCHICHIHUA: It didn't have any effect on me. They gave me that root too, but even that way the boy wouldn't straighten out, or come out. I thought I was going to become one of the *cihuapipiltin*.

XOCHIHUETZI: You mean the *mocihuaquetzqui*.

XOCHICHIHUA: That's it . . . the ones who die in childbirth.

XOCHIHUETZI: They're sacred, but leaping lizards, what a consolation!

XOCHICHIHUA: What fixed it all was a piece of ground *tlacautzin* tail. With that, what a purgative.

XOCHIHUETZI: Ugh, it must have tasted awful!

XOCHICHIHUA: At times like that, you don't even notice. And it's great, I recommend it. Later the midwife told me that a dog got into some once and ate a *tlacuatzin* and right away it started pooping out all its livers and all its guts and that nothing at all was left in its body.

(*Chicomexóchitl opens the door. Touches the jug left by Lady I.*)

CHICOMEXÓCHITL: That's how it should be. (*She picks it up, closes the door. Xochichihua and Xochihuetzi look at each other. Chicomexóchitl sticks her head out again.*) Don't go away. And don't let anybody near here. Absolutely nobody.

XOCHIHUETZI: Is it here yet, my lady?

CHICOMEXÓCHITL: The midwife is making all the pertinent invocations. It'll just be a minute, I hope.

XOCHICHIHUA: Can't we listen? It's considered good luck.

CHICOMEXÓCHITL: Come here then. Listen.

VOICE OF THE MIDWIFE: (*Recorded.*) You are present here, ladies and gentlemen, and your lord, who rules the whole world, has joined you here; here you are, old men and old women, fathers and mothers and relatives of these precious stones and of these rich feathers, that were born from you and have their beginning in you, like the thorns of the tree, like the hairs on our heads, and like the fingernails of our hands, and like the hair of our eyebrows on the flesh above our eyes . . .

   (*Chicomexóchitl closes the door. The voice is no longer heard.*)

XOCHICHIHUA: Are there many people inside?

CHICOMEXÓCHITL: No, nobody. That is, just the midwife and me.

XOCHIHUETZI: But, what about . . .

CHICOMEXÓCHITL: Those are just the words of the ritual. (*Goes in and closes the door.*)

XOCHICHIHUA: How strange! A royal birth, clandestine!

XOCHIHUETZI: What if the king comes? Do we have to stop him from going in?

XOCHICHIHUA: Well, you heard her. Nobody can go by. But the king won't come. He's gone over to La Lagunilla to receive his sister, who's coming from Tlatelolco.

XOCHIHUETZI: Chalchiuhnenetzin? Is her husband coming?

XOCHICHIHUA: I think she's coming alone. They don't get along very well. She hasn't had any children either.

XOCHIHUETZI: No? Really? It must be her fault. Or, maybe it's a family thing. You see how long it took Axayácatl. Because Moquíhuix is very hard-working when it comes to that.

XOCHICHIHUA: And how do you know?

XOCHIHUETZI: Everybody knows! He has some Pochtecans, my husband told me, who recruit fat women from all over. They trade those leather skins they tan so skillfully in Tlatelolco for the women. So, I don't know why the queen wouldn't have . . .

VOICE OF TLACAÉLEL: (*Nearby.*) Is it this way? Has my grandson been born yet?

XOCHICHIHUA: (*Frightened.*) It's Tlacaélel!

XOCHIHUETZI: (*Alarmed.*) Tlacaélel! What if he wants to go in?

XOCHICHIHUA: Well, you heard her. Orders are orders. Nobody can go inside. (*They position themselves to guard the door.*)

TLACAÉLEL: (*Entering.*) Oh! (*He stops upon seeing them.*) My dear ladies!

XOCHICHIHUA AND XOCHIHUETZI: (*Reverently.*) Your Highness!

TLACAÉLEL: You are the queen's ladies, I suppose.

XOCHICHIHUA: (*Humbly.*) Yes, my lord.

TLACAÉLEL: I'm not used to Axayácatl's modern innovations. In my day neither Izcóatl nor Huehue Moctezuma had women in their service, let alone in the palace! (*Dryly.*) Excuse me, I don't believe I know you.

XOCHICHIHUA: Of course, my lord.

TLACAÉLEL: Warriors, men! At all times and in all offices! Women, at the *metate,* at the *malacate.* Or on the *petate.* Anyway, that's his business. I am . . .

XOCHICHIHUA: (*Praising him.*) Huey Oquiztli, the Cihuacóatl: the great, the brave, the immortal Tlacaélel.

TLACAÉLEL: (*Satisfied.*) And I've come to meet my grandchild! To meet my fine little feather! To meet the fingernail of my hands! Is he inside? (*He goes towards the door. The ladies run to stop him from entering.*)

XOCHICHIHUA: He hasn't been born yet, my lord.

TLACAÉLEL: Not yet?

XOCHIHUETZI: It'll just be a moment. But the queen still can't be seen. The midwife and Lady Chicomexóchitl are with her. But no one else can go in . . . for now.

TLACAÉLEL: Okay, okay. I'll wait (*dryly*) in such gracious company. That is, if it doesn't bother you.

XOCHICHIHUA: (*Flattering him.*) How could you even think such a thing! It's not very often that we are honored with the privilege that this chance encounter brings us. To speak with none other than the builder of the Mexican Empire; we, who are poor women, ignorant, foolish . . .

TLACAÉLEL: Bright, not foolish! We don't have the letter *f* in Nahuatl.

XOCHIHUETZI: (*Quickly.*) Nor do we have the letter *b.*

TLACAÉLEL: Well said! (*Laughs. Transition.*) I have to give a speech, to welcome my grandson, as soon as he's born.

XOCHICHIHUA: We would love to hear it.

TLACAÉLEL: It's the same one as always for such occasions: the one for the rituals.

XOCHICHIHUA: I've never heard it.

XOCHIHUETZI: I have. Twice.

TLACAÉLEL: I used to know it by heart. But my memory is starting to fail me. They're nothing to laugh at, my ninety years!

XOCHICHIHUA: They become you, my lord.

TLACAÉLEL: I appreciate the compliment, my daughter and grand-child. Your name is . . . ?

XOCHICHIHUA: Xochichihua, my lord.

TLACAÉLEL: And yours?

XOCHIHUETZI: Xochihuetzi.

TLACAÉLEL: Twins?

XOCHICHIHUA: Just in our names.

TLACAÉLEL: For many years. Well, then . . . Omexóchitl sounds better to me. What were we talking about?

XOCHICHIHUA: About your speech.

TLACAÉLEL: What speech?

XOCHIHUETZI: Welcoming your royal grandson.

TLACAÉLEL: Grandson?

(*Xochichihua glances at Xochihuetzi, disconcerted.*)

XOCHIHUETZI: Axayácatl's son!

(*The door opens. Chicomexóchitl appears. Solemnly:*)

CHICOMEXÓCHITL: The son of Axayácatl is born! The first son of Axayácatl! (*Closes the door behind her.*)

TLACAÉLEL: Oh! He's born! Listen. (*He gets ready to make his speech. Reflects.*) But no. The custom is to recite the speech in front of the newly born child. I don't like the newfangledness of this clinic! Why did she close the door? No door in this empire has ever been closed on Tlacaélel, not without his fist breaking it down! (*Calms down.*) But of course, this isn't any time to break it down.

XOCHIHUETZI: Say your speech here, my lord. (*To Xochichihua.*) It's cute, you'll see. It sounds like one of Nezahualcóyotl's. (*To Tlacaélel.*) You can practice your lines. Then you can repeat them for your grandson.

TLACAÉLEL: Not a bad idea. Okay. Here goes. (*Clears his throat, recites:*) "O my grandson and my lord, person of great value, much appreciated and much esteemed, O precious stone, O emerald, O sapphire, O rich plumage, hair and fingernail of highest origin! You are welcomed to this world, you have come at the right time; you have been formed in the highest place, where the two supreme gods dwell, that is above the nine skies. Together they have molded you like a bead of gold, and have pierced you like a precious rock, very beautiful and very polished, together your father and your mother, the great lord and the great lady, and with them, our son Quetzalcóatl!"

(The door opens. Chicomexóchitl announces.)

CHICOMEXÓCHITL: The second son of Axayácatl is born! (*And closes the door.*)

XOCHIHUETZI: Another one!

TLACAÉLEL: What did she say? Why did she interrupt me?

XOCHICHIHUA: Interrupt? Hadn't you finished?

TLACAÉLEL: I was just getting through the exordium. Did she say . . . Another son! Another grandson!

XOCHIHUETZI: Continue, my lord. The line was . . . "our son Quetzalcóatl."

TLACAÉLEL: No, no. I have to start over. And use the plural now: Our grandsons, feathers, stones, fingernails . . .

XOCHICHIHUA: That won't be too hard.

TLACAÉLEL: No, no. There should be another *tlatoani* to give the speech.

XOCHIHUETZI: There aren't any others at hand.

TLACAÉLEL: One was supposed to meet me here. He must be around somewhere.

(The door opens. Chicomexóchitl announces:)

CHICOMEXÓCHITL: Another two sons of Axayácatl are born. (*And closes the door.*)

XOCHICHIHUA: Four!

XOCHIHUETZI: Four!

TLACAÉLEL: What are you surprised about? I've sired eighty-three . . . so far. And Axayácatl was cut from the same stone.

XOCHICHIHUA: But siring isn't the same. Poor woman!

TLACAÉLEL: The king must know about this. Immediately. The sacrifices to Tlazoltéotl have born their fruit. I arranged them. Two thousand children offered to Chalchiuhtlicue. It couldn't fail me. Call Axayácatl!

XOCHIHUETZI: (*Goes to the door at right. To the guards offstage:*) Call the king! (*Alternating voices, getting more distant:* "Call the king!")

(Chicomexóchitl opens the center door.)

CHICOMEXÓCHITL: Quiet! Listen.

(Tlacaélel and the ladies listen: the recorded voice of the midwife reaches them, mixed with the cries of newborn babies:)

VOICE OF THE MIDWIFE: My tender and dearly beloved children, take note of the doctrine that our Lord Yoaltecuhtli and Lady Yoaltícitl, your fathers and mothers, have left you; from between you I cut your umbilical cord. (*Little cry.*) Know and understand that your house is not here where you have been born, because you are soldiers and servants, you are the birds they call *quecholli,* you are the birds they call *zaquan,* you are the birds and soldiers of He who is in all places . . . (*Contrasting voice.*) Another three! (*The cries multiply.*)

(Chicomexóchitl goes in hurriedly and closes the door.)

XOCHICHIHUA: This is unheard of!

TLACAÉLEL: Three, and four, seven. Tenochtitlan has never had so many kings. Axayácatl is only the sixth. If they were to count me . . .

XOCHIHUETZI: Won't they need more hot water?

XOCHICHIHUA: There's another entrance, the service entry. They must be supplying themselves through there, except that this one is automatic. This is the door of honor.

(A huéhuetl is heard in the distance.)

TLACAÉLEL: Here comes Axayácatl.

XOCHIHUETZI: Is it him?

TLACAÉLEL: That's our signal system. *(He listens. A type of morse code is heard on the* huéhuetl:*)* He's bringing my granddaughter and niece. *(More signals.)* They are coming into the palace.

(The door opens. Chicomexóchitl announces:)

CHICOMEXÓCHITL: And now, two girls!

(Through the door they hear the [recorded] voice of the midwife:)

VOICE OF THE MIDWIFE: You are welcomed, my daughters, we rejoice at your arrival, very beloved maidens, precious stones, rich plumage, very esteemed things . . .

(Chicomexóchitl shuts the door.)

XOCHICHIHUA: That makes . . . nine!

(A martial rhythm on the conch shell. Enter Axayácatl, followed by Chalchiuhnenetzin. Xochichihua and Xochihuetzi kneel. Tlacaélel steps forward to receive Axayácatl. Chalchiuhnenetzin comes in second place and the ladies cross over to receive her while Tlacaélel embraces Axayácatl. When they get close to her, they retreat. They've been given the blow.)

TLACAÉLEL: My son and lord! Lucky father! I am crying, spilling copious tears of joy!

AXAYÁCATL: Dry up, old man! *(Crosses to the door. Tlacaélel goes to greet Chalchiuhnenetzin. The ladies run to prevent the king from going in.)*

TLACAÉLEL: My beloved niece, perfumed flower!

XOCHICHIHUA: *(To Axayácatl.)* Pardon me, my lord. The queen cannot receive you yet.

CHALCHIUHNENETZIN: *(To Tlacaélel.)* My grandfather!

AXAYÁCATL: Hasn't she finished? They told me . . .

TLACAÉLEL: (*Going towards him.*) She must be very fatigued. There've been . . . how many?

XOCHIHUETZI: Nine, so far.

CHALCHIUHNENETZIN: Nine! What a calamity. I've only brought enough gifts for one, or two. I'll have to send for more!

AXAYÁCATL: Don't worry about that. (*To the ladies and Tlacaélel.*) Ilan-cuéitl was always very considerate of my nervousness. And exceptionally bashful. I understand that she doesn't wish to shock me with the spectacle of her eagle hatchings. Let's go to the palace, grandpa. (*To the ladies.*) I'll return at a better time. (*To Chalchiuhnenetzin.*) If you want to stay here . . . These ladies will keep you company.

CHALCHIUHNENETZIN: As you command. But I must speak to you . . .

AXAYÁCATL: I'll wait for you in the palace. You will eat with me. (*Confidential.*) I ordered them to make *nacatamalli*s for you . . .

CHALCHIUHNENETZIN: Magnificent! I love them!

AXAYÁCATL: I know. And there aren't any there . . .

CHALCHIUHNENETZIN: No. Duck; duck every day. You get to hate it.

TLACAÉLEL: Your cold blood scares me! Nine children all at once! When you've been waiting for an heir for so long! And all you can think about is eating tamales with your family or going to the palace to negotiate with me!

AXAYÁCATL: Country comes first, Tlacaélel. You know it well. You yourself have said it many times. We all have our place. Not all our duties can be fulfilled in bed.

TLACAÉLEL: No, they don't stop there, but . . .

AXAYÁCATL: You will be pleased to know what I've decided. It's more up your alley than maternity is. Your counsel is needed, urgently. I've decided to declare war on Moquíhuix!

CHALCHIUHNENETZIN: What am I hearing! War!

AXAYÁCATL: Yes, war! Huitzilopochtli demands it! The peace agreement is over! No more cold war! The time has come for Tenochtitlan to take back the Popolocans!

TLACAÉLEL: O lucky day! O luminous day! War on the Tlatelolcans!

On the miry sons of Tezozómoc, whose tired old guts I yanked out with my own hands! Day on which nine eagles have been born to you, nine tigers, nine obsidian knives, nine *macanas!*

(The door opens. Chicomexóchitl sticks her head out.)

CHICOMEXÓCHITL: The tenth son of Axayácatl is born!

AXAYÁCATL: Let me know when she gets to a dozen.

(Exits, followed by his court, as the curtain falls.)

CURTAIN

ACT TWO

Scene 1

Axayácatl's general quarters. Near La Lagunilla. Four in the morning. Enter Axayácatl followed by Tlacaélel. Three generals escort them: Tepecócatl, Calcimehuateuctli and Cocipantli.

AXAYÁCATL: Then everything is ready to go?

TEPECÓCATL: Just as you ordered. The warriors from Cuepopan and from Aztacalco—a thousand from each district—have been out here since last night taking up their camouflaged positions among the reed groves as we planned it. When the *huéhuetl* sounds, at daylight, those from Moyotlan, with their banners and arms unsheathed, will advance to the center of the two hidden battalions to provoke an attack by the Tlatelolcans. They will carry the battle as far as possible. The Moyotlas will fake a retreat that will bring their pursuers into the ambush of the troops from Cuepopan and Aztacalco. Once they are inside the trap, we will exterminate them.

CALCIMEHUATEUCTLI: And we will go into Tlatelolco.

TLACAÉLEL: Me first! Cocipantli . . .

COCIPANTLI: Sir?

TLACAÉLEL: You will accompany me to the temple. While Axayácatl takes possession of the *tecpan,* we will get everything ready for the sacrifice of the prisoners.

TEPECÓCATL: There won't be many left.

TLACAÉLEL: There will have to be some left. My strength no longer permits me to participate in the battle. Nevertheless, by right, as the Cihuacóatl, I'm the one who gets to send as many Tlatelolcans to Mictlan as possible. It's always been that way. In the war with the Cuextecans . . .

AXAYÁCATL: (*Curtly.*) We know, Tlacaélel.

TLACAÉLEL: Well, it has to be that way. Always. Take them alive, and turn them over to me.

AXAYÁCATL: Fine. That's the way it'll be done.

TLACAÉLEL: Cocipantli . . . ?

COCIPANTLI: Sir?

TLACAÉLEL: Come with me. (*To Axayácatl.*) I'm going to . . . . (*to the bathroom, it is understood.*)

(*Exit Tlacaélel and Cocipantli.*)

AXAYÁCATL: He gets worse all the time. And he doesn't want to retire!

TEPECÓCATL: It's natural, sir. He has grown fond of his work.

AXAYÁCATL: Understood. He's held high offices and worked alongside kings for more than a *century—one of our centuries, that is.

TEPECÓCATL: That long, sir?

AXAYÁCATL: Just figure: he started with Izcóatl in 1427: a period of thirteen years; he continued with Huehue Moctezuma from 1440 to '69: twenty-nine more years. And now he's been with me since they crowned me . . .

TEPECÓCATL: Well that's true . . . But it's to him that we owe . . . our most revolutionary ideas: the true ideology of the *Revolution. For example, the idea of rewriting the History of the Empire. He had all the codices burned. A clever idea. And the idea of allowing only one official version.

AXAYÁCATL: Yes, yes. And his counsel continues to be valuable. But he's never still. I sent him to Papaloapan and he's already back here. Anyway, come here, Calcimehuateuctli . . .

CALCIMEHUATEUCTLI: At your orders.

AXAYÁCATL: What have our allies from Texcoco and Tlacopan contributed?

CALCIMEHUATEUCTLI: The people from Tlacopan have sent forces that I've reserved for the last attack, if it becomes necessary. You'll excuse me, sir, but I don't have much confidence in them: not in their skill, not in their loyalty. Remember that they are Tepanecans: relatives of Moquíhuix.

AXAYÁCATL: And those from Texcoco?

CALCIMEHUATEUCTLI: Nezahualcóyotl himself commands them. They make another two thousand. They've been in waiting since yesterday, on the eastern wing. Nezahualcóyotl has started writing an epic poem that he plans to recite when we enter Tlatelolco.

AXAYÁCATL: I don't think there will be time for literary gatherings.

CALCIMEHUATEUCTLI: I don't either; but we shouldn't contradict him. He says we need to leave the legacy of an epic poem to posterity: that that's the way all countries start off their literary traditions, and that this is the chance to write it. He's already begun.

AXAYÁCATL: Before the war? Have you heard it?

CALCIMEHUATEUCTLI: He read me the beginning. The first rhapsody.

AXAYÁCATL: Is it any good? Does it mention me?

CALCIMEHUATEUCTLI: It starts with your name. It goes: " * Sing, O muse, the wrath of the divine Axayácatl; doleful wrath that brought countless woes upon the Tlatelolcans . . ." Something like that. I don't remember any more of it.

AXAYÁCATL: (*Trying to remember.*) It sounds like . . . like . . . I think . . . Anyway . . .

TLACAÉLEL: (*Entering.*) Son and nephew! I'm proud of you! The calm wisdom with which the very lips of the * flowery war informs you of its preparations also bathes my tired eyes in tears.

AXAYÁCATL: Thank you, grandfather and uncle. (*To Calcimehuateuctli and Tepecócatl.*) All right.

TEPECÓCATL: Any other orders?

AXAYÁCATL: No more. Wait for the first light of dawn, and for the plan to go into effect. I will give the signal to attack with my little golden drum.

THE TWO GENERALS: With your permission, then. (*They salute and leave.*)

TLACAÉLEL: And now that we are alone, Axayácatl, will you explain to me the disturbing indifference with which you received the news of your long-awaited and unexpected multiple fatherhood? As Cihuacóatl and grandfather, I have, more than anybody, the right to know the reasons for your surprising behavior.

AXAYÁCATL: Now is not the time for secrets, grandfather. I'll tell you later.

TLACAÉLEL: Ten children in one blow, and you're so flippant! Don't you think Ilancuéitl deserved congratulations; celebrations; a visit from you, to meet your children before you left the city? As urgent as this war is . . .

AXAYÁCATL: Grandfather, the years have watered down your perceptiveness. I didn't think it was necessary to explain to you, Cihuacóatl, father of eighty-three children . . .

TLACAÉLEL: So far.

AXAYÁCATL: Father of eighty-three children so far, what you have always known: Ilancuéitl is sterile.

TLACAÉLEL: Sterile! And she pops out ten children!

AXAYÁCATL: Perhaps I'd better explain it to you through the euphemism of a metaphor: Can it be denied that an old mother turkey, who lavishes the periodic fever of her maternal instincts onto a nest of many eggs, would be the mother of the *totolli* hatched by her heat?

TLACAÉLEL: Of course it can't be denied! But what are you getting at with this avian simile? Is it because I called your children eagles? It's our custom to call them that.

AXAYÁCATL: But suppose that you knew for a fact, as you and I have known well for quite a while, that the decrepit old turkey has never laid an egg.

TLACAÉLEL: Is it because she lives without a cock?

AXAYÁCATL: No. And let's talk about the rooster, since you brought it up. You well know that among roosters and Nahuas it is an ancient common-sense custom that the male have an ample assortment of additional hens here and there to cajole and pin down, depending on what he's in the mood for.

TLACAÉLEL: An excellent custom. In my time, I managed to pin down, day upon day, up to three hundred concubines. Those were the days!

AXAYÁCATL: So, what is so strange, or so fortuitous, if the eggs of ten *totollas* are gathered so they can be hatched by the one hen that wasn't lucky enough to lay even one of her own?

TLACAÉLEL: You mean . . .

AXAYÁCATL: Ilancuéitl didn't lay them; she resigned herself to incubating them. My . . . *eggs, so to speak.

TLACAÉLEL: But then . . . Knock off the metaphors! My niece is no turkey hen!

AXAYÁCATL: It's very simple. Neither you nor anybody else had any reason to know: but in light of her proven sterility, Ilancuéitl suffered in anguish. From the start, she wasn't ignorant of my other details; you know: the maidens that the obsequious Mexican lords courteously offered to supply me with when I was crowned: their best products. The queen knew it, and even went along with it. She asked just one thing of me.

TLACAÉLEL: That you wouldn't make it public? But it's routine! And it isn't anything to be ashamed of.

AXAYÁCATL: She asked just this one thing: touching, really: that after five years, whenever any of my concubines gave birth, that after killing the mother, they would bring the child to her in her bed; Ilancuéitl would feign having given birth, would receive the congratulations, would have sent the lucky *cihuapipiltin* to the Tlalocan, and would counteract the humiliating reputation of her sterility. I found it to be a reasonable request. Fair, noble. And politically useful. That way we were sure of a legitimate heir to the throne.

TLACAÉLEL: Moving, really. But that doesn't explain everything. Ten at a time!

AXAYÁCATL: Everything had been arranged for just such a convenient substitution. Iztacxóchitl, my favorite, confided her pregnancy to me; Ilancuéitl confined herself to bed. The imminence of her feigned childbirth was announced. Moquíhuix and Chalchiuhnenetzin would be the godparents. And then Epcóatl had to come stick his foot into it!

TLACAÉLEL: Epcóatl? What does that little pimp have to do with it?

AXAYÁCATL: I designated him to pick up the child as soon as it was born and deliver it to his woman, Chicomexóchitl, the queen's lady, through the secret door.

TLACAÉLEL: And . . . ?

AXAYÁCATL: The imbecile brought all the children born to my concubines that day. Nine. One had twins. We've sent a whole battalion of *cihuapipiltin* to Huitzilopochtli!

TLACAÉLEL: But didn't you warn him?

AXAYÁCATL: Of course I told him, "Bring me the one that's born on the day 8-Rabbit." That should have been the one that was Iztacxóchitl's. How was I to know that he would carry out my orders so literally with all the others!

TLACAÉLEL: Oh, these people in the court; always outdoing each other just to prove how smart they are! He deserves to be punished. Have him flayed so that he'll learn.

AXAYÁCATL: I've already sent for him. Chalchiuhnenetzin is the one who came to my house to tell me all about the mix-up. She stayed there, remember? And as she was going to be the godmother, and she was the aunt, Chicomexóchitl filled her in on all the details.

TLACAÉLEL: Have her whipped for her indiscretion.

AXAYÁCATL: That's not the worst thing.

TLACAÉLEL: There's more?

AXAYÁCATL: Chalchiuhnenetzin hasn't had children either, for other reasons. And now she has come up with the idea that we should repeat the whole trick! That that way war could be avoided!

TLACAÉLEL: Oh, no! Not one step backward! No way! I don't know why we're waging this war. But it's a war, and we have to win it!

AXAYÁCATL: Calm down; you'll have your war. And Chalchiuhnenetzin won't return to Tlatelolco. I have other plans for her imminent widowhood.

TLACAÉLEL: It's starting to dawn. Isn't it time to start?

AXAYÁCATL: Yes. Take my little drum. (*Gives it to him.*) You give the signal.

(*Tlacaélel exits, happy.*
The drum beat is heard. In the distance a huéhuetl *answers. The sound of troops getting ready to march and distant shouts are heard.*)

TEPECÓCATL: (*Entering.*) The battle has begun, Axayácatl.

AXAYÁCATL: Fine. Carry on.

TEPECÓCATL: Epcóatl wants to see you. He says you sent for him.

AXAYÁCATL: Send him in!

(Exit the general.)

TLACAÉLEL: (*Returning.*) Glorious day! Let me keep playing the
drum! It makes me feel fifty years younger!

AXAYÁCATL: Play it, grandpa. (*Tlacaélel plays, thrilled.*)

(Enter Epcóatl, guarded.)

TLACAÉLEL: Here's the cretin! What are you going to do to him?

AXAYÁCATL: So, idiot, what do you have to say to me?

EPCÓATL: Do what you want with me, Axayácatl. If outdoing myself
in following your orders is a fault, punish me for it.

AXAYÁCATL: You outdid yourself by nine! Does that seem like a small
thing to you?

EPCÓATL: All of them were your children.

AXAYÁCATL: Of that I'm approximately sure. But the queen isn't a
dog! There's no way she could churn out ten! She's out of practice! One was enough! One, I told you! Clearly!

EPCÓATL: My lady the queen differed with that opinion.

TLACAÉLEL: The queen disagreed?

EPCÓATL: It was her idea. She told me you agreed, in principle . . .

AXAYÁCATL: In principle and for one, yes.

EPCÓATL: . . . and that a slight alteration of the plans wouldn't bother
you. That you had waited for ten years to have an heir; that it
was like having saved up, having all of them at once, one for
each year. And since they were all yours . . .

AXAYÁCATL: So I was a sort of warehouse for her then, a bank account? Is that it?

EPCÓATL: More or less. You'd made the deposit—the deposits—in
accounts with her name on them. There was nothing wrong
with transferring the balance to your joint account.

(Enter the general Cocipantli.)

COCIPANTLI: Sir!

AXAYÁCATL: What's going on?

COCIPANTLI: Something horrible, sir!

TLACAÉLEL: What's happening? Aren't we advancing?

COCIPANTLI: According to the plan, we provoked the Tlatelolcans into attacking into the middle of our troops waiting in ambush to cut them off.

AXAYÁCATL: But they didn't attack?

COCIPANTLI: Yes. And en masse. But we couldn't answer them with the same arms.

TLACAÉLEL: Don't we have spears? *Macanas?* Arrows?

COCIPANTLI: Yes, Cihuacóatl, but not milk!

AXAYÁCATL: Milk!

COCIPANTLI: The most hair-raising battalion of naked women burst into our ranks. They came up shouting and slapping themselves on the belly. We were so shocked we couldn't move. And when they got close to us, they squeezed their *chichis* and bathed our faces with squirts of warm, thick milk!

AXAYÁCATL: The secret weapon! The * atomizing pump!

COCIPANTLI: We don't dare attack them, unless you order us to.

AXAYÁCATL: Where are they now?

COCIPANTLI: Everywhere. There's at least one for each of our soldiers. And they have a healthy rear guard. What do we do? This didn't figure into our plans.

AXAYÁCATL: Some intelligence agency we have! Our strategists should have been able to foresee it!

TLACAÉLEL: But the Tlatelolcans! The men! Aren't there any men in Tlatelolco?

COCIPANTLI: They aren't showing themselves.

TLACAÉLEL: Cowards! Ill-bred ducks!

COCIPANTLI: Our men weren't expecting such an untimely breakfast.

AXAYÁCATL: You mean to say that . . . ?

COCIPANTLI: That after the initial upset, they started to take it laughingly. And then they started to take it . . . without laughing. They've put down their arms. The youngest are stripping their uniforms and letting themselves be chased through the cornfields. It's like mass desertion. You can see it for yourself from here, sir.

(Axayácatl crosses to see the front.)

AXAYÁCATL: *(Shouts.)* No! Not this! How awful!

TLACAÉLEL: What is it? I can't see!

AXAYÁCATL: Guerrilla cowards!

CAPTAIN: *(Entering.)* Sir, they've captured one of the fatties. She insists on seeing you.

AXAYÁCATL: Not naked!

CAPTAIN: We've already covered her with what we had. She says she's not Tlatelolcan, but Tenochcan.

TLACAÉLEL: Ah, traitor! I'll skin her!

AXAYÁCATL: Let her through!

(Exit Cocipantli and the Captain.)

EPCÓATL: May I leave, sir?

AXAYÁCATL: Are you in a hurry?

EPCÓATL: One more errand the queen commanded me to do. I have to get her ten *chichihuas* to nurse the children as soon as possible. Since we killed the mothers . . .

TLACAÉLEL: See what you've caused, cretin?

EPCÓATL: Pardon me, Cihuacóatl. I would have had to get one in any case.

AXAYÁCATL: No. Wait. I have an idea. *(Epcóatl waits to one side. Enter Tomahuazintli, pushed by the Captain and covered with a cape. She throws herself at the feet of Axayácatl.)* Get up.

TOMAHUAZINTLI: Do you recognize me, sir?

AXAYÁCATL: I've never seen you. Should I recognize you?

TOMAHUAZINTLI: I went in your sister's entourage to Tlatelolco. I am the daughter of Tecuani.

AXAYÁCATL: How did you end up here then, and naked?

TOMAHUAZINTLI: Tecónal mixed me up with the fatties that he sent to the battlefield. Moquíhuix had ordered all his concubines to join the wake-up squadron, as they called it.

AXAYÁCATL: And were you his concubine?

TOMAHUAZINTLI: Chalchiuhnenetzin had scarcely left when the guards took me by force to Moquíhuix's bedroom. He had his pleasure with me—and with another twenty Totonacans—and he retired to rest, so he said. He promised to return. But he didn't come back.

TLACAÉLEL: That coward! There's not even a word for him!

COCIPANTLI: (*Entering.*) What should we do, sir?

AXAYÁCATL: Wait! (*To Tomahuazintli.*) Go on.

TOMAHUAZINTLI: In his place came Tecónal, who corralled us all, just as we were, and put us with the others in the plaza. The fattest ones were made captains. They said they had secret orders that we should all obey to save the endangered fatherland. The rest you already know. I was unarmed, since I don't have milk. It's not that time. I managed to escape. And here I am.

AXAYÁCATL: What do you plan to do now?

TOMAHUAZINTLI: To reveal a secret to you, sir.

TLACAÉLEL: We're not interested in your secrets! They're already public!

AXAYÁCATL: About what?

TOMAHUAZINTLI: Moquíhuix.

AXAYÁCATL: What about that coward?

TOMAHUAZINTLI: He's not in Tlatelolco, and it's useless to look for him there.

AXAYÁCATL: He's fled?

TOMAHUAZINTLI: To Tlacopan. He planned it ahead of time.

AXAYÁCATL: And how do you know?

TOMAHUAZINTLI: Don't embarrass me, sir. (*Lowers her eyes.*) His valet visited my bedroom every night.

TLACAÉLEL: Cynic! Liar!

TOMAHUAZINTLI: I did it with the permission of my lady Chal-chiuhnenetzin. And every day I told her what I found out from him: of his plans against you, of his secret alliance with Tlacopan . . .

TEPECÓCATL: What should we do, sir? With the fatties! More keep coming!

TLACAÉLEL: Fence them in! Tie them up!

TEPECÓCATL: They slip away, sir.

TLACAÉLEL: Throw them on the ground!

TEPECÓCATL: We already did. They got up again. Our soldiers are the ones that stayed down.

AXAYÁCATL: Call a meeting. Call off the frontal attack.

TEPECÓCATL: How do we get past the rear guard? It's very . . . broad.

AXAYÁCATL: We'll go in lines toward Tlacopan. On the causeway.

TEPECÓCATL: To Tlacopan, you said?

AXAYÁCATL: That's what I said! Obey!

(Tepecócatl starts to leave.)

AXAYÁCATL: One moment. Haven't you taken prisoners?

TEPECÓCATL: No more than ten.

AXAYÁCATL: That's enough. Let's go, Tlacaélel. Play the drum if you want to. *(Tlacaélel plays.)* Epcóatl . . .

EPCÓATL: Sir?

AXAYÁCATL: Go with the General. *(To the general.)* Give the ten fatties to Epcóatl.

TLACAÉLEL: Is that the worst punishment for him you can think of?

AXAYÁCATL: *(To Epcóatl.)* Now you have your *chichihuas*. You know where to take them. And you, Tomahuazintli . . . *(Tomahuazintli approaches. To the general.)* You answer to me for this woman. Keep her in custody until I return.

TOMAHUAZINTLI: I'd like to go to my lady Chalchiuhnenetzin, sir. She needs me.

AXAYÁCATL: *(To the general.)* Don't let her talk to anyone. Take her away.

(The general leads Tomahuazintli out.)

EPCÓATL: I don't understand, sir. Is that how you reward a woman who's revealed Moquíhuix's hiding place to you? By imprisoning her?

AXAYÁCATL: I know what I'm doing. Hurry up! The babies haven't had breakfast!

(Exit Axayácatl, followed by Epcóatl. Double time is heard on the huéhuetl, *and gets louder as the curtain falls.)*

CURTAIN

Scene 2

A terrace in Axayácatl's palace, a day later. The old lady, and Ladies I and II.

CHICOMEXÓCHITL: (*Entering. The others follow her.*) What a shame the queen couldn't be here. The banquet is going to be splendid.

XOCHICHIHUA: Yes, a real shame. But it's understandable. Is she well? Did she get through the night all right?

CHICOMEXÓCHITL: Well, yes. Her strength is admirable.

XOCHIHUETZI: Startling.

XOCHICHIHUA: And the *pipiltzintzin*?

CHICOMEXÓCHITL: They're asleep, the angels. They're beautiful.

XOCHIHUETZI: Which of the two do they look like?

CHICOMEXÓCHITL: It's still hard to tell. By their color, like their father.

XOCHICHIHUA: There are two girls, aren't there?

CHICOMEXÓCHITL: Two. Twins.

XOCHIHUETZI: You should know. I've always been curious. Is it true that Tlacaélel is Moctezuma's twin brother? I've heard it said.

CHICOMEXÓCHITL: Twins, no. But they were born the same day. Hours apart.

XOCHICHIHUA: Obstetrics has advanced quite a bit since then. Ilan-cuéitl churned hers out all at once, almost. And ten!

CHICOMEXÓCHITL: But Tlacaélel and Moctezuma were only brothers through their father. Each one came from a different mother.

XOCHICHIHUA: Synchronized right, then.

CHICOMEXÓCHITL: That's it.

XOCHIHUETZI: Then that's why Tlacaélel is so powerful? So influential?

CHICOMEXÓCHITL: Not powerful, anymore. Ninety years don't go by without having an effect. Influential, yes. Although not as much anymore either.

XOCHICHIHUA: Nevertheless, he still went on this campaign.

CHICOMEXÓCHITL: It's his obligation as Cihuacóatl, but he didn't fight. He doesn't have the strength anymore. He had to go to the temple, to perform the sacrifices. He's had lots of practice doing that.

XOCHIHUETZI: But they help him do it.

CHICOMEXÓCHITL: The four priests hold down the blessed ones; but he gives them the final whack. He still has a magnificently steady hand.

XOCHICHIHUA: Did they take many prisoners?

CHICOMEXÓCHITL: Practically all the Tlatilolcans. As soon as they saw Moquíhuix fall from the temple, they gave up.

XOCHIHUETZI: How inspiring it must have been! So unusual.

CHICOMEXÓCHITL: Epcóatl, my husband, didn't see it either. The king had commissioned him to do something else. But my oldest son was in the whole battle. He told us.

XOCHICHIHUA: Oh, tell us!

CHICOMEXÓCHITL: There's no time now. It won't be long till Chalchiuhnenetzin gets here. They're combing her hair now.

XOCHIHUETZI: Will she take the queen's place at the banquet?

CHICOMEXÓCHITL: Who knows. She's probably not in the mood.

XOCHICHIHUA: It's true. Now she's a widow! But still a virgin, I think. So they say.

XOCHIHUETZI: Yes, there's time. Tell us.

XOCHICHIHUA: About the fatties?

XOCHIHUETZI: No, we already know about that. How horrendous! Tell us about how the king killed Moquíhuix. Hadn't he fled to Tlacopan?

CHICOMEXÓCHITL: That's what he wanted Axayácatl to believe. He took advantage of a traitor, Chalchiuhnenetzin's lady.

XOCHICHIHUA: The one they skinned today?

CHICOMEXÓCHITL: That's the one. She pretended to be a victim of Moquíhuix, loyal to Axayácatl, and wanted to send him on a detour to Tlacopan. The king pretended to believe her; but turned around and fell on Tlatelolco in a surprise attack. Moquíhuix wasn't expecting that. He thought his fatties had already finished off the Tenochcans. And that the traitors from Tlacopan would finish off Axayácatl.

XOCHIHUETZI: And there stood Troy!

CHICOMEXÓCHITL: Exactly. The little coward ran to take refuge in the temple. He still had time to let loose a battalion of naked, painted children to slow down the attack. But it didn't do him any good.

XOCHICHIHUA: Tlacaélel killed him?

CHICOMEXÓCHITL: No. Axayácatl himself. That's what I really would have liked to have seen. When he pushed him down the stairs after knocking him out with his *macana* in one-to-one combat.

XOCHIHUETZI: Beautiful! Moving!

CHICOMEXÓCHITL: Nezahualcóyotl must be finishing up his poem about now. It probably tells all about it.

XOCHICHIHUA: I'm dying to hear him read it. Will he be coming?

CHICOMEXÓCHITL: He should be; but I don't think so. He's probably gone back to his gardens in Tezcotzinco. Whenever he has to write something, that's where he locks himself up.

XOCHIHUETZI: It's beautiful. Have you ever seen it?

XOCHICHIHUA: No. It's pretty far away. Have you?

XOCHIHUETZI: Yes. We went one Sunday. They didn't let us visit the gardens, but from far away you could see it. A lot of terraces, and a swimming pool up above. It must have a splendid view.

CHICOMEXÓCHITL: Nezahualcóyotl allows himself a very good life.

XOCHICHIHUA: Well deserved. Ever since he was little, I think he's had some hard times.

XOCHIHUETZI: Why?

CHICOMEXÓCHITL: Tezozómoc wanted to kill him. He hated Nezahualcóyotl's father, Ixtlilxóchitl. His life is just like a *novel.

XOCHIHUETZI: He must have been really handsome when he was young. He still is a little.

XOCHICHIHUA: Yes, isn't that true? He's much nicer than his son.

CHICOMEXÓCHITL: Which one of all of them?

XOCHIHUETZI: Well, how many does he have? I only knew about Nezahualpilli.

CHICOMEXÓCHITL: That one's the heir; but just imagine: with five hundred concubines . . .

XOCHICHIHUA: How many?

CHICOMEXÓCHITL: Five hundred. That's what they say.

XOCHICHIHUA: Oh, how scandalous!

CHICOMEXÓCHITL: But his son has him beat. He has two thousand.

XOCHICHIHUA: Oh, no! How can that be!

XOCHIHUETZI: It must be an exaggeration. I really don't believe that with all two thousand he . . .

CHICOMEXÓCHITL: And look what happened to Chalchiuhnenetzin . . .

XOCHICHIHUA: To the one who was just widowed? Her too?

CHICOMEXÓCHITL: No. A niece of hers. That's why they gave her that name.

XOCHIHUETZI: And what happened?

CHICOMEXÓCHITL: You two are too young to remember; but it was an enormous scandal.

XOCHICHIHUA: Oh, tell, tell!

CHICOMEXÓCHITL: I don't know if I ought to . . .

XOCHIHUETZI: Why not? See how you are. You pique our curiosity and then . . .

CHICOMEXÓCHITL: It was such an ugly affair . . .

XOCHICHIHUA: What was, what was?

CHICOMEXÓCHITL: Well, that Axayácatl gave her to Nezahualpilli, for his collection. But she was so young, that Nezahualpilli ordered her to be guarded in a palace until she grew up. He stopped by to see her from time to time.

XOCHICHIHUA: Like corn, all in good time . . .

XOCHIHUETZI: And then? She grew up?

CHICOMEXÓCHITL: She didn't wait till she grew up. She started training in secret. Every night she gave big parties with the officers who tickled her fancy.

XOCHICHIHUA: And Nezahualpilli caught her? With her fancy tickled?

XOCHIHUETZI: Oh, don't jump ahead! Let's hear it all!

CHICOMEXÓCHITL: He started to get a hint of it when whenever he went to see her, her servants told him she was already in bed.

XOCHICHIHUA: Well she was, wasn't she?

CHICOMEXÓCHITL: One night he went in and found her in a very large room, full of statues with torches in their hands.

XOCHIHUETZI: Pretending to be statues?

CHICOMEXÓCHITL: She told him they were her gods. And he believed her.

XOCHICHIHUA: And they weren't?

XOCHIHUETZI: Ssh! Wait!

CHICOMEXÓCHITL: He got suspicious. And even more so when he recognized some lip-rings he had given to Chalchiuhnenetzin on two hefty officers from her guard.

XOCHICHIHUA: Ay, caray!

CHICOMEXÓCHITL: That night he went all the way to her bedroom. He felt the lump in her bed. It was a dummy. He went farther inside . . . and he finds her having a wild time with three officers in the room with the statues.

XOCHIHUETZI: How horrible it must have felt!

XOCHICHIHUA: For who? For her?

CHICOMEXÓCHITL: Can you imagine? His anger knew no bounds. He called together all the neighboring kings to witness his show of justice. They made her into mincemeat, along with the officers and her three hundred servants who had been her accomplices. Later they burned the palace.

XOCHICHIHUA: Poor girl!

CHICOMEXÓCHITL: She was a sadist, sick. What do you think the statues with the torches were?

XOCHIHUETZI: Well, standing lamps.

CHICOMEXÓCHITL: They were her lovers. She would have their skins tanned . . . afterward.

(*Enter Chalchiuhnenetzin.*)

XOCHICHIHUA: My lady!

XOCHIHUETZI and CHICOMEXÓCHITL: My lady!

CHALCHIUHNENETZIN: Good morning, friends. Am I late?

CHICOMEXÓCHITL: No, my lady. We got here early. The king told us to wait for him here. But now's a very good time.

CHALCHIUHNENETZIN: It's because I slept bad. I had dreams. I always dream the same thing.

XOCHICHIHUA: That's natural. (*Pause.*) We give you our condolences.

CHALCHIUHNENETZIN: Thank you. ("Let's talk about something else.") Have you already seen the children?

CHICOMEXÓCHITL: I have. I delivered all of them.

CHALCHIUHNENETZIN: That's right. I forgot.

XOCHIHUETZI: Have you seen them already?

CHALCHIUHNENETZIN: Yes. I just came from visiting Ilancuéitl. She's a mess, but happy.

XOCHICHIHUA: And you, my lady?

CHALCHIUHNENETZIN: Am I what?

XOCHICHIHUA: Are you . . . are you going to be the godmother . . . of all of them?

CHALCHIUHNENETZIN: I don't know what Axayácatl will work out. Moquíhuix and I were going to be the godparents. Now . . . (*Whining.*)

XOCHIHUETZI: Courage, my lady! Resignation!

CHICOMEXÓCHITL: That's how people are! How their tongues wag! They say that you and Moquíhuix didn't get along very well!

CHALCHIUHNENETZIN: We got along the best in the world. To think that his son . . . will be born without a father . . .

XOCHIHUETZI: You're expecting?

CHALCHIUHNENETZIN: Yes. And there's never been a more loving, more faithful, helpful and affectionate husband than Moquíhuix with me. (*Sighs.*) It's been quite a blow. I'm overwhelmed. I don't know what to do with myself.

XOCHICHIHUA: But then . . . the war wasn't because . . .

CHALCHIUHNENETZIN: Because of me? I already know that's what they say under their breaths. No. Some political thing, that we women can't hope to understand. And I don't even try to make sense of it. But that we didn't get along well, that's vicious slander. Moquíhuix loved the smell of my very breath.

CHICOMEXÓCHITL: Don't even think about it any more. The king loves you very much. You can stay here with us in the court. We will serve you with pleasure. Right?

XOCHICHIHUA and XOCHIHUETZI: With all our heart.

CHALCHIUHNENETZIN: Thank you. You are very kind.

CHICOMEXÓCHITL: And maybe . . . Axayácatl thinks of everything. Maybe he even has a new husband for you already.

CHALCHIUHNENETZIN: Do you think so?

CHICOMEXÓCHITL: There are kings in all the towns he's conquered recently: from Tlacotépec to Ocuilan. There might be one that's single . . .

XOCHICHIHUA: Or widowed . . .

XOCHIHUETZI: And handsome.

CHICOMEXÓCHITL: . . . and would deserve you, and be happy to make you his wife. There's no need to be discouraged . . .

CHALCHIUHNENETZIN: Do you think so?

XOCHICHIHUA: Of course! Have Axayácatl as a brother-in-law! What more could they hope for?

XOCHIHUETZI: And heir to Moquíhuix! Nothing less! I bet within a year we go to Ocuilan to dance the *areito* and baptize the first born!

XOCHICHIHUA: Or the first several! There are already precedents . . .

CHALCHIUHNENETZIN: Thank you so much for trying to cheer me up. You are very kind and discreet, but it's too soon to start thinking of that. Or too late.

CHICOMEXÓCHITL: Late, no. You are at the prime of life. So slim . . . What I would give!

XOCHIHUETZI: (*She has moved towards the entrance. With emphasis:*) I think the king's coming. Yes. He's coming with Tepecócatl and Calcimehuateuctli.

XOCHICHIHUA: What should we do?

CHICOMEXÓCHITL: He'll tell us what to do. He ordered us to wait for him here. We greet him; and if he wants us to stay, we stay.

CHALCHIUHNENETZIN: I have to talk to him.

XOCHIHUETZI: Let's go then. (*To Chalchiuhnenetzin.*) We'll wait for you outside.

CHALCHIUHNENETZIN: No. Wait in my pavilion. In the garden.

CHICOMEXÓCHITL: I have to go check up on Ilancuéitl and the ten *chichihuas*.

XOCHICHIHUA: I have to go to the kitchens. The banquet is going to be for two thousand plates.

XOCHIHUETZI: What's there going to be? Slave in *pozole?*

XOCHICHIHUA: I want a leg . . .

XOCHIHUETZI: I hope it's not too hot.

CHICOMEXÓCHITL: This dish doesn't have chile. There's just salt and corn in the stew.

XOCHIHUETZI: Will there be enough for everybody?

XOCHICHIHUA: A little bit, yes. They roasted five hundred.

    (Enter Axayácatl. Tepecócatl and Calcimehuateuctli follow.)

AXAYÁCATL: Good morning, ladies. *(The ladies bow.)* Sister!

  (Chalchiuhnenetzin approaches him. The generals stay at the door and salute bowing their heads.)

CHICOMEXÓCHITL, XOCHICHIHUA, and XOCHIHUETZI: We ask your leave to retire, sir. We were keeping Chalchiuhnenetzin company.

AXAYÁCATL: Very well. *(They start to leave.)* Don't miss the banquet. You, sister, stay. *(Chalchiuhnenetzin stops and turns.)*

CHICOMEXÓCHITL, XOCHICHIHUA, and XOCHIHUETZI: Of course, sir, we'll be there. *(They greet the generals at the door and exit.)*

AXAYÁCATL: Sister, tell them to bring us some chocolate. Come in, gentlemen. *(Chalchiuhnenetzin exits through the left. The generals approach. The king installs himself in the* icpalli.*)*

AXAYÁCATL: I'm tired.

TEPECÓCATL: And not for nothing. It was a hard journey.

AXAYÁCATL: Has Tlacaélel arrived yet?

CALCIMEHUATEUCTLI: He spent the night in Tlatelolco, but he shouldn't be long. He insisted on sacrificing the prisoners himself. The truth is he doesn't have the strength to do it any longer. He offered thirteen hearts. But he didn't come through at the cleventh.

AXAYÁCATL: He's as stubborn as only he can be.

CALCIMEHUATEUCTLI: There's no need for him to bother. That's why we assigned him trained helpers. The ceremony has progressed. I think that by night we'll have finished. There were only three hundred left.

AXAYÁCATL: Perfect. Now, Tepecócatl, while we decide whether Tlatelolco should remain independent or become a district of Mexico, you will be in charge of the government there—provisionally.

CALCIMEHUATEUCTLI: Did you say "we" decide?

AXAYÁCATL: Even though it's just a formality, I have to consult with my *allies. Nezahualcóyotl never has any objections.

TEPECÓCATL: And the one from Tlacopan has even fewer.

AXAYÁCATL: But these summits of the three greats really impress the masses. They make them think that the decision that is finally made was the best from among many proposals discussed and examined by more than one will.

TEPECÓCATL: Should I set up camp then, in Tlatelolco?

AXAYÁCATL: Set up camp isn't the word. There's no more war. Govern; that is: impose tributes, undertake public works . . . That market, for example: it's too much. It gives us too much competition. It should be turned into a branch of the one in Tenochtitlan, part of the Common Market of Anáhuac. And the causeway from Tepeyácac has to be finished, by charging a bridge toll. Anyway; so many things. We'll see.

CALCIMEHUATEUCTLI: I think there's a place, near the *tecpan* . . .

AXAYÁCATL: I know which one you're talking about: at the *ahuicalli*.

CALCIMEHUATEUCTLI: Yes. It's very large. It could serve as our quarters.

AXAYÁCATL: It has a reputation for something else. It's better to capitalize on it. We'll put the red-light district there, the *zona roja*. That way the Tlatelolcans can have the illusion that they're sharing the pleasures of Moquíhuix in situ.

TEPECÓCATL: But there aren't any small rooms. Just big halls. Moquíhuix's celebrations were, well, more like . . . assemblies.

AXAYÁCATL: We'll have to build a housing project then. Nezahualcóyotl is a very good engineer. He'll take care of it.

TEPECÓCATL: There's also a military school.

AXAYÁCATL: Dismantle it. Send the students off to war.

CALCIMEHUATEUCTLI: Off to what war? To Tlaxcala? I don't think they'd be much help. They're still very green.

AXAYÁCATL: No, not to Tlaxcala; but Tlacotépec and Ocuilan are not the only towns that I'm historically destined to conquer. There's still Cozcacuauhtenco, Callimaya, Metépec, Calixtlahuaca, Ecatépec, Teutenanco, Malinaltenanco, Tzinacatépec, Coatépec, Cuitlapilco, Teuxaoalco, Tecualoyan . . .

TEPECÓCATL: You want me to send the Tlatelolcans there? Wouldn't that be risky?

AXAYÁCATL: If they get killed, we don't lose a thing. If they are as brave as they think they are, they might even be worth something to us.

CALCIMEHUATEUCTLI: Have any provisions been made for these wars?

AXAYÁCATL: The usual ones. My ambassadors have gone to visit their kings, with splendorous gifts, to elaborate our plan for the alliance for progress, and then to ask for their cooperation. If they give it, we demand more from them, until they can't give any more and have to refuse. By doing so, they will have gone back on their promise of friendship; they will be traitors and there won't be anything left for them to do but arm themselves and fight. And once they've been beaten . . .

TEPECÓCATL: We will add them to our list of permanent subjects.

CALCIMEHUATEUCTLI: And the empire of Axayácatl will grow without limits!

AXAYÁCATL: Not mine: Huitzilopochtli's.

TEPECÓCATL: Our lord and god Huiztilopochtli's.

(*Enter slaves with* jícaras *of hot chocolate that they give to the king and to the gentlemen. Tepecócatl refuses courteously.*)

AXAYÁCATL: (*Blowing on his* jícara.) I was going to ask you.

TEPECÓCATL and CALCIMEHUATEUCTLI: Yes?

AXAYÁCATL: Among the towns I have just named . . . are there any kings that are single?

TEPECÓCATL: It's not customary. I think it's forbidden in the Constitution . . .

AXAYÁCATL: I mean: some widower . . . Or some old man, with a young single son. Because in that case, by killing off the *huehue* . . .

CALCIMEHUATEUCTLI: The one in Cuitlapilco is the oldest of all. And yes, he has a son who's single. Deaf-mute.

AXAYÁCATL: Do you know him? How old is he?

CALCIMEHUATEUCTLI: He must be about forty. I saw him once.

AXAYÁCATL: What's his name?

CALCIMEHUATEUCTLI: His name is . . . Pardon my French . . . Cuitlacuani.

TEPECÓCATL: Yuch! Coprophagist!

AXAYÁCATL: Do they have something on him, or did they give it to him without thinking?

CALCIMEHUATEUCTLI: It's his name. And it suits him. This chocolate is delicious.

AXAYÁCATL: Do you want some more?

CALCIMEHUATEUCTLI: No, thank you. (*Returns the gourd.*)

(*Exit the slaves.*)

AXAYÁCATL: You didn't have any, Tepecócatl?

TEPECÓCATL: They've forbidden it for me. My gallbladder . . .

AXAYÁCATL: Get an operation, I've told you before. Look at me. Like new. Nothing like *surgery.

CALCIMEHUATEUCTLI: What are your orders then?

AXAYÁCATL: The ambassadors shouldn't be long now. They had instructions to inform the little kings of our triumph in Tlatelolco, in order to increase our prestige and augment their fears.

TEPECÓCATL: But, how do they know already? So soon?

AXAYÁCATL: Politics is different from warfare in that politics anticipates the results of military operations at the service of politics. They left a month ago: but they knew that on the day 8-Rabbit, we would take Tlatelolco.

CALCIMEHUATEUCTLI: We couldn't fail.

AXAYÁCATL: So then, the next step is to invade those . . . twelve towns. You will command the troops. Tepecócatl will stay in Tlatelolco, but he can give you soldiers.

TEPECÓCATL: As for the *ahuianime* (the cheerer-uppers) in Tlatelolco, I think there will be enough.

AXAYÁCATL: The first town I want to fall is Cuitlapilco.

CALCIMEHUATEUCTLI: It's the poorest.

AXAYÁCATL: But it's where there is a candidate on hand. I need a single man.

CALCIMEHUATEUCTLI: Even though he's a deaf-mute?

AXAYÁCATL: Blind would be better; but something is something. You'll be ready in how many days?

CALCIMEHUATEUCTLI: Three or four.

AXAYÁCATL: And till you get back? From Cuitlapilco.

CALCIMEHUATEUCTLI: Fifteen days.

AXAYÁCATL: Perfect.

TEPECÓCATL: And . . . Sir . . .

AXAYÁCATL: Yes?

TEPECÓCATL: I wanted to remind you: with your authorization, I took the liberty of promising my most war-worn officers some compensation, some incentive . . .

AXAYÁCATL: Give them higher ranks, immediately. How many are there?

TEPECÓCATL: Two in each *calpulli:* eight all together.

AXAYÁCATL: I'll decorate them with the Aztec Eagle.

TEPECÓCATL: They would prefer . . .

AXAYÁCATL: What?

TEPECÓCATL: A few little *contracts . . .

AXAYÁCATL: Little contracts?

TEPECÓCATL: Yes: the causeways, corn, tortillas, the meat from the sacrifices . . . They have so many expenses!

AXAYÁCATL: No, no, no, and no! The contracts are for the royal family.

TEPECÓCATL: It's just that . . .

AXAYÁCATL: Don't insist! Get the promotions ready and order the decorations to be made.

(*Enter Chalchiuhnenetzin.*)

CHALCHIUHNENETZIN: Excuse me. I thought you would have finished. Did they bring you the chocolate?

TEPECÓCATL: It was delicious, thank you.

AXAYÁCATL: (*To the generals.*) Go see what's going on with Tlacaélel. I'll see you both at the banquet.

(*The generals retire, accommodatingly.*)

AXAYÁCATL: Well? You'll be happy now: free again. I did what I promised. You haven't congratulated me.

CHALCHIUHNENETZIN: For the *pipiltzintzin?* A fine mess you got me into! I didn't bring any spindles to put in their hands. How was I to know that you'd have girls . . . and two. I brought little obsidian *macanas:* two, just in case; but not eight! You should have kept me informed and up to date.

AXAYÁCATL: But I didn't know anything about it! I only authorized one! But don't worry. That's the least of it. The midwife always has lots of toys on hand.

CHALCHIUHNENETZIN: But the godmother's supposed to do it. I was supposed to do it.

AXAYÁCATL: Don't get upset. Nobody noticed.

CHALCHIUHNENETZIN: And what about the umbilical cords? They buried the girls' cords in the *tlecuilpan,* as is proper. But the boys' cords caused a problem of precedence. They couldn't remember which one was born before the others so they could bury his cord in the war field. And the rest . . .

AXAYÁCATL: Forget about the *pipiltzintzin.* They all have their *chichihuas* now.

CHALCHIUHNENETZIN: That's another thing! It really upsets me that you sent those Tlatelolcans to feed them. They're drinking the milk of Moquíhuix, as they say.

AXAYÁCATL: Well . . . he was my brother-in-law . . . If you'd had children . . .

CHALCHIUHNENETZIN: You know very well it wasn't my fault!

AXAYÁCATL: I don't understand you! I wage a war to please you; to avenge your conjugal complaints; I personally kill your husband. And instead of being happy, and thanking me for it, you act like the thousand demons had gotten to you.

CHALCHIUHNENETZIN: Don't blame that war on me! If it had been for me, you would have declared it years ago! Moquíhuix never fell for your plan, or for me, as you well knew ever since you arranged for me to marry him. He always hated me!

AXAYÁCATL: I'm starting to understand why!

CHALCHIUHNENETZIN: The fact that you wanted to take over Tlatelolco to expand Tenochtitlan is something else entirely. As if I were the pretext. And come to think of it, not even that. The last thing that occurred to you was to demand reparations from Moquíhuix, not for me, but for the merchant women who were raped!

AXAYÁCATL: You weren't even a part of that. You didn't go on that *pic-nic.

CHALCHIUHNENETZIN: You don't have to remind me. But remember that my shame is your shame. I'm your big sister. And whatever happens to me, has repercussions for your glory, or for your detriment.

AXAYÁCATL: Very well. What is it you want?

CHALCHIUHNENETZIN: I already told you, last night. To do what Ilancuéitl did: to give birth, even if it's just fake. To pretend that I'm carrying the heir of Tlatelolco in my belly.

AXAYÁCATL: Who's going to believe you. So skinny.

CHALCHIUHNENETZIN: The ladies of your court will take charge of spreading the story. I already got them to believe it, those gossips. They must already be running around the palace telling everybody.

AXAYÁCATL: Suppose they do believe you. What then?

CHALCHIUHNENETZIN: You give me another of your children. I'm sure there's no shortage. You churn them out like a factory. They attribute it to me, you be its godfather; as it grows, I govern in your name in Tlatelolco. And then, a son of yours will reign, who everybody will think is Moquíhuix's.

AXAYÁCATL: You've thought of everything, haven't you?

CHALCHIUHNENETZIN: Doesn't it seem like a good idea to you? There aren't any loose strings: my honor, Moquíhuix's heir . . . and your political interest. And a happy ending for this story to give to the people. What more is there?

AXAYÁCATL: It's not bad, in principle. But it's already too late. I've made arrangements for something else.

CHALCHIUHNENETZIN: What have you arranged?

(*Enter Tlacaélel with Nezahualpilli.*)

TLACAÉLEL: Look who I brought! (*Embraces Chalchiuhnenetzin.*) Granddaughter and fragrant flower!

AXAYÁCATL: Nezahualpilli! What a pleasure! And your father?

NEZAHUALPILLI: In Tezcotzinco, sir. The *tícitl* wouldn't let him interrupt his baths. He's sent me in his place.

AXAYÁCATL: Welcome, welcome. Do you know my sister?

CHALCHIUHNENETZIN: Of course. How are you?

TLACAÉLEL: How moving to see my grandchildren together. Fingernails of my hands, hairs from my head, eagles, tigers . . . (*To Axayácatl.*) How are the last ten?

AXAYÁCATL: Just fine, grandfather. Tired?

TLACAÉLEL: Never! I ended up with thirteen hearts. It makes me feel young again.

NEZAHUALPILLI: My father sends his congratulations, Axayácatl. And he's written two poems, which I brought with me.

AXAYÁCATL: Two?

NEZAHUALPILLI: He'd already started one. It's the epic of the war of Tlatelolco.

AXAYÁCATL: Yes, they'd told me. It must be magnificent.

NEZAHUALPILLI: The other is a short poem about your children. A *ten-liner.

AXAYÁCATL: Very appropriate.

TLACAÉLEL: My grandchildren! Eagles, tigers! I'll order that they learn it in the *tepuchcalli* and in the *calmécac*. We'll incorporate it into the official text.

NEZAHUALPILLI: My father put me in charge of giving you a reading, with your leave.

CHALCHIUHNENETZIN: Without music? Don't they have music?

NEZAHUALPILLI: They don't need it. They aren't drinking ballads, they're poems.

CHALCHIUHNENETZIN: But in any case . . . a musical background . . . helps a lot.

AXAYÁCATL: You will read them after the banquet, in front of everybody. And I will have to ask him to write another poem.

TLACAÉLEL: Another one? Is there another war?

AXAYÁCATL: No, grandpa. This one will be an epithalamium.

CHALCHIUHNENETZIN: Epithalamium? Is somebody getting married?

AXAYÁCATL: (*To Nezahualpilli.*) Your aunt Chalchiuhnenetzin . . . is going to spend a few days with you in Tezcotzinco.

NEZAHUALPILLI: It will be an honor to have her.

CHALCHIUHNENETZIN: But . . .

AXAYÁCATL: About . . . fifteen days. No more. She needs rest, to forget about her widowing, get herself back together, breathe the fresh air, eat well . . .

NEZAHUALPILLI: We will bend over backward to attend her.

AXAYÁCATL: . . . and be ready to meet the prince who has asked for her hand.

TLACAÉLEL and CHALCHIUHNENETZIN: Prince! What!

NEZAHUALPILLI: So it's my aunt who's getting married? Congratulations! (*Hugs her.*) Papá will write you a flowery song. Worthy of your aroma.

CHALCHIUHNENETZIN: And might I know who I'm going to marry?

AXAYÁCATL: He has loved you—silently—for a long time.

CHALCHIUHNENETZIN: Do I know him?

AXAYÁCATL: You don't; he does. He has foreseen you, from his distant possessions. He has been speechless before the descriptions of your talent; he has closed his ears to any other temptations. When he found out you were . . . available, his ambassadors asked me for your hand. And I have given it wholeheartedly.

CHALCHIUHNENETZIN: But, who is he? What's his name?

AXAYÁCATL: What's in a name? That which we call a rose, by any other name would smell as sweet.

NEZAHUALPILLI: That's what my father says.

AXAYÁCATL: Your father is a great poet . . . and a visionary. A name . . . does it say something? Mine: Axayácatl: face of water. Do I have a face of water?

NEZAHUALPILLI: No sir! How, of water!

AXAYÁCATL: But that the *tonalpohualli* rules us, inexorably: the crossword puzzle of destiny which makes our births coincide with the signs, benign or adverse, of the day on which it occurs: day Crocodile, day Wind, day House, Lizard, Snake, Death, Deer, Rabbit, Water, Dog, Monkey . . . Woe to he who is born on the day *Earthquake! Woe to the *five rotten days! But today is a great day.

CHALCHIUHNENETZIN: May I know his name?

AXAYÁCATL: It's . . . it's going to be . . . the king of Cuitlapilco. His name is Cuitlacuani.

TLACAÉLEL: Cuitlacuani . . . Cuitlacuani . . . Poor guy. We'll have to change his name.

(*Enter the old lady* [*Chicomexóchitl*] *and Ladies I and II* [*Xochichihua and Xochihuetzi*].)

CHICOMEXÓCHITL: Sir, your guests are starting to gather in the entry hall.

AXAYÁCATL: Are they all here?

CHICOMEXÓCHITL: Almost all. The chief of protocol has collected these invitations.

AXAYÁCATL: Read the names.

CHICOMEXÓCHITL: (*Reads: shuffling the invitations.*) Azcapotzalco, Tenayuca, Tlacopan, Coyoacan and Tizaapan, Xochimilco, Mízquic, Ayotzinco, Chimalpa, Chalco, Tlapacoyan, Cuitláhuac, Xico, Tlaltenco, Ayotla, Culhuacan, Iztahuacan, Mexicalcinco, Iztapalapa, Chimalhuacan . . .

TLACAÉLEL: So many people?

AXAYÁCATL: A few are missing: Citlaltépetl, Zumpanco, Coyotépec, Xaltocan, Tlaxomulco, Cuauhtitlan, Chiconautla, Huexotla, Coatlinchan, Atzacoalco, Tepeyácac . . .

CHICOMEXÓCHITL: They are coming from farther away but will be here on time. They all accepted the invitation.

AXAYÁCATL: Are they playing ball?

CHICOMEXÓCHITL: A few have gone to the temple to bleed themselves. They want to know if you will receive them here.

AXAYÁCATL: They won't all fit here. I will see them in the gardens. Is
the banquet ready?

CHICOMEXÓCHITL: Whenever you order it.

AXAYÁCATL: Let's go, then.

CHICOMEXÓCHITL: And . . . my lord . . .

AXAYÁCATL: What is it?

CHICOMEXÓCHITL: An emissary has arrived from Cuitlapilco.

TLACAÉLEL: From Cuitlapilco?

CHICOMEXÓCHITL: He wasn't invited; but he brought sumptuous
gifts. The chief of protocol wants to know whether to receive him.

AXAYÁCATL: He's from Cuitlapilco? Are you sure?

CHICOMEXÓCHITL: That's what he says, lord.

AXAYÁCATL: Says? He talks, then?

CHICOMEXÓCHITL: Through signs. He makes a lot of faces. He must
not know Nahuatl. He looks Otomí.

AXAYÁCATL: What day is today?

CHALCHIUHNENETZIN: Day eleven, Monkey.

AXAYÁCATL: The *tonalpohualli* never fails. Thank you, Tezcatlipoca!
Let him through! With all honors!

CHICOMEXÓCHITL: Your words are magic, sir. Here he comes.

(*Tepecócatl and Calcimehuateuctli bring, at knife point, Cuitlacuani.
They force him to stop in front of Axayácatl, who looks him over, and they
stop him from getting away.*)

TLACAÉLEL: Does he meet your needs, sir?

AXAYÁCATL: He's perfect. Take him away! (*The generals drag Cuitlacuani out.*) (*To Chalchiuhnenetzin.*) What do you think of your
new fiancé, sister?

CHALCHIUHNENETZIN: Well . . . as my late husband used to say:
"since there isn't anything else . . ." (*To Nezahualpilli.*) He has
pretty eyes, doesn't he?

NEZAHUALPILLI: But auntie! He's mute!

CHALCHIUHNENETZIN: In a ruler, that's not a defect. On the contrary: it's a rare virtue.

NEZAHUALPILLI: Yes, but . . . in a husband . . .

CHALCHIUHNENETZIN: Don't worry. I will talk for us both. You know that I can talk—your ears off!

AXAYÁCATL: (*To Tlacaélel.*) Grandfather, I think we'll have one less war. As you have seen, Cuitlapilco has turned itself over without combat.

TLACAÉLEL: Pity! But I've resigned myself. There will always be other wars, better ones. And I, the inventor of *human sacrifices, will live to see them.

AXAYÁCATL: (*To Chalchiuhnenetzin.*) Sister, it will no longer be necessary for you to wait in Tezcotzinco. Let's go. (*He offers her his arm; she takes it.*) (*To Nezahualpilli.*) Nephew, ladies, grandfather: the banquet celebrates not only my glories. It will also celebrate the honor of Queen Chalchiuhnenetzin.

THE LADIES: Queen?

AXAYÁCATL: I will announce it publicly at dessert. Now, make way for the Queen of Cuitlapilco!

> (*A moment earlier, the music of the feast has begun to be heard, and gets louder as the characters march off and the curtain falls.*)

CURTAIN

Ahuítzotl
and the Magic Water

Chapter from the unpublished *Historia de Coyoacán*
Translation of "Ahuítzotl y el agua mágica." In *Salvador Novo* by
Antonio Magaña Esquivel. Col. Un mexicano y su obra. Mexico
City: Empresas Editoriales, 1971.

Twenty-one years—the reign of Maxtla, who governed Coyohuacan from 1410 to 1431—the relative independence lasted for us Tepanecs here in Coyohuacan, long enough to install our city among the twelve great cities of the time: Xochimilco, Azcapotzalco, Cuitláhuac, Chalco, Iztapalapan, Tenayuca, COYOHUACAN, Tehuacan, Cuautitlan, Huitzilopochco, Otompan, and Mízquic. Due to Itzcóatl's treaty creating the tripartitite empire, Tenochtitlan-Tezcoco-Tlacopan, Coyohuacan came to be included among the numbers of the twenty towns directly appropriated by Tenochtitlan (*Anales de Cuauhtitlan,* 237), although it doesn't appear among the seventy-two tributaries to the Mexicans listed in the *Anales,* p. 228.

Moteuhczoma Ilhuicamina succeeds Itzcóatl and reigns from 1440 to 1469. He ascends the throne when he is forty-three years old, governs twenty-nine years, and dies in the year 3-House 1469—at the age of seventy-two. Meanwhile—always counseled and aided by his brother and Cihuacóatl, Tlacaélel, and by Nezahualcóyotl—he extends the dominion and influence of Tenochtitlan, consolidates the Alliance and regiments his tributes and rights, begins the building of the great *teocalli,* orders the carving of the *cuauhxicalli* (which is preserved in the National Museum of Anthropology, at the entrance to the Mexica Room), has his effigy sculpted in the hill of Chapultépec, and puts Nezahualcóyotl in charge of the construction of the aqueduct from Chapultépec; we Coyohuaques remain quiet, tributary, submissive; busy collecting the 1,800 quetzal feathers, 1,600 handfuls of common green feathers, 1,600 of the yellow ones, 1,600 of the flesh-colored ones, and 1,600 of the blue ones, and also forging two lip rings each year (in remembrance of our ancient specialty, *yacapíchtlica*), which the Register of Tributes in the *Codex Mendoza* reveals were our contribution to the Mexican Treasury. One more item: forced cooperation with those Xochimilcas whose grandfathers' *ears the Mexicans had cut off; we Coyohuaques helped build the causeway of Iztapallapan and its turnoff to Coyohuacan; we carved for our masters a *sun stone so enormous and heavy that it sank while transporting it across the Xóloc bridge—and we replaced it with the calendar that the reader can admire in the Museum. The Tenochcans also took advantage of our skill in sculpting the abundant stones of this region, and we provided them with masons and masters of efficacious works for the temples and palaces undertaken by Moteuhczoma. Even after the Conquest, the Tepanec stonecutters from around here still had the reputation of being so good that on "March 10, 1587, it is ordered that the Indian masons in that village [Coyoacan] present to Alonso Gómez de Cervantes, magistrate of this city [Mexico], twenty-four official Indians each week, in order to take part in the stone work that has been ordered to be laid in the street that goes from San Francisco to the *tianguez* of San Juan for as long as said project lasts; that they be paid a salary, be treated well . . . and that they be compelled to do it" (Zavala and Castelo, 14).

Of the eight children engendered by Moteuhczoma Ilhuicamina, the chroniclers only mention two males, Iquéhuac and Machimalle. The election as successor falls to neither of them after it was rejected by Tlacaélel—who had no need of the title in order to exercise maximum authority. ("Mexicans: I am grateful for the honor that you wish to grant me; but what greater honor can I have than the one I have had up till now? For the past kings have done nothing without my approval in civil and criminal affairs, and I no longer am young enough for the duty you wish to give me [he was seventy-two and his twin brother Moteuhczoma had just died], and understand that I will continue to serve and protect you with the same care until my lifetime is up, and thus, do not be disappointed, I WILL POINT OUT TO YOU WHO SHOULD BE OUR KING AND LORD, and go call King Nezahualcóyotl from the provinces of Culhuacan and King Totoquihuatzin from the Tepanec nation, because I wish to consult with them about my opinion and counsel.") (Durán, 32)

Thus Axayácatl ("aquatic fly" or "face of water") was elected to succeed Moteuhczoma in 1469 and ruled till his death in 1481 after thirteen years of government. He was the son of the prince Tezozomoctzin and the grandson of Itzcóatl.

Axayácatl has the deference to offer the sons of Moteuhczoma the position of Tlacatécatl, which they refuse, resentful for not having been elected their father's successors. Instead, they approach the Tlatelolcans, still independent, but now for a very short time to come. Their domination by the Tenochcans is consummated in 1473 through the amusing "war of the fatties," which the interested person can read about, dramatized with certain liberties, in a comedy of that title.

The haughty and lascivious Moquíhuix, a descendant of the Tepanec Tezozómoc, fourth and last independent king of Tlatelolco (and the bad husband of the sister whom Axayácatl ceded to him to win his favor—or to annoy him—the skinny, reeking Chalchiuhnenetzin), dies at the hands of Axayácatl in 1473, after fourteen years of dissolute living and rule. Chimalpahin puts the fateful words of bravado into Moquíhuix's mouth when Axayácatl invites him to the inauguration: "So he thinks he's so macho that I have to witness him take possession of the government along with his Mexicans and Tenochcans." Things did not go well for him with this kind of arrogance. Shortly afterward, Tlatelolco would be incorporated into Tenochtitlan.

After thirteen years of a government that extends his conquests as far as Tehuantépec, Axayácatl dies in 1481. Nezahualcóyotl has preceded him, in 1472, in his voyage to the Mictlan, leaving the throne of Tezcoco to Nezahualpilli. Axayácatl has engendered nineteen children, among whom it is important to remember the name of the fifth of them: Moteuhczoma Xocoyotzin.

However, it was none of those nineteen children who was elected his successor, but his brother Tizocatzin—also the brother of Ahuízotl ("dog of the waters"). Crowned in 1481, Tízoc shows himself to be less aggressive and more pacific than his predecessors during the brief six years that he governs, and during which he orders the Stone of Tízoc to be carved—a commemoration of Axayácatl's conquests that can also be seen in the National Museum of Anthropology.

Upon the death of Tízoc in 1486 (the texts insinuate that he was poisoned by those opposed to his pacifism), the Mexicans again turn unsuccessfully to Tlacaélel—who by that time had reached the ripe age of 89—to offer him the throne. Through his counsel, the election goes to Ahuízotl, his nephew, another son of Moteuhczoma according to Durán, but of Axayácatl according to Chimalpahin [Axayácatl's brother, according to the previous paragraph—Trans.], and not to any of the twelve children whom Tízoc had sworn to the pacific task of procreation.

Ahuízotl governs more to the imperialist taste of Tlacaélel. He celebrates his coronation with large parties and the sacrifice of "almost a thousand" prisoners, but there are many more, sacrificed with the skillful personal cooperation of his guests during the four days of parties and banquets for the dedication of the temple to Huitzilopochtli, whom he offers to the god and rids of suffering here in Tlaltícpac: "With the arrival of the people and the coming of the day of the party, before it was daylight, they brought out the prisoners that were to be sacrificed and made four long lines of them; the first of them went from the foot of the steps of the temple and continued to the causeway that goes to Cuyuacan and Xuchimilco, and the line was so long that it almost went on for a league; another went toward the causeway of *Our Lady of Guadalupe, no shorter than the other; another went right through the street of Tacuba, in the same way; another went toward the east until it ran into the lake. In front of each of these four lines came four sacrificial stones that had been adorned for four lords; the first and foremost, which was in front of the statue of the idol Huitzilopochtli, the dedication and renovation of whose temple was being celebrated, was where the king of Mexico, Ahuízotl, was to make sacrifices; the second was where the king of Tezcuco, Nezahualpilli, was to make sacrifices; the third was where the king of Tacuba was to make sacrifices; and the fourth was the Sun Stone, where they had prepared the one for the old man Tlacaélel to sacrifice.

With these lines in place, the three kings put their crowns on their heads and donned their earplugs of gold and precious stones and their nose rings and lip rings and their gold armbands and their socks of the same material; they put on their royal robes and their shoes and belts, and with them the old Tlacaélel, dressed the same way, whom this story says they respected as they would a king. Along with these lords, many priests dressed in the likenesses of all the gods and goddesses that there were, which, although this story might name them, would say little. All together they came out at the top of the temple, and each one of the lords, accompanied by those who represented the gods, went to their places where they were to kill them all, with their knives in hand. With the lords of all the provinces and the enemies watching from great canopies and balconies, which had been constructed for this occasion, and with the prisoners beginning to be brought from those lines, the lords, aided by the ministers that were there, who held by their feet and their hands the unlucky ones who were to die, began to kill, opening their chests and taking out their hearts and offering them to the idols and to the Sun, and after the kings were tired, they traded places, the satanic job being taken up by one of the priests representing the gods. The story says that this sacrifice lasted four days in a row, from morning till sunset, and that killed in it were, as I say, eighty thousand four hundred men of various provinces and cities, which seemed incredible to me, and which, if history didn't force me and the words were not found written and painted in many other places besides this story, I wouldn't dare include, lest I be taken as a man who writes tales.

In the year 7-Reed 1499, after thirteen years of the rule of Ahuízotl, the long-lived Tlacaélel finally dies—at 102 years of age.

Ahuízotl has perfected Tenochcan imperialism with the organization of the Pochtecáyotl—ambassadors-business agents-spies and diplomats granted a god of their own for their privileged guild: Yacatecuhtli, the Lord of the Nose, he who sniffs and shows the way. And Ahuízotl has beautified Tenochtitlan with trees, gardens, flower beds. He needs more fresh water than comes to him from Chapultépec, and he sets his eyes on the spring of Acuecuexco ("playful or boisterous water") that originates in Coyohuacan.

We again come to the question of what the name was of the man the Tenochcans had put in to govern us: it's Tozotzomatzin ("the ragged one") in Chimalpahin, Tzutzuma in Durán, Tzutzumatzin in Torquemada.

Who was Tozotzomatzin? Just in passing, Durán indicates that his death affected the king of Tacuba very much, "because he was his relative and very close to him," and farther on, he describes him as "son of the king of Azcapotzalco." We are to suppose, then, that he belonged to the conciliatory dynasty put in by the Tenochcans to govern in Tlacopan.

Let's let Chimalpahin narrate the episode:

> That was also when the Mexicans were flooded due to a water hole that broke loose in Coyohuacan, a very strong spring, which happened despite the fact that the chief of Coyohuacan, Tzotzomatzin, who was half engineer and half witch, had opposed diverting the flow of the spring Acuecuéxatl and in this sense had warned Ahuitzotzin.
>
> But when Ahuitzotzin heard the advice of Tzotzomatzin, the lord of Coyohuacan, it seemed to Ahuitzotzin that his advice was inspired by a desire to not give him water from his spring, so he immediately arranged to have an exchange of opinions with the one who was the lord of Huitzillopochco, Huitzillatzin, whom he ordered to come to Mexico for this purpose and whom he told that his reason was that Tzotzomatzin did not want the water of Acuecuéxatl to come to Mexico and that it seemed to him that such words of his about preventing the coming of the water were pure and simple insubordina-

tion and maliciousness. And they say these are the words of a witch of things of the water, an astrologer who knew the stars and the signs of the days and who lived at the place where one takes a bath and who was a very famous witch called Cuécuex, who had come to Coyohuacan, the place of the spring Acuecuéxatl to perform penitences and religious ceremonies for the Chichimecan Coyohuaques.

After Huitzillatzin had listened to this whole account, in response to Lord Ahuitzotzin, he answered: "Person of my Lord, who has told you that the water of the spring Acuecuéxatl cannot come? Tzotzoma not only is not well in the head, but he is making fun of you! Perhaps he hasn't told you that he wants those waters to go to irrigate his lands and stay there? When will I be able to watch them come into Tenuchtitlan?"

Because of this response, Ahuitzotzin fell into a rage and gave the order to kill Tzotzomatzin, by putting a cord around his neck, for having told the truth.

After this, it was ordered that the water of Acuecuéxatl be brought to Mexico, which, upon the spring bursting, came out with great force, totally flooding the city of Mexico, and when Ahuitzotzin regarded the flooding of the city he fell into a rage over it and ordered that they kill Huitzillatzin, wrapping a cord around his neck in his own town of Huitzillopochco, because he had told him lies. Thus, two lords were killed because of the Acuecuéxatl, and because of this the Mexicans also began to ask for a [certain] number of canoes, strips of wood, and stones from the Chalcas, who had to take them to them.

In Durán (48 and 49) the story is narrated more fully and colorfully: "All the beauty and fertility of Mexico depended on the city having an abundance of water because the Mexicans had made some flower beds, which, with the lack of water, dried and withered. . . . Ahuízotl orders, then, two chiefs to ask the lord of Coyohuacan for the water from Acuecuexco. Tzutzuma cannot refuse to fulfill this order, but he warns that those waters tend to increase: they could inundate Tenochtitlan, and he advises that they be happy with the water they already derive from Chapultépec."

Ahuízotl falls into a rage and orders the remiss lord to be killed. Warned, the latter lets the emissaries get as far as the chamber where he is waiting for them, converted into "a great, deformed eagle circling the seat or royal chair that the messengers were in." Then he changes into the shape of a ferocious, frightening tiger; the messengers return to inform Ahuízotl of the extraordinary events. He again sends them to the king, and now they find he has changed himself into a large, grotesque, coiled snake that attacks them, and the room breaks into flames, which forces them to flee.

At the height of indignation, Ahuízotl demands that the order be given to the people of Coyohuacan to turn over their lord immediately: if not, he will wage war on them and destroy them for rebelling against his orders. That is enough of a threat for them. Tzutzuma gives up his magic transformations and turns himself in to save his people, not without prophesying that before many days have passed Mexico will be inundated and destroyed. The Mexicans hang him and cast his body to the rocks, "where now, they say, ever since that day a fountain has flowed."

Ahuízotl asks the allied or subject cities for people and materials for the construction of the aqueduct that will bring the water of Acuecuexco to Mexico. And once it is ready, "come the given day, the king, unprepared for any sort of misfortune, ordered that the water be let loose; as it began to run toward the city of Mexico, a chief came out to meet it dressed in the likeness of the goddess of the waters and of the fountains, with a blue shirt and a sanbenito, all inlaid with green and blue stones of great value; he carried a crown on his head like a tiara, all made of white heron feathers; his face was painted red with melted rubber and his forehead blue, and hanging from his ears were two green stones and on his lower lip others and on his wrists many strings of these blue and green stones; in his hands he carried some timbrels made to look like turtles, together with a bag of blue corn flour; on his legs he wore blue and his shoes were also blue, all denoting the color of the water. With this chief came all the ministers of the temples, all with their faces painted black, with paper garlands on their heads, with large stars on their foreheads which served as ties for their headgear, all completely naked, with some paper trusses to cover their shameful parts; they carried flutes in their hands, and others some large conches and others horns, which they played in front of the one who was representing said goddess.

Other ministers came with many cages of quail and others with many paper hands, others with liquid rubber, others with resin, and as they came to the place where the water began to take its course and to run through the pipe, one of the priests began to kill the quail and to spill the blood into the tongue of water, which, as there was a lot of blood and the water brought it forward, became all bloody; at the same time the one carrying the melted resin began dripping many drops of it into the water and other drops into the pipe where it was to flow, and consequently many chips of rubber and resin were thrown on top of the water and into the thuribles with which they were incensing the water, all of which was done to the sounds of the flutes and conches, which they played noisily in front of it all, and every so often the one who was dressed in the likeness of the goddess took a handful of water and drank from it, and spilled a little of it on either side of the pipe, and spoke to it reverently, saying: "Precious lady: you have come along your path at a very good time; behold, this is the path you will follow from today on, and so I, who have come representing your likeness, I come to receive you and to greet you and to give the blessing of your arrival; behold, lady, that today you will come to your city, Mexico Tenuchtitlan"; and saying this he took out the blue flour he was carrying in the bag and threw it on top of himself, he took the timbrels and playing them, now inside the pipe, jumped and leapt spinning before the water, and after he stopped he came to the water pass, and to the debris it carried.

Down the road came all the singers of the god Tlaloc, who was the god of rain and lightning, and those of the goddess of water, all playing, dancing, and singing songs appropriate to praising the water; at the same time came many old men with pots in their hands full of live fish and water snakes, and others with frogs and leeches; in short, they brought in those pots all kinds of creatures that the water produces, offering them to the water, throwing them into the pipe itself, telling the water that they were what was going to raise Mexico and that that was the reason they had brought them.

As soon as the water arrived at the first main culvert, which was in a place they call Acachinanco, they had four children next to it, all six years old, all painted black, with blue foreheads, with their paper headdresses on their heads, with the stars on their foreheads the same as the priests we described, totally naked but for their paper trusses, with strings of little blue stones around their necks, and the first of whom, as soon as the water arrived, they stretched above the very pipe and, opening his chest, they took out his heart and offered it to the water, blood running inside the pipe; later they sacrificed another in the place that is now San Antonio, at the point of a great canal that they put there, from which the water dropped into a drain, from which all the people of the neighborhood of San Antonio and San Pablo took handfuls of water, in their canoes. The water moved forward with the same solemnity and much more, because the people had come out of the city to the reception, a great number of people with many kinds of dances, songs and dances, with different costumes and characters, and the water went on, dropping into another water tank and a drain to a place that they call Vitzilan, where the water was used by another major neighborhood, and where they sacrificed another child; from there the water went into the lagoon, where preparations had been made since the king Ahuízotl had arrived there equipped with all his greatest and chief knights, from his court as well as from other towns, and he said: "Lords, now the water has arrived at its tanks in the city. Let us greet it and give it welcome for its arrival." He came out of the palace with all his insignias and royal robes and with the crown on his head, the way he adorned himself only on solemn occasions; all the other great men also wore the robes they used in court and for festivals, all very elegant and well attired, with many jewels and stones around their necks.

When the king arrived at the place where the water fell noisily, he and the others who were with him knelt down before it, performing the ceremony of eating earth with their fingers, as was done with all the gods when one came upon their presence. After they ate the earth, the others gave the king many roses, which he offered to the water, putting them all around the canal and on the ground; then he offered it many lit *incensed straws of the kind they suck on at the banquets and parties; then they gave him many quails, which he beheaded with his own hands and offered to the water, and taking a thurible in his hand, he tossed in some incense and began to scent the water at the mouth of the canal, and having finished with the sacrifice and offering, he stood up and lifted his right hand, and said aloud:

"O powerful goddess of the water: you are very welcome in your city, whose protector and advocate is the god Huitzilopochtli, prodigious and admirable in his deeds and actions; behold, powerful lady and goddess, you come to bestow favor on your servants the Mexicans and to take the place of their miseries and needs in this passing life that we live, on the one hand so that they can drink from you, since without you nobody would be able to live, and on the other so they may find in you the resources for their crops and ordinary sustenance, with the kind of creatures that you raise with your supreme power—which is now very much a part of you and ordinary for you—and also so those same fish and animals that you raise may guard the place of the water; therefore, start today to do your task."

When he had finished this speech, he threw into the place where the water crashed from the canal into the drain many gold pieces in the shapes of fishes and frogs and a great number of stones all carved with the same design, and along with him, all the chiefs threw in jewels and stones, each according to his status and ability.

After a few days, the water, with the strong, stout dikes they had made for those springs, began to grow in such abundance that at the end of forty days it entered the city; the water of the lagoon began to grow and to overflow back into the drains of Mexico and to inundate some of the flower beds. Ahuízotl, seeing the damage that the water was beginning to cause, recalled what the lord of Cuyuacan had said when he turned himself over to the Mexicans, and consulting those of his counsel, he ordered that a great dike be built so that the waters that flowed into the lake would not be able to spill over into Mexico; and so the cities and neighboring towns were called together, and the dike was made a fourth of a league this side of El Peñón, through all the outskirts of Mexico; but the dike had no effect, because the more repairs they made to it, the more it was damaged, so that the water was soon coming into many of the lands of the neighbors, who abandoned their houses and left the city in fear; and it came to the point that the chiefs and bosses of the city and of the neighborhoods had to go to the king to beg him for a solution and a way to stop the damage and the bad things that resulted from all the water coming into the city, which had flooded all the flower beds of the subject lands and ruined all the cornfields, with the spikes not yet ripe, and all the plots of chiles and tomatoes and amaranth and roses and all the fruit they had, which moved all the people of the city very deeply when they saw their fruits and vegetables flooded and dry, and the afflicted ones abandoned the city and their houses and went to live in the nearby towns—for all of which they asked him to apply a remedy.

The king, seeing the city's suffering and the error that he had committed by having brought so much water to the city, sent for the kings of Tezcuco and Tacuba so that they could give him their ideas about the business of what should be done; and once they had come and seen the city, where one could no longer get about except in canoes, they were frightened, and when the king had proposed to them the danger they were in, he and all the people of the city, and the great damage that had been done, the king of Tezcuco, seeing the occasion at hand to speak freely and state his opinion to King Ahuízotl about the disgraceful death of Tzutzumatzin, spoke in this way:

"Powerful king, too late have you remembered to seek advice; earlier, Tzutzumatzin, lord of Culuacan, gave it to you. Too late did the fear and dread you had of the destruction of this noted city of Mexico come to you, and now you have the destruction which you ought to have considered and prevented earlier. Now you can well see that the contest is not against your enemies who have you surrounded, because these you will defeat with your courageous soul and drive from you and your city; rather, it is against an element as brave as the water, so what remedy or resistance can there be? Tzutzumatzin, the great prince of Culuacan, counseled you well, and not only did you not accept his opinion and advice, which he gave to you as a faithful vassal, but for that you took his life from him." And saying this he began to cry and to show great emotion and to say: "What did Tzutzumatzin do? What was his sin? What was his offense? Why did you so ruthlessly take his life? Was he by chance a traitor or treacherous to your Royal Crown? Was he by chance an adulterer or thief? Know, powerful lord, that you have offended and sinned against the gods, whose likeness was represented in that great lord whom the gods had charged with the government of that republic, and for that reason the Lord of Crops let this city be destroyed and depopulated. What will it look like in the eyes of our enemies who surround us if, when Mexico is depopulated, you and your chiefs are forced to flee, giving our enemies eternal vengeance on you and your chiefs? What will they say but that what your predecessors built with such toil and sweat you have destroyed in forty days? I am of the opinion that after the conduits from the fountains have been destroyed, and the water has taken its ancient course, and a solemn sacrifice has been offered to the goddess of the waters—with many jewels and feathers and with many quails and much resin and rubber and paper—to placate the wrath she has against you, and the springs have been plugged, and some children brought together to be sacrificed; maybe then we will placate her and contain her springs so that they will not put forth as much water as they put forth now."

With this speech, King Ahuízotl and all the others having been moved to tears and emotion, he then sent his messengers to all the provinces of the area and to all the towns so that they would come to his aid with the offerings and the things necessary for the sacrifice—the jewels, feathers, quails, and resin—to placate the great goddess of the waters, who is called Chalchihuitlicue. After this order had gone to all the towns and cities and villages, they complied quickly and diligently with many offerings and sacrifices, along with some skilled divers to go into the water, and once these had arrived, the three kings and all the lords and knights of the area, all dressed in their royal robes and with crowns on their heads, went to Cuyuacan and gathered around the fountains, displaying great humility and ceremony and sacrificing a few children and quail and a lot of resin, rubber, and paper and other precious things. The divers went deep into the water, carrying on their backs many jewels and feathers and precious stones that they placed inside the springs, and there they offered all that treasure, burying it in the very springs. They also placed there many other large stones made into idols, especially one made in the shape of the goddess of the waters, with which they somehow plugged the source of the water, and once the waters had gone down, the king ordered that the conduits be dismantled so that the water might follow its old course, and thus it was done.

The priests, who until that time had been swinging their thuribles and playing their little flutes and conches, stopped, and taking all their knives, they began to sacrifice themselves by bleeding their ears and their earlobes and their shins, all to placate the goddess of the water. When it seemed to them she would have been placated and they had made the townspeople believe this as well, they sacrificed another two children, and this being done, King Ahuízotl went to sit with the other kings and lords of the city of Cuyuacan, where he asked their forgiveness for the death of their lord and chose and appointed as the legitimate heir to the title a son of Tzutzumatzin; and this being done, he ordered the provinces of Chalco and Tezcuco and Tacuba and Xuchimilco and all the warm lands to come to the aid of Mexico with tributes of canoes and wooden rafts, as many as could be carved, because it was no longer possible to walk easily about the city, because the patios of the houses and temples were covered with two large palms of water; the Royal House and the lords' houses could no longer be used, and many of the houses of the plebeians were under water.

And so, with all haste a great number of canoes and rafts were brought and distributed among the lords and the common people; and they threw their belongings in them; and there they waited day and night, because the houses were uninhabitable; and for their repair, the king ordered that all the surrounding lands and the provinces subject to Mexico come to help rebuild the city. This being done, the provinces and nations responded with trees, sod, earth, and rocks, with which they cut off the water in all the places where it had come in, leaving many of the ancient buildings under water; and they turned to the rebuilding of Mexico with better and more curious and more elegant buildings, because the ones they had had were very old and built by the Mexicans themselves in the time of their poverty and were of little value, and so there were things that were very vile and base. However, this time the lords, and those who weren't lords, built them however they wanted them, because they were building with another's hand, giving each chief a town and two fiefs to build his house; and so they painted as they wished, according to the royal order, each one according to his status; and from that time Mexico was left very much ennobled and very curious and showy, with great and interesting houses, full of very elegant recreational gardens and patios, the canals very calm and lined with groves of willows and black and white poplars, with many precautions and defenses against the water so although they might be very full they would never cause any damage; all of which King Ahuízotl paid for, satisfying the officials and communities by giving them blankets, belts, cacao, chile, beans, slaves—all taken from the treasury—which made everyone very satisfied and the city of Mexico very much ennobled.

Ahuízotl derived an indirect urban benefit from the "flooding" of Tenochtitlan by the waters of Coyohuacan. Desirous of fortifying the buildings, he discovered the beautiful construction material which, from then on to this very day, is used in Mexico for its lightness, texture, and color: the *tezontle* ("stone of hair"). Torquemada (II, 68) comments "that it seems God put it there as a source for the buildings of this land, which, because it is so extremely moist, requires a light stone, and even with it God and help are needed. . . . To extract it, a call was made to all the area, and so they were able to extract quite a lot . . . and thus all the buildings were renovated and this city and all its neighbors were ennobled by them."

But the blow to the head that Ahuízotl had received three years earlier while fleeing the flooding ended his days: "And there being no human remedy, he died in the eighteenth year of his empire, leaving the people hurting for the loss of such a great lord and king."

Chimalpahin brings together the news of Ahuízotl's death and the election of Moteuhczoma: "Year 10-Rabbit 1502. This year occurred the death of Ahuitzotzin, lord of Tenuchtitlan, who governed for seventeen years. Next, Moteuhczomatzin Xocóyotl was installed as lord of Tenuchtitlan. He was a son of Axayacatzin and of a noble lady from Iztapallapan."

We will not go into too much detail on this unfortunate great lord. His story is already well known, and it relates less to the history of

Coyohuacan than does that of his predecessors here evoked, except for one anecdote that Suárez de Peralta has preserved for us: Moctezuma, coming from a battle years before the Spaniards were to arrive, and having had a masterful victory, said to the lord of Coyohuacan: "Well, now that we have conquered the provinces of Soconusco and all those surrounding it, and all their lords have surrendered and been put in the domain of Mexico, I can well say that Mexico has a foundation and a wall of iron." The chief he was talking to said to him: "Lord, one iron with another can be broken and overcome." Which seemed to be a prophecy . . . And a short time later, while the *Marqués held them like prisoners in his guest palace, Moctezuma and the lord of Coyohuacan recalled the conversation about irons and marveled over that answer, having seen the Spaniards armed; although it had been taken as disrespectful, on that occasion it was not.

This lord of Coyohuacan, companion of Moteuhczoma, could have been the Cuauppopoca whom the *Códice Chimalpopoca* establishes as Tlatoani of Coyohuacan in 1519. In that case, it is not only the father of Don Juan de Guzmán Iztolinque who is installed by Cortés as lord of Coyohuacan in 1526, but also the Cuauppopoca who marches through chapter 55 of the Fourth Book of Torquemada, a prisoner of the Conquistador who is held with Moteuhczoma, is accused of having killed Spaniards on secret orders from Moteuhczoma, and consequently is put to death by Cortés.

Cuauhtémoc

PLAY IN ONE ACT

Premiered October 19, 1962, at the Teatro Xola,
under the direction of the author.
Translation of *Cuauhtémoc: Pieza en un acto*.
Mexico City: Talleres Gráficos de la Librería Madero, 1962.

Dramatis Personae

A young Native American man   Juan Felipe Preciado
  who plays the role of Cuauhtémoc

Moctezuma   Alberto Sayán

An Aztec Captain   Pablo López del Castillo

Ixtolinque, lord of Coyoacan   Ricardo Fuentes

1st Soldier (Cortés')   Carlos Pouliot

Alfonso Yáñez (2nd Soldier)   Salvador Carrillo

Hernán Cortés   Antonio Gama

Pedro de Alvarado   Jesús Núñez

Fray Bartolomé de Olmedo   Angel Pineda

The King of Tlaxcala   Helio Castillos

Tecuichpo   Yolanda Guillaumin

Gonzalo de Sandoval   Javier Ruan

Doña Marina   Clementina Lacayo

Tetlepanquétzal   Victor Mares

Two Tiger Knights

Scenery and Costumes: Julio Prieto
(If necessary, six actors and one actress are enough to
double up on all the roles, which are played with masks, as
noted in the prologue.)

ORDER OF THE SCENES

1. The actor (Cuauhtémoc) in the proscenium
2. Inside Moctezuma's palace
3. In Coyoacan, before the Conquest
4. Inside Axayácatl's palace. A chamber.
5. The actor in the proscenium, ties into:
6. Hall of the king of Tlaxcala, returns to:
7. The actor in the proscenium, ties into:
8. Tlatelolco. Cuauhtémoc's hiding place.
9. Transition: total darkness and sound
10. Cortés' headquarters
11. Coyoacan. Torture chamber.
12. The actor in the proscenium. The actors.

Scene 1

In the proscenium

A young Native American enters through the center of the curtain, his hat in hand. He eyes the audience, smiles, and says:

Ladies and gentlemen, a very good evening to you all. Here I stand before you; my name wouldn't tell you anything: it could be Juan, or Pedro. I think it's more important that you know why a boy, like the one you see, speaks to you from up here: a Mexican—though not like you, who are also Mexican; but more so, because I am Indian—dark, with straight hair, with strong, white teeth, beardless . . . I can't stand shoes. I walk better without them, or with my *huaraches*. And I'm not cold. I cover myself with a blanket more from modesty than from the need to bundle up. And my palm hat gives me enough protection from the sun and keeps my head fresh.

Fine—that's all. Except that I'm not very communicative. I don't like to speak a lot. One doesn't have to speak to be understood by others. Often a simple glance is enough, a smile, to know if we're facing an enemy or a friend.

I was going to tell you why I'm speaking to you from here. It's because we want to put on the life of Cuauhtémoc. A group of kids from here, from this town. We've studied it and read about it in books.

We understand it is very difficult to do theater. But in any case, we decided to stage the life of Cuauhtémoc. And nobody wanted to learn the role of Cuauhtémoc. Some said that it was too long, others that it was too hard. But I think it's because they didn't like the role of the conquered, of the one who fell prisoner to Cortés, of the one who Cortés murdered after torturing him.

I liked the role of Cuauhtémoc. And I offered to do it. The others will play roles as they become necessary. We will put on masks, to pretend that we are other people. That is, the others will put them on when they speak to me, or amongst themselves. Not me. You all already know me, and there's no need for me to disguise myself. I've already told you that I will be Cuauhtémoc.

One more word before we begin: it might be that things didn't happen exactly as we are going to present them. But it's also possible that they didn't happen the way the historians tell them. It's even possible that they were the way we would like them to have been.

We can't do anything any more about whether they happened one way or the other. They are things of the past. But since we are going to relive them, to lend them our own lives, it's as if they were going to happen all over again; and in this respect we do have the right to play them another way—the way they should be: the way we would have wished they had been; the way we wish they were; the way they will be every time we portray them.

It is not known, for example, if Moctezuma and Cuauhtémoc ever talked. But we believe they did . . . in Moctezuma's palace—which is this one:

(Curtain opens.)

Scene 2

Inside Moctezuma's palace

Moctezuma enters rapidly from the right. Cuauhtémoc turns toward him and bows.

CUAUHTÉMOC: Lord—my Lord—Great Lord.

MOCTEZUMA: Cuauhtémoc! Get up, my son. I've summoned you so we could talk, not as king and subject, but as friends and relatives.

CUAUHTÉMOC: I'm listening, Moctezuma.

MOCTEZUMA: I need your aid and your counsel. You're young. I was once too. Like you, I swept our gods' temple. I bled my flesh and my tongue as an offering and as penitence. Like you, I was a Tecuhtli—and I tested my strength in the *flowery wars.

CUAUHTÉMOC: I know, Moctezuma.

MOCTEZUMA: The kingdom I received from your grandfather Ahuí-zotl grew in my hands until it reached the *jade skirts of the sea. From this little lake, Huitzilopochtli extended his ruling gaze over all the towns that today render their riches in tribute.

CUAUHTÉMOC: Fine, and so?

MOCTEZUMA: Those towns hate us, Cuauhtémoc. They are rising up against me. They have allied themselves with the white gods; they have informed them and guided them to Tenochtitlan.

CUAUHTÉMOC: Gods?

MOCTEZUMA: They are gods, Cuauhtémoc! It's Quetzalcóatl who has returned, angry and vengeful!

CUAUHTÉMOC: Have you attempted anything against them?

MOCTEZUMA: To placate them. Win them over.

CUAUHTÉMOC: With blood? With sacrifices?

MOCTEZUMA: These gods scorn our blood, and they don't want our hearts.

CUAUHTÉMOC: Then they're not gods.

MOCTEZUMA: Gold delights them and dazzles them. They throw themselves upon it like birds of prey, to pick it up and caress it. I've tried to satiate them with gold; let them carry off all the gold in their *floating houses and on their *stags—but let them leave us in peace.

CUAUHTÉMOC: The true gods scorn gold. They nourish themselves with the blood from our tongues and our ears—our silence and our listening. Take those false gods captive. Sacrifice them in the temple.

MOCTEZUMA: How could I? They have *lightning. They're like giants when they're on their stags that grunt and shout. Their *skin is impenetrable to our arrows. They are gods, I tell you. It's Quetzalcóatl who has returned for the throne that he abandoned, that your father had on loan, that I inherited—and I must return it to the *blond, bearded god.

CUAUHTÉMOC: In the *calmécac,* I learned our history. A history of constant battles: against the wind, against the sun, against the cold, against hunger. Our grandparents survived *four floods, four suns of fire. And in four centuries, they transformed this laguna into a great city. And the throne that you inherited, Moctezuma, was made safe from warriors much more numerous and fearsome than these dirty men with chalky faces . . .

Don't you realize, Moctezuma? Your empire reaches to the sea!

MOCTEZUMA: And that's where it ends! But it's where theirs begins, and it has penetrated the jade skirts of our shores like a furious pounding of waves. Cuauhtémoc, look at these paintings. That's how these invincible gods are. I'm aware of their every move.

And nothing stops them; not the gold, not the fine feathers, not the spells of our witches. In Cholula they fought against our gods—and they threw them from the temple and killed hundreds of Cempoaltecas. Now they've allied themselves with the Tlaxcaltecans, and they're coming this way, to visit me in peace. I must receive them as eminent visitors. We will go, the three kings of Anáhuac. You shall come too in the entourage, as the *Tecuhtli* of Tlatelolco that you are.

CUAUHTÉMOC: They're coming in peace, you say? Why then have they come escorted by the Tlaxcaltecans, your longtime enemies?

MOCTEZUMA: They went there first. If they had come here first, my troops would have escorted them. You know the rules of hospitality as well as I do.

CUAUHTÉMOC: Do they observe them? Do you think they're likely to follow our rules if, as you say, they are so different from us?

MOCTEZUMA: And what would you do in my place, Cuauhtémoc?

CUAUHTÉMOC: Your place is yours alone.

MOCTEZUMA: I haven't called you here to interrogate me, but to counsel me.

CUAUHTÉMOC: You said it was so I could accompany you to receive them. As eminent guests.

MOCTEZUMA: But I also want your advice, your opinion.

CUAUHTÉMOC: What good would it do? You will do your will, not mine.

MOCTEZUMA: Which is . . . ?

CUAUHTÉMOC: Destroy them—before they destroy us.

MOCTEZUMA: With our weapons? Against their lightning?

CUAUHTÉMOC: With the lightning of our wrath. With the storm of our united willpower: Tenochtitlan, Tlatelolco, Texcoco, Tlacopan . . . And all the native towns. Yes, even our enemies. It will be easy to convince them that they are more our brothers than theirs; to make them see that our destruction implies the destruction of all our race; that the slavery that these foreigners would impose on them would be much harsher, more terrible, and more definitive than the slavery they suffer under your rule.

Put me in charge of that task, Moctezuma. There's no time

to lose. I will go to Tlaxcala—to Tabasco, wherever we need to go. I will speak with the kings—I will offer them our alliance, I will invoke the alliance of their forces. Let me go, Moctezuma!

MOCTEZUMA: (*After a moment of silence.*) Fine. Go.

(*Cuauhtémoc exits. Enter a captain.*)

CAPTAIN: Lord—my Lord—Great Lord.

MOCTEZUMA: Yes?

CAPTAIN: The *teules* are advancing along the Cuauhnáhuac road. Ahead of them and guiding them are the Tlaxcaltecas, who carry their arms—and coming with the god is a woman who understands both their language and ours.

MOCTEZUMA: Yes, I know. It's all here, in these paintings. She's a slave they presented to El Malinche in . . . I don't know which town.

CAPTAIN: A slave, Lord?

MOCTEZUMA: Or—an *ahuiani*. My robes.

CAPTAIN: Are we leaving already?

MOCTEZUMA: Yes. Let's not make the . . . gods wait.

(*Enter two priests with Moctezuma's vestments—cape, crown. Darkness.*)

Scene 3

In Coyoacan

Ixtolinque, lord of Coyoacan, and Cuauhtémoc.

IXTOLINQUE: Welcome, Lord. Coyoacan, as represented by me, feels very honored to receive this unprecedented visit from the young lord of Tlatelolco—from Moctezuma's nephew—from the son of the great King of Mexico, who years ago was also our guest.

CUAUHTÉMOC: Did you ever meet my father, Ixtolinque?

IXTOLINQUE: I am old. I wasn't as old then. I met Ahuízotl, yes. I had that honor. And the pain of knowing that he would die from the wounds that he got in his flight precipitated by the flooding of his city. That's how it was, wasn't it?

CUAUHTÉMOC: I think so. I never got to know my father well. I was scarcely a boy then, just going into the *calmécac,* when he died.

IXTOLINQUE: But the flood, surely you remember it. It must have reached Tlatelolco. It was terrible for all of you. Your father was blind, Cuauhtémoc. He was determined to take all the water from Acuecuexco, despite all the warnings that he should not remove it from its source. And he had the soothsayer of ours who warned him about it hung.

CUAUHTÉMOC: That was his royal right.

IXTOLINQUE: But that was the beginning of his downfall, or his punishment. Once the waters were unleashed, nobody could stop them.

CUAUHTÉMOC: Are you speaking in parables? Do you really believe man can't contain the avalanche of water that threatens to drown him?

IXTOLINQUE: Now I'm the one who doesn't understand. But that's natural. I'm nothing more than a poor Tepanecan subject of the great Moctezuma. I ask myself to what I owe the honor of your visit.

CUAUHTÉMOC: It's about an avalanche that threatens us all—and that we all must stop, avert.

IXTOLINQUE: An avalanche? Threatening us all?

CUAUHTÉMOC: It has already swept away the towns through which it advances—from the sea that let loose its wave. It grows at every step with the treachery it embroils. It razed the temples of our gods in Cholula—and increased its volume with the Tlaxcalte-cans. It has now filtered its way to the heart of Tenochtitlan.

IXTOLINQUE: Surely you are speaking of the *teules?*

CUAUHTÉMOC: And who else?

IXTOLINQUE: But Moctezuma has received them with open arms! Perhaps you don't know that our lord Moctezuma gave my brother Cuaupopoca the distinction of guiding the *teules* to his lands?

CUAUHTÉMOC: Was that the mission charged to Cuaupopoca?

IXTOLINQUE: The very same! What other could it be? The mission of attacking their sacred personages, cutting them down in an am-bush? Moctezuma could not order that.

CUAUHTÉMOC: Why not?

IXTOLINQUE: It's not in his character—nor in our tradition. When the Mexicans take up a war, they declare it first. And they haven't declared war on the *teules*—nor have they declared war on Moctezuma, as you well know.

CUAUHTÉMOC: They've declared it on all of us, Ixtolinque. Don't feel so secure here in your states of *terra firma and bedrock.

IXTOLINQUE: My states! Twenty-three poor towns—and thirty-one or thirty-two that belong to my wife: spread between Tizapan and Huitzilopochco—Mixcóatl, Chapultépetl . . .

CUAUHTÉMOC: Does that seem like little to you? Tlatelolco isn't even the tenth part of your fifty towns.

IXTOLINQUE: But all are tributaries to Moctezuma. Like Tlatelolco, I know. We are all his servants—and have been for a long time. All year we hunt birds to gather fine feathers for the tribute. And by the way, Cuauhtémoc, do you know how much the *teules* despise feathers?

CUAUHTÉMOC: Yes. They prefer the *teocuítlatl*—the excrement of the gods.

IXTOLINQUE: We, poor Tepanecans, have neither silver or gold. Only firm, solid ground, on the shore of Moctezuma's laguna. And a road of subordination to Tenochtitlan—to carry the tribute, or the rocks we carve in Coyoacan.

CUAUHTÉMOC: I haven't come to increase your tributes, Ixtolinque. I've come, on the contrary, to free you from them. Moctezuma extends his hand to you.

IXTOLINQUE: What does he want me to put in it now?

CUAUHTÉMOC: Your loyalty—and your help.

IXTOLINQUE: My loyalty? We Tepanecans have sworn it—ever since the empire of Azcapotzalco succumbed to the Tenochcans. My help! He gets it every eighty days, in punctual payments—and whenever he wants it, in *macehuales* and stonecutters that build his palaces. What more can I offer him?

CUAUHTÉMOC: Friendship. Not forced subordination. Not passive obedience. Moctezuma has conferred on me a delicate mission; much more serious and more urgent than the one performed by Cuaupopoca your brother. I am not to approach the *teules* to beg of them a goodness they show no signs of having, nor to invite them into a fraternity they don't desire. I am to visit the kings and lords of our color, of our lands, all children of the same gods. And to make them see that these who have come are not gods, but monsters that must be destroyed before they destroy us.

IXTOLINQUE: You surprise me, Cuauhtémoc. I cannot believe that Moctezuma has changed so suddenly; that now he wants as friends those whom he has always had as slaves. Some miracle, perhaps brought on by the white gods?

CUAUHTÉMOC: Or maybe a test—to which our own kind submit their pride.

IXTOLINQUE: Would he bow down before his former servants—if it weren't that his new masters bring him to the ground?

CUAUHTÉMOC: Your tongue is sharp and cruel, Ixtolinque. But it is not my wrath nor your resentment which must reconcile us. These new masters, if they manage to become Moctezuma's master, would also be yours, and mine, everybody's. We must all unite now to prevent it, while there's still time.

IXTOLINQUE: Unite ourselves? We are united. Prevent the *teules,* if they want to, from dominating us all: how?

CUAUHTÉMOC: I don't know how yet. The first thing is the will to resist. If I've succeeded in earning yours; if I can count on it, then together we'll figure out how to exercise it.

IXTOLINQUE: In exchange for what?

CUAUHTÉMOC: Excuse me?

IXTOLINQUE: Pardon my lack of manners, Cuauhtémoc. It's just that I'm so used to bargaining . . . You taught us how, remember. Your skillful Pochtecans traveled to trade *ixtle* and cotton shawls for gold and precious stones. And we learned from them. One thing is worth another, which is given in exchange: one of our slaves, in the market you appropriated from Azcapotzalco, three or four shawls.

CUAUHTÉMOC: And so?

IXTOLINQUE: What are you offering me in exchange for the help you seek?

CUAUHTÉMOC: I can't offer you anything.

IXTOLINQUE: That's really not very much.

CUAUHTÉMOC: Lessen the tributes. Moctezuma authorized me to offer that.

IXTOLINQUE: That's still not much.

CUAUHTÉMOC: Defend you—and yours.

IXTOLINQUE: Defend me? Is someone trying to attack me?

CUAUHTÉMOC: The *teules!* Don't you understand?

IXTOLINQUE: I'm a little slow, excuse me. I thought I was the one who could defend you from them. I haven't even seen them. Cuaupopoca told me that they arrived in great wooden houses, like fish or seabirds. Those houses, do you think they could navigate on the laguna? The only boats that can even get close to shore here in Coyoacan—and over in Tezcoco—are the *acalli* that we of Ixtapalapa use to carry fruits and vegetables to your parties . . . But they could launch larger boats from here . . . the laguna is wide . . . like those they have in the sea . . . Are you leaving so soon, Cuauhtémoc?

CUAUHTÉMOC: Yes. A long journey awaits me. I must visit many other lords.

IXTOLINQUE: May the gods—the good gods—guide you. You have taken possession of your house—the one where your father lived. My heart rejoices. But I won't keep you. Maybe some-day—soon—you'll return to Coyoacan . . .

(Darkens)

Scene 4

Axayácatl's palace, residence of Moctezuma's Spanish guests. A chamber.

SOLDIER 1: (*To the second, who enters.*) Have you already eaten?

SOLDIER 2: Yes, and you?

SOLDIER 1: Like a prince. These savages never tire of giving us presents. Right here they served us so many strange meats that you didn't know which one to try. And all of them were hot, with coals underneath. They're spicy, but tasty.

SOLDIER 2: They make me sick. Those *tamali*, with meat inside, wrapped in leaves. I can't stop thinking it might be human flesh. They eat one another! You know? I escorted the Capitán when they took him to Tlatelolco, and we saw the *tianguis*. They sell a little of everything there. There was a shrunken arm, blackish, and it was supposed to be eaten! The Indian laughed because the Capitán was dumbstruck when he saw it.

SOLDIER 2: Today I saw the Montezuma eat. He invited the Capitán and Alvarado and Fray Bartolomé. An enormous room, near here. They sat on the floor, they were given perfumed water for their hands, and the parade of dishes began. There couldn't have been less than a hundred. The Montezuma scarcely tried them. They ate in silence, it was like he was in a trance. Then they gave them *straws to suck that made a smoke that smelled very good, and flowers. And then after that some popes came in with gifts of gold and feathers. That's all I saw. The Capitán gave me the signal to take the gifts to his quarters, and I carried them, which I could barely do.

SOLDIER 2: Did you eat there?

SOLDIER 1: No. I kept guard near the Capitán, at the door. But later they brought me food here. Almost the same thing they had served them.

SOLDIER 2: I wonder when we'll go back to Spain—if we are going back.

SOLDIER 1: Do you want to go back?

SOLDIER 2: Naturally! With all the gold I've talked people out of, I have enough, and with what the Capitán owes us . . . I hope he'll keep his word about splitting the booty with us.

SOLDIER 1: You're never happy with anything! I'd like to stay here.

SOLDIER 2: You're crazy! Stay! Do you think these Indians would let us? There's scarcely a handful of us—they're like ants. They could do away with us in an instant if they wanted to.

SOLDIER 1: But they don't want to! They take us for gods! The Capitán at least.

SOLDIER 2: Yes. But you've already seen what they do with their gods. From here you can see the Temple—from the terraces. That big urn up there is for the victims' blood. It could be filled with ours.

SOLDIER 1: But there's gold, gold! It's worth all the risks. And it's medicine for the melancholy you suffer from now. Were you present in Vera Cruz when the Capitán told Montezuma's ambassador that he had a heartache—and that it could only be relieved with gold and more gold? It was a good idea—just like him! That's when they brought him that *golden sun. How much do you think it's worth, once it's melted down, of course?

SOLDIER 2: What I saw was horrible. I responded to the shouts. One of those ambassadors or popes was offering Cortés a flask—a *jícara*, they call it.

SOLDIER 1: With *octli!* It's delicious, sweet . . .

SOLDIER 2: No! It was blood! They had killed one of the men they brought with them—they took out his heart—and they offered the blood to Cortés to drink! It infuriated him, and he had them killed.

SOLDIER 1: Blood! Indian blood!

SOLDIER 2: You already know that the Capitán rarely loses his temper. He always treats these savages like people—although he well knows they aren't. But he's . . . diplomatic. By letting them do it, he finds out their ways and customs. That's how he found out in Tlaxcala that they hated the Montezuma.

SOLDIER 1: And how well he's used that to his advantage! They have come along to carry the arms! They are our "allies."

SOLDIER 2: But that sure got him mad.

SOLDIER 1: Is that why he was angry all the way to Cholula?

SOLDIER 2: That was something else. It was necessary to take precautions, knock down the demons, and plant our Holy Cross.

SOLDIER 1: Here we'll have to do exactly that—take good precautions, as you say. I don't like this peace. I didn't get on that boat for this. I want action—and here there's nothing but gifts and pampering. These Indians! The Montezuma has a bath. And he bathes himself completely every day!

SOLDIER 2: Every day! That's not possible!

SOLDIER 1: I've seen the bath! And what about the beds? They have awnings and feather blankets! I sleep like a king! But enough is enough; I want war!

SOLDIER 2: We'll get our war. (*Walks around the room, feels the walls.*) Look! Come here!

SOLDIER 1: What is it?

SOLDIER 2: This wall. It looks like it's been covered recently. It was a door and now they've closed it off with stones.

SOLDIER 1: Why, it's true!

SOLDIER 2: It would be easy to pull them out. Shall we do it?

SOLDIER 1: What can there be behind the wall? Why would they have closed it off?

SOLDIER 2: Some secret passage. Some danger for the Capitán. They had given him the whole palace. This is suspicious. It must be serious.

SOLDIER 1: I'm going to warn the Capitán.

SOLDIER 2: No! Wait! Let's open it ourselves. Give me your sword.

SOLDIER 1: Here.

SOLDIER 2: Help me. This rock is already giving way. Pull here.

SOLDIER 1: There it goes! (*They struggle; pull out a stone.*)

SOLDIER 2: (*Sticking his head in the hole.*) Look!

(*Enter: Cortés, Alvarado, Fray Bartolomé de Olmedo.*)

CORTÉS: What are you doing here?

SOLDIER 1: The wall, Capitán. There's a door that's been covered recently. We took out this stone to look.

SOLDIER 2: Gold! Mountains of gold!

(*Cortés goes forward, brusquely pulls Soldier 2 away, and puts his head in.*)

CORTÉS: Gold! Gold! Up to the ceiling! Without a doubt this is Montezuma's treasure! It *was* Montezuma's treasure!

FRAY BARTOLOMÉ: God be praised!

ALVARADO: Amen. Finish opening that door!

CORTÉS: No! Not yet. On the contrary, replace that stone. Don't let them notice that we've discovered it.

(*The soldiers replace the stone, disconcerted.*)

ALVARADO: Are you going to leave that treasure there?

CORTÉS: And where would it be better off than in my palace? (*To the soldiers.*) Leave, hurry! (*They leave.*)

ALVARADO: Good thinking, Capitán! It's not a good idea to let the soldiers know we've come across the treasure. We could tear this door down ourselves.

CORTÉS: And where would we take it? Don't you understand that we are still Montezuma's prisoners, just like that treasure is a prisoner to those walls? What we need is to change the terms of our situation.

ALVARADO: I don't understand.

CORTÉS: I didn't expect you to. Nevertheless, any jurist could explain to you that possession entails a right; but that the right is predecessor to possession.

ALVARADO: And so?

CORTÉS: First we must establish the right. On a basis so firm that nobody can dispute it.

FRAY BARTOLOMÉ: The Holy Church . . .

CORTÉS: That's it. The Holy Church, our Mother, derives the divine right from God our Lord, the exercise of which is furnished to the kings, our lords on earth.

ALVARADO: But these pagans . . .

CORTÉS: They are ignorant of it. It's necessary to teach them. And it won't be difficult. They've been molded to the obedience of Montezuma—of the mortal Montezuma—and when he disappears, they will go on cheerfully obeying whoever takes his place. That's how they've been doing it for centuries.

ALVARADO: And who will take the place of Montezuma? Do you think that the king, our lord . . .

CORTÉS: And who else? Of course, it will be by delegation. The king himself is a delegate of God. Our mortal eyes cannot see God. To see the king is the privilege of a few men; but his authority is exercised, in turn, through delegation. The Ayuntamientos: Do you remember, in Villa Rica? There, the will of all of you, my dearest companions, obeyed in unison the divine inspiration to serve God and our king in the best possible way. With it was established a right—of the most legitimate lineage and substance: what one day men may perhaps call . . . "democracy." I

was favored by your votes to do not my will, but yours, in service to God and the king. Again, by delegation. I am thus the
last link in a chain that bonds us all . . .

FRAY BARTOLOMÉ: . . . With God.

CORTÉS: With God. The real one. Do you understand now?

ALVARADO: A little, yes. But—that treasure?

CORTÉS: This treasure, this palace, this city, these lands, these thousands of men—all will render themselves to the service of God
and the king, as soon as we, their delegates: I, your Capitán,
establish the right that will give us legitimate and complete possession of what today is paid in tribute to the devil and to the
pagan Montezuma.

ALVARADO: And that right . . .

CORTÉS: Emanates from God—is infused in the king—comes down
to my fist—and finally is delegated in my sword. Father . . .

FRAY BARTOLOMÉ: Yes, Capitán?

CORTÉS: Have you gone to Montezuma to insist that he convert to
our holy faith?

FRAY BARTOLOMÉ: As many times as I've been able. But I'm starting
to believe that it's useless.

CORTÉS: What a shame. Keep insisting. His body doesn't matter. We
all have to die. But it would be so edifying to save his soul . . . If
there's still time . . . Let's get out of here, Capitán Alvarado . . .

(They leave.)

Scene 5

In the proscenium, with the curtain open

Enter the young Native American; he approaches the audience:

Thus the *teules* came upon Moctezuma's treasure—and thus they sen-
tenced him to death. I, in the meantime, had visited other lords to
demand help for Tenochtitlan. But without success. The lord of Coyoacan was not the only one who was resentful toward the Tenochcans,

and all of them were blinded by their rage, so that they were unable to foresee the common danger.

Scene 6

Hall of the king of Tlaxcala

Enter the Tlaxcaltecan king.

KING: So what you're proposing to us is that we now become Moctezuma's allies?

CUAUHTÉMOC: Not his. His person is mortal. Of all of us—those of us born here—the same in Tlaxcala as in Huexotla, or in Cholula, or in Oaxaca: those of us who are equal.

KING: Equal? That's certainly not the way Moctezuma sees it. We Tlaxcaltecans, deprived of salt, have survived in independence, not because Moctezuma respects us but because he scorns us. He wants a flock of slaves at hand that will be amusing to capture in the flowery wars—and to carry off and sacrifice, in triumph, in the temple. We have witnessed the ceremony, Cuauhtémoc, many times. We arrived under cover of night, on special invitation from your king, and we saw ours die, and we returned fearful of you, to continue begetting victims.

CUAUHTÉMOC: All that will change.

KING: Of course! It has already started to change. Thanks to our alliance with the *teules*.

CUAUHTÉMOC: Your alliance with them is merely subordination to the ends of the foreigners.

KING: Their ends coincide with ours. There is no subordination, there's cooperation. They bring us their powerful weapons—and their new faith, which they explain to us . . .

CUAUHTÉMOC: A new faith? New weapons to impose it with blood and fire?

KING: That's how yours was imposed on us. From what we've seen, there is no other way to establish any faith among men, except through blood and fire.

CUAUHTÉMOC: Think it over well, King. Don't let your anger toward
  Moctezuma blind you. What will the *teules* offer you? Have
  they given you anything? Have they done anything besides take
  control of the riches from the temples of the places they pass
  through—and raze them, and put a cross in their place?

KING: They give us hope—of an eternal life in the sky, with angels
  and music, if we are good; if we help them kill the Mexicans; if
  we swear off our gods and receive baptism. I've already received
  it—and all my family. Otherwise, on dying we would go to hell.
  A horrible hell, full of flames, of boiling oil . . . and forever . . .
  for all eternity . . . (*Exits.*)

Scene 7

In the proscenium

CUAUHTÉMOC: (*To the audience.*) When I returned to Mexico, Moctezuma had been assassinated. Cuitláhuac was ascending a
  wavering throne. But he at last managed to awaken the wrath of
  the Mexicans in his desperate decision to face the *teules,* who
  had taken their perfidiousness to the limit by killing the priests
  and the townspeople and the guests and the women, during
  the ceremony of Tezcatlipoca at the Templo Mayor. Alvarado
  consummated that act. And the town burned with rage, and it
  armed itself as best it could, to expel the intruders: fighting at
  night, destroying their horses, forcing them to flee toward Tlacopan. Many died rich, by sinking into the marsh before they
  could lighten themselves of the gold they had loaded themselves
  down with.

  But Cuitláhuac only governed us for eighty days. An illness
  unknown to us, and brought by the Spaniards, covered his body
  with pox and a fever while his city prepared for the defense,
  since the *teules* again attacked us.

  It was then that I was elected Tecuhtli of the Mexicans.
  And I carried forth the struggle of Cuitláhuac. Once again we
  were being left alone to defend ourselves as we had been at the
  beginning: harassed by the barbarians of earlier times—and by
  the new barbarians. But if we had indeed survived, we could

again struggle against all odds, against everyone, in order to preserve our way of life.

Scene 8

Tlatelolco. Cuauhtémoc's hiding place

TECUICHPO: (*Entering.*) Cuauhtémoc . . .

CUAUHTÉMOC: Tecuichpo! What are you doing there?

TECUICHPO: Praying—for my father—and for my husband, Cuitláhuac. They have already reached the good land. They fly now, *hummingbirds, among flowers that don't die.

CUAUHTÉMOC: : Yes, Tecuichpo. Come into my arms. You're shaking.

TECUICHPO: Everything is so horrible! How could those men kill my father? He received them in peace, as friends; he let them have my grandfather's palace; he loaded them with gifts . . .

CUAUHTÉMOC: You can't understand it, Tecuichpo. You are scarcely a child.

TECUICHPO: And already a widow, and an orphan.

CUAUHTÉMOC: My wife. The wife of the Tlacatecuhtli. Let's cheer ourselves up, Tecuichpo. If none of this had happened, I would be no more than the Tecuhtli of Tlatelolco—and your poor cousin, although we've loved each other in secret since we were children. Moctezuma would not have let us get married.

TECUICHPO: Your father was Ahuízotl the Great.

CUAUHTÉMOC: But I was not his only son. Not even the first born. I was the last: the one with the ominous name of the *Falling Eagle.

TECUICHPO: My love!

CUAUHTÉMOC: And I will fall. On them! With all my wrath. To avenge your father and Cuitláhuac, and to ease the anger of our gods! For more than sixty days we have resisted. We will go on fighting, without stopping.

TECUICHPO: Today I stepped out to the streets. Everything is in ruins. The water sprouts cadavers.

CUAUHTÉMOC: Don't look, Tecuichpo. Close your eyes, close your ears. This is a bad dream you will wake up from. Go now to the side of your little girl. Play with her, smile. Teach her to know you.

TECUICHPO: You don't want to eat, Cuauhtémoc? You haven't eaten since yesterday. Look, I've cut these herbs from the garden. They're sweet. There's nothing else.

CUAUHTÉMOC: You eat them, Tecuichpo. I'm not hungry.

(Enter two *Tiger Knights. They carry the heads of two Spaniards and two horses impaled on spikes. They stop upon seeing Tecuichpo.)

CUAUHTÉMOC: Go in, Tecuichpo. Don't set your eyes on this rubbish. (*Tecuichpo exits, covering her eyes.*) (*To the warriors.*) Fine. These then are the immortals, the white gods; what a terrible expression they have on their pale faces!

KNIGHT: We've sent other heads and feet and hands and stag heads to Huexotzingo and to Xochimilco, and to other towns that believed they were untouchable. Some are starting to have doubts—others promise their help and alliance.

CUAUHTÉMOC: Let's not count on them too much. Especially on the Xochimilcans. We will go on fighting alone—at night, when Tezcatlipoca favors us. Be ready to cut the bridges as soon as it gets dark, and rig the *acalli* so we can attack the brigantines en masse.

KNIGHT: And these heads?

CUAUHTÉMOC: Take them to the *tzompantli*. Let them look toward the sun, their ally, their accomplice. Have you eaten their bodies?

KNIGHT: We tried them. Their flesh is bitter, inedible.

CUAUHTÉMOC: Naturally. Go now. Prepare yourselves for combat.

KNIGHT: Did you receive their messengers, Cuauhtémoc?

CUAUHTÉMOC: For the third time. And again I've consulted the elders. The answer is the same: fight to the death. El Malinche asked me to avoid, through the submission he calls peace, the suffering of women, elders, and children—which he has unleashed against them. He is unaware that the children, the old, and the women are unafraid of either suffering or death.

KNIGHT: It's getting dark.

CUAUHTÉMOC: Sound the battle conch.

Scene 9

Transition

Total darkness. Above the long lament of the war conch, little by little, in constant crescendo, are heard shouting voices and war cries in which can be heard at intervals the war cry, "México, Tenochtitlan, México"; the beating of lances and macanas *against bucklers and shields; bodies that fall in the water. Fifteen seconds. The sound cuts off abruptly at its climax and there is an absolute silence for ten seconds.*

Scene 10

Cortés' tent

When the lights come on, Cortés is on the scene with Sandoval, Alvarado, and Fray Bartolomé.

CORTÉS: Seventy-five days since we encircled the city! And not one of them without difficulties, dangers, and misfortunes!

FRAY BARTOLOMÉ: God be praised! It's Tuesday today, Capitán: August 13, the day of Saint Hipolitus. Memorable day.

CORTÉS: We will consecrate a temple to Saint Hipolitus. I'm glad, Alvarado, that it wasn't you who took Guatemocín prisoner. I know your impetuousness.

ALVARADO: You ordered me to stand guard in the market. Sandoval was the one in charge of attacking their forts.

SANDOVAL: And García Holguín had the good fortune of being the one to sight his canoe and to give it chase. The Capitán had ordered that they not be killed. I also don't understand why.

CORTÉS: Let's call it . . . reciprocity. You know very well how many times I found myself in danger of death at their hands. And if I saved my scalp, it's because they wanted me alive, for their gods.

FRAY BARTOLOMÉ: God protects you, Capitán.

CORTÉS: That must be it, without a doubt. That, and this medallion of the Holy Virgin always over my chest.

FRAY BARTOLOMÉ: What a mortal silence there was all of a sudden! After days and days of deafening us with shouts, drumbeats, and conches!

CORTÉS: A mortal silence. The *stones have gone mute. As if they'd all been knocked down. Is Guatemocín there?

SANDOVAL: With the other *caciques. And with his wife. His wife is beautiful, Capitán.

CORTÉS: I know her. Moctezuma's daughter. But bring Guatemocín in alone. (*Exit Sandoval and Alvarado.*) Are you there, Doña Marina?

MALINCHE: (*Entering.*) At your side, Lord. I was waiting for your call.

CORTÉS: You will tell Guatemocín to have no fear whatsoever. That I have always wished to be his friend. That I forgive him the war he waged on me, and that if he swears loyalty to our king—and is baptized—I will see that he governs his people, as before.

MALINCHE: His people no longer exist, Lord. They've all died. Can't you hear the silence?

(*Enter Cuauhtémoc. At his sides, Sandoval and Alvarado. He and Cortés regard each other for an instant. Cuauhtémoc advances to face Cortés.*)

CORTÉS: Be welcome, Guatemocín. Take a seat.

(*Cuauhtémoc remains standing.*)

CUAUHTÉMOC: Here I am, Malinche. I did what I was obliged to do in defense of my city and my people.

CORTÉS: It was your duty, Cuauhtémoc. And I admire you for it. But you refused peace, many times. And your people suffered, and the town is in ruins.

(*Cuauhtémoc quickly grabs Cortés' knife. Sandoval and Alvarado intervene to protect the Capitán, who dismisses them with a motion of the hand. Cuauhtémoc returns the knife by the hilt and offers it to Cortés.*)

CUAUHTÉMOC: Finish your work, Malinche. Give me a clean death. Bury your knife in my chest.

CORTÉS: No, Guatemocín. (*Sheathes the knife.*) Now we are no longer enemies. You will come with your family and with me to Coyoacan, while Tenochtitlan is being reconstructed. And then . . . (*To the others.*) Let's go outside, men. Doña Marina needs to speak with our royal guest.

(*They exit. Cortés gives the signal to Doña Marina. La Malinche and Cuauhtémoc are left alone.*)

MALINCHE: Wouldn't you like to sit down, Lord? (*Cuauhtémoc doesn't respond.*) The Capitán has put me in charge of speaking with you. He's not going to do you harm. His God is good, you know? I have been baptized, and I go to mass and take communion every day . . . Why are you turning your back on me, Lord?

CUAUHTÉMOC: I don't understand your tongue, Malinche.

MALINCHE: Do I speak the language of Anáhuac badly?

CUAUHTÉMOC: You speak a language—that I will never know.

(*Darkness.*)

Scene II

Coyoacan. Torture chamber

Cuauhtémoc and Tetlepanquétzal seated on the ground, tied with chains. We are in Coyoacan, days after the downfall.

CUAUHTÉMOC: Are you crying, Tetlepanquétzal?

TETLEPANQUÉTZAL: No, my lord. It's the smoke from that fire outside. It's gotten in my eyes.

CUAUHTÉMOC: Xiuhtecuhtli. The god of fire. He has deserted those livid flames. He's not there. He neither recognizes us nor claims our sacrifice. We are unworthy of his love, Tetlepanquétzal. Two prisoners. Two slaves. Chained.

TETLEPANQUÉTZAL: United, sir: you and I—the last kings. What will they do with us now?

CUAUHTÉMOC: I know. They will go on asking us what we did with the treasure. They will promise clemency and food and to take off the chains, if we tell them.

TETLEPANQUÉTZAL: They have a sinister laugh. Yesterday they had a dance and a banquet. They ran around the tables drunk, with their women.

CUAUHTÉMOC: That must be their religion. Some sacred ceremony.

TETLEPANQUÉTZAL: They're preparing for a voyage. I heard them talk about it.

CUAUHTÉMOC: You see and hear many things, Tetlepanquétzal.

TETLEPANQUÉTZAL: You don't?

CUAUHTÉMOC: Yes. Many. But I am quiet.

TETLEPANQUÉTZAL: Pardon me, sir.

(Enter Ixtolinque. He dresses Spanish style. And he emphasizes the fact.)

IXTOLINQUE: You have returned to Coyoacan, Cuauhtémoc. To my lands. I told you, remember?

CUAUHTÉMOC: I remember it well, Ixtolinque.

IXTOLINQUE: Don't call me that. I've been baptized. I am now Don Juan de Guzmán.

CUAUHTÉMOC: It's about time!

IXTOLINQUE: I've given the Capitán all the land of mine he wants to make his house, and Doña Marina's, and a temple, and a monastery, and . . .

CUAUHTÉMOC: Was it necessary for you to give him what was already his?

IXTOLINQUE: You're wrong, Cuauhtémoc. Cortés doesn't take anything by force. He represents a lord—a great king of all the earth, whom all the kings of the earth obey. They have sworn obedience to that great king. And once sworn, it's treason to resist his demands, a sin of infidelity, of disloyalty. And it's punishable, of course.

CUAUHTÉMOC: Of course. Is that what you've come to tell me?

IXTOLINQUE: To obey, on the other hand, to submit oneself, to collaborate brings with it great advantages. The king can grant us favors: give us titles and arms and recognize our properties and tributes.

CUAUHTÉMOC: Has he already given you a title? Another, different from the one you deserve?

IXTOLINQUE: Lord of Coyoacan. Don Juan de Guzmán. On my coat of arms I will be able to use the symbols that the king chooses. And I will retain the lordship of my lands. Without any more tributes to the king of Mexico.

CUAUHTÉMOC: Just to the king of Spain, is that it?

IXTOLINQUE: Yes. I've learned his name: Sacra, Augusta, Cesárea, Católica, Real Majestad. If you'd like . . .

CUAUHTÉMOC: If I'd like what?

IXTOLINQUE: If you weren't so stubborn, like your father . . . If you would confess where the treasure is . . .

CUAUHTÉMOC: You too! Do you believe like they do that I ate the treasure? That I've hidden it where their fingernails and their eyes can't lay hold of it? Have they already forgotten that they robbed all of it? All of it! From Axayácatl's palace, when Cuitláhuac besieged them and drove them out to Tlacopan? Don't they know that it's the gold that sank their bodies in the lake?

IXTOLINQUE: They don't believe it, Cuauhtémoc. And their patience and their tolerance have reached the limit. They've sent me to warn you, for the last time, sure of our common blood, and because I am old, and of your race, that I will persuade you to confess. Otherwise . . .

TETLEPANQUÉTZAL: Otherwise what?

IXTOLINQUE: That bonfire, you see? The smoke and the glow of the fire even reach in here. It's for you, Cuauhtémoc. They're going to torture you over the fire until you confess.

CUAUHTÉMOC: Has Cortés arranged it?

IXTOLINQUE: He's opposed. But the others have compelled him to do it, Alderete the treasurer, above all. Cortés never does anything more than he's obliged to do. If you persist in refusing, what is he to do?

CUAUHTÉMOC: (*He sits up, painfully. The chains rattle.*) Thank you, old man. Now you can go. I'm ready.

IXTOLINQUE: To confess?

CUAUHTÉMOC: Stir the fire, Ixtolinque. Throw your staff in it, your ruler's cane. The *teul* will give you another, richer one.

IXTOLINQUE: Fool! (*Exits.*)

CUAUHTÉMOC: Let's go, Tetlepanquétzal! Xiuhtecuhtli, the god of
fire, has reconciled himself with us, and he calls us!
> (*They exit toward the blaze of the bonfire.*)
> (*An instant of music.*)

Scene 12

The young actor steps forward to the proscenium.

ACTOR: What followed, you already know. Crippled by the torture,
Cuauhtémoc remained a prisoner of the *teul*—and was taken in
his entourage on the expedition to Las Hibueras, to Tabasco, or
Chiapas. All that, Cortés told in his long Letters of Relation
to the Sacra, Augusta, Cesárea, Católica, Real Majestad. And in
the fifth of those letters, with a few short lines, he explains how,
through the renegade Mexicalcingo (Cristóbal, by his Christian
name), he discovered that Cuauhtémoc and Tetlepanquétzal
were still conspiring, and he says succinctly, "In this way these
two were hung, and the others I let loose, because it didn't seem
that they could be blamed for anything more than having heard
them, although that alone was enough to deserve death."
  So in this way the life of Cuauhtémoc was ended: his body
left hanging from a ceiba tree in Acalan—bouncing in the wind
while the conquistadors headed out, in search of more gold. But
I like to imagine that Cuauhtémoc has not died. I sense him in
the earth, germinating at night under the infinite battle of the
stars—and sprouting forcefully in the harsh, wrathful dawn of
the nopal and the maguey; in the water, that colors the flowers;
in the air that caresses my hair, straight like his, and fills my
lungs; in the hummingbird, that sucks the precious stones from
the tiny iris.
  Now the earth has digested all the old hatreds. It has swal-
lowed up the dead: Cortés. (*Cortés appears. He takes off his mask.
Under it there is a Mexican boy who has played his role.*) Alvarado.
(*Same game.*) Fray Bartolomé. (*Same game.*) (*One by one they
each leave their masks on the ground, as if they were burying them
and then reappearing, free from them and transformed.*) They will

have gone to their heaven, or their bodies will have turned into stone—or into trees, returned to us by the earth, our Mother.

And Cuauhtémoc hasn't died. I know that he is in me; that he will live forever, in me and in my children and in those who come afterward—to be born in the land of Mexico, molded with the bones of our ancestors, nourished like the sun with the blood of our hearts.

CURTAIN

Cuauhtémoc and Eulalia

A DIALOGUE

Translation of *Cuauhtémoc y Eulalia*. In *Diálogos*. Los Textos de la Capilla, vol. 2. Mexico City: Editorial Stylo, 1956.

EULALIA: Excuse me, young man. I seem to have lost my way. You're from here, aren't you? Tell me please, is this the way to Ichcateopan?

YOUNG MAN: Yes, this is it, ma'am. Do you see that mountain? On the other side is Ichcateopan. Ten hours or so, on foot.

EULALIA: On foot! There's no road?

YOUNG MAN: Yes, there's a road. Not a very good one, but there's a road.

EULALIA: It's not that I have a car, or a truck either. Alfonso Caso didn't want to lend me the one from the Institute. He's done everything to try and stop me, because he knows . . . But you don't want me to spend ten hours on foot, all the way to the other side of that hill, do you?

YOUNG MAN: I don't want anything, ma'am. I'm just telling you that from here to Ichcateopan, it's a ten-hour walk.

EULALIA: Yes, of course, that's the way it is. Excuse me. But, how long would it be by horse? Couldn't I get a horse?

YOUNG MAN: I don't know what you're talking about.

EULALIA: You don't know what a horse is?

YOUNG MAN: The bottom part of a Spaniard. I know perfectly well. Or, if you wish, let's say a Spaniard is the top part of a horse.

EULALIA: Great! That's how Cuauhtémoc would have defined them!

YOUNG MAN: You were saying?

EULALIA: Nothing. Your definition surprised me. And that, in the midst of the twentieth century, a young Native American would be speaking like his ancestors.

YOUNG MAN: Do you know my ancestors?

EULALIA: That's exactly what I have come in search of. I'm going to Ichcateopan to find the remains of Cuauhtémoc.

YOUNG MAN: The remains of Cuauhtémoc!

EULALIA: Yes. Let me introduce myself. May I sit down a moment? I'm a little tired.

YOUNG MAN: Make yourself right at home, ma'am. Can I bring you something to drink? Some flowers?

EULALIA: No, thank you. I was going to introduce myself. My name is Eulalia Guzmán. I'm an archaeologist. That is, I research the past.

YOUNG MAN: That's a curious profession. Individuals' pasts? I didn't know they called the police archaeologists.

EULALIA: Not individuals' pasts; the past of a people.

YOUNG MAN: Yes, but you were telling me about one person: about . . . Cuauhtémoc.

EULALIA: But Cuauhtémoc wasn't a person; not just any person. He was the emperor of the Mexicans, and consequently, is the symbol of a race; of my race; of our race.

YOUNG MAN: And has he died?

EULALIA: Yes, of course; centuries ago, at the hands of the Spanish, the conquistadors. But, my boy! How can you not know? What kind of schools do we have, for God's sake!

YOUNG MAN: You can see what kind. But it's never too late to teach me. You were going to tell me about your profession, ma'am—archaeology. You research a people's past. May I ask you, with what end?

EULALIA: Pure science has no end other than knowledge of the truth.

YOUNG MAN: The truth of the past?

EULALIA: Truth is timeless. There's only one truth. But yesterday explains today; it clarifies it and lets us deal with it better.

YOUNG MAN: And you think you will be able to deal with the present better by discovering the remains of, let's say, my ancestor?

EULALIA: Yes.

YOUNG MAN: By proving that he's dead?

EULALIA: That he's alive. That he existed; finding his bones to glorify them, to bring the cult of his virtues back to life among the Mexicans.

YOUNG MAN: His virtues? Was he a virtuous man? What they call a Saint? In the churches I have seen ex-votos, relics. The priests preach that the saints they teach us to worship are made in the image of the virtuous men of the Christian church. Without a doubt, it must be comforting for the Christians to see in the saints the possibility of becoming like them. Those saints give the faithful a contact, an indirect communication with the saints of their devotion. Is that what you hope to do with your reconstruction of Cuauhtémoc? Try to get them to canonize him?

EULALIA: No pope would ever dare do it, of course, though few martyrs have suffered what Cuauhtémoc has. But that's not what I'm hoping to do.

YOUNG MAN: What then?

EULALIA: Cortés' remains, we know where they are. For many years, the preservers, the Hispanophiles, kept them secret. Finally, after the time of resentment had passed, they revealed their whereabouts. They are sealed inside a box, no bigger than a shoebox, in the chapel of the Hospital de Jesús, which he founded. Now then: it's absolutely absurd that we don't know, on the other hand, where Cuauhtémoc lies. This is his homeland. We owe him the honor of rescuing the relic of his mortal remains from the dust.

YOUNG MAN: To put them opposite Cortés'?

EULALIA: Not to stand opposite them. To stand above them.

YOUNG MAN: A posthumous triumph. The contest of the bones. Will they, do you think, turn out to be better preserved than Cortés'?

EULALIA: What doubt can there be! The Conquistador suffered from shameful diseases, which had already sapped him while he was alive, and which the examination of his corroded bones has just revealed. Besides, he was a dwarf. The portraits the painters made of him favored him. He wasn't the dashing bearded knight that they want to make us believe. Through *scientific reconstruction, we can tell he was a monster, as if his deeds hadn't already made us suspect it. Cuauhtémoc, on the other hand . . .

YOUNG MAN: Do you know what he was like?

EULALIA: He was . . . a hero. Even his name says it: the falling eagle. It's wonderful how the Native Americans chose names that described the virtues they displayed: Huémac, the builder, the one with the big hands; Ilhuicamina, the archer of the stars . . .

YOUNG MAN: But aside from his name, do you know what Cuauh-témoc was like?

EULALIA: His deeds are enough to describe him. A young prince, who rebelled against the cowardice of the conformists, of those who accepted through superstition the foreign yoke; who confronted the blond gods, owners of iron and of the lightning bolt; and who, with unequal arms, fought against them.

YOUNG MAN: Excuse me for insisting, ma'am, but that alone doesn't help me visualize Cuauhtémoc. You say there are portraits that remain of Cortés, although you hasten to add that they are flattering and false. Aren't there any of Cuauhtémoc?

EULALIA: No authentic ones. The indigenous painters didn't know about perspective. The codices, which were both their writing and their painting, reject likenesses for symbols. They are expressionists in that sense, like the beautiful native pre-Cortesian sculpture.

YOUNG MAN: What about statues? Aren't there any of Cuauhtémoc?

EULALIA: No contemporary ones. Pre-Cortesian religious and funereal sculpture avoided realism and didn't use living people as its models. Later, yes. In the Paseo de la Reforma there's a statue of Cuauhtémoc. A real disgrace: like a figure from opera or ballet, adorned with feathers and in the act of throwing a javelin. That image of him has unfortunately been popularized on beer bottles.

YOUNG MAN: So, there's no way to know what Cuauhtémoc was like.

EULALIA: That's why I'm searching for his skeleton, or what remains of it. Archaeology has many more resources now, more methods that come from the related sciences like anthropology. It's been possible, based on a vertebra discovered in an excavation, to reconstruct the dinosaurs of the most distant past in their natural size. I intend to do the same with Cuauhtémoc when I find his remains.

YOUNG MAN: But, supposing you succeed in imaginarily reconstructing Cuauhtémoc, it would be a physical reconstruction. Would that tell you what Cuauhtémoc was like?

EULALIA: Undoubtedly. You're referring to his character, right? Well then, the old Lombrosian phrenology has been perfected and made scientific. We already know the mutual effect of an organism's soma on its soul and vice versa. Studies by Kreschmer, Viola's *Biotypology,* have conferred on us an understanding of character through one's physiological features and through the individual's physical conformation.

YOUNG MAN: So, once you have reconstructed Cuauhtémoc, you could, with all certainty, how should I say it, make him talk and set him walking?

EULALIA: That's the way it is.

YOUNG MAN: In service of the present? A minute ago you said that you were interested in revealing the past in order to serve the present. In what ways would we benefit by having, thanks to your noble efforts, a Cuauhtémoc pieced back together from his ashes, from his bones, like a jigsaw puzzle? Don't you fear being disappointed if you find he is anachronistic, or so different from the image you've formed of him that you would have to lie, as you say the iconographs have lied about his enemy, Cortés?

EULALIA: No. I'm not afraid. In my quest, in my research, I have proceeded, first, by intuition, and then, with scientific method. Really, I'm not looking for, not aiming for, anything more than material proof for what I already know from the start. Cuauhtémoc was young. That, all the chroniclers admit. He must have been tall, handsome; serene, but capable of great anger; sweet and cruel at the same time; stoic and sybarite.

YOUNG MAN: Excuse me, ma'am. I'm guilty of shooting more than one question at you in a single round. What I would like to know is why you believe that it would be of service to Mexico to find Cuauhtémoc's remains.

EULALIA: I have already told you. We need to venerate them, raise an altar for them. It's gross. In Mexico City there's one that's called the *Rotonda de los Hombres Ilustres. That's where everyone goes who dies in vogue and eminence: generals, singers, ex-presidents. That's where Father Hidalgo is, and that's fine. He gave us Independence. But much earlier, Cuauhtémoc had already begun the protest. And we don't even know where his bones are!

YOUNG MAN: To rebury them, now in the company of the Illustrious Men and in their . . . Rotunda, you said?

EULALIA: Yes. Or separately. In his own solemn monument that would be the symbol of our gratitude for his unequaled heroism.

YOUNG MAN: That would be better. I suppose he would be more

comfortable away from the illustrious men. But what if, even more comfortable than in such a monument, Cuauhtémoc rests and germinates there, wherever he is, where for so many centuries he has managed to avoid just such veneration that presumes and accepts his death? Where he has avoided the adulteration of the statues which, like the one you mentioned, can in a few years be both successively beautiful and horrendous?

EULALIA: Would you prefer that his remains weren't discovered? The remains of your ancestor?

YOUNG MAN: No, it's not that I would prefer it. It's just that I know, ma'am, that you will never find them. Nor anybody else either.

EULALIA: I will. I'm certain of it. I will come across them, even if I have to dig them up with my own fingernails. Even if everybody denies it; even if they make fun of me and say I'm crazy.

YOUNG MAN: Not you. Not anybody. Because it would be like the painful certification of his death. Like making him equal to Cortés, in a coffin, even in an altar, sumptuous as it might be. And Cuauhtémoc hasn't died.

EULALIA: What!

YOUNG MAN: He will never die. The Spaniards didn't succeed in killing him. No foreigner will succeed. Cortés, Maximiliano, Wilson . . . They all pass and die. Cuauhtémoc remains. They exploit him, they rob him, they whip him, they deceive him, they praise him, they humiliate him, they sack his treasures, they indenture him to work the lands that were his. But he doesn't die.

He is the land, in which you, ma'am, vainly search for his remains: the air, which caresses his straight, black hair; the water that colors his flowers; the dark flesh that knows how to keep quiet under the stars and last throughout centuries without dying . . .

EULALIA: What strange things you say! Who are you? What's your name?

YOUNG MAN: Oh! Should we get *personal? Whatever you want. You can, for example, call me . . . Cuauhtémoc.

CURTAIN

Malinche and Carlota

A DIALOGUE

Translation of *Malinche y Carlota*. In *Diálogos*. Los Textos de la
Capilla, vol. 2. Mexico City: Editorial Stylo, 1956.

MALINCHE: Another cup of tea?

CARLOTA: Yes, thank you. No sugar this time. Thank you. You're not
going to have any?

MALINCHE: No. One's enough for me.

CARLOTA: *Tea is so nice at five! It gives a tonicity, as the doctors
say . . . In your country, I could never get used to your famous
*chocolate.

MALINCHE: My country! You say it as if it weren't yours as well!

CARLOTA: Well, no it wasn't. My loved one, yes, but not my lover.
There's a difference.

MALINCHE: But you reigned in Mexico. Just a short time, that's true;
but no less than any president. Things have never lasted very
long there.

CARLOTA: They threw me out. I would have wanted to stay there forever. To have a child, a Mexican child, born there, in that sullen
silence . . .

MALINCHE: A child? Of Maximiliano's?

CARLOTA: Are children of their father? No more than the fruit or the
flower are of the farmer who deposits the seed in the earth.

MALINCHE: A child of the earth then?

CARLOTA: Mine, and of that land. Twice hers, or doubly mine. That
way our dynasty could have begun. You were more lucky.

MALINCHE: No. Not me either. But I never thought of having a baby.
I never ever considered it.

CARLOTA: And, nevertheless, you had them. The Mexicans. It's all your blood, fortified by Cortés', the blood that flows in their veins.

MALINCHE: But they hate me. To them I symbolize treason, surrender.

CARLOTA: Just as I, the intruder, the foreigner, the Johnny-come-lately. And, nevertheless, I didn't wish for anything more than to surrender myself, humbly and passionately, to Mexico.

MALINCHE: I loved Cortés. He was the only thing that mattered. My smooth, sweet race left me cold. The rough, red skin of that blond god inebriated all my senses. Was that a betrayal of my people, of my race? I believe it was more loyalty to myself.

CARLOTA: Without a doubt. But we historical women are not completely free to follow the impulses of our hearts. Nevertheless, I understand you well. You aren't aware of your destiny.

MALINCHE: And you, did you know yours?

CARLOTA: Since I was little they had prepared me, trained me, to rule. Where, and how, my empire was to end I couldn't have said, but I accepted it from the start.

MALINCHE: To reign together with your loved one; to share with him the triumphs and the anxieties. It's a noble destiny. I never dreamed of it.

CARLOTA: And, nevertheless, you gave him a kingdom.

MALINCHE: I received him when he came. Like I would a guest, who is owed the honors of hospitality. I was assigned that mission by my parents, my lords. For many generations, they had been awaiting the return of Quetzalcóatl.

CARLOTA: And with Cortés, they believed he had arrived.

MALINCHE: He arrived. With him. For me at least.

CARLOTA: But Quetzalcóatl was a god. He had taught your people crafts, arts. He hadn't come to kill and destroy, like Cortés.

MALINCHE: The gods destroy. That's what they're made to do. Quetzalcóatl himself, in order to civilize my people, had to annihilate their ignorance.

CARLOTA: But Cortés annihilated their wisdom.

MALINCHE: In order to give them another. Even Christ . . .

CARLOTA: Don't say such blasphemy.

MALINCHE: There's nothing blasphemous in it. Christ was a man. I learned it from Cortés—from the man who was a god for me. And he too destroyed in order to edify.

CARLOTA: It seems to me that you preserve a . . . pagan notion, let's say, of Christianity. The terrible, destructive gods were your gods: Huitzilopochtli, blood thirsty. Not the God of the Christians; not Jesus, who was all humanity, forgiveness, resignation . . .

MALINCHE: I was humble, submissive, even before I was baptized as a Christian. But Cortés was too, in my arms, upon returning from battle, in the silence of a night brimming with risks. Then he slept, in my breath he breathed the warm, magic air of my land. What did his greed and cruelty matter then? His ambition rested, languidly, like all his muscles. I felt him dream his dreams of gold; his endless boyish dreams of power and riches. But I caressed the living gold of his hair. The treasure of his body that breathed, that lived, was mine. To keep him next to me, I would have opened the doors to a hundred cities for him.

CARLOTA: Then you don't regret what the Mexicans call your betrayal?

MALINCHE: Not for a minute. Never. I would do it all over again if by doing it I could live those moments over again.

CARLOTA: In a way, I envy you.

MALINCHE: Why? Maximiliano was blond and handsome.

CARLOTA: Yes. Blond and handsome.

MALINCHE: I would have loved him the same as I did Cortés. But I no longer existed then. And then . . . He came with you. Cortés came alone. He needed me, he claimed me; as if he had dreamed me; as if for me he had undertaken the voyage.

CARLOTA: Quetzalcóatl. Yes, Max was Quetzalcóatl. By the right of God, he had been born a prince. Through the call of the Mexicans, he came to their land. Not for adventure, for robbery and killing, like Cortés; but to be your friend, your father, your pastor. To defend you, against yourselves. Blood, hate, betrayal! One cruelty had betrothed another when you got together with Cortés. The Christ the Spaniards brought was the bloody god, the crucified god. Max was the young, smiling Christ that was close to children. He would have been a friend of Juárez'.

MALINCHE: Juárez . . . I've seen him, yes. I know him. Even here, he doesn't give up his patient custom of waiting in the antechamber. Nobody would say that he is of my race. Well, of mine, yes. But not of Cuauhtémoc's.

CARLOTA: Why do you say that?

MALINCHE: I don't know. It embarrasses me a little. I know I have no right to talk. Even without intending to, I facilitated the conquest of my people. But I didn't go in search of the conquerors. They just came.

CARLOTA: We came too, Max and I. You had called us, you had gone in search of us. But Juárez rejected us.

MALINCHE: He was incapable of love. He thought a lot, meditated, which is different. From what it seems, he saw legal orthodoxy as politically convenient for the autonomy and freedom of his people. And he went to find godparents, while you were offering yourselves as parents.

CARLOTA: Political convenience! That's exactly what led Napoleon III to use us as instruments. The ignoble origin of our coming to Mexico. But we would have cut ourselves off from his tree in time, in order to put down far-reaching roots; in order to be Mexican through our children, just like yours by Cortés. That way we would have redeemed ourselves from the original sin.

MALINCHE: Without a doubt; but Juárez, inside his frock, under his funeral hat, was hateful and resentful. Three centuries afterward, he took his revenge on Cortés out on Maximiliano.

CARLOTA: He was taking revenge on you . . .

MALINCHE: Following in my footsteps, but not as nobly. It's been said that it was for love of his people. But how can someone not love his people? Besides, love of oneself is sterile, and the peace born from the respect of another's rights, which can't be defined or described except in the texts, is dead and frozen. Life is only fertilized through surrender, which means absorption and conquest.

CARLOTA: You're saying he's right, when you are trying to deny there was any reason for his actions.

MALINCHE: I'm trying to explain it, but I'm not able to justify it. I said he was incapable of love; that it couldn't have been love for the Americans that inspired him to make a deal with them against you, but hate for what you represented, what you incarnated, in his dark, vengeful mind. The Tlaxcaltecans had done the same thing earlier. They too hated the Mexican emperor. And blind, they also failed to foresee the servitude their alliance would forever impose on them.

CARLOTA: I've forgiven Juárez. Forgiveness is love, you must be right. I never hated him. I never hated any Mexican.

MALINCHE: Nor did they hate you, I'm sure.

CARLOTA: Maybe. But they didn't love us.

MALINCHE: You've never understood how we Mexicans love? With cruelty, with blood. Perhaps we made Maximiliano ours when we offered his heart, like that of a chosen youth, to Huitzilopochtli. On the other hand, Juárez died without glory; a bourgeois death, satisfied to be like Lincoln and to be known as the *Do-Gooder of America.

CARLOTA: You hate him . . .

MALINCHE: No. I'm just judging him, describing him, that's all. And it hurts me a little to think he altered the course of a life that was born from my love for Cortés.

CARLOTA: I've come to admire Juárez. His obstinance, his unwavering tenacity, his disdain for the throne, his blind confidence in the righteousness of his cause, his impassiveness . . . Those are the best virtues of your race. He incarnated them.

MALINCHE: He incarnated the past, static and sterile. Under the guise of modernity, with independence as a lure. An idol in a silk hat.

CARLOTA: Why do you say that he altered the course of the life of Mexico? Maybe, on the contrary, he saved it. At least that's what he proposed to do, what he fought for.

MALINCHE: What's worse is that he was the unwitting instrument for a tragic return to the past, and this time forever.

CARLOTA: To the past? Maybe we represented the past. The monarchy, the throne. He restored the Republic.

MALINCHE: Government of the people, by the people, and for the people. I know the phrase, the "slogan," as they call it, the inventors of mottoes, of congresses, conventions, campaigns: "America for Liberty"; "The Pause that Refreshes"; "Remember

Pearl Harbor"; "The Good Neighbor Policy"; "Follow the Three Movements of Fab." That's what Juárez opened the door to, by closing it on Europe.

CARLOTA: He couldn't have known. That's not what he was proposing.

MALINCHE: Because hatred is blinding. Because revenge drags in the past. Love is what looks toward the future, forging it. Without intending to either, but because an act of love is an act of immortal creation.

CARLOTA: Hatred is blinding, true enough. That which you profess toward Juárez leads you to the aberrant statement that Juárez procured for Mexico a step backward. On the contrary, he made it move forward. He removed the residue of all the evil the Spaniards had imposed before: something neither the priest Hidalgo, nor Morelos, nor any of the insurgents had time to do. He combated fanaticism . . .

MALINCHE: To substitute it, with what faith? With the naked ambition of gold that doesn't go toward the splendor of beautiful altars, but to be hoarded in the crypts of the banks, and to circulate in checks? With the worship of the machine? With the religion of work, not understood as creation and as a game that produces useless and beautiful objects; but as punctuality, speed, anxiety?

CARLOTA: That would have happened without Juárez too. You can't blame him. The world is all like that, now.

MALINCHE: I know. But I resist understanding it and accepting it.

CARLOTA: Do you think things could have been any other way?

MALINCHE: You are the one who can answer that question. Juárez is from your time, not mine.

CARLOTA: No, there is no time for us anymore. Not yours, not mine. That's why we can get together now and judge the past, the present, yours, ours, the Mexicans'.

MALINCHE: And do it without regrets. But also without hope?

CARLOTA: You can harbor hope in your children. In the ones you didn't want, that you didn't plan to have when you loved Cortés. Not me. I didn't have them, not by Maximiliano, not by Mexico.

MALINCHE: And mine were born of passion. They are mine even when they detest and deny me.

CARLOTA: You can't say that. On the contrary. The very same Juárez whom you hate, what he committed, by your own judgment, was nothing more than an act of . . . malinchismo.

MALINCHE: No! If the new conquerors fused their flesh with fertile women of Korea, of China, of Mexico, of Germany, of Africa, then I would admire them! Then they would be like my Cortés! But they don't do it. In the name of democracy, they give the orders; and in the name of freedom, they drown it. And they do it without even a shadow of passion, of surrender, of love: through calculations, through laws, through conventions, through agreements, through convenience. The red-hot iron that marked the backs of the slaves has become the brand names of the merchandise on people's backs. Indenture has reappeared with the braceros. They lock up the peoples of the world in reservations, like the ones they use to confine their Indians, to condemn them to a freedom that is so guaranteed it's sterile!

CARLOTA: It frightens me to hear you talk like that.

MALINCHE: It doesn't frighten me; but it surprises me. Pardon me. We have carried on a conversation unfit for a five-o'clock tea. I don't know how it began!

CARLOTA: I don't remember either. Oh, yes! We were talking about Mexico. I said that it had been my loved one, but not my lover.

MALINCHE: And we talked about Cortés . . .

CARLOTA: And about Juárez . . .

MALINCHE: No. We talked about love. About Cortés . . .

CURTAIN

In Ticitézcatl
or
The Enchanted Mirror

OPERA IN TWO ACTS

Translation of *In Ticitézcatl o El espejo encantado: Opera en dos actos*.
Serie de Ficción, no. 67. Xalapa, Mexico: Universidad Veracruzana, 1966.

Dramatis Personae

(In order of appearance)

Tezcatlipoca (basso profundo), later the Tourist Guide
Chorus
Tenor
Soprano
Contralto (Coatlicue)

NOTE TO *IN TICITÉZCATL*

The mix of characters in *In Ticitézcatl* may seem a bit strange or confusing to readers unfamiliar with the Aztec legends that provide the background for the opera. Using a technique he applies in a few of his other plays—for example, *Yocasta, o casi*—Novo has projected the roles of legendary figures of the past onto modern characters; specifically, he has imposed the roles of Tezcatlipoca, Quetzal-cóatl, Quetzalpétatl, and Coatlicue onto, respectively, the Tourist Guide (the bass), the desperate young man (the tenor), the student of archaeology (the soprano), and her aunt/the young man's mother (the contralto). The chorus that Novo has chosen to include is a device that was used in both classic Western opera and classic Nahuatl epic songs. Novo takes the chorus a step further by allowing it to interact with the characters.

As mentioned in the Introduction, Angel María Garibay Kintana's *Literatura de los aztecas* (1964) and his earlier *Epica náhuatl* (1945) were Novo's primary sources for *In Ticitézcatl,* along with the more ancient *Anales de Cuauhtitlan*. For additional background information to the opera, readers may want to refer to the legend of Quetzalcóatl compiled from the Aztec codices and other early texts by Garibay Kintana in *Literatura de los aztecas*.

The episode in *The Enchanted Mirror* that gives the opera its name also has its basis in Aztec legend. Garibay's version of it, again reconstructed from the early codices, appears in his book *Epica náhuatl,* a less arcane collection of legends than his *Literatura de los aztecas,* and incidentally, one of "the books they sell in the stores [that] don't give this version of the story," mentioned by the chorus in the last minutes of the opera. It evades the issue of Quetzalcóatl's incest.

In Ticitézcatl's many allusions to contemporary archaeologists have been explained in the Glossary.

ACT ONE

The action takes place in the archaeological zone of Teotihuacan.
Modern day.

After the overture by the orchestra ("El crepúsculo" or "Los cuatro soles").
Left vibrating in the air is a chord that clearly says:

Tezcatlipoca! Tezcatlipoca!

The curtain opens to darkness. Using a dimmer, the light comes up to a
mysterious glow. We see Tezcatlipoca enter the stage, with a mask and a
feather headdress.

BASS

Who dares pronounce my name? Who invokes
the great Tezcatlipoca from the bottom of time?
How can they say my name without burning their mouths?
They show they have little
(judging from their foolishness)
understanding of magic.

From the bottom of the Mictlan I have come to these temples
built by giants—oh!—during better times!
Quetzalcóatl and I were lords of this place
and here I did my tricks, I mean, my metamorphoses.
Now one comes by car; comfortably by car
to this place where I reigned as god of the night;
and there's no one to scare any more
even if I disguise myself as an *océlotl* or a tiger.
The Moon Temple, by *Dávalos Hurtado
—so competently cared for;
. . . transmitted by everyone
the old *Avenue
of the Dead, who lie stretched out on their cots
and about whom Leopoldo Batres didn't know a thing.
And here next to it, the *Palace of the Butterflies
with its green, red, and yellow paintings
in the Tea Room
discovered by the tenacious Laurette Sejourné.

Everything has changed so! But there is nothing that surprises
     me:
since we gods change, won't men change too?

History renews itself, history repeats itself:
but there's no way to take the danced tributes away from a god.
My memory is already fading: memories get worse
with the passage of time, which sours everything;
I'm not sure anymore whether it was in Teotihuacan
or if the affair happened somewhere near Tula.
The thing is that, irritated by the wisdom
of the king of the Toltecs—a *feathered serpent,
person of resources, influential official,
and a man who hoarded riches—one day
I decided to annoy him. "Let his fame be smeared,"
I told myself; and I resolved to run him up the flagpole.

How did I do it? You'll see. I'll tell you:
Quetzalcóatl lived in luxury and comfort
in an impenetrable house beyond comparison
with the condominium we gods inhabit
in the heavens. There wasn't a single old thing, or a dirty thing,
      in it.
It was made of seashells, with walls of emerald like
the kind Chalchiuhtlicue makes her skirt from.
To get in there, I had to be pretty sly:
I disguised myself (I like to disguise myself) as an old man.
I requested, in the usual manner, an audience,
which was conceded to me. And in his august presence,
I put the magic of my mirror in front of his eyes.

A mirror! That's all. A mirror! A window
through which daily we observe the spectacle
of our deterioration; which serves us as a staff
to lean on, when each morning
patient makeup covers up the wrinkle,
hides the pimple, dries up bleary eyes,
and a little dye disguises a gray hair!
Quetzalcóatl looked at himself in my magic mirror.
He was horrified to discover that he was already very old.
And that's when I slipped in my perfidious advice:
"You can be a *telpuchtli* again," I told him,
"Let me paint your body with creams and ointments."

He obeyed submissively. I worked his head
with synthetic hormones and monkey glands;

to make a long story short, I really worked him over,
and on his wrinkled face I applied a thick layer of makeup.

He looked at himself again in this magic mirror
that I so slyly manage
and found he was no longer old, nor musty, nor worn,
and he exclaimed enthusiastically, "But what am I complaining
    about?
No one even comes close to me,
since besides being king, I look as fresh as a mango!
Let them all come see me! Let's celebrate with a meeting
of the lords of the kingdom! Let them organize a parade
and proclaim this day of the *Rabbit a holiday!
Who will the idiot be who takes me for an old man?"

"You see, Lord," I told him, "what my science can
do; but you still must have a little patience.
You should take counsel, which I will give you,
and it is to try a sip of this delicious pulque."

He resisted at first:
it was a *new drink in this neighborhood,
but he agreed to taste it: some cured with a cactus apple
the way they no longer do in any cantina.
And here begins the meat of my true story:
with the pulque, a most fertile euphoria came upon him.
He was overcome by a desire more appropriate to a younger age
and burning with love, his head lost,
he ordered that they serve him the princess at room
    temperature,
and the princess was—get this—his sister!

Incest was consummated. *Black god of the night,
I paved the way for his downfall with nefarious loves.
And that was the beginning
of the fall of the Toltecs and of this city.
Because the next morning, after his nocturnal adventure,
the king had a taciturn hangover.
He lamented the sin, regretted everything
and couldn't think of any better form
of penitence for his horrendous sin
than to leave his town in flight, in shame,
accompanied only by a few little dwarfs.

About the exodus of the king, there are a few poems.
Read them in translation, by Father Garibay.
In courtly stanzas
his deeds and punishments are told;
how he suffered the beatings and cruelties of the cold north
       wind,
how he left the imprint of his behind in a rock.

I, who am an evil god, am still celebrating.
At the end of his harsh pilgrimage,
he at last arrived at the *land of red and black,
and in a sea of serpents, that is, of his *brothers,
armed with a match, he gave himself over to the rays
of the most frightful and ardent combustion.

In a luminous spark his heart burst
from the burning bonfire that left him fried like a pig skin.
He ascended quickly: he set the record
for the space travel
they have taken up nowadays—Oh, what a deluded couple—
the Russians and the North Americans!

His shining scalp, since converted
into a star, today is known as the light of the dawn.
And since your language has no *rhyme in "utli,"
I'll say its name by itself: "Tlahuizcalpantecuhtli."

History repeats itself. Circumstances change,
but not human passions and anxieties.
Quetzalcóatl swore, when he left, to return;
and in this land, anything can happen:
perhaps Quetzalcóatl has been born again,
perhaps on the staircase, or perhaps on the scaffolding
which the wise Manuel Gamio used to explore these sites,
even now he endangers the virtue of a man
held captive in the traps of pulque and women,
which snare both age and youth alike.

I would be happy if it were that way. I would be happy
to go back to my wanderings and show off my power:
power, in its idleness,
insidious, perfidious, envidious:

the power, in the end, of my mirror
over the young and over the old.

There in the distance I see a woman coming
and on the other side, a young lad . . . And there's a noisy racket
from either tourists or students from the *Polytechnic.
I'll hide! I've already said a whole *huehuetlatolli!*

(He hides. Enter the chorus of youngsters.)

(At the foot of the Pyramids of Teotihuacan.)

CHORUS
In this district
that is so different,
so misunderstood,
so renowned
for its pyramids
"For its pyramids."
"The one to the Moon."
"That is one of them."
"But there are two."
"There are more than that."
"There are more?"
"There are more?"
"There are many more uncovered
on the Avenue of the Dead."
"Many more what?"
"I'll tell you:
there are monuments;
not decayed,
but robust,
though very ancient
and dusty;
stairways
that can only be climbed on all fours.
There are attractions,
and incentives,
and archaeology.
Oh, what joy!
Daily they make discoveries

of extraordinary monuments,
and even a restaurant is operating.
Everything answers to the wise plan
to increase tourism,
designed by the man himself,
Don Miguel Alemán."
"The monuments
bring gracious moments
to the tourists
and the artists
who usually come
to see their attractions.
To this district
that is so different,
so renowned,
so restored,
we have come."

Let us strip off our chlamydes
to climb the pyramids.
"Let us listen to the archaeologists
intoning their wise monologues
and revealing to us the past
of this solitary place."
Let's go there!
Let's go there!
Let's go there! (*They begin an exit. They stop.*)

But, what do we see?
We pause
to look;
someone is coming toward our group.
He comes alone. How did he know?
When we planned this outing,
we invited no strangers.
"Something in my heart tells me:
let's hide ourselves so we can listen
to what this brave young lad
has to say to himself."
"Let's cover our heads with our chlamydes,
and he will believe we are pyramids."

"A very good idea."
Ea, ea.
"Let it be so." (*They hide.*)

TENOR (*Entering.*)
Oh, how wonderful is solitude
when the soul is oppressed by pain!
When it is one's only lover,
faithful, quiet, and young!
When pain deadens the soul
insipidly like the foam
of a *Moctezuma beer!
Moctezuma, did I say? Well, yes.
O cruel and tyrannical destiny!
It was a pre-Hispanic impulse
that brought me this far.

CHORUS
He's penitent, there's no doubt!
Something very serious is going on with him.
Let's listen.

TENOR
Tezcatlipoca!
My voice invokes your ghost!
Here, where you, according to history,
deprived a king of glory
and with your wand of virtue
returned him to youth,
look at mine, destroyed.
Well, fate had a reason
for me to be born a foundling,
and of my parents, I know nothing!

CHORUS
He alludes to a past event
and is misinformed;
he turns his stallion into a mule,
since according to opinion,
what he says, happened in Tula.
Sssh! Quiet, he continues,
let's let him finish

the complaint he modulates with his voice,
no matter whether it's Teotihuacan or Tula.

TENOR

Come to me, violent death;
quickly, that I may not feel it!
The pain makes its siege
and leaves me no alternative.
My life will go out in a blur
when I throw myself from the high tower.
And if there's no tower, a pyramid
will be my
double feature death. My life,
scarred by bitter deception!

CHORUS

What is the meaning of all this crying?
If he wants to commit suicide, let it be hara-kiri!
Let him get on with it!
He must be the victim of an Oedipus complex!
But, let's watch! Attention!
A drama is beginning to take place here,
a superhuman drama, of course;
I sense it, because a lady,
with a voice that is clearly soprano,
is coming and singing a song.

(Enter the soprano.)

SOPRANO

This is the place, historic, and pleasant too.
I'm going to walk through it frontward and backward.
I will climb its tall steps,
and from above, I will look out
upon the little hamlets;
anyway, I'm not really so old,
so I won't get tired. (*Begins to climb.*)

CHORUS

And who is this little woman
who walks in among us like this?
Aren't we going to be alone?

TENOR

A strange sight!

CHORUS

Oh, for shame!
Can you believe he made a date with her for here?
Let's observe.

TENOR

Oh, señorita!

SOPRANO

Were you talking to me?

TENOR

Talking to you, an understatement.
Don't take me for a crazy man.

SOPRANO

I didn't say . . .

TENOR

Not saying either.
I neither talk nor say: I invoke.

SOPRANO

And you say that you're not crazy?
But you were talking to yourself . . .

TENOR

That's true.
And I was complaining about my fortune;
and I got as far as wishing for death
as the remedy for my suffering.

SOPRANO

Is it that bad?

TENOR

It doesn't even have a name.
And neither do I!

SOPRANO

Oh, good man!
State your woes, then.
I am here to listen patiently;
and if my little science is able

to cure you, you can be sure
that I will try to help.

TENOR

Would you perhaps be a fairy?
Nothing in the world
can bring me relief
or cure the ills
of my painful orphanhood!

SOPRANO

No, I'm not a fairy; no, not at all;
yet my virtuous wand
will be enough to cure the health
of an agonizing man, and even a dead one.
There's nothing on terra firma or at port
that Youth cannot penetrate!

TENOR

Youth is an illusion;
I've discovered for myself.
To the pains that cripple us,
youth is the same as old age.
But it's worth little to be a lad
if one drinks from a bitter chalice;
it's not worth a thing to be a bachelor
if—I dare not say it!—
our loyal, faithful heart
has been broken like an egg
because our chest has been pierced
with the cruel knowledge of not having a mother!
It's not worth a thing to be a spring chicken;
in any case, things are going to go wrong.
But . . . here I have been discourteous,
neglectful of the presence
of your fragrance and essence,
I speak of myself, a faux pas.
I ought first to have asked you
what you are doing here where I am;
why are you outside and not inside
these walls . . .?

SOPRANO

> Answer you
> I will . . .

TENOR

> To know about your person,
> apparently very refined,
> what you apply your talents to
> and who you are . . .

SOPRANO

> You see, a girl;
> not so much a girl any more . . .

TENOR

> Yet everything indicates that you are
> a girl, and cute besides.
> Did you come alone?

SOPRANO

> Just as I wanted it.

TENOR

> And you're looking for . . .?

SOPRANO

> Let's say . . . I'm exploring.

TENOR

> Prospector, veins of gold?

SOPRANO

> My profession is homologous
> to the prospector's. I look for
> gold from time gone by. I've reduced
> my anthropologist's ambition to that.
> My talent is extraordinary;
> which is why they call me a talent;
> and at the moment I am applying it
> to visiting this monument,
> to a seminarian's task
> which I diligently document.
> And by so doing, I fulfill the requirements
> that they deem necessary
> for my college degree

—just as my aunt wishes—
of Doctor of Philosophy.

TENOR

Do you mean your aunt
has thrown you into philosophy?

SOPRANO

That's what I said. Why?

TENOR

Oh, nothing.

SOPRANO

Do you perhaps know my aunt?

TENOR

No, I don't believe so.

SOPRANO

She's very famous.
And I admit, without being ashamed,
that she is today the best contralto
whose breast abounds in trills.
Because I am not envious.
Besides, it's a moot point:
she's a contralto, and I'm a soprano.

TENOR

Yet she gives you orders, or governs you?
And why has she disposed that you should study
how two times three make six,
such a deep, eternal career?

SOPRANO

I'm an orphan; and my aunt,
whom I've lived with since I was little,
down by Taxqueña,
acts as my mother, and . . . she's determined
that I study *philosophy.

TENOR

Are you studying at the *C.U.?

SOPRANO

Of course not! *Qu'en pensez-vous!*
I am from the most upright column

of extra-fine education,
that is, I'm enrolled, as a student,
in the Feminine University.

TENOR

If my memory isn't material for an apologue,
you said you were an anthropologist.

SOPRANO

From *anthropos,* "man"; as for *logos,*
even the pedagogues know:
"study of." As for me, the subject I get into deepest,
gloomily and seriously, is Man, astray or in the flock.

TENOR

Vile subject!

SOPRANO

That depends . . .

TENOR

I assure you!

SOPRANO

Do you speak for yourself?

TENOR

(*Aside.*) (It's a deep trance!)
I speak for myself.

SOPRANO

Now it's time for you
to state your problem. And for me to try
to cure you.

TENOR

Oh, good fairy!
Why would you have come at such a good time
to this site to hear my woes?

CHORUS

How's the match seem to you?
Let's lend, let's lend an ear!
Let's lend, let's lend an ear!
He, tame as a lamb;
She, sly as a weasel;
let's lend, let's lend an ear!

TENOR

> And will your philosophical stone
> be able to heal my ill?

SOPRANO

> I'm suggesting we try.
> Let's sing—Do you want to?—a duet.

CHORUS

> They're getting close. Pair of simpletons!
> Let the orchestra begin!
> They are looking at each other and holding hands
> like a club sandwich!

TENOR

> I've found you in my path.

SOPRANO

> You crossed my path.

TENOR

> Like a bird that trills its song.

SOPRANO

> Because Destiny willed it.

TENOR

> Its trill, its trill, its trill,
> because Destiny willed it.

SOPRANO

> I long to know man.

TENOR

> I want to research my origin!

SOPRANO

> I dedicate my days to studying.

TENOR

> Me, what I'm looking for is a miracle.

SOPRANO

> Well this site is miraculous.
> You have come to a good place.
> Here we are both to find fortune,
> you and I . . .

TENOR

> You fill me with joy
> with such a beautiful prediction!

SOPRANO

Here we are to find fortune.
Let there be no more pain, no more mourning.
Let us unknit the gloomy brow,
and together, we shall ascend the stairs,
because he who picks a good tree
(I'm speaking of the tree of Science),
with diligence and patience,
surely reaches the top.

BOTH

What peace! What a delicious calm
the countryside fills the soul with!
Hope appears, precious,
like the one who doesn't want it!
And in the ruins of Teotihuacan
two kindred souls come together!
Let us open our souls and mouths
to invoke Tezcatlipoca!
Tezcatlipoca! Tezcatlipoca!

CHORUS (*Strophe*)

Fools! Do they know, perhaps,
what a dangerous step they've taken
onto the turf of Alfonso Caso
by invoking the terrifying god
who, perhaps, perhaps,
—Oh, Saint Sulpice, what punishment!—
will find their flesh edible
and carve them into a sacrifice?

(*Antistrophe*)

When dealing with the past, one shouldn't
try to get sound from a *chicharrón!
He who dares is foolish,
since he shouldn't, and shouldn't drink
or remove the ashes or the snow
from that magic bonfire.

(*Epode*)

In any case, goodbye to our outing.
We no longer enjoy
the scenery that we see,

much less
these elegant sites.
We were going to be actors,
but we are simply spectators.
That couple, I envy them;
but look at them, how fastidious!
But let's keep our mouths closed,
the one coming, is it Tezcatlipoca?

TEZCATLIPOCA (*Reappears disguised.*)
Who are you calling? It seemed to me
that you were invoking Tezcatlipoca.

TENOR
Yes.

SOPRANO
Indeed.

TEZCATLIPOCA
There's not even a trace
of those gods left. They have all been
exiled by the Baptists.

SOPRANO
Who might you be then?

TEZCATLIPOCA
A tourist guide.
Can I be of service to you? Would you like
to visit that which you see?
For me to explain what you are looking at?
For me to go with you to five or six
corners, and to visit
among these ruins, the famous
*bedrooms of the butterflies?

SOPRANO
No, good man. When it comes to that,
I'm fine by myself. I'm an anthropologist.

TEZCATLIPOCA
Then . . . I strive to serve you.
How might I? If there's a way, just ask.
Are you interested in buying idols?
I might be able to get some for you . . .

SOPRANO

They must be fake.

TEZCATLIPOCA

There are all kinds;
but I can find the way.
Here I have a mirror, for example,
found near that temple.
It's obsidian, nothing phony;
it's not like the plastic ones.
So polished, so shiny,
as if it were recently made.
And nevertheless, I assure you
that its origin is very obscure.
Look at yourselves in it. What do you see?

SOPRANO

My face.
What's so unusual about the thing?

TENOR

Let me see . . . the devil!

TEZCATLIPOCA

What do you see?

TENOR

Something that leaves me with a *six on the die.
I'm looking at myself, it's me . . . my eyes
burned out, my face tarnished . . .
My heart gives a start!
Am I this decrepit old man?

TEZCATLIPOCA

You're going to be. This dark mirror
reveals what the future will be.

TENOR

How soon?

TEZCATLIPOCA

As soon as you like.
Today, if you find it right,
you will enjoy the tranquility,
virtue, and chastity
that come only with age.

You will experience unheard-of joy
hidden to the infant and to the youth,
perturbed in adolescence
by the ephemeral gaiety
that encourages their vanity.
But . . . why are you making such a face?
Isn't that what you are aiming for?

TENOR
Of course not!

SOPRANO
What he's aiming for,
you surely don't understand.
You are ignorant of his origin. He has come here
to see if he can put it into oblivion.

TEZCATLIPOCA
That's easy. Look in the mirror;
to be oblivious is to be old.
And you, what do you want?

SOPRANO
To know
man.

TEZCATLIPOCA
Is it *twelve already?
And what's wrong with this one? You don't know him?

SOPRANO
I mean Man in general.

TEZCATLIPOCA
Well, this one, does he seem bad to you?

SOPRANO
Not really . . .

TEZCATLIPOCA
Listen to my advice:
Look at yourselves together in the mirror.
Put your heads together in it,
and through the spell of this artifact,

you will see how, in the act,
your woes dissipate.

CHORUS

It's time for us to intervene
in the spell we are watching.
There's no doubt. This place
is bewitched and unique.
Here, deposit of time,
a few vestiges still live
waiting for the *Usiglos
—I mean, because he's such a nice person—
to come to give dramatic life
and to enrich our waning dramaturgy
with their liturgy.
What will become now
of this man and this woman?
I don't trust them;
with this *uncle
they're surely going to sing a trio.
Although a trio, with more respect,
in opera is called a tercet.

TENOR

This mirror
makes me old.
How dear
life turns out to be!
How avaricious,
how mischievous
it artfully
dares
to whiten and unhair my head!

Come to me, wine!
Cruel destiny!
I, a boy,
get drunk;
I prove well
that that's the way I escape
from the phantom

that immobilizes me,
O memory, how you curse and swear!

SOPRANO (*Simultaneously.*)
To see my face
how well I face up to it;
what a jewel
of a figure!
What a doll
would describe me!
What beauty!
What nobility!
You can tell Palmolive takes care of it!

Come, wine glasses!
Let the wine run!
He, squeamish,
is here no more!
I ask him
to forget
his aboriginal
origin,
which happens sometimes, but not often!

BASS (*Simultaneously.*)
They've fallen
into the trap!
Long live drunkenness
when this mirror
that I leave them
stops working
—an ugly thought—
because it will warm them up
and confuse both of them with its spell!
Now the wizard
gives them a drink;
restless,
voluptuous,
virtuous he
will become.
They will feel it,

if not from the pulque
then from what they ask for and are served on the rocks!

CHORUS

Old fox, or *tlacuache* or *cacomizqui!*
He's going to wrap them up in a spirit of whiskey!
And once submerged in its fumes,
they will act like husband and wife!
Let's throw ourselves into it
to prevent—opium dream!—
them from consummating such a union
in this historic building,
because it's not exactly the appropriate place!

(*Da capo.*)

TEZCATLIPOCA

I invite you to a drink
of a celebrated liquor
that was bottled
on site in Europe.
Thus let us celebrate
the pleasure of running into each other here again.

TENOR

I gratefully accept, because I could really use it.
And if need be, I will even accept again.

TEZCATLIPOCA

And you, my lovely lady,
won't you toast with the young man?

SOPRANO

I will toast, take the chance,
just to see how it feels,
because I, a decent person,
have only tried eggnog.

TEZCATLIPOCA

Cheers, then. The cup is thrown,
as is the custom in Europe,
from where clothing is imported
and, at times, children's toys.
In this mischievous life

there's nothing like the *jícara*.
Even Tezozomoctli
was inclined to *octli*. (*They drink.*)

TENOR
I have emptied the glass.

SOPRANO
Yes, we see. Yes, we see.

TENOR
What happened to you?

SOPRANO
I'm thirsty, I'm thirsty.

TEZCATLIPOCA
Well, drink again,
have another sip,
and try
happiness.

TENOR (*Simultaneously with Soprano*)
What pleasure!
To drink!
Through the influence of the liquor
I feel my sadness going away.

A kiss you will give me
and infuse my adoring soul
with life, yes.
A magnificent occasion
that corner provides us.

SOPRANO (*With Tenor.*)
To drink!
What pleasure!
Come declare your love for me!
Rid yourself of woes!

At last you will dare
to leave behind
the pains that brought you here!
A wanton kiss
will get you my heart.

BOTH (*Together.*)
I'm dying of love for you.

(*Exit, hugging.*)

TEZCATLIPOCA
Go, my little ones!
Taste the poison pleasures of love!
Be one of the other
like the cat of the tom and the mare of the stallion!
Enrapture yourselves!
Coo to each other!
Delight in each other!
Throw yourselves
into the chaos of carnal delight!
Then, when finally tomorrow you wake up exhausted,
I won't answer for the sudden fright that awaits you!
Ha! Ha! Ha! Ha! Ha! Ha! Ha! Ha!

(*Exits.*)

CHORUS (*Strophe*)
I'm paralyzed with stupor
by these machinations that fill me with horror!
That perverted god, that evil god,
proceeds in an unworthy manner with people.

(*Antistrophe*)
He shows the boy the mirror
and with it he makes him
think that he is old, and that he should make merry
now, before he is no longer able.
As for the woman,
he induces her to love him
and to desire him and to provoke him!
This old anthropoid
is nothing more than a schizoid
and the most vile alkaloid!
"Why does he laugh so sinisterly?
What ending has he planned,
this master
of magic?"

(*Strophe*)

    I have guessed it! Horror! Could it be what I suspect?
    That bed, which is conjugal, will it be familial?
    She doesn't have any parents; she lives with an aunt
    who has enrolled her in the School of Philosophy;
    he lacks a mother . . . Oh, what a horrible thought!
    Could it be? Is it possible?

(*Epode*)

    But what can we do
    in such unusual circumstances?
    Nothing! Wait patiently;
    and fulfill our purpose here
    to pull, to pull, to pull
    the curtain, the curtain, the curtain!

CURTAIN

ACT TWO

SOPRANO (*Alone.*)

    Night of delight,
    night of glory,
    night of incomparable
    love.
    Oh, how many times I've dreamed of you
    under the friendly light of a star!

    It was so perfect,
    so delicious;
    the lord gave me
    everything giveable.
    Oh, I unsheathed my shy rose
    in the Palace of the Butterflies!
    I made him forget
    his ancient woes,

    I left him
    weak and helpless;
    I made him swear
    that he would love me

the same on land as in the sea!
He still sleeps,
rests,
now unstirring,
tamed,
oh! what wild beast took hold in my breast
when we passed from fortune to bed!

I am a new person,
I no longer am
the one I was yesterday, the one I was yesterday.
Now I am really the woman
who at last has known
who at last has known
who at last has known
at last has known man!

How right my aunt was
to steer me toward
philosophy
and to the theory
of knowledge!
Oh, what wonders
anthropology
had saved for me!

Did Doctor Gamio foresee
my glorious epithalamium
when he explored these ruins?
I don't know, I don't know.
But I feel the effluvium
of my matrimonium
sprouting from a day
when I was another woman!
A princess, perhaps?
Maybe a queen?
Ah, ah, ah, ah, ah!
Let Alfonso Caso worry about it,
it means nothing to me! Ah, ah, ah, ah, ah!

If I were a poet,
I would rush,
blushing perhaps,

to take hold the calamus
to describe in detail
the delicacies of the bridal thalamus.

But no; I am more discreet
than any poet
full of vanity;
and to the air alone will I give
the incandescent fire
of my private happiness!

Oh, happy nightingale
of sweet throat,
my luck is so great, so great,
that it proclaims my love!

I shall see if my enchanted prince
has already awakened.
Yes, the door is open!
I shall run, shall run to his side!
Ah, ah, ah, ah, ah!

> (*Exits. If the applause justifies it, she returns to thank the audience.*)

CONTRALTO (*Enters.*)
Stop!
Stop!
Stop!
Where are you going so fast
after leaving me—foolish, crazy girl!—
waiting for you at home
all night,
worried, nervous,
seeing that you hadn't come home from school?
Stop! Stop!
Stoooooooop!

SOPRANO
What a fright!
Is it my aunt, the contralto?

CONTRALTO
Stop!
Come here, misguided girl,
and look me in the eyes!

You have nothing to say to me?
Won't you justify yourself
or explain your behavior,
that is, if it has an explanation?
To spend the night out,
and perhaps, with a man!
Ah!
Is that it? Is that it?
There's a guilty lip print
on your mouth and on your cheek!
Ah, you're humbled, you're humbled!
Explanation! Explanation!

SOPRANO

But, Aunt! I'm not a vandal!
There's no reason to make such a scandal!

CONTRALTO

And why not!

SOPRANO

Well, there isn't, I assure you!

CONTRALTO

Do you swear?

SOPRANO

I swear!
I was going to come, you knew that!

CONTRALTO

But not to spend two days!

SOPRANO

It's because the car broke down on me
and . . . I had to spend the night
in a hotel . . .

CONTRALTO

And couldn't you
—anger burns in my chest
at your gall!—
have sent me a telegram
or at least a telephone call?

SOPRANO

I didn't think you would be angry,
since it's not really such a big deal!

CONTRALTO

But, my god!
Why not!

SOPRANO

Well, it isn't.

CONTRALTO

Yes, it is!
You're the only one I have!

SOPRANO

As well I know! As well I know!

CONTRALTO

I dedicate myself to my duties,
I worry about your education,
and make sure you don't become
the grotesque mockery of men!

SOPRANO

I take that as flattery,
but I wasn't born to become a nun!
One needs a profession to transcend men.
Some day,
O aunt of mine,
in spite of your vain efforts,
I will find the man of my dreams!

CONTRALTO

Ah, libertine!

SOPRANO

Me, libertine?

CONTRALTO

Come, hemlock!

SOPRANO

Me, libertine?
Who says so?
Don't use such a hirsute word!

CONTRALTO

Well, I see that the feared
and long-awaited time has come
when I must make the grave confession

of my justifiable
horror of men.
Listen closely:
it concerns you.
It's a grisly story,
pay attention.

SOPRANO

I'm all ears.

CONTRALTO

We are descended from an ancient family
which brings together two illustrious bloodlines:
a mother, born in Morelia,
and father, who came from Sicilia.
They called my sister Celia,
and they named me Emilia:
my mother, born in Morelia,
wanted to rhyme with Sicilia.

SOPRANO

Well, they could have named you Cecelia.

CONTRALTO

Don't interrupt this tragic story!
My sister has already gone to her glory.
Yes, your mother! My twin sister,
since Emilia was twin to Celia!
One night, we were sleeping peacefully
—as is usual in good families—
in the bedroom of Celias and Emilias,
when a man, woe is me! I never knew
how he got in, whether like a lightning bolt or like
a ray of starlight,
or if he was looking for Lupe,
who was our nanny or maid.
· The truth is that he raped us,
who was first or last? Who knows!
Faced with such a sudden, serious attack,
we shouted every which way.
But . . . it didn't help at all. And exactly
nine months later, as is the rule

—recalling the occasion moves me!—
the feared event took place.
We both gave birth,
we both gave birth;
that has been my cross to bear,
that, the atrocious memory!

Because—I tremble to think of it—we conceived twins,
twins like ourselves, after atrocious sleepless nights;
in pairs, and furthermore: one boy and one girl
Celia and I each had inside the crib.

Our father found out
and in his offended honor, as he was from Sicily,
he cursed our progeny, stains on the family,
while he cruelly murdered . . . our mother!

He said—I tremble to remember such fiery words!
(there's no doubt; he was rather bothered)—
that it would be for us like it was for those
cloistered nuns who lived before, under the old regimes,
fighting among themselves, and committing crimes
of which the most horrible was incest.

Immediately, as if they were kittens,
he gave the four innocent bambini away to the neighbors.

SOPRANO
    And I am . . .

CONTRALTO
    You guessed it? One of them!

SOPRANO
    Your daughter!

CONTRALTO
    How would we know?

SOPRANO
    You don't know?

CONTRALTO
    I don't know. There were four of you.
    I was able to steal you later. And I adore you!
    I stole you—and hid you behind the grinding stone,
    and I had you at my side, raising you until you were weaned.

But of your three siblings, what has become of them? Do I
   know?

SOPRANO

If you're not my mother . . .

CONTRALTO

I already told you that she died.
Since then I have only lived
in fear of what treacherous Destiny will bring:
The paternal curse!
Because gloomy Destiny
will try anything—
on you, incest.
And that is why, why . . .
Do you understand now?
I don't want you to come across any man, tyrant,
for it could turn out to be my nephew or your brother!

SOPRANO

But my dear aunt! You worry in vain;
among so many, how would I run across my brother?

CONTRALTO

An ounce of prevention is worth a pound of cure, I
   know.
A bird in hand is worth two in the bush.
The paternal curse threatens our lineage;
worse things you can see in Greek tragedies;
and if you run around loose,
I can't guarantee that you,
for being footloose and fancy-free,
won't run into your twin brother.
Everything is possible in this world,
and you would agree, girl, that it would be horrible!
Let's go home now. This place gives me the creeps.
It reeks of oracles—Delphic and Pythian.
Let's get out of here.

SOPRANO

No. Wait.

CONTRALTO

Wait?

SOPRANO

> Yes, wait.
> I can't go without saying goodbye to him.

CONTRALTO

> (Ah, why do I tremble?) To whom, may I know?

SOPRANO

> You'll see him in a second.
> Here he comes.

TENOR (*Entering.*)

> My love!
> Why have you abandoned me,
> why, why did you leave me,
> when the cold was coming in,
> in a bed, warm before, but without you, empty?

CONTRALTO

> What do I hear! What do I see!
> What terrible surprise comes up the walk!
> I don't want to believe it, ah, I can't believe it!
> Chronos seems to have turned back his calendar!
> This is the man who raped us twins!

SOPRANO

> It's not possible!

CONTRALTO

> The very one!
> May the earth swallow me up!

SOPRANO

> No! No! He would already be an old man!
> Without a doubt, this is someone else, since with all due respect,
> the man you see now could be your grandson!

TENOR (*Aside.*)

> My heart goes tictoc;
> could it be the effects of the cognac?
> Seeing this aging lady,
> a pluperfect emotion,
> an ancestral memory is injected
> into my desolate orphanhood.
> I have seen, I have seen those wrinkles!
> Ah, my past is being uncovered!

Oh, I have suckled from that udder
in puerile times, smiling
in the shade of Tepeyac!
My heart goes tictoc
like an ox among bric-a-brac!

BASS

The ancient legend is reborn!
This is the man! How it pleases me!
It's Quetzalcóatl, resurrected,
product of an illegitimate procedure!
It's only necessary to verify
that Coatlicue was his mother,
because there is no mother more ancient
—much proof testifies to it—
than the one who was *chichihua* to all:
the one with the big feet and big breasts,
the *rubbish eater,
the one about whom Justino Fernández
brings so much news!

CONTRALTO

And who is this who spouts off
here where no one calls him?
New person in the drama!
What's your name?

BASS

Tezcatlipoca!

CONTRALTO

Such a name!

BASS

Don't be startled!
I'm a god, not a man.
If you had listened to the prologue
that I made longer with a monologue . . .

SOPRANO

He's as tame as a dove;
he's nothing more than a tourist guide
in the service of the Museum,
except he's always joking.

He sells postcards and magazines
to those who come to visit
this place, which isn't so ugly
since it has some good views
and even recreation rooms
with modernist decor.

CONTRALTO

And what I see—
is it also the robes of Hymen?
Ah! I'm fainting! Give me a cane!
I think the oracle has come true!
This man—tell me—did he taint you?
Rob you of honor and innocence?
Leave us alone, Tezcapote!

TENOR

Ah, form that becomes corporeal!
I remember that stentorian voice!
As if in a dream, in a fog . . .!

BASS

Here the smoke screen of my mirror!
Here my tuft of feathers!
Woman who, incensed, shouts so furiously:
give in to the influence of my hypnotic,
inflexible, mischievous, and despotic power,
and tell me, do you recognize me?
Look at yourself in this magic mirror!
Stop using such a tragic tone!
What do you see, tell me?

CONTRALTO

I see my face.

BASS

Look again: what do you see behind you?

CONTRALTO

My face is blurring, my features erasing . . .
Saints above preserve me, help!
Your face appears behind me . . .

BASS

> That shows
> that you are my sister Coatlica.

CONTRALTO

> Me, Coatlica? I'm ice and rock!

BASS

> Just as I am Tezcatlipoca.
> We are both of Toltec background,
> we were gods, and we are brother and sister;
> and we carry out our arcane plans
> as we walk from one place to another.
> The family tree of which we
> are robust branches is ancient,
> except that they never write plays
> about our lives, which isn't logical.
> Today we are reincarnated: I, as a tourist
> guide, and you, as the aunt
> of a student of archaeology.
> Thus it is explained
> how you can be a mother like Coatlica
> of this decrepit tenor,
> and I can repeat the tricks
> I played in remote times,
> provoking incestuous love
> consummated in fraternal bed
> with the soprano and the tenor.
> Fake it, it's the easiest way!
> No use crying over spilled milk!

TENOR

> Mother! At last! At last I find you in my path!

CONTRALTO

> Ah, curse! Ah, destiny!
> If this isn't my son, then it's my nephew!

TENOR

> The heart is never wrong!
> Tezcatlipoca was right!

CONTRALTO

> Don't let mention of Tezcatlipoca
> fall from your lips!
> (Let's fake it, as is proper,
> making an effort to forestall.)
> I, your mother? How if I'm unmarried
> and a virgin inside and out!

TENOR

> Beloved mother,
> long lost,
> found at last!
> Sweet pleasure!
> In tender embrace
> give me your arms!
> Take the broken pieces
> of my love!

SOPRANO (*Simultaneously.*)

> He has already forgotten
> that I am his life!
> He doesn't try to coax me
> today as he did yesterday!
> Soon he will leave,
> leave me falsely,
> he doesn't hear
> the complaint of my love!

BASS (*Simultaneously.*)

> What a conflict
> when I dictate
> that this convict
> should look for a wife!
> Today as in yesteryear
> —what a case!—
> multiple damages
> I have caused again!

CONTRALTO (*Simultaneously.*)

> My forehead sweats,
> full of doubt
> that I should have to see

such a rude thing!
A son or a nephew,
tragic,
though at least I have one
—O wretched world!

(*The four repeat in unison. Then:*)

SOPRANO

I sought man diligently
to document my thesis:
Man is relative to all,
thus I discovered.
My wedding night I celebrated happily,
the sweet bridal thalamus I enjoyed,
I sinned without knowing I sinned,
I dreamed without knowing I dreamed!

TENOR

I beg your forgiveness,
I acted like a thief,
I was searching for my mother and ended up finding my sister;
my suffering is double,
it's preferable to die languishing
and disappear,
better to die.

SOPRANO

No, no, you're not right,
listen to my song,
I can be your mother although your sister or cousin in the end I
    come to be.
Good luck and pleasure
brought me to meeting my brother,
what blame have I
for being a woman?

CONTRALTO

Enough already,
enough already,
neither here
nor there.

If Papa decreed this,
what am I to do
if in the end
it happened?

BASS

Let subtle, anapestic meter
settle this domestic squabble.
And like any respectable opera,
let's close with a quartet.

SOPRANO

If that's what the Manes have planned,
let's fold, let's fold our hands.
It's obvious we are inane,
assuming we are human.

Let's sing together, let's sing!
We will celebrate the tragic ending
singing the deeds of Tezcatlipoca
with all our lungs!
Sing!

TENOR

Sing!

BASS

Sing!

CONTRALTO

Sing!

CHORUS

It's obvious we have been forgotten
seeing as they don't even invite us to sing;
but here we are, it would be a dishonor
if, at the end of an opera, the chorus didn't appear!

(*Quartet follows.*)

TENOR

Wretched
Destiny,
what do I seek
so foolishly?
Pain catches me by surprise and writes me off

writes me off
writes me off
writes me off!
An orphan I,
Thebian I
soon discovered
very early on
that the fatal destiny of the cloister
awaited me
and that all the women would flee from me
because I reek.
Ah! Ah! Ah! Ah! Ah!

SOPRANO (*Simultaneously.*)
    I trill
very well,
I shine
like a princess
and my throat sings, because
I love to, because I love to
point out
yes, to point out,
yes, to point out,
yes, to point out:
if he's my brother,
all is in vain!
*Hummingbird,
my tyrant,
he won't be worse off for it
than other husbands
like those who go to the supermarket
with the shopping cart!
Bah! Bah! Bah! Bah! Bah!

CONTRALTO (*Simultaneously.*)
    The divine
road,
I deduce,
is miserable;
it ruins and arouses,
arouses my relative,
my parturient

relative.
Siciliano
che diranno!
Ci lasciammo
E così!
The fates were fulfilled,
the unfair fates!
I was ready for anything, except
this!

BASS (*Simultaneously.*)
    With wine
    I incline
    the crude one
    and the refined one,
    and the throat accepts
    and doesn't wretch with
    the diligent
    diligent
    diligent
    cloak
    that I, the tyrant,
    served them
    with my hand
    early on!
    As with the king Quetzalcóatl,
    I inebriated their senses.
    And happily they consummated
    incest!

CHORUS
    Incest! Incest!
    I was ready for anything, except this!
    The books they sell in the stores
    don't give this version of the story!
    Incest! Incest!
    I was ready for anything, except this!
    Mystery! Mystery!
    Let the flute and the guitar sound!
    Let the *teponaxtle* and the conch echo
    the new version of Quetzalcol,

who inebriated his senses in alcohol,
and in misery drowned—
a serious thing—
the people we called the *Pueblo del Sol!
Ah! Ah! Bah! Bah! Ya! Ya! Ha! Ha! Ha!

(*Da capo: As a quartet, then alternating.*)

TENOR

Such a terrible tragedy humbles me
and fills me with horror and moderation.
I have come to see that I was born in Morelia
and nothing will save me or preserve me.
Me, born on Tarascan *petates!*
Me, author of incestuous absurdities!

SOPRANO

Well, as long as we have a family
Michoacan is the same to me as Morelia;
if it's a girl, we'll call her Celia;
if there are two, the other will be Emilia.
It's the custom to grind on *metates,*
and in this house, to give birth to *cuates!*

CONTRALTO

We are descended of an ancient family
that brings together two illustrious bloodlines.
My deceased mother, born in Morelia,
and papa, who came from Sicilia!
Thus they planned it, my vengeful
penates, Italians, lunatics!

BASS

The past is at last reconciled
when I return to play my tricks.
The ballet of Copelia is not as good
as the tragedy of Celia and Emilia!
I have once again beaten you in combat, Quetzalcóatl,
my fine-feathered twin!

CHORUS

The evil idols
are everywhere;
I sense them and smell them

here in Teotihuacan.
*Ten-dollar words and symbols
infiltrate the arts
with sorcerers in disguise that appear here wholesale.

It's tragic and it's valid
to search for them in History,
in the story of a magician
who showed them his phony mirror;
squalid, vandalous,
the affair is notorious;
he repeated the dipsomaniacal and apostate deed!

FINAL CHORUS
Worthy of eternal memory,
our gods are resuscitated here.
They reside in archaeological sites
all around Tenochtitlan.

The plans were carried out,
and the Toltec gods avenged:
the ancestors came back to life
brought together by me at these ruins.

Let us sing a hymn of glory
that convokes foreign tourism
and places the Fatherland
of this story in an eminent position!

ALL
Victoria! Victoria! Victoria! Victoria!

CURTAIN

Appendix A

MEXICANS LIKE 'EM FAT

Translation of "Los mexicanos las prefieren gordas." In *En defensa de lo usado*. In *Toda la prosa*. Mexico City: Empresas Editoriales, 1964.

In few countries does the feminine struggle against obesity take on characteristics more anguished, or more sterile, than in Mexico. Within the last few years, American cinema, with its overwhelming strength, has imbued our public, munching on salted peanuts as it contemplates the screen, with an idea of beauty that consists of its perfumed incarnations deincarnating themselves until they weigh as few kilos as possible. The occasional reading of one or another pamphlet or an article in *Popular Science* laying out the healthy advantages of being slender adds to the objective proof offered by the movies; and the not-so-technical books like *Gordos y Flacos* by Dr. Marañón—that Dr. Cabanes of the morning—have come to preoccupy our better halves, setting them on the conquest of an ideal figure, one that would reduce them to being our better thirds.

But let us set aside till later this discussion of whether such an ideal is really our ideal and whether it succeeds in its ulterior motives by provoking our admiration. Do they work? Fasts, massages, walks, kneebends and thyroid pills; total abstinence from sweets, a few puffs on a Lucky Strike in their place; as little water as possible, food without salt—this complete modern calvary leads to nothing but peremptory convalescence. Once the goal measured by the scale has been reached, the spirit relaxes, the *enchiladas suizas*—called that because of the cream that garnishes them, despite the fact that they're unknown in Switzerland—are delicious, and the adipose waves again reach high tide. Or else the patient was single, and the happiness of marriage has begun to spill over onto the hips and the double chin. Aldous Huxley, brother of a biologist after all, gracefully perceives the trajectory of Mexican beauty. "Etla," he says, "was painfully fashionable. A beauty contest has been held, and the results of this contest were found sitting next to their mothers, near the town mayor. They looked like six bulls in a cattle contest. Nevertheless, all youth retains a certain charm. What was horrible was to see in their mothers the future of that flesh!"

Of course, one can never expect a foreigner to tell the truth about any country. I don't quote Huxley here because I agree with this description or any other of the very offensive descriptions that he makes of the Mexicans of the fair sex, but precisely, girls, to demonstrate to you just how inappropriate it is to combat a Latin idiosyncracy by acquiring a Saxon one. The governesses in all the English novels were as skinny as the one must have been who wouldn't let Huxley eat suspiciously colored sweets; and Freud says that apart from our mammas, our nurses are our first ideal love, the one that determines, forever on, our tastes and inclinations. The Puritans of New England are brought back to life in the nineteenth century in the form of the American suffragists. They are, like the Puritans and the English governesses, true mummies, with eyeglasses and convictions. Overcome again, the resurrection of their bones is achieved through the perfidious weapons of the cinematographer for their propaganda. Those women must know what they are doing and why, how many Huxleys prefer, on embracing their loved ones, to create the squeaky illusion of a battle of old chairs. The Historia Patria, supported by historical materialism and by Mexican reality, teaches us that if, on the other hand, we want to be authentic, we should conduct ourselves in our feminine preferences as our ancestors did, for one thing, and for another, more importantly, as the "masses" or the "social conglomerates" of our so-called socialist country do. And it is notoriously known that although the odious intellectual elite, born into the mental straits of a corset, today likes skinny women, *campesinos,* workers and soldiers—the very nerve of our society, as they say—are the standard bearers of an unpolluted tradition that impels them, with decided predilection, to fall in love with the plumpest and softest comrades.

In support of my thesis, I can produce more evidence than would fit in an essay. The women in our history who have registered the most numerous amorous successes have never weighed less than two hundred pounds, whenever there have been scales to verify it. Opposite the young adipose sensation of Tetrazzini we can place our memory of Angela Peralta, the Mexican nightingale with habits of a hen and an absolutely soprano voice, who married three times—which is a lot for us. One of the reasons Carlota wasn't liked much in Mexican society was her slenderness, and the fact that, in contrast to the aristocratic ladies of her time, she drank only tea, while they put down large cups of chocolate, which is so fattening. And, as we know, her slenderness led to her disastrous end. Maximiliano Mexicanized himself to such a degree that he fell in love with a chubby peasant girl; and he was Mexicanized to such a degree that the Mexicans killed him. And Carlota lost so much weight that, as we know, she went crazy.

Given that pre-Cortesian art in Mexico has the disadvantage of being so futuristic that it disdains, as a general rule, painting the human figure, we cannot use it as a means to prove how fat Moctezuma's sandaled houris must have been. We can, nevertheless, deduce their weight from their dark-skinned great-great-great-great-great-granddaughters, who still use huaraches.

Malinche was the Eve of this Mexican paradise, and the robust Cortés played the happy role of a white, heavily-bearded Adam. And because he fell in love with her, she must have offered, in his eyes, an exuberant personality. He had come—and it had been a very long voyage—from a country in which the Gothic idea of beauty had not triumphed over Baroque aesthetics; a country in which Jimena, the honorable wife of El Cid, and that early Juliet named Melibea, "de dulce carne acompañada," plant a solid matron's foot firmly on the land; a country that King Roderick lost to the Moors simply because of the fat pair of legs he saw when he surprised La Cava in the palace garden in the act of showing them to her friends; a country in which the bony angels of El Greco have in Velázquez a vigorous carnal response that can, even in the Menina that's next to the dog, or even better, in *La Monstrua* by Carreño de Miranda (Museo del Prado), come close to showing myxedematous characteristics.

And Cortés brought with him a Latin artistic tradition that boils down to nothing more than a racial preference. Let us think for a minute of the art of the Renaissance. Gothicism liquidated, in architecture there is a return to heavy lines which are adorned with human figures, who, recovered now from the medieval fast, are well nourished and muscular. The Adams and Eves we are shown by painters from then on, beginning with the bas-relief of Jacopo della Quercia, Il Sodoma, Titian, even Van Eyck (in whose work, even though she is slimmer, Eve still preserves an abdomen in need of massage) are, if we want to make the example absolutely clear, quite fat. Stripped of the clothes that deceive us, we can surprise the women in the bathroom, with their identity completely revealed, and ascertain for ourselves, with the fingers of our eyes, their adiposities. The *Shepherd and Nymph* or *Diana and Actaeon* of Titian, by opening the door to Rubens for his pot-bellied Bacchanal, prepare the bath for the Susana of Tintoretto and clear the way for the curvilinear horizon of her Via Lactea. The Allegories of the man from Verona would later be no less wide, nor the idea of fertility and abundance that Jordaens and Proudhon would have, successively. The bathers of Boucher, of Daumier, of Courbet, of Millet, and of Renoir, who is content to caress them with the paintbrush as they brush their hair or put on their makeup—all these illustrious examples are shouting eloquently to us that the real truth of the matter is that we Latins like 'em fat. In the ample women of Picasso, in his *Repos de Moissonneurs,* one must see, more than anything else, a racial preference which in the Spaniards manifests itself preeminently.

The same does not occur, naturally, in Saxon art. To go no further, though in Hogarth's or Reynolds' work women and children are healthy and of good appearance, their robustness is bland and provisional like an apple, artificial and due to diets and sports, never sensual or luscious. Gainsborough's *Portrait of Mrs. Mordey and Her Children* is the most complete example of a skinny aristocratic beauty, vaporous and intellectual, that says nothing to the senses, and who, though the skinny Mr. Huxley might miss her in Mexico, would have sent Cortés back to Spain posthaste if he had found her instead of Malinche. And where would we be now?

The type of women in vogue has always responded to the architecture and industries of its times (architecture, this industry of yesterday; industry, this architecture of today). Not long ago I noticed a curious coincidence between car fenders and skirts (fenders, those skirts of cars; skirts, those fenders of women). In the earlier models, let's say till 1931, fenders and skirts were high, leaving the wheels revealed. From then till now, they have gradually covered more and more; the more expensive the car—or the more formal the dress—the more there is of them. The same with weight. These large old stone houses that the slender American tourist comes to visit in the enchanting Old Mexico, were occupied by lazy, robust matrons. One of them, Josefa Ortiz de Domínguez, sporting a Spanish veil and double chin, helped Hidalgo win independence for us in 1810. Now those who live there, in the skinny apartments that are our idea of skyscrapers, are thin girls who have about them an unforgivable air of kinship to those *machines à vivre,* with their tall, unadorned lines, that make up the modern household. Irreparably, we are letting ourselves be dragged down an alienating, industrial current. Mr. Stuart Chase, who would love us to remain authentic and primitive, is going to be greatly disappointed. Let's pause, then, to meditate on it.

A Mexican philosopher stated, not too long ago, that the national complex, and its multiple expressions of boastfulness and killing, is the much-touted inferiority complex. I regret I do not share his opinion; but my observations lead me to conclude that, if we suffer from any kind of national complex, some illness that identifies us as a race, it is the Oedipus complex. Mother's Day, recently imported to Mexico from a country in which the children remember her only on that exact day, turns out to be inappropriate in our country, where everybody lives with their mother until they die, and then she goes on living. All the people we run into on the street make us think of our mothers, no matter what time of day. We don't say Fatherland, but Motherland. And all this would mean nothing more than that we are, and it should be applauded, very good children. But the pathology begins when we begin to have fun. We go to the movies, quite clearly because it is a dark place, and there we happen to see American beauties that weigh forty pounds. We watch them indifferently, hand in sweaty hand, leaving our girlfriend with one free hand for the important business of consuming her submarine sandwich. But we prefer the theater. And as there are no theaters in Mexico, we go to the variety shows in the circus tents. The tents are adorable barracks, replete with all classes of proletarians. Tourists are cordially invited to admire these salty, picturesque theaters so similar to those in Shakespeare's time. Here we see how truly intelligent the Mexicans are, and how the Mexican Revolution has produced a communistic mishmash of jobs and diversions for the working classes. But keeping our object in mind, we see more. A young slender woman with no voice appears on the stage (because sometimes we produce this type, but we are always quick to export them, as Lupe Vélez and Dolores del Río prove conclusively). She knows how to sing and dance, but nobody applauds. That is then followed by the appearance of a fortyish siren, a true whale of jello. The auditorium goes crazy. Her song is a song of morbid origin for all of us. The young think of their mothers; the prosperous politicians look upon her as the pinnacle of their numerous aspirations. And from the enthusiastic shouts we can conclude from our indefinable, but not irrational, expectations that Mexicans prefer fatties.

Appendix B

LINEAGE CHART OF THE KINGS OF TENOCHTITLAN
AND NEIGHBORING CITIES

Incorporates information from *Chimalpahin's Historia Mexicana:
A Short History* (Massachusetts: Conemex Associates, 1978).

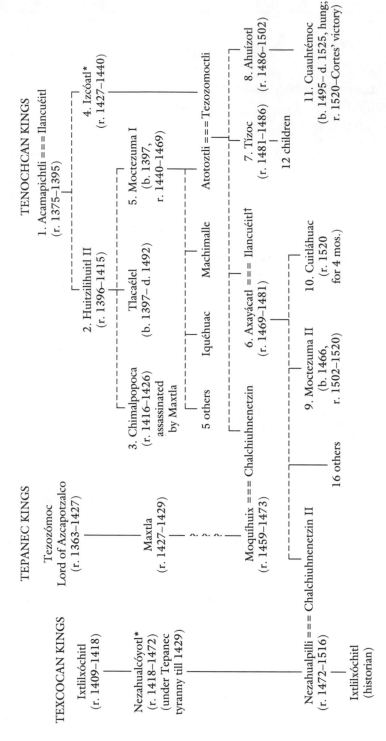

TENOCHCAN KINGS

TEPANEC KINGS

TEXCOCAN KINGS

1. Acamapichtli === Ilancuéitl
(r. 1375–1395)

4. Izcóatl*
(r. 1427–1440)

Tezozómoc
Lord of Azcapotzalco
(r. 1363–1427)

2. Huitzilíhuitl II
(r. 1396–1415)

Tlacaélel
(b. 1397– d. 1492)

5. Moctezuma I
(b. 1397,
r. 1440–1469)

Atotoztli === Tezozomoctli

7. Tízoc
(r. 1481–1486)

8. Ahuízotl
(r. 1486–1502)

12 children

11. Cuauhtémoc
(b. 1495– d. 1525, hung;
r. 1520–Cortes' victory)

Maxtla
(r. 1427–1429)

3. Chimalpopoca
(r. 1416–1426)
assassinated
by Maxtla

Iquéhuac   Machimalle

6. Axayácatl === Ilancuéitl†
(r. 1469–1481)

10. Cuitláhuac
(r. 1520
for 4 mos.)

? ? ?

Moquíhuix === Chalchiuhnenetzin
(r. 1459–1473)

5 others

9. Moctezuma II
(b. 1466,
r. 1502–1520)

Chalchiuhnenetzin

16 others

Ixtlilxóchitl
(r. 1409–1418)

Nezahualcóyotl*
(r. 1418–1472)
(under Tepanec
tyranny till 1429)

Nezahualpilli === Chalchiuhnenetzin II
(r. 1472–1516)

Ixtlilxóchitl
(historian)

*Original integrants of the Triple Alliance with the king of Tlacopan against Tepac domination.

†As noted by Novo in the "Notice" to *The War of the Fatties*, in real life Ilancuéitl was the wife of Acamapichtli, not of Axayácatl.

Appendix C

MAP OF ANÁHUAC AND CENTRAL MEXICO

Redrawn based on maps from *National Geographic*, December 1980, vol. 158, no. 6 (Washington, D.C.: National Geographic Society), p. 7704A; Hubert Howe Bancroft's *The History of Mexico*, vol. 1 (San Francisco: A. L. Bancroft and Company, 1967; reprint of 1888 edition), p. 583; and *Encyclopedia International*, vol. 12 (New York: Grolier, 1965), pp. 14–15.

ANÁHUAC
The Valley of Mexico

To Tula

Xaltocan

●Tultepec
●Cuauhtitlan

Teotihuacan ●

Ecatépec ●

Aztacoalco

Texcoco   Tezcotzingo
                  ●

Tenayuca

Azcapotzalco ●   ●Tepeyácac   ● Huexotla

LAKE
TEXCOCO

Tlacopan
(Tacuba)   ● Coatlinchan
Chapultépec   ●Tlatelolco
               ●Tenochtitlan   ● Chimalhuacan

Coyoacan
Tizaapan
        ●Iztapalapa
Huitzilopochco   + Cerro de la Estrella
Mexicalcinco   Culhuacan
               Tlahuac   LAKE
                                CHALCO
               LAKE   Xico
               XOCHIMILCO   ●Mizquic Chalco
                           Cuitláhuac
        Xochimilco
  +   ● Mixquic
Cerro Xitle   ● Ayotzinco
+
Volcán Ajusco   Volcán Iztaccíhuatl +

                      + Volcán Tlaloc
To Cuauhnáhuac
(Cuernavaca)   + Volcán Chichinautzin
                                    Volcán Popocatépetl
               Chimalhuacan ●   +

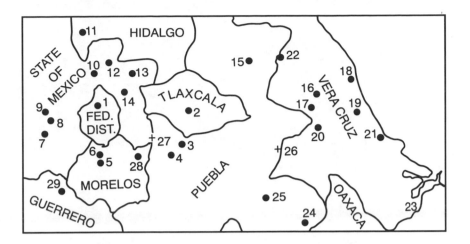

1. Mexico City
2. Tlaxcala
3. Puebla
4. Cholula
5. Cuauhnáhuac
   (Cuernavaca)
6. Ocuilan
7. Malinaltenanco
8. Toluca
9. Calixtlahuaca
10. Cuauhtitlan
11. Tula
12. Zumpango
13. Teotihuacan
14. Texcoco

15. Chiconautla
16. Xalapa
17. Coatépec
18. Villa Rica
19. Cempoala
20. Tlacotépec
21. Vera Cruz
22. Tlapacoya
23. Papaloapan River
24. Tzinacatépec
25. Tehuacan
26. Orizaba
27. Popocatépetl
28. Yacapichtla
29. Ichcateopan

Glossary

Novo wished to educate his audience about all aspects of the Aztec culture. Consequently, his text includes many Nahuatl terms that were often as foreign to Mexican audiences as they are to most English speakers. These Nahuatl terms have been included in the translation, though directors may wish to add or substitute a gloss or otherwise adjust the text according to the needs of a specific audience. The following glossary should be helpful not only to pronounce and interpret these words, but also to get a more in-depth understanding of character names.

Pronunciation. The spelling of all the Nahuatl names and terms in these works comes from transcriptions by the Spaniards. Consequently, knowledge of the Spanish alphabet is helpful in pronouncing the terms included here. All the letters are identical to the way they are pronounced in modern Spanish, with the exception of the *x,* which is often pronounced like the *sh* in *ship,* as it was in fifteenth-century Spanish. The position of stressed syllables also varies as rules for accentuation in Nahuatl differ from Spanish. (In Nahuatl, stress is always on the penultimate syllable, never the ultimate.) Approximate pronunciation appears in parentheses.

Place names. Except where noted here (e.g., *Tepanec*), adjectives and nationalities are formed by adding the suffixes *-ca(n)* and *-teca(n)*.

Acachinanco (ah-cah-chee-NAHN-coh). Name of the site of one of the water tanks in Tenochtitlan, near where Pedro de Alvarado eventually settled; lit., "place of the reed fence."

Acalan (ah-KAH-lahn). The ancient city near Tenosique, Tabasco, where Cuauhtémoc was hung by Cortés' troops.

Acallan (ah-KAH-lahn). Alternate spelling of Acalan.

acalli (ah-CAHL-lee). Lit., "water house," that is, boat or canoe. As suggested by Ixtolinque's conversation with Cuauhtémoc, Cortés' eventual construction and use of small launches marked the pivotal point in the battle for control of the lake.

Acamapichtli (ah-cah-mah-PEECH-tlee). First king of Tenochtitlan, ruled from 1375 to 1395, husband of Ilancuéitl.

ácatl (AH-cahtl). "Reed"; name assigned to certain days and years in the *tonalpohualli,* one of the Aztec calendars. Quetzalcóatl, born on the day 1-Reed (*ce-ácatl*), is often referred to by this name.

Acolhuacan (ah-cohl-WAH-can). Alternate name for Texcoco (Nezahualcóyotl's kingdom); from *atl,* "water" + Culhuacan.

Acosta, Padre (ah-COHS-tah), 1539–1600. Spanish chronicler, author of *Historia natural y moral de las Indias.*

Acuecuéxcatl (ah-kweh-KWESH-cahtl). The spring in Coyoacan, source of the Río Churubusco, which flooded Tenochtitlan; lit., "playful water."

Acuecuexco (ah-kweh-KWESH-coh). Site of Acuecuéxcatl; lit., "place of the waves."

ahuiani (ah-wee-AH-nee). See *ahuianime.*

ahuianime (ah-wee-ah-NEE-meh). Plural of *ahuiani.* Novo's gloss, "cheerer-uppers," was included in the original text. Early Spanish-Nahuatl dictionaries listed it as "one who likes pleasure," "whore."

ahuicalli (ah-wee-CAHL-lee). House of pleasure, brothel.

Ahuítzotl (ah-WEE-tsohtl). Alternate spelling of Ahuízotl.

Ahuitzotzin (ah-wee-TSOH-tseen). Alternate spelling of Ahuízotl; the *-tzin* suffix means "noble" or "beloved."

Ahuízotl (ah-WEE-sohtl). Eighth Tenochcan king, ruled from 1486 to 1502; brother of Axayácatl, Tízoc, and Chalchiuhnenetzin; father of Cuauhtémoc; uncle of Moctezuma II.

Alderete, Julián de (hoo-lee-AHN deh ahl-deh-REH-teh). His Majesty's Treasurer, arrived with reinforcements for Cortés' crew.

Alemán, Don Miguel (dohn mee-GHEL ah-leh-MAHN). President of Mexico from 1946 to 1952; notorious for his government's corruption, nepotism, and rapid development of Mexico's tourist industry, which made him a millionaire. Though he was the first civilian president after a long string of military men who had played a part in the Revolution, he was nevertheless considered a "strong" president and exerted his power accordingly. Like Calles and Cárdenas, he reorganized the ruling party, incorporating the "popular sector" (i.e., small business), and gave the party the oxymoronic name it still carries today, the Institutional Revolutionary Party (PRI). Though Novo satirizes him here, he is indebted to Alemán for taking him off the blacklist, allowing Novo to be named theater director of the National

Institute of Fine Arts by Carlos Chávez, an event that sparked Novo's major theatrical production.

alliance for progress. Although the character here refers to the Triple Alliance, Novo also alludes to President John F. Kennedy's program with this name.

allies. Axayácatl's treatment of his allies here provides Novo with a chance to satirize the ruling party of Mexico, the Institutional Revolutionary Party (PRI). Like the Triple Alliance, the PRI is, in theory, a coalition of equals: of government, urban labor, and peasant groups; however, the interests of the latter two groups are often overruled, and their support taken for granted.

Alvarado, Pedro de (PEH-droh deh ahl-vah-RAH-doh). Commander of one of Cortés' ships in voyage to mainland. He gave the order for the massacre of the Mexicans that is described in Scene 7 of *Cuauhtémoc*.

Anáhuac (ah-NAH-wahk). Valley of Mexico (i.e., Mexico City); lit., "near the water," since Lake Texcoco once nearly filled the valley.

areito (ah-RAY-toh). Popular song and dance of the Native Americans of the Caribbean and Central America.

artificial, oversized island. Tenochtitlan, like Tlatelolco, was built on an island on Lake Texcoco that had been enlarged through the use of *chinampas*.

atomizing pump. Novo's play on *bomba atómica* (the secret weapon) and *pompa atomizadora* doesn't quite come through in the English.

Avenue of the Dead. Name of the major street in the ancient ceremonial district of Teotihuacan.

Axayácatl (ah-shah-YAH-cahtl). Son of Moctezuma I or of Tezozomoctzin, accounts vary; father of Moctezuma II, Cuitláhuac, and Chalchiuhnenetzin (the second); sixth king of Tenochtitlan, ruled from 1469 to 1481; lit., "face of water."

axin (AH-sheen). A yellow or orange greasy substance produced by the insect *Llaveia axin*.

Axayacatzin (ah-shah-yah-CAH-tseen). Alternate form of Axayácatl (-*tzin* is an affectionate diminutive denoting royalty).

Ayotla (ah-YOH-tlah). City conquered by Ahuízotl, southwest of Mexico City in state of Puebla; lit., "place of the turtle"; now Ayutla.

Ayotzinco (ah-yoh-TSEEN-coh). City to south of Lake Chalco, in what is now the state of Mexico.

ayuntamiento (ah-yoon-tah-meeYEHN-toh). The Spanish form of government most used in colonial times. The Ayuntamiento de Villa Rica (Vera Cruz) was where Cortés burned his ships and proclaimed his allegiance directly to the king of Spain, thus circumventing the pesky authority of Diego Velázquez, governor of Cuba.

Azcapotzalco (as-cah-poh-TSAL-coh). City to northwest of Tenochtitlan.

Its kings, Tezozómoc and Maxtla, dominated the lake area, including Tenochtitlan and Texcoco, from 1376 until 1429 when the Triple Alliance under Izcóatl, Axayácatl's grandfather, was formed to overthrow them. Moquíhuix of Tlatelolco is the most visible descendant of the kings of Azcapotzalco. The rulers of Tlacopan (Tacuba), Coyoacan, and Ixtapalapan also occasionally, even after the rise of Tenochtitlan, claimed allegiance to the Tepanecs (i.e., the people of the Azcapotzalcan empire).

Aztacalco (ahs-tah-CAHL-coh). City near Chapultépec.

Aztacoalco (ahs-tah-coh-WAHL-coh). City on the northern shore of Lake Texcoco, in what is now the state of Mexico.

B. *B* is not a sound native to Nahuatl.

Batres, Leopoldo (leh-oh-POHL-doh BAH-tres). The earliest modern archaeologist mentioned by Novo; Mexican Inspector General of Archaeological Monuments (1900) and author of *Teotihuacan; o, La ciudad sagrada de los Toltecas* (1889). *See* Bibliography.

bedrooms of the butterflies. *See* Palace of the Butterflies.

black god of the night. One of Tezcatlipoca's many names; the four cardinal directions were assigned to Tezcatlipoca: the north was the Black Tezcatlipoca of the Night; the south, the Blue Tezcatlipoca, the Sun God (or Huitzilopochtli); the west, the Red Tezcatlipoca (or Xipe); the east, the White Tezcatlipoca (or Quetzalcóatl, for his association with Tlahuizcalpantecuhtli, i.e., Venus, the morning star).

bleed. The Aztecs occasionally pricked or pierced their tongues, earlobes, genitals, or legs with maguey spines, offering the blood in sacrifice to the gods.

blond, bearded god. A reference to Cortés and Quetzalcóatl.

brothers. Quetzalcóatl is half snake, half bird, so snakes are his brothers.

bug-eaters. Moquíhuix's insult is not unfounded; the Aztecs considered water-fly eggs a delicacy, much like we do caviar. Grasshoppers were also eaten.

cacique (cah-SEE-keh). "Chief"; not a Nahuatl word; an Arawakan word Spaniards took with them to Mexico from the Antilles.

cacomizqui (cah-coh-MEES-kee). Lit., "grazing lion" (i.e., an ocelot).

Calcimehuateuctli (cahl-see-meh-wah-tehOOK-tlee). Tenochcan general.

Calixtlahuaca (cah-leesh-tlah-WAH-cah). City conquered by Axayácatl, east of Tenochtitlan in what is now the state of Mexico.

Calles, Plutarco Elías (KAH-yes), 1877–1945. Fought in Mexican Revolution, later made general; after holding important positions under presidents Carranza (1917–1920) and Obregón (1920–1924), he was elected president. He is best known for his founding of the National Revolutionary Party, predecessor to the now-ruling Institutional Revolutionary Party, and for his strong-arm approach to politics, justified as necessary to consolidate the Revolution, for which he earned the title Jefe Máximo de la Revolución, or Maximum Boss of the Revolution. Besides being president himself (from 1924 to 1928), he personally chose and dominated the four presidents who succeeded him, until Cárdenas, the fourth, exiled him in 1935. Though originally considered a radical president, mainly for the restrictions he imposed on the Catholic Church, he also is known for the coopting and corruption of labor leaders which took place under him. Calles is a favorite target of Novo's satire, especially as he was responsible in the end for the exile (for opposing Calles' candidate in the 1929 election) of José Vasconcelos, minister of education under Obregón, and one of Novo's and the Contemporáneos' mentors.

calli (CAHL-lee). "House"; name assigned to certain days and years in the *tonalpohualli,* one of the Aztec calendars.

Callimaya (cahl-lee-MAH-yah). City conquered by Axayácatl, in Toluca, eleven leagues from Tenochtitlan; now Temapaxalco.

calmécac (cahl-MEH-cahk). A school for the noble children (the *pipiltin*) for learning reading and writing, astronomy, religion, and crafts; Novo calls its students "cadets from the military school" in allusion to the military school in modern-day Mexico City.

calpulli (cahl-POOL-lee). District, troops.

cantina (cahn-TEE-nah). Spanish for "bar."

caray (cah-RAEE). Spanish exclamation of disgust.

Cárdenas, Lázaro (CAHR-deh-nahs), 1895–1970. Fought in Mexican Revolution of 1910, later made general; president from 1934 to 1940. Although chosen by Calles for the presidency, he promptly moved to consolidate his own administration by removing Calles' favorites from power and later exiling Calles. He, like Calles, took an interest in developing institutional support for his power, reorganizing and renaming Calles' party, which later became the PRI, ruling today. Cárdenas is portrayed as the last true representative of the Mexican Revolution, mainly for his nationalization of the oil industry and expansion of agrarian reforms. Though he paid lip service to the socialist sectors, for example, by declaring education in Mexico to be "socialist" without implementing any substantial changes, and by granting asylum to Leon Trotsky, Cárdenas cannot be considered to have done much to advance socialism. Like Calles, Cárdenas retained much of his power after leaving office, often to the dismay of government officials. During World War II, he held a nominal military command and later exerted influence as an "influential elder statesman" and "consultant" to the government until his death in 1970. Cárdenas' son, Cuauhtémoc Cárdenas, a disgruntled PRI official who ran for president under an umbrella coalition of leftist parties, was the major opposition to PRI candidate Pedro Salinas in 1988. Charges of PRI electoral fraud brought thousands of citizens to the streets. His candidacy constitutes the biggest threat to PRI domination of the government in Mexico in recent years.

Carlota (cahrr-LOH-tah), 1840–1927. Charlotte Amelie, Princess of Belgium, appointed with Maximilian of Austria by Napoleon III to serve as Emperor and Empress of Mexico. She and Maximilian desperately tried to be accepted by Mexican society by naïvely donning serapes and eating tortillas. After Maximilian's execution, she returned to Europe to plead support from Napoleon. She eventually lost her mind and lived her last sixty years in a deranged state, for which she is better known in Mexico as "la loca Carlota" and has become the subject of ridicule and pity. She died during Novo's lifetime, in 1927, the same year he was setting up Teatro Ulises. *See also* tea; Juárez, Benito.

Caso, Alfonso (ahl-FOHN-soh CAH-soh), 1896–1970. Director of the Instituto Panamericano de Geografía e Historia and the Instituto Nacional Indigenista, and author of numerous important studies of pre-Columbian Mexico (*see* Bibliography), including *Pueblo del Sol,* which Novo ridicules in *The War of the Fatties* for its stereotypical characterization of Native Americans. He is mentioned in both *Cuauhtémoc and Eulalia* and *In Ticitézcatl.*

causeway. Tenochtitlan, an island on Lake Texcoco, was linked to the shores by four major stone causeways, to Tepeyácac, to Tlacopan (Tacuba), to Ixtapalapa, and to Coyoacan. *See* map, Appendix C.

Cava, La (lah CAH-vah). Nickname for Florinda. *See* Roderick.

Celestina (seh-lehs-TEE-nah). *See* Rojas, Fernando de.

Cempoala (sem-poh-WAH-lah). City in what is now the state of Veracruz; one of the first and most important cities to side with Cortés against Moctezuma.

century. Fifty-two years. The Aztecs named each year by combining the names of four days (rabbit, reed, house, flint knife) from the *tonalpohualli* with the numbers 1 to 13. A total of fifty-two (4 × 13) combinations was possible. Each time the combinations had to be repeated, a new century, or "cycle," began. The end of every century coincided with the end of the 260-day *tonalpohualli* cycle. It was celebrated with the kindling of a "new fire" for the empire. Aztecs let the fires in all the kingdom burn out, then in a ceremony atop a hill above Culhuacan, a new fire was lit on the chest of a sacrificial victim, transferred to torches, and carried throughout the kingdom. The end of every other century coincided with the end of a "Venus count," an important occasion as Venus was thought to be Quetzalcóatl. *See also* five useless days; Earthquake.

chalchíhuatl (chahl-CHEE-wahtl). Water; lit., "jade water."

chalchihuites (chahl-chee-WEE-tehs). Jade stones.

Chalchihuitlicue (chahl-chee-wee-TLEE-kweh). Goddess of lakes and rivers, sister or wife of Tláloc; lit., "jade-skirted lady." She is the goddess repeatedly addressed in "Ahuítzotl and the Magic Water."

Chalchiuhnenetzin (chahl-cheeoo-neh-NEH-tseen). Lit., "noble jade doll" or "noble jade vulva." 1. Axayácatl's sister, Moquíhuix's wife. 2. Moctezuma II's sister who was married to Nezahualpilli but killed for infidelity.

Chalco (CHAHL-coh). City on eastern shore of Lake Chalco, in what is now the state of Mexico; lit., "place of the jade."

change. As noted by Novo in the "Presentation," the Aztecs did not have fractionary currency; however, they did use a sophisticated system of currency using cocoa beans, tin tokens, and feathers filled with gold dust.

Chanticon (chahn-TEE-cohn). A goddess of fire.

Chapultépec (chah-pool-TEH-pehk). City and forest on the western shore of Lake Texcoco; lit., "hill of the grasshoppers." Toward the end of their "wandering nation" period, before the founding of Tenochtitlan, Mexicas settled here among the people of Chapultépec and stayed until the Mexicas' raids into neighboring territories for wives brought on a punitive attack from larger kingdoms. Some of them were forced to move to the island of Tenochtitlan, others were forced into serfdom in Culhuacan, then the dominant force on the lake and identified with the Tepanec empire. Moctezuma I commissioned King Nezahualcóyotl of Texcoco (part of the Triple Alliance) to build an aqueduct linking Chapultépec and Tenochtitlan, crucial to the survival of the great city. Chapultépec is now a park in Mexico City and was once the home of Maximiliano and Carlota, who lived in the Castle of Chapultépec. *See also* ears.

Chapultépetl (chah-pool-TEH-pehtl). Alternate name for Chapultépec; lit., "mountain of grasshoppers."

Chiapas (cheeAH-pas). State in southeastern Mexico bordering Guatemala.

chicharrón (chee-chah-RROHN). A snack of deep-fried pork skins; the chorus in *In Ticitézcatl* is referring to Quetzalcóatl, who according to legend set himself on fire, and according to Novo in Act I is left "fried like a pig skin"; the meaning of the whole line is akin to "Let sleeping dogs lie."

chichi (CHEE-chee). To suckle; breasts.

chichihua (chee-CHEE-wah). "Breast-woman" (i.e., wet-nurse).

Chichimeca (chee-chee-MEH-cah). A Nahua tribe, originally from northern Mexico, which conquered the Toltecs and settled in Texcoco.

They are considered nomads and "uncivilized" in comparison with the Toltecs. The Tenochcans are thought to be descendants of the Chichimecas.

chicle (CHEE-kleh). Spanish for "chewing gum"; "deformed" version of the Nahuatl *tzicli;* this is probably the origin of the brand name Chiclets.

Chicomexóchitl (chee-koh-meh-SHOH-cheetl). Lady of honor to Queen Ilancuéitl; her name is lit., "7-flower" (i.e., the day of her birth).

Chiconautla (chee-coh-NAOO-tlah). 1. City on eastern shore of what once was a strait linking Lake Texcoco to Lake Xaltocan, in what is now the state of Mexico. 2. City in northeastern Puebla.

Chimalhuacan (chee-mahl-WAH-cahn). 1. City to southeast of Tenochtitlan and directly west of Mt. Popocatépetl, in what is now the state of Mexico. 2. City on eastern shore of Lake Texcoco.

Chimalpa (chee-MAHL-pah). City to northeast of Tenochtitlan, near Lake Atocha, in what is now the state of Hidalgo.

Chimalpahin (chee-mahl-PAH-een), 1579–1660. Native historian; complete name is Domingo Francisco de San Antón Muñón Chimalpahin Cuauhtlehuanitzin.

Chimalpopoca (chee-mahl-poh-POH-cah). Lit., "smoking shield." 1. Third Tenochcan king, reigned from 1416 to 1426; consolidated the autonomy of Tenochtitlan, but was assassinated by the king of Azcapotzalco, Maxtla, Tezozómoc's son. Chimalpopoca was succeeded by Izcóatl, who avenged his death by conquering Azcapotzalco. 2. The *Códice Chimalpopoca* is an alternate title for *Anales de Cuauhtitlan* (*see* Bibliography), an important source for the stories depicted in *In Ticitézcatl.*

chinampas (chee-NAHM-pahs). Floating islands made of mud and aquatic vegetation, layered onto a woven frame and anchored by stakes and trees; these were used to create the floating gardens of Xochimilco (still in existence) and greatly extend the islands of Tenochtitlan and Tlatelolco in Lake Texcoco.

chocolate. A reminder that chocolate was an Aztec drink before it was exported to the Old World. The word, in English, Spanish, and other European languages, comes from the Nahuatl, *xocóatl.*

Cholula (choh-LOO-lah). City in what is now the state of Puebla; site of an important battle with Cortés.

Cid, El (ehl SEED). Legendary Spanish warrior, based on the life of Rodrigo Díaz de Vivar (1043?–1099), famous for his battles against the Moors, and the subject of many epics, notably *El cantar del mío Cid.*

Cihuacóatl (see-wah-COH-ahtl). High priest of Tenochtitlan, Tlacaélel's title; also, name of the fertility goddess who raised Quetzalcóatl; lit., "woman-snake."

cihuapactli (see-wah-PAHK-tlee). Type of plant used for inducing labor; *cihua*, lit., "woman" + *pactli*, "plant."

cihuapipiltin (see-wah-pee-PEEL-teen). Name given to women who die in labor; lit., "noble woman person"; from *cihua*, "women" + *pipiltin*, "nobles."

cíhuatl (SEE-wahtl). Woman.

Citlaltépetl (see-tlahl-TEH-pehtl). Mountain now known as the Pico de Orizaba on the border between the present-day states of Puebla and Veracruz.

cóatl (COH-ahtl). Snake.

Coatépec (coh-wah-TEH-pehk). City conquered by Axayácatl, to south-west of Tenochtitlan, in what is now the state of Mexico; lit., "hill of the snakes."

Coatlica (coh-ah-TLEE-cah). Alternate spelling of Coatlicue.

Coatlicue (coh-aht-LEE-kweh). Aztec god of mothers, mother of Huitzilopochtli, mother and sister of Tezcatlipoca; mother of four hundred sons (the stars) and one daughter (the Moon); also, according to some legends, mother of Quetzalcóatl (Venus); lit., "snake-skirted lady"; represented in sculpture as having a face of twin serpents; said to eat garbage.

Coatlinchan (coh-ah-TLEEN-chahn). City near the eastern shore of Lake Texcoco, in what is now the state of Mexico; lit., "house of snakes."

Cocipantli (coh-see-PAHN-tlee). Tenochcan general; lit., *coci* is a drum-beat, *pantli* is "banner" or "warrior."

coconete (coh-coh-NEH-teh). Regional Spanish for "boy" or "girl."

Cohuaxólotl (coh-wah-SHOH-lohtl). Name of a god similar to Queztalcóatl and Huitzilopochtli, possibly used interchangeably. Lit., *cohua* is "snake," Xólotl is the name of a god whose significance varies, possibly Quetzalcóatl's twin. Some accounts attribute the war on Tlatelolco to that city's attempt to build a temple honoring Cohuaxólotl to rival Tenochtitlan's great temple to Huitzilopochtli.

combustion. After Cuauhtémoc's capture, Cortés was pressured by his troops (led by the royal treasurer Alderete) to torture Cuauhtémoc until he revealed the hiding place of "Moctezuma's treasure." His feet and hands were burned, hence his "combustion"; however, all Cuauhtémoc could tell them was that the treasure had already been carried off by Spanish troops and sunk to the bottom of the lake with them during the battle of the Noche Triste. The king of Tlacopan was also tortured, as described here in *Cuauhtémoc,* Scenes 11 and 12. Novo also refers to the combustion of Quetzalcóatl, who lit himself on fire before ascending to the heavens as Tlahuizcalpantecuhtli.

contracts. President Miguel Alemán was notorious for giving lucrative "little contracts," like those described in *The War of the Fatties,* to his relatives.

Copolco (coh-POHL-coh). Ancient district of Tenochtitlan near Tlatelolco.

Cortés, Hernán (ehr-NAHN cohr-TEHS), 1485–1547. Besides conquering Mexico, Cortés had previously participated in the conquest of Cuba with Diego Velázquez, and later, in expeditions to Honduras and California. (*See* ayuntamiento.) He was awarded the title Marquis of the Valley of Oaxaca.

Coyoacan (coy-yoh-AH-cahn). Important city on the western shore of the strait between Lake Texcoco and Lake Xochimilco, where one of the causeways to Tenochtitlan began, now a neighborhood of Mexico City; lit., "place of the coyotes." Cortés built his house in Coyoacan after the Conquest, so it was initially the seat of the colonial government. Novo also lived in Coyoacan and established a theater there, where a street was named after him. His book *Breve historia de Coyoacán* (*see* Bibliography) gives an excellent overview of the town's history.

Coyohuacan (coy-yoh-WAH-cahn). Alternate spelling for Coyoacan.

Coyohuaque (coy-yoh-WAH-keh). Adjective for someone from Coyohuacan.

Coyotépec (coy-yoh-TEH-pehk). City north of Tenochtitlan, in what is now the state of Mexico; lit., "coyote hill."

Cozcacuauhtenco (cohs-cah-kwaw-TEHN-coh). Ancient city conquered by Axayácatl.

Cristóbal (krees-TOH-bahl). Traitor to Cuauhtémoc and Tetlepanquétzal, as described in *Cuauhtémoc,* Scene 12. His name before baptism was Mexicalcinco.

C.U. (seh-OOH). An abbreviation for Ciudad Universitaria, name for the campus of the Universidad Nacional Autónoma de México (UNAM). Novo uses it to rhyme with *Qu'en pensez-vous!* Despite its excellent scholarship, many members of the Mexican elite shun the UNAM because it is a public school.

cu (coo). Temple; like *cacique,* the word was brought from the Antilles by Spaniards.

cuani (kwah-NEE). Eater.

cuate (KWAH-teh). Mexican word for "twin."

Cuauhnáhuac (kwaw-NAH-wahk). City to south of Tenochtitlan where Cortés eventually settled; now Cuernavaca in the state of Morelos.

Cuauhtémoc (kwaw-TEH-mohk). 1. Eleventh and last Tenochcan king, Ahuízotl's son, Axayácatl's nephew; resisted Spaniards and opposed Cortés after death of Moctezuma II; was later tortured and put to death by Cortés' troops on the way to Honduras; lit., the "falling eagle." 2. Cuauhtémoc is also the first name of the 1988 opposition leader Cuauhtémoc Cárdenas, son of Lázaro Cárdenas. Recollection of the heroic resistance of his Aztec namesake could only have had a positive impact on his candidacy.

Cuauhtitlan (kwaw-TEET-lahn). City five leagues to the northwest of Tenochtitlan, in what is now the state of Mexico; lit., "near the trees."

cuauhxicalli (kwaw-shee-CAH-lee). Lit., "eagle's cup"; a stone box or cup for holding human hearts during rituals. The large *cuauhxicalli,* eight feet around and two and a half feet thick, ordered by Tízoc is also called a "sacrificial stone."

Cuaupopoca (kwaw-poh-POH-cah). Ixtolinque's brother.

Cuauppopoca (kwaw-poh-POH-cah). Alternate spelling of Cuaupopoca.

Cuécuex (KWEH-kwesh). The witch who warned Ahuízotl of the dangers of diverting the water from Acuecuéxatl.

Cuepopan (kweh-POH-pahn). Ancient town that helped Axayácatl defeat Moquíhuix.

Cuextecans (kwesh-TEH-cahns). Natives of Cuextlan, city conquered by Axayácatl, in present-day state of Veracruz; now called the Huasteca.

cuitla (KWEE-tlah). Feces; from *cuítlatl.*

Cuitlacuani (kwee-tlah-KWAH-nee). Prince of Cuitlapilco; lit., "dung eater," from *cuitla* + *cuani,* "eater."

Cuitláhuac (kwee-TLAH-wahk). Lit., *cuitla* plus *tlahuac,* "an edible algae found in the lake." I. Axayácatl's son, king of Mexico for eighty days in 1520, after his brother Moctezuma II's death; forced the Spaniards to flee Tenochtitlan to Tlacopan on what the Spaniards call the "Noche Triste"; died of a disease brought by the Spaniards. 2. City in central Veracruz. 3. City of Tlahuac on Lake Chalco, in what is now the state of Mexico.

Cuitlapilco (kwee-tlah-PEEL-coh). City conquered by Axayácatl.

Cuiuacan (kwee-WAH-cahn). Alternate spelling of Coyoacan.

Culhuacan (cool-WAH-cahn). City on Iztapalapan peninsula, on the strait between Lake Texcoco and Lake Xochimilco.

Cuyuacan (kwee-WAH-cahn). Alternate spelling of Coyoacan.

Dávalos Hurtado, Eusebio (DAH-vah-lohs oor-TAH-doh). Mexican anthropologist and author; among the subjects he wrote about are Mexican cooking (like Novo; *see* Bibliography), cranial deformation of Tlatelolcans, and physical anthropology.

deciphered. A reminder that the Aztecs did use an alphabet.

de dulce carne acompañada (deh DOOL-seh CAHR-neh ah-cohm-pah-NYA-dah). "Accompanied by sweet flesh" (i.e., plump).

del Río, Dolores. *See* Río.

Do-Gooder of America. A liberal translation of Juárez' sobriquet, "el Benemérito de las Américas."

dogs. The native dogs of Mexico, the *izquintli,* were mute and were considered a delicacy by the Aztecs. Modern Mexican Spanish has taken *escuintle* or *escuincle* to refer humorously to children.

Doña Marina. *See* Marina.

Durán, Fray Diego (fry deeEH-go doo-RAHN), 1537?–1588. Spanish chronicler, author of *Historia de las Indias de la Nueva España.* (*See* Bibliography.)

ears. Before the founding of Tenochtitlan, the Tenochcans living under Culhuacan rule were forced to fight alongside the Culhuacans in a war against the Xochimilcans. Taking prisoners, the Tenochcans cut an ear from each of them. However, because the Tenochcans did not hold the prisoners captive themselves, but instead sent them to be held with the prisoners the Culhuacans had taken, it appeared at the end of the battle that the Tenochcans had been unable to take any prisoners. When the chief of Culhuacan criticized the Tenochcans for their failure to take prisoners, the Tenochcans answered by producing the missing ears of the thirty prisoners that had only one.

Earthquake. Name (sometimes translated as "movement") assigned to one of the days and years of the *tonalpohualli;* considered unlucky because the fifth sun (*see* Quetzalcóatl) was predicted to be destroyed on 4-Earthquake; instead, Cortés arrived during a cycle of 4-Earthquake.

Ecatépec (eh-cah-TEH-pehk). City conquered by Axayácatl, on the northern shore of Lake Texcoco, in what is now the state of Mexico.

eggs. In Spanish it is a burlesque pun on eggs and testicles.

enchiladas suizas. Lit., "Swiss enchiladas."

El Cid. *See* Cid, El.

El Malinche. *See* Malinche, El.

Epcóatl (ehp-COH-ahtl). Axayácatl's court minion; lit., "rattle snake."

estaba muy buena (ehs-TAH-bah MOO-ee BWEH-nah). Lit., "she was very good"; an expression perhaps better applied to ripe fruit, it is often used to describe a voluptuous woman.

Eulalia (ehoo-LAH-leeah). See Guzmán, Eulalia.

extinction. According to legend (and the *tonalpohualli*), the Aztec world had already been destroyed four times by the time Cortés arrived, once by jaguars, once by wind, once by fiery rain, and once by water (a flood). Predictions said the fifth extinction would come during the cycle 4-Earthquake. *See also* Quetzalcóatl; Earthquake.

F. F is not a sound native to Nahuatl.

Falling Eagle. Literal translation of Cuauhtémoc's name.

feathered serpent. Literal translation of Quetzalcóatl's name.

Fernández, Justino (hoos-TEE-noh fehr-NAHN-des), 1914–1977. Mexican painter and sculptor, author of *Coatlicue; estética del arte indígena antiguo.* See Bibliography.

five useless days. To supplement the 260-day calendar cycle of the *tonal-pohualli,* the Aztecs also used a calendar based on the solar year, like the Gregorian calendar. The year was composed of eighteen 20-day months, for a total of 360 (18 × 20) days. The remaining five days of the solar year were not assigned to any month and were considered useless and unlucky days: there were limitations, like blue laws, on the type of work that could be done, pregnant women stayed inside for fear of being turned into wild animals, and people let their fires burn out, to be relit from a flame kindled on the chest of a sacrificial victim. *See also* Earthquake; century.

floating house. See *acalli.*

Florentine Codex. An alternate name for Sahagún's *General History of the Things of New Spain.*

flowery wars. Prearranged, ritual wars between the Tenochcans and other nations for the purpose of capturing men to sacrifice; the Nahuatl word for the wars, *xochiyaotli,* comes from *xóchitl* or "flower," often used as a metaphor for blood.

four floods. *See* extinction; Quetzalcóatl; *tonalpohualli.*

Fox. Novo has used poetic license here since there was no day of the Fox; however, he represents the logic of "unlucky days" fairly accurately. See *tonalpohualli.*

Fray Bartolomé. *See* Olmedo.

Gamio, Manuel (mah-NWEHL GAH-meeoh), 1883–1960. Mexican Director of Anthropology, author of important works on Teotihuacan, including a guide for tourists viewing the ruins. *See* Bibliography.

Garibay, Father (gah-ree-BY), 1892–1967. An important researcher and translator of Nahuatl literature. His work served as an important source for Novo's opera. *See* Bibliography.

golden sun. A gift from Moctezuma, sent to Cortés in Vera Cruz, since melted down for bullion.

Gómez de Cervantes, Alonso (ah-LOHN-so GOH-mes deh cehr-VAHN-tes). Magistrate of Mexico City in 1587.

Gonzalo de Sandoval. *See* Sandoval.

Guatemocín (gwah-teh-moh-SEEN). The Spaniards' mispronunciation of Cuauhtémoc's name.

Guzmán, Eulalia (eh-oo-LAH-leeah goos-MAHN). Mexican historian, archaeologist (a Ph.D. with studies in Mexico and Germany), and educator who in 1949 discovered what she alleged to be the remains of Cuauhtémoc, based on the oral tradition of the town where she found them, Ichcateopan. Local residents produced documents, guarded as family heirlooms, allegedly signed by the monk Motolinía, known as "Defender of the Indians," telling the story of Cuauhtémoc's birth and reign in Ichcateopan and how his body had been secretly carried from Acallan, site of his death in 1525, to Ichcateopan for burial in 1529. In the early 1950s, an investigation of Guzmán's findings was carried out by a hostile group of anthropologists, the Gran Comisión Investigadora de los Restos de Cuauhtémoc, accused of paying more attention to politics than to science. The political nature of the investigation was compared to Galileo's testimony before the church tribunals of his time. Perhaps the best quote describing the controversy surrounding Eulalia's claims comes from Arturo Arnaiz y Freg, "History will bring nothing to light through the new industry of tomb seekers, although this kind of research will indeed help us to get to know our contemporaries much better." Guzmán's claims were not affirmed. However, in 1975, a presidential decree declared the town a historic city, without admitting to the validity of Guzmán's claims. In 1976, the evidence was re-examined by a commission from the National Institute of Anthropology and History and again found the evidence insufficient, though not fraudulent, as had been suggested in 1951. In 1978, by order of the governor of Guerrero—the state where the grave had been discovered—the skeleton was reconstructed to be displayed in a marble and glass tomb at the church where it had been found. Mysteriously missing from the skeletal remains, which had last been handled by the investigating committee, were the atlas, the first cervical vertebra, and the misshapen third metatarsal, which had been key factors in asserting the identity of its owner, since Cuauhtémoc had been tortured by burning his feet. Guzmán's story is told in the *Códice de Cuauhtémoc* by Dolores Roldán. *See also* Bibliography; *Cuauhtémoc;* and the Introduction, Part III.

Guzmán, don Juan de (dohn hwahn deh goos-MAHN). Christian name of Ixtolinque, lord of Coyoacan.

hermaphrodite. Novo, of course, knew the difference between a lesbian and a hermaphrodite. He uses the term here as Sahagún did.

Hibueras, Las (lahs ee-BWEH-rahs). The Gulf of Honduras.

Hidalgo, Father (ee-DAHL-goh), 1753–1811. Priest, martyr, and father of Mexican Independence of 1810; gave the famous Grito de Dolores which allegedly initiated the struggle.

Hill of Toltecs. Literal translation of Tultépec, city to north of Teotihuacan.

Historia Patria (ees-TOH-reeah PAH-treeah). The official history of a country. Novo, not a historical materialist, is being facetious. *See also* Izcóatl.

Holguín, García (gahr-SEE-ah ohl-GHEEN). The Spanish soldier who captured Cuauhtémoc.

Hospital de Jesús (ohs-pee-TAHL deh heh-SOOS). Hospital in downtown Mexico City established through Cortés' last will and testament.

hour of the flute playing. 9 o'clock P.M.

huaraches (wah-RAH-chehs). Mexican sandals.

huehue (WEH-weh). Old; old man; senior (see *huey*).

Huehuecuauhtitlan (weh-weh-kwaw-TEET-lahn). Lit., "place next to the old tree"; place where Quetzalcóatl stopped in his exodus.

huéhuetl (WEH-wehtl). Name of a type of vertical drum.

huehuetlatolli (weh-weh-tlah-TOHL-lee). Lit., "tales of old people" or "talk of the ancients" (i.e., history). This is the title for a speech Novo gave commemorating Cuauhtémoc.

Huémac (WEH-mahk). 1. Astrologer priest who lead the Toltecs to found Tollan (Tula), predecessor to Teotihuacan; lived to be three hundred years old; wrote book of history and prophecies that included the prediction of Quetzalcóatl's return. The "no good end" Huémac came to, mentioned in *The War of the Fatties,* resulted from his demand that tribute owed him by the Nonoalcans be paid in women whose hips measured four outstretched hands across. His rejection of anything less angered his subjects and led to his downfall. 2. Alternate name of Quetzalcóatl, king of Tula, who brought civilization to the Toltecs; he abandoned them to go to the East because the people did not learn from his teachings.

Huexotla (weh-SHOW-tlah). City near eastern shore of Lake Texcoco, in what is now the state of Mexico.

huey (WAY). Old; senior. Huey Moctezuma is Moctezuma I, as opposed to Moctezuma II, who is the one Cortés met.

Huitzillatzin (wee-tsee-LAH-tseen). The lord of Huitzillopochco; lit., "noble hummingbird."

Huitzillopochco (wee-tsee-loh-POHCH-coh). Alternate spelling of Huitzilopochco.

Huitzilopochco (wee-tsee-loh-POHCH-coh). Ancient name of the river and neighborhood of Mexico City now called Churubusco, known for its spring; lit., "place of Huitzilopochtli."

Huitzilopochtli (wee-tsee-loh-POHCH-tlee). Aztec god of war, patron of Tenochtitlan; lit., "left-handed hummingbird." Left-handed people were thought to be good fighters and for that reason were used to deliver the coup-de-grace in some sacrificial ceremonies.

human sacrifice. Tlacaélel would indeed have lived during the period when human sacrifice was perfected in Tenochtitlan, that is, beginning in the reign of Izcóatl, when Tlacaélel first took office.

hummingbird. A native American bird; metaphor for warrior and for Huitzilopochtli.

Hymen. The Greek god of marriage.

icpalli (eek-PAH-lee). Throne.

Ichcateopan (eech-cah-teh-OH-pahn). City in Guerrero where, in 1949,

Eulalia Guzmán discovered under the main altar of a 16th-century church what she alleged were the remains of Cuauhtémoc. *See* Guzmán, Part III of the Introduction. Cuauhtémoc's mother, Cuayauhtitali, according to various early codices, may have been from Ichcateopan.

Ihuimécatl (eel-wee-MEH-cahtl). Sorcerer of feathered belts.

Ilancuéitl (ee-lahn-KWAYTL). Lit., "skirt of an old woman"; in *The War of the Fatties,* she is Axayácatl's sterile wife; in real life (1349–1383), according to Novo, she was Acamapichtli's wife; other accounts suggest she was his mother.

Ilhuicamina (eel-wee-cah-MEE-nah). *See* Moctecuhzoma Ilhuicamina.

in (een). The.

in situ. Latin for "in the site."

incensed straws. Straws filled with herbs to smoke.

Iquéhuac (ee-KEH-wahk). One of Moctezuma I's sons; took refuge in Tlatelolco after Axayácatl was chosen instead of him to be Moctezuma's successor.

Ixtapalapa (eesh-tah-pah-LAH-pah). City and peninsula on the southern shore of Lake Texcoco where one of the causeways to Tenochtitlan began; it nearly divided the waters of Lake Texcoco and Lake Xochimilco; hence, lit., "place across the water."

ixtle (EESH-tleh). Textile made from woven agave.

Ixtlilxóchitl (eesh-tleel-SHOW-cheetl). Lit., "flower face." 1. King of Texcoco, Nezahualcóyotl's father; died in battle defending his kingdom against Tezozómoc. *See also* Triple Alliance. 2. Historian Fernando de Alva Ixtlilxóchitl, ca. 1577–ca. 1648, author of *Historia de la nación chichimeca. See* Bibliography.

Ixtolinque (eesh-toh-LEEN-keh). Lord of Coyoacan.

Izcóatl (eesh-COH-ahtl). Lit., "obsidian snake"; fourth Tenochcan king, ruled from 1427 to 1440. Through Nezahualcóyotl's urging, he helped form the Triple Alliance, which brought an end to Tenochcan domination by Maxtla and Tezozómoc, Moquíhuix's grandfather. As mentioned in *The War of the Fatties,* Act II, Scene 1, Izcóatl did indeed promptly burn all records of the past in order to rewrite history, thus anticipating Orwell by over five hundred years. The confusion over the exact year Tenochtitlan was founded, noted in the "Presentation," is a direct consequence. *See also* Revolution.

Iztacxóchitl (ees-tahk-SHOW-cheetl). Axayácatl's mistress; lit., "white flower."

Iztahuacan (ees-tah-WAH-cahn). City on the border of the Chichimec empire; lit., "place of the plains" or "desert."

Iztapalapa (ees-tah-pah-LAH-pah). Alternate spelling of Ixtapalapa.

jade skirts. A metaphor for the sea and for Chalchihuitlicue, the "jade-skirted lady," goddess of lakes and rivers.

jícara (HEE-cah-rah). A gourdlike fruit, whose shell, when dried, is used as a cup.

Jimena (also spelled Ximena, hence, shee-MEH-nah). Wife of El Cid.

Juárez, Benito (beh-NEE-toh HWAH-rehs), 1806–1872. Leader of the liberal constitutional Reform movement in Mexico in the 1850s, which included limits on the powers of the Church. Jailed by President Santa Anna in 1853, he took asylum in the U.S. after his escape. Later, when President Comonfort fled in the face of a conservative revolt, Juárez, as Minister of Justice and legal successor, declared himself president (and was recognized by the U.S.). Debts incurred during the consequent civil war between Liberals and Conservatives were one of the pretexts for the French intervention in 1861 that established Maximiliano and Carlota as rulers. Juárez set up government in El Paso del Norte, now called Ciudad Juárez, and hoped to play U.S. expansionism against French imperialism. After the withdrawal of Napoleon's troops, he captured and executed Maximiliano and won reelection in 1867 and 1870, but died in office. His government was constantly broke, and in an effort to raise money, once sold off 4.5 million acres of government land, mostly to hacendados and large industrialists, and offered transit rights across the Tehuantepec Isthmus to the U.S., for which he was much criticized. Born of humble Zapotec parents in Oaxaca and orphaned early in life, his story is often compared to Lincoln's—for his sobriety, humble origins, faith in the constitutional system, and as noted in the Dialogue, for his habit of wearing a frock and top hat, which he wore, in part, to hide his indigenous origins at a time when there was still much prejudice against Native Americans. He worked as a lawyer before entering politics.

La Cava. *See* Cava.

Lagunilla, La (lah lah-gooh-NEE-yah). Lit., "the little lake," a lagoon midway between Tenochtitlan and Tlatelolco.

La Malinche. *See* Malinche, La.

land of red and black. *See* black god of the night.

lightning. The way the Aztecs described gunfire.

macanas (mah-CAH-nahs). Obsidian-edged machetes or swords.

macehuales (mah-seh-WAH-lehs). See *pipiltin*.

Machimalle (mah-chee-MAHL-leh). One of Moctezuma I's sons; took refuge in Tlatelolco after Axayácatl was chosen over him to be Moctezuma's successor.

machochtli (mah-CHOCH-tlee). Not derived from the Spanish *macho*, as

Novo's suggestive question mark might lead readers to believe, though its true meaning may be related—it is possibly a combined form of *maitl,* "hand."

maguey (mah-GAY). Maguey plant, used for making pulque (an alcoholic drink) and rope.

malacate (mah-lah-CAH-teh). Loom.

Malinaltenanco (mah-lee-nahl-teh-NAHN-coh). City conquered by Axayácatl to the southwest of Tenochtitlan, in what is now the state of Mexico.

Malinche, El (ehl mah-LEEN-cheh). This nickname, usually applied today to doña Marina, was also applied to Cortés.

Malinche, La (lah mah-LEEN-cheh). Nickname (considered derogatory) for doña Marina.

malinchismo (mah-leen-CHEES-moh). Term taken from the nickname for doña Marina to describe either a preference for foreign things or a betrayal of Mexico.

Marina, doña (DOH-nyah mah-REE-nah). A Native American woman, by varying accounts a slave, a prostitute, or the orphan daughter of nobility (with a story similar to Moses'); she was given to Cortés as a gift in Tabasco; she served as his interpreter and companion and bore him two sons. Cortés later gave her away to another Spaniard.

Marqués (mahr-KEHS). One of Cortés' titles after the Conquest was Marqués del Valle de Oaxaca.

Maximiliano (mahk-see-mee-leeAH-noh), 1832–1867. Ferdinand Maximilian Joseph, Archduke of Austria, and later, in 1864, installed by Napoleon III—supposedly through the invitation of "an assembly of [Mexican] notables" and a trumped-up plebiscite—as emperor of Mexico. Caught between the Liberals and Conservatives who had been at war, faced with intense nationalism, and having little experience as a ruler, he was never able to gather a base of support. His tragicomic reign ended when Napoleon withdrew French troops from Mexico to send to Prussia. Maximiliano was captured and executed by Benito Juárez. His wife was Carlota.

Maxtla (MASH-tlah). 1. Son of Tezozómoc; ruled Texcoco from 1427 to 1429, until his defeat by Nezahualcóyotl and the Triple Alliance. 2. Lord of Coyoacan from 1410 to 1431.

maxtli (MASH-tlee). Loincloth.

Melibea (meh-lee-BEH-ah). One of the two main characters in *La Celestina,* the Spanish Juliet.

metate (meh-TAH-teh). Grinding stone.

Metépec (meh-TEH-pehk). City to southeast of Tenochtitlan, in what is now the state of Puebla.

Mexica (meh-SHEE-cah). Name of unknown origin given to the Aztecs by their god Huitzilopochtli after relocating to the Valley of Mexico.

Mexicalcinco (meh-shee-cahl-SEEN-coh). City to the south of Tenochtitlan on the Iztapalapan peninsula, on the edge of Lake Texcoco.

Mexicalcingo (meh-shee-cahl-SEEN-goh). Renegade, informed on Tetlepanquétzal and Cuauhtémoc.

Mexican. Used interchangeably to denote either the Nahuas (Tenochcans) or the modern Mexicans.

Mexicáyotl (meh-shee-CAH-yohtl). Mexican.

Mexico. 1. Tenochtitlan. 2. The Valley of Mexico (i.e., Anáhuac). 3. Modern-day Mexico City. 4. Mexico, the country.

Michoacán (mee-choh-ah-CAHN). State in southwest Mexico; capital is Morelia.

Mictlan (MEEK-tlahn). Lit., "place of the dead."

Mixcóatl (meesh-COH-atl). City on Lake Texcoco; lit., "snake-fog."

Mizquic (MEES-kweek). Also spelled Mixquic; city south of Lake Xochimilco, now part of the Federal District.

mocihuaquetzqui (moh-see-wah-KEHTS-kee). Women who die in childbirth; lit., "a few precious, full women."

Moctecuhzoma Ilhuicamina (mohk-teh-coo-ZOH-mah eel-wee-cah-MEE-nah). *See* Moctezuma I. Lit., Moctecuhzoma is "angry lord," Ilhuicamina is "archer of the stars"; hence, "wrathful lord who shoots for the stars."

Moctezuma (mohk-teh-SOO-mah). A brand of Mexican beer.

Moctezuma I (mohk-teh-SOO-mah). Axayácatl's father; an accomplished leader in Izcóatl's wars, he became the fifth Tenochcan king and ruled from 1440 to 1469 with Tlacaélel's counsel.

Moctezuma II (mohk-teh-SOO-mah). Axayácatl's son; ninth Tenochcan king, ruled from 1502 to 1520; killed in an attack while held prisoner by Cortés.

Montezuma (mohn-teh-SOO-mah). Spanish mispronunciation of Moctezuma. The soldiers in *Cuauhtémoc* refer to him as *the* Montezuma, mistaking his name for his title.

Moon Temple. One of the pyramids in Teotihuacan.

Moquíhuix (moh-KEE-weesh). King of Tlatelolco, reigned from 1459 to 1473; lit., *moq* is "full of," *huix* is a maguey spine; figuratively, a pulque drinker.

Moquihuixtli (moh-kee-WEESH-tlee). Alternate spelling of Moquíhuix.

Morelia (mo-REH-leeah). Capital city of the state of Michoacán.

Morelos (mo-REH-los). José María Morelos y Pavón, 1765–1815. Priest and hero of Mexican Independence, often portrayed wearing a tight cap.

Moteuhczoma Ilhuicamina (moh-teh-ook-SOH-mah eel-wee-cah-MEE-na). *See* Moctecuhzoma Ilhuicamina; Moctezuma I.

Moteuhczoma Xocoyotzin (moh-teh-ook-SOH-mah shoh-coy-YOH-tseen). *See* Moctezuma II. Lit., "Moctezuma ("angry lord") the Younger."

Moyotlan (moy-YOH-tlahn). Ancient city that aided Axayácatl in battle against Tlatelolco.

nacatamalli (nah-cah-tah-MAHL-lee). Meat (*nácatl*) tamales.

Nahua (NAH-wah). An Aztec.

Nahuatl (NAH-wahtl). Language of the Aztecs.

Napoleon III, 1808–1873. Emperor of France from 1852 to 1871; sent troops to Mexico with the pretext of collecting debts incurred during that country's civil war. Intended to establish a puppet state with Maximiliano and Carlota at the head. *See also* Juárez.

new drink. Pulque was introduced to Teotihuacan during the reign of Iztaccaltzin (833–885), coincidentally about the same time the cults to Huitzilopochtli and Tezcatlipoca began to replace those to Quetzalcóatl and Tlaloc, and shortly before the end of the abandonment of Teotihuacan.

Nezahualcóyotl (neh-sah-wahl-COY-yohtl). Nezahualpilli's father; the engineer, poet, and king of Texcoco. He built the Chapultépec aqueduct and served as the "brain" of the Triple Alliance. He was known as the most cultured of the classical kings. Lit., the "fasting or hungry wolf."

Nezahualpilli (neh-sah-wahl-PEE-lee). Prince of Texcoco; lit., the "fasting prince" or the "hungry prince."

Nonoalco (noh-noh-WAHL-coh). A district of ancient Mexico; lit., "place of the foreigners."

novel. Nezahualcóyotl did not, of course, write a novel. However, many of his poems that tell of his life have been preserved and translated. Some are included in Gabriel Zaid's *Omnibus de poesía mexicana* (Mexico: Siglo XXI, 1971, 1972) and in compilations by Miguel León Portilla.

Oaxaca (wah-HAH-cah). City and state of southern Mexico.

océlotl (oh-SEH-lohtl). An ocelot.

octli (ohk-tlee). Wine.

Ocuilan (oh-KWEE-lahn). City to southwest of Tenochtitlan, in what is now the state of Mexico.

Olmedo, Fray Bartolomé de (fry bahr-toh-loh-MEH deh ohl-MEH-do). One of the church men on Cortés' expedition.

Omexóchitl (oh-meh-SHOW-cheetl). Clever name Tlacaélel proposes for Xochichihua and Xochihuetzi; lit., "2-Flower" (i.e., a day from the Aztec calendar). See *tonalpohualli*.

One-Reed. Quetzalcóatl's name before initiation as a warrior. The name is based on his birthdate, One-Reed. See *tonalpohualli*; *ácatl*.

Oquiztli (oh-KEES-tlee). Another title of Tlacaélel's; see *Quilatzli* for origin.

Orozco y Berra, Manuel (oh-ROHS-koh ee BEH-rrah). Contemporary Mexican historian. *See* Bibliography.

Ortiz de Domínguez, Josefa (hoh-SEH-fah ohr-TEES deh doh-MEEN-ghes), 1764–1829. Also known as "la Corregidora de Querétaro," heroine of the Mexican independence struggle.

Otomí (oh-toh-MEE). A native race and language of Mexico, found in the present-day states of Guanajuato and Querétaro; the Otomís were pushed north by the Texcocans and Tepanecs, thus Cuitlacuani could well have been Otomí.

Otompan (oh-TOHM-pahn). One of the twelve great cities of pre-Cortesian Mexico, to the northeast of Tenochtitlan, in the state of Mexico; now called Otumba.

Our Lady of Guadalupe. Catholic virgin said to have appeared at Tepeyácac in Azcapotalco. The causeway is usually called the causeway of Tepeyácac.

Pahuacan (pah-WAH-cahn). Site of one of the water tanks in Tenochtitlan.

Palace of the Butterflies. A temple in Teotihuacan where paintings of butterflies are ubiquitous. They have been interpreted by Séjourné as representations of the human soul or fire.

Papaloapan (pah-pah-loh-AH-pahn). River passing through what are now the states of Oaxaca and Veracruz; lit., "place of the butterflies."

Paseo de la Reforma (pah-SEH-oh deh lah reh-FOR-mah). A major boulevard going from downtown Mexico City to Chapultépec, beautified, incidentally, by Maximiliano, who lived in Chapultépec.

personal. The original reads "¿nos tuteamos?" Cuauhtémoc notes that Eulalia has stopped using the formal "usted" form of address.

petate (peh-TAH-teh). Spanish word for *pétatl*.

pétutl (PEH-tahtl). A finely woven palm mat, used to sleep on.

philosophy. In Mexico, the school of philosophy is similar to the college of letters and science in the United States.

pic-nic (PEEK-neek). The Spanish word *pic-nic* has been borrowed from the English, but is here used humorously by Novo because of its phonetic similarity to many Nahuatl words.

pipiltin (pee-PEEL-teen). Noble people, as opposed to the *macehualtin* (the masses), and the *mayeques* (the peasants and slaves).

pipiltzintzin (pee-peel-TSEEN-tseen). The noble children; lit., "beloved beloved people."

pochtecan (poch-TEH-cahn). Merchant travelers; defined by Novo as combination ambassadors, business agents, spies, and diplomats. *See also* Yacatecuhtli.

Pochtecáyotl (poch-teh-KAH-yohtl). Alternate form of *pochtecan*.

Polytechnic. One of the large universities in Mexico City, rival to the Universidad Nacional Autónoma de México (UNAM).

Popoloca (poh-poh-LOH-cah). In Nahuatl, "barbarian"; also, as previously in European languages, someone from another nation or one who speaks another language.

pozole (poh-SOH-leh). Mexican soup of hominy, chile, and meat.

Pueblo del Sol (PWEH-bloh dehl SOHL). Lit., "people of the sun"; name used by Alfonso Caso to describe the Aztecs in the title of one of his books (*see* Bibliography). Novo objects to its romantic connotations, and pokes fun at Caso in the "Presentation" for *The War of the Fatties* and in *In Ticitézcatl*.

pulque (POOL-keh). An alcoholic drink made from fermented maguey juice. *See* new drink.

quecholli (keh-CHOHL-lee). A certain kind of bird with fine plumage.

quetzal (KEH-tsahl). A brightly colored bird with extremely long tail feathers (which look like a snake when the bird is in flight; *see* Quetzalcóatl), found in Mexico and Central America. Because its feathers were highly valued by the Aztecs, the word also came to mean "precious."

Quetzalcóatl (keh-tsahl-COH-ahtl). Lit., "quetzal-snake"; the wind god and the god of civilization who gave the Aztecs agriculture, art, metalworking, and the calendar. Quetzalcóatl was a god the Aztecs inherited from the Toltecs, along with the Toltecs' more advanced civilization. Quetzalcóatl is also the name of a Toltec king (*see* Huémac). The war between Quetzalcóatl and Tezcatlipoca mentioned in the "Presentation" for *The War of the Fatties* involved a fight over who would be the sun. It began at a time when Tezcatlipoca was sun. Quetzalcóatl knocked him out of the sky and into the water, making himself the sun. The fight repeated itself four times, and each time the sun was destroyed, humans were transformed into a different animal shape. Hence, the Aztecs were living in the age of the Fifth Sun when Cortés arrived. *See also* extinction; Earthquake; four fires; *tonalpohualli*.

Quetzalcol (keh-tsahl-COHL). Shortened form of Quetzalcóatl.

Quetzalhua (keh-TSAHL-wah). Name of the Tenochcan officer who, according to Torquemada, killed Moquíhuix.

Quetzalpétatl (keh-tsahl-PEH-tatl). Quetzalcóatl's sister; lit., "precious sleeping mat."

quexquémetl (kesh-KEH-mehtl). Aztec muumuu.

Quilaztli (kee-LAHS-tlee). Name of a witch or god; lit., "plant stork" or "green stork."

rabbit. Name assigned to one of the days and years of the *tonalpohualli*, one of the Aztec calendars. *See also* century. Given that Quetzalcóatl's fall was in part caused by Tezcatlipoca's mirror carved in the shape of a rabbit, it is appropriate that the date it occurs is also a day of the rabbit.

refugees. Tenochtitlan was founded when the Tenochcas were forced to flee from Chapultépec.

Revolution. Tepecócatl refers to Tenochtitlan's war of independence against Tezozómoc under Izcóatl; however, Novo also alludes to his government's various reinterpretations of the Mexican Revolution of 1910 in this passage. *See also* Izcóatl.

rhyme in "utli." The Spanish version of *The Enchanted Mirror* is rhymed; Spanish has no native words that can rhyme with "Tlahuizcal-pantecuhtli."

Río, Dolores del (doh-LOH-rehs dehl REE-oh), 1905– . Mexican movie actress.

road of subordination. Ixtolinque is referring to the causeway that linked the town with Tenochtitlan.

Roderick. Also known as Don Rodrigo; last Visigoth king of Spain; overcome in 711 by the Moors in the battle of Guadalete. According to legend, his rape of La Cava led Count Julián of Cueta, her father, to side with the Moors and to encourage their invasion and subsequent seven-hundred-year stay.

Rojas, Fernando de (fehr-NAHN-doh deh ROH-hahs), 1510–1538 or 1541. Author of *La tragicomedia de Calisto y Melibea,* also known as *La Celestina*. The name of its main character, Celestina, who intervenes in the relationship of Calisto and Melibea, has come to mean "matchmaker."

Rotonda de Hombres Ilustres (roh-TOHN-dah deh OHM-brehs ee-LOOS-trehs). Monument in Mexico City for the tombs of national notables. Novo wrote a short comic play set there, called *Diálogo de ilustres en la Rotonda,* 1966.

rubbish eater. Coatlicue.

Sacra, Augusta, Cesárea, Católica, Real Majestad (SAHK-rah, aoo-GOOS-tah, seh-SAH-reh-ah, cah-TOH-lee-cah, reh-AHL mah-heh-STAHD). Holy, August, Caesarian, Catholic, Royal Majesty.

Sahagún, Fray Bernardino de (saah-GOON), 1499?–1590. A Spanish-born Franciscan monk, he enrolled the help of many Native American informants to write and illustrate one of the most important sources on pre-Hispanic culture, *General History of the Things of New Spain,* in Nahuatl with a (loose) translation to Spanish by Sahagún.

San Antonio and San Pablo. Sites of watering holes built by Ahuízotl in Tenochtitlan.

Sandoval, Gonzalo de (gohn-SAH-loh deh sahn-doh-BAHL). A very important soldier and skillful commander in Cortés' troops; a hard-liner.

scientific reconstruction. Though not necessarily scientific, one unflattering reconstruction of Cortés caused quite a scandal when Diego Rivera revealed his mural in the Mexican National Palace. Rivera also sketched a rendition of Cuauhtémoc based on the shape and size of the skull found by Eulalia Guzmán and by using various archaeological charts on cranial measurements. It is reproduced in Roldán's *Códice de Cuauhtémoc. See* Bibliography.

Séjourné, Laurette. French anthropologist, author of several books on archaeology, art, and religion of Teotihuacan, including a book describing the Palace of the Butterflies.

Si vis pacem, para bellum. Latin for "If you wish peace, prepare for war."

"Sing, O muse . . ." Axayácatl cannot quite remember where he has heard the line before because it is the opening line of Homer's *Iliad*.

six. A six on a die is bad luck in craps.

skin. By some accounts, the Native Americans initially mistook the Spaniards' armor for their skin.

smoking papers. *See* incensed straws.

Soconusco (soh-coh-NOOS-coh). Now the state of Chiapas.

sométicos (soh-MEH-tee-kohs). Archaic form of *sodomitas,* Spanish for "sodomites."

sorcerer. Tezcatlipoca.

stag. A horse, since there were no horses in the New World before the Spaniards brought them.

stones have gone mute. This is an oft-quoted line from historians' descriptions of the Conquest. It has also served as the title of at least one book.

Suárez y Peralta, Juan (SWAH-res ee peh-RAHL-tah), 1537–c. 1590. Mexican historian. *See* Bibliography.

sun stone. A carved circular stone used for sacrifices to the sun, mistakenly referred to as the calendar.

supinos (sooh-PEE-nohs). Sahagún's use of this word as a noun is unclear. As an adjective it means "in a horizontal position, like that of the palms facing up when the hands are extended perpendicular to the body." He may perhaps have meant something akin to "eunuchs."

surgery. The Aztecs did indeed perform surgical operations.

Tabasco (tah-BAHS-coh). State in southeastern Mexico that gave its name to tabasco sauce.

Tacuba (tah-COO-bah). Modern name for Tlacopan.

tamali (tah-MAH-lee). A tamale; meat packed in cornmeal and steamed inside banana leaves or corn husks.

Tarascan (tah-RAHS-can). Name of the fifteenth-century civilization around the lake of Pátzcuaro in Michoacán, Querétaro, and Guanajuato; known for its fierce warriors who were able to keep the area from becoming part of the Aztec empire. Axayácatl reportedly lost 20,000 warriors in a single battle with the Tarascans.

Taxqueña (tahs-KEH-nyah). An important street in the southern part of Mexico City.

tea. In his essay "Los mexicanos las prefieren gordas" ("Mexicans Like 'em Fat"), Novo has this to say about Carlota and tea: "One of the reasons Carlota wasn't liked much in Mexican society was her slenderness, and the fact that, in contrast to the aristocratic ladies of her time, she drank only tea, while they put down large cups of chocolate, which is so fattening. And, as we know, her slenderness led to her disastrous end. Maximiliano Mexicanized himself to such a degree that he fell in love with a chubby peasant girl; and he was Mexicanized to such a degree that the Mexicans killed him. And Carlota lost so much weight that, as we know, she went crazy." Novo is, of course, being facetious.

Tecónal (teh-COH-nahl). Moquíhuix's prime minister.

tecpan (TEHK-pahn). Palace.

Tecualoyan (teh-kwah-LOY-yahn). City conquered by Axayácatl.

Tecuani (teh-KWAH-nee). Tomahuazintli's father.

Tecuichpo (teh-KWEECH-poh). Cuauhtémoc's cousin and wife; Cuitláhuac's widow; Moctezuma's daughter.

Tecuhtli (teh-COO-tlee). Lit., "prince" or "grandfather"; title given to exceptional warriors, and a suffix to many of the men's names.

Tehuacan (teh-WAH-cahn). City in what is now the state of Puebla.

Tehuantépec (teh-wahn-TEH-pehk). 1. City conquered by Axayácatl on the Pacific coast of southern Oaxaca. 2. Isthmus between the Gulf of Mexico and the Gulf of Tehuantépec (Pacific Ocean).

telpuchtli (tehl-POOCH-tlee). Young stud.

Temacpalco (teh-mahk-PAHL-coh). Lit., "place of the hand prints."

temazcalli (teh-mahs-CAHL-lee). Sweathouse, sauna.

Tenayuca (teh-nah-YOO-cah). City to the north of Tenochtitlan, now part of the Federal District.

ten-dollar words. The original reads "esdrújulos," that is, words stressed on the antepenultimate syllable, pronunciation which was considered fashionable and more cultured at one time.

ten-liner. The original reads "décima," a form of poetry in Spanish with stanzas of ten eight-syllable lines. Axayácatl jokes that it is appropriate for Ilancuéitl's ten children.

Tenochcan (teh-NOHCH-cahn). Person from Tenochtitlan.

Tenóchcatl (teh-NOHCH-cahtl). Aztec singular form of Tenochca(n).

Tenochtitlan (teh-nohch-TEE-tlahn). Lit., "place of the prickly-pear cactus"; city with an estimated 300,000 inhabitants at the height of the empire. *See* Chapultépec for an explanation of its founding in 1325.

Tenuchtitlan (teh-nooch-TEE-tlahn). Alternate spelling of Tenochtitlan.

teocalli (teh-oh-CAHL-lee). Temple; lit., "house of the gods."

teocuítlatl (teh-oh-KWEE-tlahtl). Gold; lit., "excrement of the gods."

Teotihuacan (teh-oh-tee-WAH-cahn). Capital city of the Toltecs, to the northeast of Tenochtitlan, in what is now the state of Mexico; site of the Sun and Moon Pyramids; lit., "place where the gods come."

Tepanecans (teh-pah-NEH-cahnz). The people of Azcapotzalco, from which Moquíhuix and the Tlatelolcans are descended. The Tlacopans were once also part of the Tepanec empire—which explains why Calcimehuateuctli does not trust them—as were the people of Coyoacan, which is one reason Cuauhtémoc has difficulty gaining Ixtolinque's cooperation. *See also* Tezozómoc; Triple Alliance.

Tepecócatl (teh-peh-COH-cahtl). Tenochcan general.

Tepeyac (teh-peh-YAHK). *See* Tepeyácac.

Tepeyácac (teh-peh-YAH-cahk). City on the north edge of Lake Texcoco, in ancient times joined to Tenochtitlan and Tlatelolco by a causeway; site of the alleged apparition of Our Lady of Guadalupe.

teponaxtle (teh-poh-NASH-tleh). A two-tongued horizontal, cylindrical drum.

tepuchcalli (teh-pooch-CAHL-lee). Trade school for the artisan class (*macehualtin*) to learn farming and warfare; compare *calmécac*.

terra firma. Unlike Tenochtitlan and Tlatelolco, which were built on *chinampas* in the middle of Lake Texcoco, Coyoacan was built on solid ground.

Tetlepanquétzal (teh-tleh-pahn-KEH-tsahl). Lord of Tlacopan, executed with Cuauhtémoc in 1525.

teul, pl. *teules* (tehOOL, tehoo-lehs). Lit., "gods"; word used by the Aztecs to refer to Cortés and his troops.

Teutenanco (tehoo-teh-NAHN-coh). City conquered by Axayácatl.

Teuxaoalco (tehoo-shah-WAHL-coh). City conquered by Axayácatl.

Texcoco (tesh-COH-coh). City on eastern edge of Lake Texcoco, in what is now the state of Mexico; ruled by Nezahualcóyotl, founder of the Triple Alliance; like the Toltecs, the Texcocans were considered to be more highly civilized than the Tenochcans.

Tezcapote (tehs-cah-POH-teh). Shortened form of Tezcatlipoca.

Tezcatlipoca (tehs-cah-tlee-POH-cah). The supreme god, the original god; lit., the "smokey mirror." The war between Tezcatlipoca and Queztalcóatl mentioned by Novo may refer to the fall of Tula, the city of King Quetzalcóatl, and to the legendary fight for control of the sun, described under "Quetzalcóatl." *See also* black god of the night.

Tezcoco (tehs-COH-coh). Alternate spelling of Texcoco.

Tezcotzingo (tehs-coht-TSEEN-coh). City to the east of Texcoco, now Molino de Flores (Flower Mill) National Park, in the present-day state of Mexico.

Tezcuco (tehs-COO-coh). Alternate spelling of Texcoco.

tezontle (teh-SOHN-tleh). The light porous stone used in the reconstruction of Tenochtitlan; a red porous amygdaloid.

Tezozómoc (teh-soh-SOH-mohk). Moquíhuix's grandfather (reigned from 1363 to 1427); he succeeded in subjugating the Texcocan king Ixtlilxóchitl, Nezahualcóyotl's father and Nezahualpilli's grandfather. The Tenochcan kings from Acamapichtli to Izcóatl were also Tezozómoc's tributaries. His daughter married Huitzilhuitl II, second king of the Tenochcans. His vicious son Maxtla succeeded him, first killing his own brother and later Chimalpopoca, third king of the Tenochcans and Tezozómoc's grandson. Their ruthless tyranny brought about the formation of the Triple Alliance.

Tezozómoc, Fernando Alvarado (fehr-NAHN-doh ahl-vah-RAH-doh teh-soh-SOH-mohk), 1519–1598. Historian, author of *Crónica mexicáyotl.*

Tezozomoctli (tch-soh-soh-MOHK-tlee). Chalchiuhnenetzin and Axayácatl's father, according to Torquemada.

tiánguez (teeAHN-ghehs). Spanish for *tianquiztli.*

tianguis (teeAHN-ghees). Spanish for *tianquiztli.*

tianquiztli (teeahn-KEES-tlee). Open air market, especially that of Tlatelolco.

Ticitézcatl (tee-see-TEHS-cahtl). Lit., "the mirror doctor," i.e., Tezcatlipoca.

tícitl (TEE-seetl). Doctor.

Tiger Knights. One of the special, high orders of Aztec knighthood reserved for exceptionally skilled combatants; they wore war dress made of ocelot skin.

Titlacahuan (tee-tlah-CAH-wahn). One of the names of Tezcatlipoca; translated by some as "we are his slaves"; lit., *titlan* is "messenger," *cahuan* is "to catch on fire."

Tizapan (tee-SAH-pahn). City southwest of Tenochtitlan, near Coyoacan and what is now San Angel, part of the Federal District.

Tizaapan (tee-sah-AH-pahn). Alternate spelling of Tizapan.

Tízoc (TEE-sohk). Lit., "chalk leg"; seventh king of Tenochtitlan, ruled briefly from 1481 to 1486, after Axayácatl. He was poisoned by his generals for lack of military prowess and for a nonviolent outlook.

Tizocatzin (tee-soh-CAH-tseen). Alternate name for Tízoc. The -*tzin* suffix means "noble."

Tlacaélel (tlah-cah-EH-lehl), 1397?–1492. The Cihuacóatl of Tenochtitlan, said to be the twin brother of Moctezuma I, ninety years old at the time of *The War of the Fatties; tlácatl* is "man."

Tlacatécatl (tlah-cah-TEH-cahtl). One of Tlacaélel's titles.

Tlacatecuhtli (tlah-cah-teh-COO-tlee). Lit., "prince of men"; the highest political and military title in Tenochtitlan; it is balanced by the religious position of Cihuacóatl.

Tlacopan (tlah-COH-pahn). City, now called Tacuba, on the western edge of Lake Texcoco, joined to Tenochtitlan in ancient times by a causeway; Cortés' troops were chased to this city after their catastrophic defeat, called the Noche Triste or Sorrowful Night.

Tlacotépec (tlah-coh-TEH-pehk). 1. City on what is now the Morelos-Puebla border, near Popocatépetl. 2. City in what is now the state of Veracruz, near the border with Puebla.

tlacuache (tlah-KWAH-cheh). See *tlacuatzin.*

tlacuatzin (tlah-KWAH-tseen). Opossum, a native American animal; its tail was used as a laxative.

Tlahuizcalpantecuhtli (tlah-wees-cahl-pahn-teh-COO-tlee). Lit., "lord of the house of dawn," i.e., Venus, the morning star; according to legend, Venus was created upon Quetzalcóatl's ascension to the sky.

Tlaloc (TLAH-lohk). 1. Rain god, liked sacrifices of children; from *tlalli* "earth" and *octli* "wine," that is rain or "wine of the earth." 2. Name of volcano south of Mexico City.

Tlalocan (tlah-LOH-cahn). Cemetery; lit., "place of Tlaloc."

Tlaltenco (tlahl-TEHN-coh). Ancient city; lit., "place at edge of the earth."

Tlaltípac (tlahl-TEE-pahk). Name of the site of the sacrifices described in "Ahuítzotl and the Magic Water"; lit., "above the world."

Tlapacoya (tlah-pah-COY-yah). City on the eastern edge of Lake Chalco, now in the state of Mexico.

Tlatelolco (tlah-teh-LOHL-coh). Lit., "mountain of earth"; originally a separate island to the north of Tenochtitlan, it was joined to the island of Tenochtitlan through the use of the *chinampas;* today part of Mexico City, site of the Plaza of Three Cultures, and of the 1968 repression of the student movement.

Tlatelulcaten (tlah-teh-lool-CAH-tehn). Alternate spelling for Tlatelolcan, pertaining to Tlatelolco.

Tlatelulco (tlah-teh-LOOL-coh). Alternate spelling of Tlatelolco.

Tlatilolco (tlah-tee-LOHL-coh). Alternate spelling of Tlatelolco.

tlatoani (tlah-toh-WAH-nee). Soothsayer; governor; lit., "he who speaks well."

Tlaxcala (tlahsh-CAH-lah). Lit., "city of bread"; city and state east of Tenochtitlan; protected by fierce warriors and the Sierra Madre Oriental, it maintained its independence from the Aztec empire, though through the "flowery wars," it often ended up providing captive warriors for Moctezuma's sacrificial celebrations—one of its motives in becoming Cortés' most important ally against Moctezuma.

Tlaxomulco (tlah-shoh-MOOL-coh). Ancient city.

Tlazoltéotl (tlah-soh-TEH-ohtl). A night god, interpretation varies; is patron of thieves and lovers, both considered to be most active at night; lit., "god of trash."

tlecuilpan (tleh-KWEEL-pahn). Cemetery; lit., "the place of the paintings," i.e., a temple.

Tohuenyo (toh-WEH-nyoh). Name of the chile vendor whose form is taken by Titlacahuan; lit., "naked offering."

Toltecs (TOHL-teks). The people from Tula, the Aztecs' most highly civilized predecessors.

Tomahuazintli (toh-mah-wah-SEEN-tlee). Chalchiuhnenetzin's maiden; Novo has invented her name, combining Nahuatl words, intending it to reflect her large behind.

tonalpohualli (toh-nahl-poh-WAHL-lee). The Aztec calendar, lit., the "sun counter," used for divination purposes; identified each day of its 260-day cycle with a combination of one of twenty names (crocodile, wind, house, lizard, snake, death, deer, rabbit, water, dog, monkey, grass, reed, jaguar, eagle, vulture, earthquake or movement, flint knife, rain, flower) with the numbers 1 to 13. Like Catholics who are sometimes named after the patron saint of the day they were born, Aztecs sometimes assigned their children the name of the day they were born (e.g.: Chicomexóchitl, "7-Flower"; and Ce-ácatl, "One-Reed," Quetzalcóatl's birthname). Some days, like Earthquake, were considered unlucky. The sun was predicted to be destroyed on 4-Earthquake, and Cortés arrived during a week beginning with 4-Earthquake. *See also* extinction; century; five useless days; Quetzalcóatl.

tongue. *See* bleed.

Torquemada, Juan (tohr-keh-MAH-dah), born between 1557 and 1565; died in 1624. Spanish monk and historian, author of *Monarquía indiana*. *See* Bibliography.

totolla (toh-TOHL-lah). Female turkey.

totolli (toh-TOHL-lee). Turkey chicks.

Totonacan (toh-toh-NAH-cahn). A Huastecan, someone from the area to the east of Mexico City, especially along the Gulf Coast.

Totoquihuatzin (toh-toh-kee-WAH-tseen). A Tepanec king.

Tozotzomatzin (toh-soh-tsoh-MAH-tseen). Alternate spelling of Tzotzomatzin.

Triple Alliance. Alliance formed in 1429 by Tenochtitlan (King Izcóatl), Tlacopan, and Texcoco (King Nezahualcóyotl), originally to overcome Maxtla, Tezozómoc's successor, king of Azcapotzalco. The Tepanec domination was brought to an end, and King Nezahualcóyotl regained his father's kingdom. *See* Izcóatl.

Tula (TOO-lah). Capital of the Toltec civilization—original city destroyed in 1116—in what is now the state of Hidalgo north of Mexico City.

twelve. Possibly a humorous reference to Cinderella's curfew.

tzicli (TSEE-klee). See *chicle*.

Tzinacatépec (tsee-nah-cah-TEH-pehk). City conquered by Axayácatl, in what is now the state of Puebla, near the Oaxaca border.

tzompantli (tsohm-PAHN-tlee). A skull rack.

Tzotzoma (tsoh-TSOH-mah). Alternate form of Tzotzomatzin.

Tzotzomatzin (tsoh-tsoh-MAH-tseen). Lord of Coyoacan; son of Tezozómoc; lit., "ragged one."

Tzutzuma (tsoo-TSOO-mah). Alternate spelling of Tzotzomatzin.

Tzutzumatzin (tsoo-tsoo-MAH-tseen). Alternate spelling of Tzotzomatzin.

uncle. The title is used for any relative or respected man, not necessarily the brother of one's parent.

Usiglos (oo-SEE-glohs). Novo has Hispanicized the name of Rodolfo Usigli (1905–1979), Mexican poet, essayist, and dramaturge, to fit the rhyme scheme. *See* Bibliography.

Vera Cruz (beh-rah CROOS). Complete name for this town, founded by Cortés in 1519 on the eastern coast of Mexico, is Villa Rica de la Vera Cruz, lit., "rich village of the true cross." *See* ayuntamiento.

Villa Rica (bee-yah REE-cah). *See* Vera Cruz; ayuntamiento.

Vitzilan (wee-TSEE-lahn). Site of one of the water tanks in Tenochtitlan; lit., "place of the hummingbird."

Vitzilopuchtli (wee-tsee-loh-POOCH-tlee). Alternate spelling of Huitzilopochtli.

Wilson, Thomas Woodrow, 1856–1924. U.S. president from 1913 to 1921, he refused to recognize the government of Victoriano Huerta who had come to power in a coup against Francisco Madero (first Mexican president after the overthrow of Díaz); sent troops to occupy Vera Cruz and to block an arms shipment to Huerta, and sent a punitive expedition into northern Mexico to capture Francisco (Pancho) Villa.

Xaltelolco (shal-teh-LOHL-coh). Former name of Tlatelolco; lit., "mountain of sand."

Xaltocan (shal-TOH-cahn). City on the edge of the ancient lake of the same name, to the north of Tenochtitlan, in what is now the state of Mexico; lit., "place of the sand."

Xico (SHEE-coh). City on an island in Lake Chalco, south of Tenochtitlan, in what is now the state of Mexico.

Xiuhtecuhtli (sheeoo-teh-COO-tlee). God of fire.

Xihuacan (shee-WAH-cahn). Lit., "place where the turquoise is."

Xochichihua (shoh-chee-CHEE-wah). Lady (I) of the Tenochcan court; lit., "flower-breast lady."

Xochihuetzi (shoh-chee-WEH-tsee). Lady (II) of the Tenochcan court; lit., "flower smile."

Xochimilco (shoh-chee-MEEL-coh). Town built on *chinampas* in Lake Xochimilco south of Tenochtitlan, where Tenochcans got their flowers; lit., "place of the fields of flowers"; called "Moctezuma's floating gardens" in tourist guides.

xóchitl (SHOH-cheetl). Flower; figuratively, blood.

Xóloc (SHOH-lohk). Fort and bridge about half a league from Tenochtitlan along the Ixtapalapan causeway.

yacapíchtlica (yah-cah-PEECH-tlee-cah). Stone carving; derived from Yacapichtla (lit., "place of the subtle arts"), city south of Tenochtitlan.

Yacatecuhtli (yah-cah-teh-COO-tlee). Lord of the Nose; he who orients; patron god of the Pochtecáyotl.

Yáñez, Alfonso (ahl-FOHN-soh YAH-nyehs). Cortés' second soldier.

Yoaltecuhtli (yoh-ahl-teh-COO-tlee). Male childbirth god; lit., "lord of the night."

Yoaltícitl (yoh-ahl-TEE-seetl). Female childbirth god; lit., "night doctor."

zaquan (SAH-kahn). A kind of bird with brightly colored feathers.

zona roja (soh-nah ROH-hah). Red-light district; also possibly a pun on *zona rosa,* an area in downtown Mexico City which has been extravagantly renovated.

Zumpanco (soom-PAHN-coh). City, today called Zumpango, north of Mexico City, in the state of Mexico.

Bibliography

Abbreviations used in the Bibliography:
Col.   = Colección
IMSS = Instituto Mexicano del Seguro Social
INAH = Instituto Nacional de Antropología e Historia
INBA = Instituto Nacional de Bellas Artes
UNAM = Universidad Nacional Autónoma de México

FOR AN EXCELLENT QUICK INTRODUCTION

National Geographic, December 1980, vol. 158, no. 6. Washington, D.C.:
National Geographic Society. Includes: "The Aztecs," by Bart Mc-
Dowell, photographer David Hiser, artist Felipe Dávalos; "Tenoch-
titlan's Glory," by Augusto F. Molino Montes; and "The Great
Temple," by Eduardo Matos Moctezuma. Map p. 7704A "Visitor's
Guide to the Aztec World," and "Mexico and Central America."
"Following Cortés: Path to Conquest." In: *National Geographic,* Octo-
ber 1984, vol. 166, no. 4. Washington, D.C.: National Geographic
Society.

TEXTS AND AUTHORS MENTIONED BY NOVO

Acosta, José de. *Historia natural y moral de las Indias.* Seventh Book. "On
the Death of Tlacaélel and the Deeds of Axayácatl." Valencia: Valencia Cultural, 1977 [originally 1596].
Alva Ixtlilxóchitl, Fernando de. *Historia de la nación chichimeca.* Germán
Vázquez' edition. Madrid: Historia 16, 1985.

Alvarado Tezozómoc, Fernando. *Crónica mexicana*. [*Crónica mexicáyotl*.] 2d ed. Notes by Manuel Orozco y Berra. Mexico City: Editorial Porrúa, 1975.

Anales de Cuauhtitlan (Códice Chimalpopoca). Mexico City: UNAM, Instituto de Investigaciones Históricas, 1975.

Batres, Leopoldo. *Teotihuacan: o, La ciudad sagrada de los Toltecas*. Mexico City: Talleres de la Escuela Nacional de Artes y Oficios, 1889.

Caso, Alfonso. *The Aztecs: People of the Sun*. Norman: University of Oklahoma Press, 1959.

———. *Los barrios antiguos de Tenochtitlan y Tlatelolco*. Mexico City: Academia Mexicana de la Historia, 1956.

Chimalpahin Cuauhtlehuanitzin, Domingo Francisco. *Anales de Chimalpahin Cuauhtlehuanitzin*. Sixième et Septième rélations. Translated by Rémi Siméon. Bibliothèque Linguistique Américaine, vol. 12. Paris: 1889.

Codex Mendoza: Aztec Manuscript. Comment by Kurt Ross. Miller Graphics, ca. 1978.

Dávalos Hurtado, Eusebio. *La deformación craneana entre los tlatelolcas*. Mexico City: Secretaría de Educación Pública, 1951.

———. *Temas de antropología física*. Mexico City: INAH, Secretaría de Educación Pública, 1965.

Durán, Diego. *The Aztecs: The History of the Indies of New Spain*. Translated, with notes, by Doris Heyden and Fernando Horcasitas. New York: Orion Press, 1964.

Fernández, Justino. *Coatlicue: Estética del arte indígena antiguo*. Mexico City: UNAM, Centro de Estudios Filosóficos, 1954.

———. *A Guide to Mexican Art from Its Beginnings to the Present*. Translated by Joshua C. Taylor. Chicago: University of Chicago Press, 1969.

Gamio, Manuel. *Guide for Visiting the Archaeological City of Teotihuacan*. Mexico City: Secretaría de Agricultura y Fomento de Turismo, 1972.

———. *La población del valle de Teotihuacan*. Mexico City: Instituto Nacional Indigenista, 1979.

Garibay Kintana, Angel María. *Épica náhuatl*. Mexico City: UNAM, 1945.

———. *Flight of Quetzalcóatl*. Translated by Jerome Rothenberg. Brighton: Unicorn, ca. 1967.

———. *Historia de la literatura nahuatl*. 2 vols. Mexico City: Editorial Porrúa, 1953.

———. *La literatura de los Aztecas*. Mexico City: Joaquín Mortiz, 1964.

———. *Veinte himnos sacros de los nahuas*. Mexico City: UNAM, Instituto de Historia: Seminario de Cultura Nahuatl, 1958.

Guzmán, Eulalia. *La escuela nueva o de la acción*. Mexico City: Secretaría de Educación Pública, 1923.

————. "Genealogía y biografía de Cuauhtémoc." *El Diario de Culiacán.* (Sinaloa) n.d.

————. *Pruebas y dictámenes sobre la autenticidad de los restos de Cuauhtémoc.* Mexico City: Gran Comisión Investigadora de los Restos de Cuauhtémoc, INAH, 1951.

————. *Los relieves de las rocas del cerro de la Cantera, Jonacatepec, Morelos.* Mexico City: Secretaría de Educación Pública, 1934.

————. *La tradición de Ichcateopan.* N.p. 1949.

————. *Cartas inéditas de Hernán Cortés a Carlos V sobre la invasión de Anáhuac: aclaraciones y rectificaciones.* Mexico City: Libros Anáhuac, 1958.

Leander, Birgitta. *In xóchitl in cuícatl. Flor y canto: La poesía de los aztecas.* Mexico City: Instituto Nacional Indigenista, 1972.

León Portilla, Miguel. *The Broken Spears: The Aztec Account of the Conquest of Mexico.* English translation by Lysander Kemp. Boston: Beacon Press, 1962.

————. *Trece poetas del mundo azteca.* Mexico City: UNAM, Instituto de Investigaciones Históricas, 1967.

————. *Visión de los vencidos: Relaciones indígenas de la conquista.* Mexico City: UNAM, 1959.

Orozco y Berra, Manuel. *Historia antigua y de la conquista de México.* Mexico City: Editorial Porrúa, 1960.

Sahagún, Bernardino de. *General History of the Things of New Spain: Florentine Codex.* Translated by Arthur J. O. Anderson and Charles E. Dibble. Santa Fe, N. Mex.: School of American Research; Salt Lake City: University of Utah, 1950–1982.

————. *Hablan los aztecas: Historia general de las cosas de Nueva España.* Edited by Claus Litterscheid; prologue by Juan Rulfo. Barcelona: Tusquets, 1985.

Séjourné, Laurette. *Burning Water: Thought and Religion in Ancient Mexico.* Berkeley, Calif.: Shambhala, 1976.

————. *Un palacio en la Ciudad de los Dioses, Teotihuacan.* Translated by Arnaldo Orfila Reynal. Mexico City: INAH, 1959.

————. *El universo de Quetzalcóatl.* Translated by Arnaldo Orfila Reynal. Mexico City: Fondo de Cultura Económica, 1962, 1984.

Suárez de Peralta, Juan. *La conjuración de Martín Cortés y otros temas.* Mexico City: UNAM, 1945.

————. *Noticias históricas de la Nueva España.* Madrid: Imprenta de M. G. Hernández, 1878.

Torquemada, Juan de. *Monarquía indiana.* 4th ed. Mexico City: Editorial Porrúa, 1969.

Usigli, Rodolfo. *El gesticulador, pieza para demagogos en tres actos, con un epílogo sobre la hipocresía del mexicano, y doce notas por Rodolfo Usigli.* Mexico City: Letras de México, 1944.

————. *México en el teatro.* Mexico City: Imprenta Mundial, 1932.

Zavala, Silvio, and María Castelo. *Fuentes para la historia del trabajo en Nueva España.* Vol. 2, 1579–1581. Mexico City: Fondo de Cultura Económica, 1940.

OTHER WORKS OF INTEREST

Alcocer, Ignacio. *Apuntes sobre la antigua México-Tenochtitlan.* Mexico City: Tacubaya, 1935.

Bancroft, Hubert Howe. *The History of Mexico.* Vols. 9 and 10. San Francisco: A. L. Bancroft and Co., 1883–1888.

Davies, Nigel. *The Aztecs: A History.* London: Macmillan, 1973.

Díaz del Castillo, Bernal. *The Discovery and Conquest of Mexico, 1517–1521.* Genaro García edition. Translated by A. P. Maudslay. Farrar, Straus & Cudahy, ca. 1956.

Fuentes, Carlos. *Todos los gatos son pardos.* Mexico City: Siglo XXI, 1970, 1983.

Gillmor, Frances. *Flute of the Smoking Mirror: A Portrait of Nezahualcóyotl, Poet-King of the Aztecs.* Albuquerque: University of New Mexico Press, 1949.

González Martínez, Enrique. *Poesías Completas.* Asociación de Libreros y Editores Mexicanos. Mexico City: Talleres Gráficos de la Nación, 1944.

Horcasitas, Fernando. *The Aztecs Then and Now.* Mexico City: Editorial Minutiae Mexicana, 1979.

Paz, Octavio. *The Labyrinth of Solitude.* New York: Grove Press, 1985.

Prescott, William Hickling. *The Conquest of Mexico; The Conquest of Peru.* New York: Random House, n.d.

————. *World of the Aztecs.* Minera, 1970.

Qualli amatl, chicome calli. Conquista de Tlatilolco; anónimo náhuatl traducido al castellano por Porfirio Aguirre. Mexico City: Vargas Rea, 1950.

Robelo, Cecilio Agustín. *Diccionario de mitología nahuatl.* Mexico City: Navarro, 1951.

Roldán, Dolores. *Códice de Cuauhtémoc: Biografía.* Orión, 1984.

Schafer, Robert Jones. *A History of Latin America.* Lexington, Mass.: D. C. Heath, 1978.

Soustelle, Jacques. *Daily Life of the Aztecs on the Eve of the Spanish Conquest.* Translated from the French by Patrick O'Brian. Stanford, Calif.: Stanford University, 1970.

Thompson, John Eric. *Mexico before Cortez*. New York: C. Scribner's Sons, 1933.

Vaillant, George Clapp. *Aztecs of Mexico: Origin, Rise, and Fall of the Aztec Nation*. Harmondsworth, England: Penguin Books, 1955.

WORKS BY NOVO

Plays

Divorcio: Drama Ibseniano en cinco actos. April 30, 1924. *El Universal Ilustrado*. Also in *Toda la prosa*.

Le señorita Remington. May 15, 1924. *El Universal Ilustrado*, vol. 8, no. 366, pp. 27, 91.

Le troisième Faust: Tragédie brève. 1937. Paris: Soixantedixneuf. (Written in 1934.) Published in Spanish as *El tercer Fausto*, included in *Diálogos*.

Don Quixote: Farsa en tres actos y dos entremeses. 1948. Mexico City: INBA. 2d. ed., Monterrey: Universidad de Nuevo León, 1961.

El Coronel Astucia y los Hermanos de la Hoja. 1948. Adaptation of Luis G. Inclán's novel *Astucia*. Mexico: INBA.

La culta dama: Comedia en tres actos. 1951. Mexico City: Imprenta Veracruz. Also in Celestino Gorostiza's *Teatro mexicano del siglo XX*, vol. 3. Mexico City: Fondo de Cultura Económica, 1956.

El joven II: Monólogo en un acto. 1951. Mexico City: Imprenta Muñoz. Also in *Diálogos*.

A ocho columnas: Pieza en tres actos. 1956. Los Textos de la Capilla, vol. 1. Mexico City: Editorial Stylo.

Diálogos. 1956. Los Textos de la Capilla, vol. 2. Mexico City: Editorial Stylo. Contains: *El joven II, Adán y Eva, El tercer Fausto, La güera y la estrella, Sor Juana y Pita, Malinche y Carlota, Diego y Betty,* and *Cuauhtémoc y Eulalia*.

Yocasta, o casi: Pieza en tres actos. 1961. Los Textos de la Capilla, vol. 3. Mexico City: Editorial Stylo.

Cuauhtémoc: Pieza en un acto. 1962. Mexico City: Talleres Gráficos de la Librería Madero. Also in *In Ticitézcatl*.

Ha vuelto Ulises: Pieza en un prólogo y un acto. 1962. Col. Alacena, no. 3. Mexico City: Era.

In Pipiltzintzin (Los niñitos) o La guerra de las gordas: Comedia en dos actos. 1963. Col. Letras Mexicanas, no. 75. Mexico City: Fondo de Cultura Económica. Also in *El teatro mexicano* by Antonio Magaña Esquivel, Col. Aguilar, 1965.

El sofá: Obra teatral en un acto. August 1963. *Cuadernos de Bellas Artes*, vol. 4, no. 8. Also in *In Ticitézcatl*.

In Ticitézcatl o El espejo encantado. 1966. Serie Ficción, no. 67. Xalapa, Mexico: Universidad Veracruzana. Includes: *Cuauhtémoc, El sofá,* and *Diálogo de ilustres en la Rotonda.*

Sor Juana recibe. 1972. In *Las locas, el sexo, los burdeles.* Edo. de México: Novaro.

Plays Translated by Novo

Jean Anouilh, *Leocadia (Léocadia).*
Marcel Aymé, *Los pájaros de la luna (Les Oiseaux de lune).*
Robert Bolt, *Un hombre contra el tiempo (A Man for All Seasons).*
Guido Cantini, *Daniel entre los leones (Daniele tra i leoni), Los girasoles (I girasoli),* and *Paseo con el diablo (Passeggiata col diavolo).*
Henrik Ibsen, *Espectros (Ghosts).*
Allan Jay Lerner, *Brigadoon.*
Donagh MacDonagh, *Feliz como Larry (Happy as Larry).*
André Obey, *Lázaro (Lazare).*
Jacques Offenbach, *Orfeo en los infiernos (Orphée aux enfers).* Libretto by Héctor Cremieux.
Eugene O'Neill, *Diferente (Diff'rent)* and *Ligados (Welded).*
Terence Rattigan, *Ross* and *Mesas separadas (Separate Tables).*
Rodgers & Hammerstein, *El rey y yo (The King and I).*
André Roussin, *La vidente (La voyente)* and *Helena o La alegría de vivir (Hélène ou Joie de vivre).*
William Shakespeare, *Otelo (Othello).*
George Bernard Shaw, *Santa Juana (Saint Joan).*
William P. Shea, *El dólar plata (Silver Dollars).*
Robert E. Sherwood, *Camino a Roma (The Road to Rome).*
Jean Tardieu, *Teatro de cámara (Théâtre de chambre).*
Carlo Terrón, *Proceso a los inocentes (Processo agli innocenti).*
Giulio Cesare Viola, *El Presidente hereda.*
Oscar Wilde, *El abanico (Lady Windermere) (Lady Windermere's Fan).*

Novels

El joven: Novela mexicana. 1928. With a drawing by Roberto Montenegro. La novela mexicana, vol. 1, no. 2. Mexico City: Editorial Popular Mexicana. 2d ed. with preliminary notes, Mexico City: Imprenta Mundial, 1933. Also published in *La Antorcha* vol. 1, nos. 20–22 (February 14, 21, 28, 1925); and in reduced form as "¡Qué México! novela en que no pasa nada" in *La Falange* no. 6 (September 1923).

Lota de loco: Fragmentos de novela. 1931. Supplement of *Barandal.*

Poetry

Poemas de infancia and *Poemas de adolescencia*. Unpublished until 1955. In *Poesía, 1915–1955*.

Adytias, poemas. 1924. Selections read by their author at the Feria del Libro, *El Universal*.

XX poemas, con un poema de Carlos Pellicer. 1925. With a portrait by Roberto Montenegro. Mexico City: Talleres Gráficos de la Nación. Also included in *Ensayos* as *Ensayos de poemas*.

Espejo: Poemas antiguos. 1933. Mexico City: Taller de La Mundial.

Nuevo amor. 1933. Mexico City: Imprenta Mundial. 2d ed. with a new poem, "Elegía," Mexico City: Talleres Gráficos de la Compañía Editora y Librera ARS, 1948. (See translation section below.)

Canto a Teresa. 1934. Mexico City: Editoriales Fábula.

Décimas en el mar. 1934. Drawings by Julio Prieto. Mexico City: Imprenta Mundial.

Frida Kahlo. 1934. Mexico City. Also included in *Poesía* and *Poesía, 1915–1955*.

Never Ever. 1934. Mexico City. Also included in *Poesía* and *Poesía, 1915–1955*.

Poemas proletarios. 1934. Mexico City. Also included in *Poesía* and *Poesía, 1915–1955*.

Romance de Angelillo y Adela. 1934. Mexico City: Imprenta Mundial.

Seamen Rhymes. 1934. With drawings by Federico García Lorca. Buenos Aires: Casa de Don Francisco A. Colombo.

Un poema. 1937. With an illustration by Julio Prieto. Mexico City: PLYCSA.

Poesías escogidas. 1938. (Selections from previous books with a new poem.) Cuadernos México Nuevo, no. 2, published with Elías Nandino. Mexico City: Talleres de Angel Chápero.

Decimos: "Nuestra tierra." 1944. Mexico City. Also included in *Poesía* and *Poesía, 1915–1955*.

Dueño mío. 1944. Mexico City: Talleres de Angel Chápero. Also included in *Sátira, el libro ca.* . . .

Florido laude. 1945. Drawings by Mary Helen Morgan. Mexico City: Cultura. Also included in *Poesía* and *Poesía, 1915–1955*.

Dieciocho sonetos. 1955. Mexico City: Private edition. Includes the four sonnets of *Dueño mío*.

Poesía, 1915–1955. 1955. With drawings by Federico García Lorca. Col. Lince, no. 1. Mexico City: Impresiones Modernas. Includes: Prologue by Novo; *Poética (1915)*; *Poemas de infancia, 1915–1916*; *Poemas de adolescencia, 1918–1923*; *XX poemas*; *Espejo: Poemas antiguos*; *Nuevo amor*; *Seamen Rhymes*; *Romance de Angelillo y Adela*; *Décimas en el mar*; *Poemas proletarios*; *Frida Kahlo*; *Never Ever*; *Dueño mío, cuatro sonetos*; *Florido* laude; *Decimos: "Nuestra tierra"; Dieciocho sonetos; Soneto al terminar el año y comenzar el nuevo: 1955;* and the translations: "La poesía norteamericana moderna, 1924–1925"; and a bibliography.

Sátira. 1955. With drawings by Federico García Lorca. Col. Lince, no. 2. Mexico City: Editores Alfonso Alarcón y Socios.

Antología poética. 1961. Introduction by José Emilio Pacheco. Voz del Autor, Serie Voz Viva de México, no. 8. Mexico City: UNAM.

Poesía. 1961. Letras Mexicanas. Mexico City: Fondo de Cultura Económica. Includes: *Poemas de adolescencia, 1918–1923; XX poemas; Espejo; Nuevo amor; Seamen Rhymes; Romance de Angelillo y Adela; Poemas proletarios; Never Ever; Frida Kahlo; Florido laude; Decimos: "Nuestra tierra"; Seven sonnets, 1955–1961.* The 1977 edition also includes *Mea culpa; Adán desnudo;* and sonnets for 1962–1971.

Salvador Novo: Antología 1925–1965. 1966. Colección de escritores mexicanos. Mexico City: Editorial Porrúa. Prologue by Antonio Castro Leal. Also contains some theater.

Adán desnudo. 1969. Bilingual Spanish/English edition. Translated by Robert Graves and Laura Villaseñor. Mexico City: Novo's private edition.

Mea culpa. 1969. Bilingual Spanish/English edition. Translated by Laura Villaseñor. N.p. Ed. EPSA, J.M.R., y F.T.

Sátira, el libro ca. . . . 1978. Mexico City: Diana.

Translations of Novo's Poetry

Nuevo amor. Translated by Edna Worthley Underwood. Portland, Maine, 1935.

Nouvel amour. Translated by Armand Guibert. Túnez, 1936.

See also *Adán desnudo* and *Mea culpa* above.

History, Essay, and Literary Criticism

Note: Many of Novo's writings appear in *Ulises,* the magazine he edited with Xavier Villaurrutia, and the other magazines mentioned in the Introduction. These have been reprinted by the Fondo de Cultura Económica as recently as 1980.

"Los corridos mexicanos." *El libro y el pueblo,* vol. 3, nos. 10–11 (October–December 1924): 235–236.

"Algunas verdades acerca de la literatura mexicana actual." *El Universal Ilustrado* (February 19, 1925).

"Notas sobre la literatura de México." *La Antorcha,* vol. 1, no. 25 (March 21, 1925).

"Veinte años de la literatura mexicana." *El libro y el pueblo,* vol. 9, no. 4 (June 1931): 4–9.

"La era bibliofílico." *El libro y el pueblo,* vol. 10, no. 1 (March 1932): 1–5.

"Leños, libros y amigos." *El libro y el pueblo,* vol. 11 (1933): 90–96.

Ensayos. With a portrait by Roberto Montenegro. Mexico City: Novo's private edition, Talleres Gráficos de la nación, 1925. (Includes *Ensayos* and *Ensayos de poemas,* a.k.a., *XX poemas*). In *Toda la prosa.*

La educación literaria de los adolescentes. 1928. Mexico City: Talleres Gráficos de la Nación.

Return Ticket: Viaje a Hawai. 1928. Mexico City: Editorial Cultura. In *Toda la prosa.*

Jalisco-Michoacán: 12 días. 1933. Photos by Roberto Montenegro. Mexico City: Imprenta Mundial. Also in *Toda la prosa.*

Continente vacío: Viaje a Sudamérica. 1935. Madrid: Espasa-Calpe. Also in *Toda la prosa.*

En defensa de lo usado y otros ensayos. 1938. Mexico City: Editorial Polis. In *Toda la prosa.*

Nueva grandeza mexicana: Ensayo sobre la ciudad de Mexico. 1946. Mexico City: Editorial Hermes. 2d ed., 1946. 3d ed., Col. Austral, no. 797, Buenos Aires: Espasa-Calpe, 1947. 4th ed., Populibros La Prensa, 1956. In *Toda la Prosa.*

La televisión. 1948. (Study.) Mexico City: INBA.

Diez lecciones de técnica de actuación teatral. 1951. Mexico City: Secretaría de Educación Pública.

Este y otros viajes. 1951. Mexico City: Editorial Stylo. In *Toda la prosa.*

Las aves en la poesía castellana. 1953. Drawing by Miguel Prieto. Letras Mexicanas, no. 10. Mexico City: Fondo de Cultura Económica. In *Toda la Prosa.*

"La actuación teatral." 1958. In *Enciclopedia del arte escénico.* Barcelona.

El teatro inglés. 1960. Illustrated ed. Mexico City: INBA, Departamento de Literatura. In *Toda la prosa.*

Breve historia de Coyoacán. 1962. With notes and drawings by Dr. Atl and photos by Ricardo Alcázar. Col. Alacena, no. 6. Mexico City: Ediciones Era.

Letras vencidas. 1962. Cuadernos de la Facultad de Filosofía, Letras y Ciencias, no. 10. Xalapa, Mexico: Universidad Veracruzana. In *Toda la prosa.*

"Huehuetlatolli, discurso por Cuauhtémoc." 1963. In *Homenaje a Cuauhtémoc.* Mexico City.

Toda la prosa. 1964. With a jacket note by Emmanuel Carballo and a prologue by Novo. Mexico City: Empresas Editoriales. Includes: *Ensayos; En defensa de lo usado; Return Ticket; Continente vacío; Este y otros viajes; Jalisco-Michoacán; Nueva grandeza mexicana; Las aves en la poe-*

sía castellana; Letras vencidas; Prólogo a la Reseña histórica del teatro en México.

"Salvador Novo." In *El trato con escritores.* 1964. Mexico City.

La vida en México en el período presidencial de Lázaro Cárdenas. 1965. Prologue by Novo; preliminary note by José Emilio Pacheco. Mexico City: Empresas Editoriales.

La vida en Mexico en el período presidencial de Manuel Avila Camacho. 1965. Mexico City: Empresas Editoriales.

Crónica regiomontana: Breve historia de un gran esfuerzo. ca. 1965. Monterrey: Cervecería Cuauhtémoc.

"Juárez, símbolo de la soberanía nacional." 1966. Speech. Mexico City: Secretaría de Hacienda y Crédito Público. (12 pp.)

La ciudad de México, del 9 de junio al 15 de julio de 1967. 1967. Mexico City: Editorial Porrúa.

Cocina mexicana; o, Historia gastronómica de la ciudad de México. 1967. Mexico City: Editorial Porrúa.

México, imagen de una ciudad. 1967. Mexico City: Fondo de Cultura Económica. Photos by Pedro Bayona.

La vida en México en el período presidencial de Miguel Alemán. 1967. Mexico City: Empresas Editoriales.

Apuntes para una historia de la publicidad en la ciudad de México. 1968. Edo. de Mexico: Novaro.

La vida y la cultura en México al triunfo de la República en 1867. 1968. Mexico City: INBA, Departamento de Literatura.

"El tesoro del indio." *Ponch* 1 (August 15, 1968): 4.

Las locas, el sexo, los burdeles (y otros ensayos). 1972. Edo. de Mexico: Novaro.

Los paseos de la ciudad de México: Antología. 1974. Mexico City: Fondo de Cultura Económica.

Historia de la aviación en México. 1974. Mexico City: Compañía Mexicana de Aviación.

"Memoir." In *Now the Volcano.* 1979. Edited by Winston Leyland. San Francisco: Gay Sunshine Press.

Anthologies by Novo

Antología de cuentos mexicanos e hispanoamericanos (10 países). 1923. Mexico City: Cultura.

La poesía francesa moderna. 1924. Mexico City.

La poesía norteamericana moderna. 1924. Translated, selected, and with notes by Novo. Mexico City: Publicaciones Literarias Exclusivas de El Universal Ilustrado.

Lecturas hispanoamericanas. 1925. Selected and with notes by Novo. Mexico City: Secretaría de Educación Pública.

Lecturas para el tercer ciclo, I y II grados. 1928. Mexico City: Herrero Hermanos. (Many editions; 6th by 1944.)

Lecturas. Antología para el tercer ciclo, I y II grados. 1946. Mexico City: Herrero Hermanos.

Teatro de Lope de Rueda. 1946. Selected by Novo. Mexico City.

Prosa selecta de Manuel Gutiérrez Nájera. 1948. Special edition for the Círculo Literario. Mexico City: W. M. Jackson Inc.

Joyas de la amistad, engarzadas en una antología. 1963. Col. "Sepan Cuantos . . . ," no. 23. Mexico City: Editorial Porrúa.

Mil y un sonetos mexicanos. 1963. Selections and prologue by Novo. Col. "Sepan Cuantos . . . ," no. 18. Mexico City: Editorial Porrúa.

Breve historia y antología sobre la fiebre amarilla. 1964. Mexico City: Secretaría de Salubridad y Asistencia/Prensa Médica Mexicana.

101 poemas, antología bilingüe de la poesía norteamericana moderna, compilada por Salvador Novo. 1965. Mexico City: Editorial Letras.

CRITICAL STUDIES AND BOOKS ABOUT NOVO

Blanco, José Joaquin. *Crónica de la poesía mexicana.* Col. Textos Americanos. Guadalajara, Mexico: Departamento de Bellas Artes, Gobierno de Jalisco, 1977.

Carballo, Emmanuel. *Diecinueve protagonistas de la literatura mexicana del siglo XX.* Mexico City: Empresas Editoriales, 1965, pp. 231–262.

———. "Salvador Novo: Nuevo examen y disección de 'Contemporáneos.'" *México en la Cultura* 490 (August 4, 1958).

Colín, Eduardo. "Salvador Novo." In *Rasgos.* Mexico City: Imp. Manuel Leon Sánchez, 1934.

Dauster, Frank N. "La poesía de Salvador Novo." *Cuadernos americanos* 116 (1961): 209–233.

Forster, Merlin H. *Los contemporáneos, 1920–1932: Perfil de un experimento vanguardista mexicano.* Col. Studium, no. 46. Mexico City: Ediciones de Andrea, 1964.

Kuehne, Alyce de. *Teatro mexicano contemporáneo, 1940–1962.* Mexico City: 1962.

———. "'La realidad existencial' y 'La realidad creada' en Pirandello y Salvador Novo," *Latin American Theatre Review* 2/1 (Fall 1968): 5–14.

Lamb, Ruth Stanton. *Bibliografía del teatro mexicano del siglo XX.* Mexico City: 1962.

Lambert, Jean Clarence. *Les poésies mexicaines.* Paris: Seghers, 1961.

Magaña Esquivel, Antonio. *Medio siglo de teatro mexicano (1900–1960).* Mexico City: INBA, Departamento de Literatura, 1964.

———. *Salvador Novo.* Col. Un mexicano y su obra. Mexico City: Empresas Editoriales, 1971. Includes Magaña Esquivel's biography of Novo, an excellent bibliography, selections of Novo's work, and important articles and reviews on Novo.

———. *El teatro contrapunto*. Mexico City: Fondo de Cultura Económica, 1970.

Magaña Esquivel, Antonio, and Ruth S. Lamb. *Breve historia del teatro mexicano*. Manuales Studium, no. 8. Mexico City: Ediciones de Andrea, 1958.

Mendoza-López, Margarita. *Primeros renovadores del teatro en México, 1928–1941: Vivencias y documentos*. Mexico City: IMSS, Subdir. de Prestaciones Sociales. Coord. de Teatros, 1985.

Monsiváis, Carlos. *La poesía mexicana del siglo XX*. Mexico City: Empresas Editoriales, 1966, pp. 31–34, 37–39, 489–490.

———. "Salvador Novo: Los que tenemos unas manos que no nos pertenecen." In *Amor perdido*. Mexico City: Era, 1977.

Muncy, Michele. *Salvador Novo y su teatro: (Estudio crítico)*. Madrid: Atlas, 1971.

Reyes de la Maza, Luis. *En el nombre de Dios hablo de teatros*. Mexico City: UNAM, 1984.

Roster, Peter J., Jr. *La ironía como método de análisis literaria: La poesía de Salvador Novo*. Madrid: Gredos, 1978.

Thompson, Alan Reynolds. *The Dry Mock, a Study of Irony in Drama*. Berkeley: University of California Press, 1948.

Unger, Roni. *Poesía en Voz Alta in the Theater of Mexico*. Columbia: University of Missouri Press, 1981.

Usigli, Rodolfo. *México en el teatro*. Mexico City: Imprenta Mundial, 1932.

Villaurrutia, Xavier. *Textos y pretextos*. La Casa de España en México. Mexico City: Fondo de Cultura Económica, 1940.

———. *Cartas de Villaurrutia a Novo, 1935–1936*. Prologue by Salvador Novo. Mexico City: INBA, Depto. de Literatura, 1966.

BIBLIOGRAPHIES OF NOVO'S WORK

Arce, David N. *Nómina bibliográfica de Salvador Novo*. Mexico City: Biblioteca Nacional, 1963.

Ocampo de Gómez, Aurora Maura, and Ernesto Prado Velázquez. *Diccionario de escritores mexicanos*. Mexico City: UNAM, Centro de Estudios Literarios, 1967.